A
SONG
OF
MOUNTAINS
AND
MEMORIES

Copyright © 2022 Rachel L Brown
Cover Design © 2022 Rachel L Brown
First Edition
All rights reserved. No part of this book may be reproduced or used in any manner without the prior written permission of the copyright owner, except for the use of brief quotations in a book review.
ISBN: 978-0-578-29300-4 (paperback)
All characters, places and events in this book are fictitious. Any similarity to real places or real persons, living, dead, undead, or immortal, is coincidental and not intended by the author.
Printed in the United States of America
Published by Rachel L Brown
500 E Whitestone Blvd #1272 Cedar Park, TX 78630
www.rachellbrown.com

A Song

Of

Mountains

and

Memories

By

Rachel L Brown

Eastern Marshes

The Violet Mountains

Realm of Ruin
Portal
⊛

Divine Realm
Portal
⊛

The Cave
★

Larni
▪

Pavento
◇

The Farm

Mezzadia
▪

The Kingdom of Roltia
Duchy of Pavento Region

Legend

Current Portal Location: ⊛

City: ◇   Town with unreadable sign: ▪

Town: ▪

Chapter One

The balcony mocked her with its promise of freedom. Saderna leaned over the railing, trying to get a better glimpse of the meadow that surrounded her temple. A pair of songbirds flew overhead, oblivious to her plight, and landed in a circle of glittering blue flowers. Spring had come to the Divine Realm, and everything was enjoying new life. Except for her. She could only view it from a distance.

A shimmering wall of hard air formed in front of her pushing her back onto the balcony. Runes carved into the stone railing lit up, showering the temple walls with silver and gold light. Other gods might have thought it was a delightful display. But to Saderna, it was yet another reminder of her fate.

She was the Goddess of Peace, locked in a gilded cage. Ever since she'd been created, around twenty cycles ago, she'd only known the temple. She watched the seasons change year after year, wondering what the earth would be like under her feet. Wondering what the other divines were doing in their shining cities.

"Can you please let me go into the meadow?" She asked the runes as they faded into the stone. The iridescent barrier remained, blocking her from escaping and keeping the warm breeze from entering.

Saderna gave one last look at the meadow. She would come back later once the runes calmed down. She headed deep into the heart of her sanctuary, through a labyrinth of corridors and chambers. Most of which lay vacant.

Unlike the rest of the temple, which was a stark white, her main chambers were filled with color. Ornate tapestries covered the bare walls while stained glass windows and skylights filtered the sunlight into various colors. An array of plants in white vases lined the walls of her rooms.

"Good morning, my friends," Saderna said to an apple tree. The tree bowed slightly when she entered the room. This was the most sacred place in her temple.

A large, turquoise-colored pool was at the center; silver and gold runes were carved into the stone at the bottom. Above was a vast domed ceiling made of transparent glass so clear it looked like nothing was there at all.

Goddess of Peace, hear my plea…

A voice drifted out of the pool, creating ripples in the water. Saderna gathered her magic around her and floated over to the source of the sound. Runes carved into the stones below told her it was a human asking for help.

She listened quietly to the tale of yet another soul torn apart by war. Once again, Einar, the God of War, had gotten the upper hand. There was little she could do to stop his rampages across the Mortal Realms. At least not while locked inside the temple.

Once the human had finished with their petition, Saderna summoned a pitcher and imbued the water within it with some of her essence. She then poured the water into the pool, directing the streaks of blue and gold toward the petitioner. It wasn't much, but hopefully, the human could sleep.

More petitions came in from mortals in nearly every realm. It would be impossible for her to finish before sunset. War had broken out in many realms.

"Damn you, Einar," she muttered under her breath. A part of her wished he would pop up and try to justify himself, but she knew he wouldn't. No one visited. Well, almost no one.

"You can create a spirit to aid you with the more mundane tasks." As if on cue, a cool voice drifted across the room.

"I wouldn't have anything to do," Saderna let the pitcher float back over to its table before she turned to face her visitor.

Bedisa, Goddess of Fates, stood in the doorway. Unlike the last time she'd visited, when she came as a giant snake, Bedisa had come in her typical form. It was a human female with long black hair, tanned skin that had iridescent runes painted onto it, and gold eyes. Though her ears were different; they were long and slender and came to a sharp point.

Bedisa smiled and brushed an ear while Saderna exited the pool. "Do you like them? They're in honor of the new elf god!"

"What's an elf?"

Bedisa waved her hand, and an image of a tall humanoid race with pointed ears appeared next to her. "They are the newest species to be created, and their god was recently born!"

Saderna frowned. "I saw nothing new in my pool."

"You wouldn't have. The elves don't have a Goddess of Peace," Bedisa paused, "yet."

"I look forward to meeting them someday. It's always fun to see new mortals."

"Oh, that's the best part! They're immortal! Kind of. They can still die from egregious wounds, and I think there is a plague that can kill them…"

Saderna tuned her out as she prattled on. She ambled over to a fig tree and pretended to check the rune carved into the pot. Something wasn't right. Bedisa always had a task or a favor to ask of her. Last time she asked her to bless a mortal for reasons she wouldn't divulge.

"Bedisa, as happy as I am to see you. What task do you have for me today?" She asked while Bedisa admired her reflection.

"Hmm?" Bedisa's brow creased with confusion before her eyes lit up. "Ah, this time I don't have a task for you. Because of some recent events, Vilmantas is requesting your presence at the Great Palace."

Saderna's mouth dropped open, and her vision wavered.

"I get to leave?" She squeaked out.

"Yes."

Saderna walked over to a stone bench and sat on it before her legs gave out.

"Why now? Is my magic finally strong enough to withstand corruption?"

The reason she'd never been able to leave was because the other gods feared her magic was easily corruptible. Perhaps she'd matured enough that they no longer believed that was the case.

Bedisa eyed the runes on the walls. "He doesn't want to talk about it outside of a secure location. We're trying to keep things from leaking out into the rest of the realms."

"How is this not a secure location? I can't leave, and no one aside from you can enter."

"Because he didn't create this place." Bedisa flicked a stray hair back and folded her arms. "Vilmantas is a bit paranoid these days."

"This is ridiculous. My temple is perfectly safe!"

"We can either go peacefully, or I'll have to drag you out of here," Bedisa cocked her head to the side. "I thought you'd be more excited about leaving."

Saderna shook her head. Something inside her was screaming, but she couldn't make out the words. Wasn't she just longing for freedom on the balcony? Why was she hesitating now when freedom was within her grasp?

"This place is the only one you've ever known," Bedisa said softly.

"Yes, but…"

"It's only natural for you to hesitate. But I can promise you that nothing will happen to you."

Bedisa's eyes glowed and she spoke with the authority of the fates. Yet, that nagging voice in the back of her mind refused to shut up. She backed away from Bedisa until she bumped against a vase. Her fingers caressed the tree behind her, drawing strength from it's magic.

No, she would not let her fear of the unknown ruin this moment. She could always come back.

"I'll go."

Bedisa smiled and swept her arms to her sides. A burst of brown sparkles floated around her, and the wards imbued in the temple walls flickered, then vanished.

"We leave at once."

Before Saderna could react, Bedisa grabbed her arm, and a swirling vortex of light brown and gold surrounded them.

"Don't focus on anything!" Bedisa shouted over the hum.

The world rushed past until it was a colorful blur. Then, without warning, everything went still. They were now standing in a courtyard with a huge apple tree. Stone benches covered in ivy were scattered about.

Saderna studied her feet, trying to quell the disappointment that arose within her. She wanted to see a forest, not more buildings. She took a step forward, and her body swayed.

"Take a few deep breaths. It's never fun the first time around," Bedisa said with a concerned tone in her voice, but a hint of amusement glimmered in her eyes.

"That was awful," Saderna said. "I never want to do that again!"

"That is what they all say. Now let's go do some exploring before your meeting."

"What? Don't I need to meet Vilmantas first?"

"You will, but we have some time, and I'm sure you'd much rather see the city before we meet with the old man."

Bedisa smiled and led her toward a pair of silver doors; golden vines were etched into the metal. She could hear the city beyond as millions of souls were just outside the door. Electricity crawled on the inside of her skin.

"Are you sure we must go out there? Can't you just whisk us into the palace?"

"No, it's warded against fast travel," Bedisa said and opened the door. She gently shoved Saderna through it and onto the street.

Tall buildings of ice-blue stone towered above them. Banners glittering with runes and jewels hung from enormous open windows. Most of the banners were for shops or other services. The streets themselves were paved with golden crystals that had tiny streams of violet sparks moving through them.

Immortals of many shapes and sizes passed by them—some had the body of a horse and the head of a goat, while others looked like humans with elf ears. The amount of energy they were giving off was nauseating. It was like she was standing too close to the sun.

"This way!" Bedisa grabbed her hand and led her through another wide street with even more banners. The energy was still too much despite the street being less crowded.

"Don't worry, it all becomes background noise at some point," Bedisa said with a sympathetic smile.

The stone road gave way to a large courtyard lined with silver trees and thousands of tiny shimmering flowers. Bedisa pulled her into an alleyway before Saderna could get closer.

"Hey! I wanted to see more of the courtyard!"

"You will, but you have an appointment, and I don't want to be late."

Saderna raised her eyebrows. "I thought we'd be seeing the city."

"We will! After this appointment."

She paused at a large ornate door with silver runes surrounding an engraved needle. A tall woman with hair that looked like smoke stepped out as the door flew open. She smiled at Bedisa.

"Ah, there you are! I was starting to think you weren't going to show!" She exclaimed; the excitement on her face dimmed when she noticed Saderna. "And who is your friend?"

"I'm Saderna, the Goddess of Peace," Saderna said.

"Ompelija, Goddess of Sewing," she said. Her gaze swept over Saderna's clothes. "You're the one who's been locked up since her creation, right?"

"Yes, I am."

"Let's get you out of those ancient rags and into something a tad more…fashionable."

Saderna brushed her skirt. The dress was a simple one with one shoulder showing and had gold vines woven throughout.

She rather liked her clothes, but, despite her protests, the other two goddesses quickly pulled her into the shop.

Hours later, Saderna wore a flowing turquoise and gold dress cinched at the waist and a diamond belt around her hips. Ompelija tried to get her to wear the elf ears, but Saderna wasn't about to change her form that drastically.

She was following Bedisa down a wide road that led straight to the steps of the Great Palace. Her gaze never left the large building that loomed in front of them. The scrolls she'd read in her temple didn't prepare her for the sheer majesty of the building in front of her.

A hundred steps led up to an enormous building made of shimmering gold stone. There were thousands of arched windows with balconies jutting out from underneath each one. At the top of the steps were two large doors with a sentinel in silver armor on either side.

Bedisa led her into a large hallway filled with all sorts of divines. Some looked human, while others were a mishmash of creatures.

Saderna sidestepped an immortal who resembled an ox and hurried after Bedisa.

It wasn't long before she paused in front of a large doorway. Large scroll-like runes were engraved on either side. It was the divine rune of the God of Knowledge.

"Are you ready?"

Saderna nodded and followed her through the doorway. They entered a room with a high ceiling, painted to look like an afternoon sky. Light runes, carved into a circle, bathed the room in a warm light. The walls were lined with shelves, filled to the brim with scrolls and books.

In the center of the room was a large stone table. Various magical devices and dried plants were scattered about. A tall male sat at one end, reading a scroll. His skin shimmered like a rainbow when the light hit it. His dark hair was longer than Saderna's, nearly reaching the floor. He looked up when they drew closer. His dark purple eyes softened when he smiled.

He was Vilmantas, the God of Knowledge. Saderna had met him only once, the day she'd been created. But he was a god that was hard to forget.

"Ah, Saderna, thank you for coming," Vilmantas said and

gestured for her to sit.

"I had little choice," Saderna said with a sidelong glance at Bedisa. Vilmantas narrowed his eyes at the goddess, who shrugged in response.

"I decided it would be better to make her come."

"Before you make such decisions, could you please inform me?" Vilmantas said before he turned back to Saderna. "Forgive us for all the secrecy, but it is necessary."

"What is going on? Is there going to be a war?"

"There is no war…. yet."

"What do you mean?"

Vilmantas drummed his fingers against the scroll he'd been reading.

"Do you know about the treaty we have with Casimir? The God of Ruin?"

"Every thousand years, one side has to hand over a divine as tribute?"

"Yes, that's the one. It was our turn this time."

Saderna frowned. The exchange usually took place two weeks before the Spring Equinox. She glanced over at the elaborate rune calendar on the wall. Equinox was in three days. They should've sent the tribute by now, unless there was a delay?

"Did something happen with the tribute?"

Vilmantas let out a heavy sigh. "We sent Zimri, the God of Music, to his realm almost two weeks ago. Apparently, Zimri was miserable, and his music became so insufferable that Casimir sent him back."

Sent back? Since the forging of the treaty, no god or goddess had ever been returned to their old realm. Despite this knowledge, no electricity swelled within her, and no warnings of war between the realms rang in her thoughts.

"Does this mean the treaty is broken?" Saderna asked.

"No, but some adjustments are required."

Visions of meetings and scrolls being signed flashed through her mind. Did they want her to forge a new treaty? Saderna straightened and smoothed out her skirts.

"Let me see the treaty. I will make sure whatever adjustments are needed won't cause unnecessary bloodshed."

Vilmantas raised an eyebrow, "That's not what we need you to do. You-"

"Then do you need me to oversee any negotiations? I promise I won't let you down!"

"Saderna, will you let me finish!" Vilmantas snapped and she recoiled.

"Sorry."

"We are not changing anything in the treaty. Casimir has agreed not to attack us if we send you to his realm in Zimri's place."

Saderna shivered like a wave of cold water had been splashed upon her. The small flame of hope she'd been keeping died. She would not be free. No, she was going to trade one prison for another.

"But why me? I'm a new goddess, and you locked me up in the temple to keep me from getting corrupted by gods like Casimir."

"We have no choice. Casimir made it very clear that we send you or plunge into war. The last time that happened, most of the Mortal Realms were destroyed, and countless gods and goddesses lost their lives. Even though it was eons ago, we're still recovering. Most of the dead divines haven't been reborn yet."

"You can say no, but you will be responsible for the deaths of entire realms," Bedisa chimed in. Her voice was bright and cheery, a stark contrast to her words.

Saderna stared at her hands. Freedom was so close, and now it was being snatched away. She was starting to understand why the mortals cursed the fates so much.

Perhaps she could end the stalemate and convince Casimir to rejoin the Divine Realm and end his foolish crusade to rule over everything. Maybe she could show them all she didn't need to be locked up.

She caught Bedisa looking at her with a proud smile plastered on her face. She'd already seen her decision.

Vilmantas leaned forward in his chair with an eager expression.

"Fine, I'll do it. But I would like to make a few stipulations if I may," she said, and Vilmantas gave her a slight nod. "He cannot keep me locked in a temple for the rest of my existence. I also want all my plants from my temple to be transferred."

Vilmantas's eyebrows rose. He glanced at Bedisa, who answered his silent question with a shrug.

"She needed something to do."

"But are plants truly that important?"

"Yes, they're important," Saderna said and crossed her arms. She glared at Vilmantas, who let out another sigh.

"Fine, I will inform Casimir of your requirements. Though I'm unsure if he will let you roam his realm freely."

"I'm sure he can be negotiated with," Bedisa added when

sparks raced up Saderna's arms.

"We shall see. Now, if you'll excuse me, I have to get back to my research," he rose from his chair and walked over to a box filled with scrolls.

Saderna fled the room and slammed into an immortal carrying a large silver tray filled with wine goblets. A couple of them tipped over, causing the wine to spill onto the pristine floors.

"Watch it!" The immortal snarled at her.

Saderna mumbled her apologies and grabbed the fallen goblets. She hastily placed them back on the tray before hurrying down the hall.

"Saderna!"

Bedisa called out to her, but she didn't stop until they were on the steps outside the palace.

"Saderna, wait for me!"

She took a few deep breaths before she faced the goddess.

"How could you do this to me?"

Bedisa's face fell. "I'm sorry."

"You could've given me a warning."

A flurry of brown and gold sparks whirled around Bedisa.

"No, you wouldn't have left your temple if I told you."

"What if I didn't agree to go to Casimir's realm? Would you have dragged me there against my will?"

Bedisa bowed her head, and Saderna walked away.

"You've done the right thing. Your actions today will save countless lives!" Bedisa called after her.

She's lying.

A voice from deep within her said. Goosebumps formed on

her skin.

For the first time in her existence, she wished she was back in her temple.

Chapter Two

The smell of blood and fear hung in the air like an invisible fog. The forest had become quieter than a tomb.

"Something isn't right," Aiden whispered. A seeking rune floated around him. "The creature should be right in front of us. But there isn't anything but trees and dead logs."

Henry let a wave of orange swirls arc out of him and into the surrounding forest.

"Anything?"

"Quiet, I need to concentrate," Henry said and closed his eyes. His vision transformed into a sea of grey and orange swirls; there was no sign of life.

"This is looking like a bunch of hogwash," Aiden grumbled when Henry opened his eyes.

"We saw the mangled corpses, and we haven't seen nor heard a bird in days."

"Maybe the animals in the forest are afraid of us?"

Henry held up his seeking rune. "It's here somewhere, and we need to find it before things get worse."

Aiden pressed his lips together and glared at his rune. "I think it's broken."

"Only a fool says his tools are the problem."

"Since when did you start trying to spout wisdom? Are you finally taking the mantle of the God of Justice and Mercy seriously?"

"Big words coming from the God of Truth, who doesn't even have a temple."

"Maybe we're not cut out for this. We're only half-divine, and what if this creature is stronger than us?"

"You want to turn back? Right in the middle of a hunt?"

Before Aiden could come up with a reply, a low growl reverberated through the forest. Their seeking runes lit up like small suns; Henry shoved his into his pouch before the light blinded him. He reached for his axes and let magic flow from his body into the weapons. A lightning rune etched into the metal glowed a soft orange. Energy crackled around him as he shifted into a defensive stance.

"Come on out, you big lug; I'm tired of chasing you!" Henry shouted while Aiden unsheathed his sword. Unlike Henry, he didn't enchant his weapons. He was always rambling on about keeping the metal pure.

"Oh, let's piss it off further," Aiden mumbled, just loud enough for him to hear.

"What the hell is wrong with you?" Henry peered into the forest.

"Nothing," Aiden grumbled.

"No, something is wrong," Henry whirled to face him, "spit it out!"

The blood drained from Henry's face when he saw a large red gash on Aiden's stomach. His tunic was torn to shreds.

"When in the hell did that happen?"

"Just now," Aiden said with gritted teeth and inclined his head toward a looming shadow.

Henry unleashed a curse and pulled out a shielding rune. It created an invisible shield around his body just as the shadow raced toward him. A swirl of darkness surrounded him for a moment, then faded when the creature retreated a few steps. The thing turned back to Aiden, who had a protection rune hovered above him while he used a healing rune to stem the flow of blood from his body.

"Aiden, you need to use a shielding rune on this thing!" Henry shouted and flung a wave of air towards the creature.

"What? That's absurd! Shielding is meant for light, magical blows!" Aiden shouted.

"Just do it!"

Aiden summoned his shielding rune, but it was too late, and the shadow creature tossed him against a tree like he was nothing.

Henry poured more magic into his axes and threw one at the creature. The shadow didn't move, and, instead, the axe froze in front of the creature. A tendril of dark smoke wrapped itself around the handle. The light inside the steel sputtered, and shadows spewed forth from the lightning rune. In the blink of an eye, the axe disappeared.

Shit. Henry tamped down on the wave of fear that swept through his body. He needed to stay calm. His mortal half screamed at him to run, but if he ran, it would mean his death.

"Henry, do something!" Aiden shouted as the creature advanced toward him.

Henry shoved his remaining axe back into its sheath and tugged out his divine runestone. Aiden's eyes widened at the sight of the two orange triangles.

"Not that!"

"I don't have a choice!"

Henry gripped the rune in his hand and filled it until it was almost unbearable to hold. His senses heightened, and he could feel every living thing within a hundred-mile radius. He took a breath and narrowed his focus on the creature in front of him. His body vibrated while the intense energy overwhelmed his mortal form. The air crackled around him, and time slowed.

The shadow let out a screech and began moving towards him faster than it should. Aiden was shouting something, but Henry couldn't hear him over the sound of the crackling orange energy. Right before his body reached its limit, he formed a ball of lightning in his hand and slammed it into the shadow creature.

The creature let out an ear-shattering scream and exploded. Scattered shadows filled the air before they dissolved into ash.

Henry fell to his knees, and the runestone went dark. His fingers dug into the dirt; he struggled to keep his mortal side from fading away.

"Henry," Aiden called out to him.

His eyes flew open, and he rushed to his friend's side. Aiden had pressed his hands to the gaping wound in his stomach. The wound would have killed a mere mortal, but thanks to his half-divine blood, he was still breathing. For now.

"Can you walk?"

Aiden stared at him incredulously. "No!"

"Just checking," Henry said, and Aiden groaned.

"The damn creature drained me dry," Aiden held up a healing rune. Not a drop of magic was in the stone.

"Can you use your divine rune?"

The runestone in question floated out of his pouch. It was carved to look like a flaming chalice. But no light shimmered in the carvings. The rune was empty.

"Gods above, is the God of Ruin making shadow vampires now?" Henry muttered to himself.

"Henry, can you stop your musing for five seconds and heal me?" Aiden asked. His skin was turning an odd shade of purple. Henry could feel Aiden's divine half struggled to keep his mortal half from succumbing to his injuries.

Henry's healing rune floated out of his pouch, and he let it do its work. He ignored the dull ache in his bones. He was getting close to his limit, but he didn't care. He would not lose his friend to a damn shadow.

After what felt like eons, Aiden's wound stopped bleeding, and Henry collapsed onto the ground. He crawled over to a tree and rested his head against the rough bark. The soothing energy of the forest eased his nerves.

"What in the hell was that thing?" Aiden asked.

A bird started singing somewhere deep in the woods, signaling to the other creatures there were no monsters nearby. For the first time in days, Henry let himself relax a bit.

"I don't know."

"Should we tell the others?"

Henry sighed and stared at the canopy of branches above him.

"Henry, if we could only fight off the creature by using dangerous levels of magic, how are the humans going to fare?"

"They don't listen, Aiden. Unless it's a direct threat to their existence, they won't lift a finger to help."

"Yes, but that thing drained my magic! My *divine* magic."

"Remember, we're not full gods. Maybe our mortal blood makes us weaker."

"I remember; you remind me every damn day." Aiden rose to his feet; Henry was quick to follow. Aiden patted his stomach a few times before he gave Henry a withering look.

"No, I don't," Henry said and checked the area for any sign of the monster they'd vanquished.

"What is it?"

"We have nothing to show the townsfolk," Henry ran a hand through his hair and tried to quell his rising frustration. They had barely enough money to get him a new axe, much less afford a meal.

"We're hunting our dinner tonight, aren't we?" Aiden took a step forward, but he swayed so much he had to lean against a tree to keep from falling.

"No, it means *I'm* hunting," Henry gestured to a dead tree. "When you've got enough strength, see if you can make a fire. The smoke will let the people know the forest is safe."

He ventured off into the forest before Aiden could protest.

The next morning, Henry awoke to the sounds of a forest filled with life. A small smile crossed his lips. For a moment, the world was restored to what it had been before the God of Ruin had unleashed his creations. From across the smoldering fire, a low groan had him scrambling to his feet. He readied his axe in one hand and a fire rune in another.

Instead of a monster, Aiden was curled up on his bedroll. His skin was a dark grey with angry red welts scattered all over his body.

"Aiden? Can you hear me?" He knelt next to him, careful not to brush his skin.

"Yes," Aiden said, his voice was barely above a whisper.

Henry pulled out his healing rune, but it didn't make a difference. Aiden took a shaky breath.

"It seems I caught some kind of plague," he said and tried to rise.

"Stay down, and I'll go fetch a Vestral."

"Henry, a Vestral isn't strong enough to heal this." Aiden held up a hand. His skin was turning translucent.

Henry sat back on his heels. He was right. No Vestral, not even one who served the God of Healing, could fix this. It would require too much energy to channel, and the human body wasn't made to handle an extreme amount of divine magic.

He pulled out a small map and his seeking rune. The portal moved constantly, and the only way to find it was to use a seeking rune. This was supposed to keep curious mortals from finding it, but it wasn't foolproof, and sometimes a mortal would enter; never to be seen again.

The rune hovered over the map while Henry visualized

the portal they used to traverse between realms. The rune spun around, and both men watched it stop. Henry let out a breath when it informed them the portal wasn't far away.

"The Goddess of Fates must be on your side today," he said and helped him to his feet, doing his best not to grip too hard. They stumbled through the underbrush; Henry gripped his seeking rune. The stone heated the closer they got to the portal.

"How much farther is this damn thing?" Aiden asked. More parts of his body were becoming translucent. His mortal self was hanging on by a thin thread.

Henry used a fire rune to burn away a thick brush and sighed with relief. A portal, made of black and blue stones, hovered a few feet above the ground. Henry pulled out his divine rune, and the portal hummed as they approached.

"Take us to the God of Healing's residence," he said to the rippling mirage. Before Aiden could say a word, Henry used a wind rune to propel them through.

The momentum carried them through the gateway and across the bridge that connected to the portal in the Divine Realm. They moved so fast; Henry barely had time to adjust to his divine form. He gritted his teeth as the realm's influence wove into his mortal side, sending electric shockwaves through his body. His mortal half had to be shielded the entire time he was in this blasted place; otherwise, he'd perish.

Appearance-wise, it wasn't much different from his mortal form; his hair would be a lighter shade of red. Unlike full gods, he was stuck in the form he was born in.

They slammed into a wall. Aiden crumpled to the ground; his body was still fading.

"What in all of creation is going on?" A voice boomed.

Henry looked up from Aiden's fallen form to find Errapel, the God of Healing, staring at him slack-jawed.

"We need help!" Henry said and gestured to Aiden. The shock in Errapel's face was replaced with a grim determination. He swept back a lock of long dark hair away from his eyes and clapped his hands. A pair of divines dressed in flowing light pink dresses joined him at his side. They all could have passed for a human if it weren't for the long-pointed ears.

"Take him to the Healing Well," Errapel said. His assistants swept up Aiden with ease and hurried out of the room.

"How long will it take him to heal?" Henry asked when the door slid shut.

Errapel's dark pink eyes narrowed, and he gestured at the hole in the wall Henry had created.

"You destroyed my painting! And you had no right to use my personal portal! Do you know how long it took me to get one?"

Henry clenched his fists at his sides. "I had no choice."

"Bah, you should've come the moment Aiden got injured. You could have gone the proper route! Now, I've got to do a mountain of paperwork!"

It took every fiber of Henry's being to keep himself from smashing his fist into the god's face. Why mortals loved the divines who ruled over them so much was beyond him.

"Are you seriously going to give me a lecture on portal usage when my friend is dying?"

"He'll be fine. His mortal side is still attached to his body," Errapel said and waved at the door. "I'll send word when he's healed."

"But—"

Errapel shoved him out the door and slammed it shut. Henry scowled and banged on the door. When it became clear Errapel wasn't coming back, he stormed away.

A tall sentry dressed in plate armor moved toward him.

"Excuse me. It seems you have brought undocumented weapons from the Mortal Realm. Please hand them over so we can have the Temple of Portals store them during your visit."

Henry groaned but quickly handed over his axe and his rune pouch. The last thing he needed was a reason for Vilmantas to summon him. The weapons were useless here.

"Guess I'll just sit at the tavern and wait," he muttered. He watched a pair of immortals float past him. Like Errapel and his assistants, they were in human form and sported the strange ears. Divine fashion sense was a strange thing. The last time he was here, everyone had spider-like legs.

He headed into the city proper, weaving through the crowded streets. He stepped into an alleyway that led to the back door of the tavern but was blocked by a large, cloaked figure. They lowered their hood to reveal a skeleton with glowing red eyes. Henry summoned a vortex of orange lightning around him. The light caused an amulet hanging from the creature's neck to glow. It had two crimson x's in the center hanging from the creature's neck. It was the divine rune for the God of War.

"Einar, that form is much more suitable for the God of Death than the God of War," Henry said with a grin. The skeleton transformed into a tall man with dark hair and scarlet eyes. Crimson runes were painted onto the god's bronze skin, giving the impression he was ready to head out onto a battlefield at any moment.

"Does anything scare you?"

"Nope."

"Hah, I don't believe you. Someday I will find what you are truly scared of!" Einar clapped him on the back, "Where is Aiden?"

Henry quickly recounted the events of the last few days. When he was done, Einar's eyes glowed a deep ruby.

"Oh, I would love to get my hands on one of those… things," he said.

"Come to my realm, and you just might."

"You know I can't. Vilmantas still doesn't trust me."

Einar had been sent as a tribute from Casimir a few thousand years before Henry was born. Vilmantas rarely let the god out of his sight.

"That's no surprise since you insist on trying to scare the divinity out of everyone. Maybe Vilmantas thinks you're planning something."

Einar let out a bitter laugh. "Old bastard is getting more and more paranoid with each passing year. I never want to go back to that shithole."

They stepped aside to let a pair of glittering divines pass.

"What is up with the ears, and why don't you have them?"

"New god was born; he's supposed to rule over the newest species. They call themselves elves," Einar said with a shrug. "The ears are part of their charm apparently, but it doesn't go with my aesthetic."

"Ah, I wonder why I wasn't summoned for a big welcoming

party."

"Zimri got sent back."

Henry's blood ran cold. Was this the reason Casimir's monsters had gotten worse over the past few days?

"What do you mean sent back?"

Einar glanced around and lowered his voice. "Zimri pissed Casimir off, and now they are sending Saderna to his realm to keep things from escalating. Vilmantas tried to keep the information from spreading, but you know how it goes. It only takes one spirit to send things into a tizzy around here."

"Saderna is…who again?"

He could never keep track of all the divines who lived here. His mother had only taught him the important names.

"The Goddess of Peace, the one who's been kept away from us. You were there to celebrate her creation; it was only twenty years ago!"

"Oh, now I remember. She wasn't there."

Henry recalled a vague memory of a rather dull party whose only saving grace was the large wine fountains. The goddess had been whisked away to a temple the moment she'd been created for reasons Vilmantas never specified.

"Yes, it rather ruined the fun. What's the point of a welcoming party if the person you are throwing it for is already under lock and key?"

"Speaking of fun, why don't you join me at the tavern? It will be a while before Aiden is ready to return."

"Before you do, Vilmantas would like to speak with you," a shrill disembodied voice said.

Henry gave Einar a sympathetic look when Airi, the

messenger spirit favored by Vilmantas, appeared. She was a silver humanoid with bright yellow eyes.

"Good luck, my friend, and I'll save a spot for you," Henry turned on his heel and started toward the tavern.

Airi floated around them and pointed at Henry. "He wants to see you."

Einar snorted and laughed when Henry's jaw dropped.

"Me?"

"Vilmantas is not in a patient mood. I suggest you hurry," the spirit said before she vanished.

"I'll save you a seat," Einar clapped him on the shoulder and sauntered away.

He paid little mind to the immortals in the street. They were busy perusing the marketplaces, boasting goods from all the realms. He focused solely on the door of the Great Palace. Vilmantas would likely sense his presence before he even arrived.

He shoved his way through the great doors, sending a few spider-like immortals to hug the walls.

Once he reached the doors of Vilmantas's quarters, he took a breath and pushed them open. Vilmantas was staring out a window with his hands clasped behind his back. The god was one of the tallest divines in existence. Like the other divines, he was also sporting the elf ears.

He didn't move when Henry stormed into the room.

"It's rather rude to enter without knocking first," Vilmantas said.

"You knew I was coming."

Vilmantas turned to face him. His dark purple eyes were bright with anger. With a flick of a finger, a clear crystal orb appeared in front of him. Runes flashed across the smooth surface. It was a rune used to monitor the magic levels of a realm.

"Would you mind explaining why there was an extreme amount of divine magic flowing out of your realm?"

Henry quickly went over the fight with the creature. Vilmantas had him repeat it a few times while a spirit took notes. When he was finished, the anger had faded from Vilmantas's eyes. He tapped the orb, and it vanished from sight.

"I was not aware such a thing existed," Vilmantas said.

"Perhaps Casimir is hiding things from you?"

Purple smoke churned around Vilmantas while his face remained impassive.

"That is impossible because I am knowledge itself."

"Everyone has a weak spot."

Vilmantas went still, and Henry thought he turned to stone. Every divine had a weakness. Not even the God of Knowledge could escape that fact. Henry was lucky; his weakness was simple—he was half-divine. Other divines could go for eons not knowing what their weakness was and become comfortable with the idea they had none.

"I don't have a weakness," Vilmantas snapped and stormed across the room. His sudden movement caused Henry to jump back.

"If you don't have a weakness, why don't you get off your arse and help me get these damn creatures out of my realm!"

"Watch your tone, Huestace."

Henry bristled at the use of his divine name.

"That's *not* my name."

Vilmantas laughed. "Yes, it is. The name Henry has no power."

"Forgive me if I prefer the name that was given to me by my parents instead of an ancient waste of air."

They stared at each other, then Vilmantas's right eye twitched.

"If you are so concerned with the mortals, why don't you forgo your mortal side and embrace your role as the God of Justice and Mercy."

"I do; besides keeping them safe from monsters, I give a sparkle show at the temples every month."

"Your mother had thousands of realms worshipping her because of her work, and you've reduced it to one. I bet she could've taken on Casimir's creatures without blinking an eye."

"Don't you *dare* bring my mother into this," Henry snarled. His fingers twitched, and his magic strained to the point he thought his skin was going to melt off. "You're the one who doomed her and my father."

"They did that to themselves," Vilmantas snapped; the air between them became taut with electricity. There was no way Henry would win the fight, Vilmantas was a full divine and didn't have the confines of mortality swimming in his veins.

"I need you to expand your horizons."

"How do you expect me to do that and keep my realm safe from these damn creatures? I'm asking for your help!"

"Try harder."

Henry tensed and clenched his hands at his sides. Sparks of orange flame danced on his skin. This bastard dared to tell him to try harder when he was doing everything he could to ensure his realm didn't fall to the hands of Casimir?

"I am doing everything I can. Why don't you help?" he

asked, keeping his voice cool.

"I will not interfere; if I did, I'd never stop. There are too many realms to keep track of. Besides, Saderna will head to Casimir's realm soon enough, and I'm sure she can persuade him."

Henry scoffed. "You must be joking; she's been locked up in a temple for almost two decades, and you expect her to get him to stop? What is she going to do? Flutter her eyelashes at him?"

"She is the Goddess of Peace, and she will do what she must to ensure the treaty holds," Vilmantas shrugged, then narrowed his eyes. "Once Casimir has reined in his abominations, I expect you to step up in your duties."

"Or what?"

Vilmantas stalked over to him and grabbed him by his shirt collar.

"Or I'll have you put into a temple so remote and so isolated, the only thing you'll be able to do is answer the damn petitions," he hissed and gave Henry a good shove.

Henry took a deep breath and straightened his shirt. He needed to calm down before he really got in trouble.

"All right."

Vilmantas blinked. Surprise flickered across his face.

"Truly?"

"I promise to step up my duties. I will have my statues sparkle *twice* a month," he said, resisting the urge to laugh as Vilmantas's face turned red, then purple.

"You—"

"You never set the terms," Henry held up his hands and gave Vilmantas what he hoped was an innocent smile.

"Get. Out." Vilmantas said through clenched teeth. Henry hastened out of the room before he'd reached the end of the god's patience.

The three moons shone brightly in the sky as he sprinted down the steps with a flurry of violet sparks surging past him.

He didn't stop until he was at the tavern where he found Einar drinking at a table nestled in the corner. The tavern was not like a human one; it was in the open air where the patrons could enjoy the moonlight. A few divines glanced in his direction, but most were engrossed in their liquor.

"What did you do now?" Einar asked when Henry grabbed the tankard from his hands and finished the last of the ale.

"Bastard wanted to give me a lecture," he said.

"With the amount of magic Vilmantas let out, I thought you'd be a walking ember."

Einar summoned the tavern spirit who set down a couple more tankards of ale.

"I almost was. He wasn't thrilled about the creature Casimir let loose."

"Is he going to do anything?"

"No, he's too busy trying to get that goddess prepped for her sacrifice."

"Do you want to take a bet on how long she'll last in Casimir's realm?"

Henry stared into his tankard and watched the brown liquid swirl around before he raised an eyebrow at Einar.

"If she doesn't last, we go to war."

Einar shrugged and held out a small gem pouch, "I'll bet this entire bag she lasts a day."

Henry reached into his own pouch and held up two gold coins.

"Two months."

"You have that much faith in the Goddess of Peace?"

"No, but it gives me time to prepare."

If war was coming, he needed all the time he could get.

Chapter Three

Saderna collapsed onto a settee; the entire day had been nothing but meetings and introductions to immortals she'd never see again.

A chorus of laughter had her rising from her seat and over to the window. A pair of young immortals were flittering about the large bushes that encircled the courtyard below.

She wished she could walk around without a care in the world. Instead, she was being shuttled around like an object.

The air shimmered, and Saderna braced herself.

"Hello, Saderna," Airi materialized next to her. "You've been summoned."

"By whom?"

"I've been sworn to secrecy."

"I didn't know you could be made to hold secrets."

The spirit merely blinked and inclined her head towards

the door.

"If you could please hurry, I have many tasks to accomplish today."

She followed the spirit out of the room and into the cavernous hall. Immortals stared at her as she hurried after Airi; she ignored them. It wasn't long before they were in a room filled with crystal chandeliers and walls covered in gilded roses.

A short god with blond hair stood in the center, clutching a lyre to his chest. He whirled around to face her when Airi slammed the door shut.

"Thank you for coming," the god said.

"And you are?" Saderna asked since there were no runes on the god's silver tunic. Nothing about him seemed familiar.

"Zimri, the God of Music."

A surge of power flooded her veins.

"You're the god responsible for almost plunging us into an inter-realm war," Saderna said, unable to keep the iciness out of her voice. "I'm not sure if I should thank you for getting me out of my temple or curse you for condemning me to Casimir's realm."

"You don't understand. That realm is absolute torture for a divine like me," Zimri sighed and shook his head.

"If you're here to beg for my forgiveness, you will not receive it. Ask me in a few thousand years once the repercussions of your actions have been fully realized." Saderna spun on her heel and marched toward the door.

"Wait!" Zimri surged ahead of her and flung himself in front of the door.

"Get out of my way," Saderna snapped.

"Please, you need to listen to me!"

"About what?"

"The Realm of Ruin, you don't know what it's like."

Saderna rolled her eyes. She'd already received a hundred different lectures on how Casimir's realm operated, and she didn't need one from him. It was taking every ounce of her willpower to keep from throwing him into a chandelier. He ruined her life, not that she had much of one in the first place, and this was all his fault.

"They've already given me the speech on how it's an exact copy of this realm, but much drearier and filled with decay."

"It's worse than that!" Zimri cried, grabbing her arm.

A gust of air flew out of her hands and flung Zimri into a wall.

"Countless gods and goddesses have been traded between realms. You're the only one who took the route of a coward! Now I must pay the price for your actions. All because you couldn't handle it!" She shouted as swirls of gold and blue pulsed around her.

"His realm was eating away at my soul! Every song I created turned into a bastardized version of itself! I was changing!" Zimri shot back.

Saderna scoffed. "I've been told the opposite by every divine that came from there."

Zimri clasped his hands together and fell to his knees.

"You must believe me. You're the Goddess of Peace! What if you get corrupted and turned into something else!"

"That is impossible."

"Trust me. I saw many divines who came from this realm

and how much they changed."

"Changed? How? Did they start wearing Casimir's colors?"

"They became the opposite version of themselves."

Saderna laughed. The sound rang hollow in her ears. "I hate to break it to you, but the God of War already exists."

"Maybe you'll change into something else!"

"Like what?"

"Zimri, what in all of creation are you doing!" Vilmantas stormed into the room, preventing the god from replying.

A surge of violet lightning swept past Saderna as Vilmantas grabbed Zimri by the collar of his tunic. He lifted the god off his feet and let him dangle in the air.

"What did he tell you?" He asked Saderna, his gaze never leaving Zimri, who was trying in vain to free himself.

"That the Realm of Ruin will corrupt me."

Vilmantas's tense shoulders relaxed a fraction before he threw Zimri onto the ground. He grabbed the lyre and broke it half. He tossed the remains onto the floor. Zimri dropped to his knees as tears streamed down his face.

"If you continue to spew lies, I will have you stripped of your divinity and sent into a backwater realm."

Zimri curled up into a ball. The god started whimpering while Vilmantas used his lightning to break the lyre into smaller pieces.

Despite her anger towards him about his actions in Casimir's realm, it was hard to watch him crawl towards his ruined instrument.

"You didn't have to break his lyre," Saderna said when Vilmantas motioned for her to follow him.

"Zimri is lucky I enjoy his music. If any other divine had been kicked out of Casimir's realm like he was, they'd be long gone by now."

Vilmantas led her back through the palace towards her temporary chambers, and Saderna couldn't help but replay Zimri's words in her mind.

"Is it true?"

"What?"

"Does the Realm of Ruin cause a divine to change?"

Vilmantas laughed. "No, it doesn't, at least not in the way Zimri was implying. You would have to give yourself over to the realm's influence and let it twist you."

"Was Zimri allowing himself to be changed?"

"He claims he wasn't allowing it, but Zimri is a fickle god. He's done odd things to gain my favor before."

"But what if he's telling the truth? You told me the reason I was locked up was to keep me from being corrupted."

Vilmantas paused and rested a hand on her shoulder.

"I can understand if you're hesitant, but please remember, Zimri likes to embellish things, especially now that the guilt is hitting him. He's going to do everything he can to justify his actions and make it seem like he's innocent in this matter."

Saderna sighed. "I hate this."

"Trust me; if there were another way or another divine I could send, I would send them." Vilmantas started walking again. "You are my prized jewel, and Casimir has been clamoring to have you ever since you were created."

Before Saderna could respond, a tall willowy male rounded the corner ahead of them. He was followed by a crowd of immortals, all of them clamoring for his attention. With brown hair that fell below his long-pointed ears, golden skin, and a strong jawline, it was easy to see why he'd gained such a following.

"Vilmantas!" The male cried and rushed over to them. He gave Saderna a puzzled look. "Who is this?"

"Tarmo, this is Saderna, the Goddess of Peace," Vilmantas said.

Tarmo smiled widely at her, causing his already handsome features to almost be unbearable to look at.

"I'm the God of the Elves," he said. "I'm afraid my people don't yet worship you, but perhaps I could make an exception."

His gaze swept her up and down. Something inside of her recoiled. Vilmantas cleared his throat.

"Save your seductions for something else. Saderna is leaving tonight."

"You're no fun, Vilmantas," the elf god said, but he waved to his followers and continued down the hallway. He flashed Saderna another grin before he sauntered through a doorway. Vilmantas let out a long sigh.

"I've always hated new gods and their desire to sleep with anything that moves."

"I never had that problem."

Vilmantas nodded. "Only because I kept you away from everyone. Which is something I might need to do with Tarmo until he cools down and finds his divine purpose. Or he finally sets his sights on some poor mortal in his realm."

Vilmantas flicked a lock of his hair over his shoulder.

"But enough of such talk, let's get you back to your chamber. You have a long journey ahead."

Hours later, Saderna was standing at the entrance of the Temple of Portals. The temple was a giant elm tree. The inside was hollowed out and held most of the portals to various realms within its branches.

She'd changed into a flowing black gown with tiny silver stars that had been embroidered into the fabric. It was the finest piece of clothing she'd ever owned, and it would be in tatters by the time she got to Casimir's palace.

"Are you ready?" Bedisa asked.

Saderna nodded. She hadn't spoken to the goddess in days.

Bedisa must've sensed she wasn't going to start speaking to her because she gave a sharp knock on the doors.

The doors flew open to reveal a large chamber filled to the brim with immortals.

In the center of the room stood a large portal made of obsidian and a blue stone Saderna couldn't identify. Runes carved into the stones flickered like a candle, bathing the room in a silver light. The center of the portal had a shimmering grey barrier that hummed a rather gentle tune.

The portal was hovering a few feet above the ground, not too far from a steep flight of stairs. Sentries in shining plate armor stood at either side of the stairs, keeping curious divines from getting too close.

"Good evening, gentle ones!" A voice called from the crowd. "The portal will open shortly!"

Saderna's heart started pounding as Bedisa led her through the crowd of immortals. Most of whom bowed their heads when she passed. A brush of her magic told her most of them were filled with relief, except for two outliers who had annoyance seeping out of them.

She let her powers sweep through the crowd as curiosity got the best of her. It settled over Einar, who was glaring at a tall redheaded male. Neither of them noticed her invisible threads weaving around them.

Unlike the other immortals, the readhead was more solid. His presence was nothing like she'd ever felt before. She moved towards them, drawn in by that strange aura. She stopped when another male joined him.

He looked similar to the redhead, though his hair was a dark shade of auburn, and he wasn't nearly as handsome.

"Who are they?" She asked Bedisa, who cast a dirty look at the two males.

"The redhead is Henry, God of Justice and Mercy, and the dull one is Aiden, God of Truth. They are half-human," she said with a hint of disdain.

"Can I talk to them? I've never met a half-god before."

Before Bedisa could respond, Vilmantas appeared at the base of the steps underneath the portal.

"Gentle ones, tonight we will be making history and sending another tribute to the Realm of Ruin after our dear Zimri was kicked out. Zimri is currently composing new music and he will join us shortly."

A chorus of murmurs swept through the crowd.

"I wondered why we had no music," a goddess murmured to her companion.

"Well, at least our parties won't be so boring. Two weeks

without Zimri's melodies was absolute *torture*."

"Saderna, don't do it," Bedisa whispered as blue and gold sparks slithered up her skin.

"They don't realize how close we came to war, and they're concerned about music? Someone needs to set them straight," she whispered back.

"Yes, but you don't need to get on Vilmantas's bad side."

Saderna clenched her fists at her sides, keeping herself from doing something she'd regret later. She cast a withering glance at the two deities, who merely nodded and raised their goblets at her.

"Please give Saderna a warm round of applause as she embarks on one of the most sacred and important duties in our realm!" Vilmantas shouted, and Bedisa gave her a light shove towards the portal.

The applause died down when she made it to Vilmantas's side.

Vilmantas handed her a scroll made of silver paper and sealed with Vilmantas's divine rune.

"As is tradition, Saderna will give Casimir a copy of the peace treaty and sign it once she has crossed over."

The crowd let out another cheer as Vilmantas led Saderna over to the stairs. The shimmering grey center of the portal changed to a dark blue.

"Good luck Saderna, and may you bring peace to us all," Vilmantas leaned down and whispered in her ear. "If you fail, we will plunge into war, and the blood of millions will be on your hands. Remember your place and make sure you follow all the rules."

Saderna could only nod. A lump had formed in her throat, keeping her from talking. She cast one last glance around the room; everyone was smiling at her. Probably more excited that their party would resume the moment she left. She took a breath and headed up to the portal.

She reached a hand out towards the shimmering field. A flash filled the space, and Saderna was sent flying backward into a wall.

Her vision swam with crimson, and a loud ringing filled her ears. The portal was now a pile of smoking rubble, and the crowd was fleeing in terror as several large grey wolves with ruby eyes rose from the wreckage.

Magic flared to life within her, healing her body enough to stand before she could attack the creatures in front of her. Bedisa appeared and pulled her toward the door, flinging air at anyone who got into their way.

"We need to stop them before more people get hurt!" Saderna screamed. An immortal close to her was grabbed and torn in half by a giant wolf.

"We need to get you out of here," Bedisa tightened her grip on Saderna's arm.

A glimpse of orange sparks caught her eye as Bedisa continued to pull her towards the door. The half-god, Henry, was running straight toward a wolf. Orange lightning wove around him in a blaze of fury. Einar was close behind him; pure glee was all over the god's face.

Henry jumped onto the beast, and Bedisa shoved her through the door, slamming it shut.

"We need to help them!" Saderna tried to open the door,

but red runes flared in the wood and shoved her back, causing Bedisa to stumble on her skirt.

"Saderna, there are immortals in there who have eons of combat experience."

"But maybe I can calm the situation?"

Bedisa sighed. "You can't."

"Does this mean we're going to war?"

"I don't know," brown smoke swarmed around her. "How could this slip by me?"

A chill swept through Saderna's blood.

"You didn't see this?"

"No, I saw nothing of the sort. Everything was fine," Bedisa's voice dropped to a whisper. "This doesn't make any sense."

"Has this ever happened before?"

"Once, but I was tied up with many different fates that day. Sometimes I can miss small things, but I was only focused on your ceremony today."

When they made it to her chambers, sentries were now posted on either side of the door. Runes had been carved into the wood. The same ones that had been used to keep Saderna from leaving her temple.

"What is this?"

Bedisa's brow furrowed. "I don't know."

"Vilmantas's orders," Airi said when she appeared in front of the door. "You are not to leave until we have ensured all threats have been neutralized."

"But I can help!"

"That is not my concern. You can either get into your chambers without causing a scene, or I can use my magic on you and get you inside."

"This isn't fair! I can help!" Saderna shouted. Airi's golden eyes turned red, and she grabbed Saderna's arm.

In the blink of an eye, Saderna was standing alone inside her chambers. She slammed into the door with all her might, but the wards pushed her back.

She threw herself at the doors again and was almost thrown into a wall.

"Saderna, stop it! You're going to hurt yourself! I promise you won't be stuck in there forever," Bedisa's voice drifted into the room. "I'll be right back."

Saderna slumped against the door, listening to her footsteps fade.

Her magic was in turmoil, and her divine purpose swept through the realm, searching for any signs of war. There was nothing aside from the chaos in the Temple of Portals. She didn't move from the door until the screaming faded.

She wandered over to a window that looked out at the Temple of Portals. The tree showed no outward signs of the chaos within.

Saderna replayed the event over and over in her mind. If Casimir wanted her so badly, why would he try to have her killed? Was he trying to force her to be reborn?

And what about those wolves? She'd never read about any such creature in her library. Then again, she had limited material.

She rested her head against the glass. There were too many questions and not enough answers.

"Saderna?" Bedisa called from the door.

"Yes?"

"You're going to have to stay here for a day or so. Vilmantas has ordered a complete sweep of the city. Don't worry, he'll allow you to have company once he's sure they won't try to attack you."

Saderna let out a long sigh. "Are we going to war?"

"Vilmantas is trying to contact Casimir."

Bedisa's aura becomes inundated with concern.

"You don't sense any signs of war?" She asked after a minute.

"No, and I'm assuming you can't see the future?"

Bedisa remained silent.

"Bedisa?"

"Saderna, no matter what happens, promise me you will stay true to yourself and don't trust anyone," Bedisa paused, and when she continued, her voice was thick with sorrow. "Promise me that when you find someone worth fighting for, you won't give up on them. Promise me you will forgive them for hurting you."

"Bedisa? Are you seeing my future?"

Her answer was the goddess's footsteps echoing down the hall.

Saderna sighed and pushed away from the window. She headed into her bed-chamber and changed into a simple grey tunic with black pants. She was done with finery for the time being. When she made her way over to the bed, she spotted a small scroll with a blue tulip tucked underneath it.

Smiling to herself, she grabbed the tulip and inhaled. The smell soothed her frazzled mind while she grabbed the small scroll.

It was sealed with a divine rune she didn't recognize. It was a hand covering what looked like a mouth.

She carefully unrolled the scroll.

Sorry about the mess.

She dropped it onto her bed and backed away. What in all of creation was going on? Had someone deliberately destroyed the portal? Was someone trying to make them go to war?

Again, she had more questions than answers.

She grabbed the scroll and scanned it. There wasn't a trace of magic inside of it. She shoved it into a pocket and left the bedchamber. She checked every room, making sure something wasn't lurking in the shadows. Once she was sure she wasn't going to be attacked, she went over to the two doors with glowing runes.

"Hello? Is anyone out there?" She called out, hoping the sentries would hear her. When she received no response, she started pounding on it.

Don't trust anyone. Bedisa's warning rang in her ears. She withdrew her hands, and slid down onto the floor.

"What do I do now?"

Her words were met with silence.

Chapter Four

"This is ridiculous. We've been stuck here for almost a week," Henry grumbled and grabbed a pint of ale. He was sitting in the open-air tavern next to Einar and Aiden. Vilmantas had ordered every portal shut until further notice and no one was allowed to leave the city.

Since the portals were closed, there was nothing for him to do except listen to his petitioners and drink at the tavern. How anyone could live a life this boring was beyond him.

"At least we aren't him," Einar said and tilted his tankard to where Tarmo was sitting. He was, as usual, surrounded by the fairest and most handsome divines in the realm. All of them vying for his attention and the opportunity to rule his realm at his side. Tarmo, however, did not seem interested in their conversation and was staring into space.

"Just wait till another divine is born; they'll move on."

"Why hasn't he started ruling over his realm? I've heard rumors the elves are in complete chaos at the moment."

"Everything is in chaos," Henry muttered and took a long drink.

"I wonder why Casimir didn't request him. The Goddess of Peace is too valuable," Einar said. "Tarmo, over there, is much younger and could be persuaded to join his cause."

"Maybe Casimir wants to draw up a new treaty?" Aiden asked, and Einar shrugged.

"Who knows, but it would've been much more entertaining if they sent him," Einar nodded at a goddess who was batting her five eyes at Tarmo. "I'd pay good coin to see what would've happened if he tried this shit in Casimir's court."

"Aye, he gives you a run for your money Henry. He doesn't even have to appear interested, and he still has them falling all over him." Aiden said, and Einar raised his eyebrows.

"I didn't take you for a flirt Henry."

Henry shrugged. "I had little else to do before Casimir's monsters showed up."

"I bet you couldn't get any of them to take their eyes off of Tarmo."

Einar held out a small pouch of gemstones and tilted his head toward a group of giggling goddesses. Henry licked his lips at the sight. Those gemstones would be enough to buy that island he'd been eying.

"Double it. I'll have all their eyes on me in mere moments," Henry said and rose. A powerful gust of wind knocked him back onto his chair, and before he knew it, Airi was floating above him.

"You've been summoned by the Sacred Council," she said.

The Sacred Council was a group comprised of the oldest divines. They were supposed to make sure that the realms ran smoothly, and no god interfered with the natural order of things. But for some reason, they turned a blind eye to Casimir's actions.

Vilmantas was a member and Henry really didn't want to talk to him today.

Henry groaned. "I'm not going. I want to go home."

"It is not a suggestion," Airi said, "If you don't come willingly. I have been authorized to use force."

Henry shuddered. His mortal side shrank back at the thought of Airi using her summoning magic on him. She'd done it once. The experience was enough for him to jump to his feet and follow her without complaint.

It wasn't long before he was back in the Great Palace, but instead of Vilmantas's chambers, he was taken to a large meeting hall. It was supposed to be a replica of human architecture, but they got the hearth wrong. It was floating in the center of the room where a table should be.

Vilmantas stood near the fire with Bedisa, along with Burvis, the God of Magic, and Legurta, the Goddess of Marriage and Family. Dearil, the God of Death, was consulting with a flickering shadow.

"Huestace, thank you for joining us," Legurta said before Vilmantas could say anything.

Henry bristled at the use of his divine name but kept his mouth clamped shut. It was one thing to tell off Vilmantas, but he would be an utter fool to reproach Legurta. She was Vilmantas's bond mate, but she was also one of the oldest divines in the room. Most mortals referred to her as the Goddess of Marriage and Family, but she had another lesser-known name. Goddess of Bonds, and she could rip him to shreds without lifting a finger.

"The portal to Casimir's realm has been destroyed," Burvis said.

"Thank you for stating the obvious," Legurta said, and Burvis scowled. Henry swallowed the laugh that threatened to come out.

"We've discovered who destroyed it," Burvis said and plucked some imaginary lint off his shirt.

"Did Saderna do it? Or one of those wolves?"

"Neither of them was the culprit. Something else destroyed it."

"Something else?"

Burvis snapped his fingers, and a dead monster appeared out of thin air and floated next to him. It looked like a snake, but it had a split tail with claws on the end.

"We found this eating the remains of the stones."

"Do you have any idea what type of creature this is?" Vilmantas asked.

Henry raised an eyebrow. "You don't know what it is?"

"I'm afraid Casimir has learned how to cloak these creatures, and I have no idea how he's making them."

Henry frowned. Casimir had found Vilmantas's weakness.

"I was hoping you'd know more," Henry said, and Vilmantas sighed. Legurta walked over and rubbed his back.

"I will have to perform a more intense autopsy," Burvis said and with another snap of his fingers, the monster's corpse disappeared.

"What does this mean? Are we going to war?"

"No, Casimir claims he wasn't the one who destroyed the portal," Legurta said. "He still wants Saderna to join his realm."

"Speaking of realms, how are things in your little one?" Burvis asked.

Henry stared at him and wondered if he was joking, but Burvis stared straight back. Annoyance flickered across his features.

"Wonderful, aside from the monsters Casimir keeps sending."

"And just how strong is Casimir's influence?"

"Well, seeing as he's creating creatures we've never seen before, I'd say pretty strong."

Burvis pursed his lips at this and glanced at Vilmantas with concern. Vilmantas paid him no mind as he clasped his hands behind his back.

"Is the portal to Casimir's realm hard to reach?" Legurta asked.

"For a human? Yes. For a divine? I'm not sure." Henry shrugged. The gods fell silent again, and he could feel Bedisa's gaze upon him.

"It seems we have no choice but to do that plan of yours," Burvis said to Vilmantas.

"What plan?" Henry asked.

Were they going to make him lead an army through the realm? He wasn't sure he could handle being around that many divines for weeks on end.

"We need you to escort Saderna to the portal," Vilmantas said.

Henry's mouth dropped open. Leading an army was one thing, but escorting a goddess who'd been stuck in a temple for most of her life? That was a death sentence.

"I'm not strong enough to protect her. I could barely keep Aiden alive," Henry said. He glanced at Bedisa, who was now studying the floor.

"You don't need to protect her," Burvis paused and looked at Vilmantas for approval. He continued when the other god nodded. "We're more concerned about your safety."

"What could she possibly do to me?" He huffed, trying to sound brave. But he knew full divines could wreak havoc on his mortal half.

"She's destroyed an entire realm before."

"What? That's impossible! She's only been around for twenty cycles!"

"Twenty cycles in this incarnation," Bedisa whispered.

The hair on the back of Henry's neck stood up.

"What in the hell is going on?"

Vilmantas's mouth curled up at the mortal curse word.

"Saderna isn't just the Goddess of Peace. She's also the Goddess of Destruction. We learned it the hard way when she destroyed a realm and almost plunged us into a never-ending war."

Henry knew gods and goddesses could be reborn if they died, but they kept their memories. Saderna didn't seem like an ancient divine at all. Her energy was too new, too hopeful.

"If she's so dangerous, why are you sending her away?"

"Each time she reincarnates, we've chipped away at her mind, hoping to remove the destructive forces within her. This is the first time she's reformed without memories."

"I've scanned her energy, and the destructive part is tucked away deep inside of her," Burvis said. He was now holding a dagger with a silver blade and a copper hilt. A small blue crystal was embedded in the pommel.

"What happens if she goes to Casimir's realm and that part of her is woken up?"

"It's a risk we are willing to take," Vilmantas said with the ease of someone talking about the weather and not a goddess potentially destroying an entire world.

Bile rose in his throat, and he backed away, shaking his head. No, he would not risk his entire realm for some crazy plan. Let the fates choose another way.

"Where are you going?" Vilmantas asked. Violet smoke wove around him like snakes ready to strike.

"I will not be used as a pawn in this sick game you're playing. Get Airi to watch her," Henry snapped and started to leave when an icy wind filled the room. The mortal side of him wanted to flee in terror. Tendrils of black and white smoke curled around the door. In a flash, Dearil stood in front of him. Unlike the other divines, his face was covered by a checkered veil. No one was allowed to see his face.

"Your parents," the god hissed. His voice sent shivers down Henry's spine. "If you agree to escort Saderna through the realm, I will release their souls to the Divine Realm."

Henry swallowed, his hands trembled, and he tried to keep his expression passive.

"And I will grant them minor godhood's," Vilmantas added with a gleam in his eye.

Henry bowed his head, a part of him screaming not to take the offer. But they had found his weakness. His parents deserved to be freed from their prison in the afterlife. He looked at Bedisa. Her face was impassive, though he detected a flicker of pity in her aura. He clenched his fists at his sides.

Damn these arseholes into the darkest pits of the afterlife.

That's rather rude, don't you think? I go there to get away from them. Dearil's voice crept into his skull.

If you don't like my thoughts, then stay out of my head.

I can't help it. You know that.

I'm just thinking!

Stop thinking so loudly.

Henry pulled his magic close and formed a shield in his mind. He didn't need the other gods to poke around his head. It was yet another disadvantage of having mortal blood. Unlike full divines, his mortal half made it so other divines could force their thoughts into his.

"Henry? Do you have an answer for us?" Vilmantas asked.

"I'll do it."

"Excellent!" Burvis rushed forward and handed him the dagger he was still holding along with a small sheath. Tiny streaks of blue lightning danced across the blade.

"What do I need this for?"

"We created this dagger to force a divine to reincarnate if they step out of line. If Saderna loses control, use that dagger on her. It's the only way you can stop her."

"What! If I stab her in that realm, it could take hundreds of years for her to be reborn, and she could *actually* die!" Henry shouted. Dearil took a step toward him. The air chilled further, and Henry clamped his mouth shut.

"It's highly unlikely you'll even have to use it," Burvis said with a yawn. "Saderna is more concerned about plants and her petitioners. She won't be in your realm long enough to cause harm."

"If she doesn't go, then all the realms, including your precious mortal one, will be thrust into a war that would kill millions," Legurta said. She stepped towards him; her eyes flashed with anger. "Are you truly so selfish that you would doom us all to such a fate? Saderna is the Goddess of Peace, and times like this are the reason for her existence."

"Think of your parents," Dearil rasped. Henry did his best to ignore him and turned to Bedisa. The goddess had locked down her aura, though it did little to hide the uncertainty in her face.

"And what do you think? Is this a good idea?"

"Saderna is my friend, at least…she was," Bedisa said, her voice was still so quiet. Her golden gaze searched Henry's, and a sad smile crossed her lips. "We have no other option. If she isn't taken, we will plunge into war."

Henry glared at the dagger and then at the divines around him. He shoved the dagger into the sheath and secured it onto his belt.

"Let's get this over with."

Chapter Five

Saderna twisted the small handkerchief in her hands. Bedisa had informed her about the plan to get her to Casimir's realm. Now she was in a tailor's shop getting ready for her trip to the mortal lands.

She'd not received any more mysterious notes since the day the portal blew.

"We are ready for you," the tailor's assistant said.

They led her into a room filled with mirrors of all shapes and sizes. Boxes filled with fabric and bones were scattered about. With a blinding flash, a circle of runes appeared on the floor and an immortal stepped out from behind a mirror.

He was tall with a long neck and long arms. His skin was a grey-blue, and his eyes were a prism of light. He wore a long tunic made of silver and gold threads so thin a breeze would tear it apart. The runes woven into the cloth identified him as the tailor.

"Welcome, Saderna, and please—"

The door flew open, and Henry and Aiden rushed in, followed by a flustered-looking assistant. The tailor's skin shifted to a dark crimson, and he glared at his assistant.

"We're here to make sure she doesn't choose the wrong form," Henry said. He flipped a chair around and straddled it. He gave the tailor an impatient look before his gaze flickered over to her.

"I'm Henry, and this is Aiden," he said and nodded toward his companion.

"Sorry about this," Aiden whispered and took a seat next to Henry.

"This is a private event," the tailor glared at them.

Henry snapped his fingers, and a letter bearing Vilmantas's seal appeared in his hand. The letter floated over to the tailor, who eyed it with disdain before he plucked it out of the air. He skimmed the contents before he tucked the letter into a pocket.

"As you can see, I'm under orders from Vilmantas himself," Henry said.

The tailor's skin flashed multiple colors before it returned to its original hue, and he waved his assistant out of the room.

"Fine, now where was I?" The tailor frowned then pointed at a circle of runes painted on the floor. "Saderna, please stand in the circle, and please don't leave until I tell you to."

Saderna did as instructed, and the tailor wove shimmering smoke into the mirrors. Runes appeared in the glass and shone so bright she had to close her eyes. When she opened them, she stared at her reflection. It was her, but it also wasn't her. The woman in the mirror had dark brown hair, golden-brown skin, and light brown eyes speckled with gold.

"What is this?"

"You are here to choose your mortal form," the tailor continued when Saderna didn't reply.

"This is in the style of a peasant woman from…" the tailor paused. He glanced at a large map that appeared in one of the mirrors.

"The Kingdom of Roltia," Henry chimed in and pointed at the center of the map.

"Right," the tailor cleared his throat. The image in the mirror changed to a woman with silver hair, green eyes, and pale skin.

"Acrilla," Henry said before the tailor could speak.

The image changed again to a dark-haired woman with grey eyes and dark brown skin.

"Eastern Marshes," Aiden chimed in and shrank back in his chair when the tailor turned his sharp gaze to him.

He snapped his fingers, and the image changed to a woman with bright red hair, blue eyes, and tan skin. She looked like she could be a sister to Aiden and Henry.

"Sodervia."

"I cannot work in these conditions! You two need to keep your mouths shut!" The tailor shouted at the two of them.

"We don't have time to go through every damn country in the realm. We've got a deadline to meet," Henry said.

The tailor moved quickly, sorting through hundreds of different mortal shapes and sizes in the blink of an eye. But nothing caught her attention. She was staring at the eyes of strangers, not her own.

"Excuse me?" Saderna asked quietly. The tailor turned to

her; his expression softened.

"Yes?"

"Is there a way I can look like myself?"

The tailor clasped his hands behind his back and paced around the room. He walked up to a mirror and flicked through a few options before he turned to Saderna.

"Close your eyes and only open them when I tell you. Now I must weave into the deepest parts of yourself. It may get uncomfortable."

The moment she closed her eyes, a tingling sensation swept across her skin. The prickling energy seeped into her bones as something clamped itself into her divine soul. A shell she could use to navigate the Mortal Realm.

She resisted the urge to cry out as icy claws pierced her flesh and her body. Then as quickly as the sensations appeared, they vanished.

"You can open your eyes now," the tailor said. Something in his voice changed. He sounded terrified.

Saderna's eyes flew open, and she carefully studied her reflection. Not much had changed, but her hair was a dark brown with hints of red woven throughout. Her eyes were a soft brown with tiny flecks of gold and blue.

"This is perfect!" She smiled at the tailor who gave her a weak one in return.

"Is something wrong?" She asked when Henry shot out of his chair.

"No! You'll fit in nicely," he said and tossed a coin at the tailor. Tendrils of silver smoke swept through the room, and the tailor's posture relaxed. When he looked at Saderna again, the terror in his eyes was gone. Henry had used a calming spell on him, before she could ask why the tailor cleared his throat.

"Your mortal form will attach itself once you pass through the portal. When you get to Casimir's realm, you'll be able to change forms at will if you wish. Or, if you prefer, a tailor there can remove the form if you tire of it."

One of his assistants entered the room when he clapped his hands, carrying a bundle of clothing.

"Thank you."

"Good luck with those two buffoons," the tailor said and shooed them out of the room.

She followed Henry and Aiden through a maze of crowded streets and corridors till they came to a large fenced-off courtyard filled with immortals drinking from tall silver tankards.

"Where are we? I thought we were leaving?" Saderna asked when they were seated at a large table, and Henry waved a woman over carrying a large tray. She set down several large tankards filled with a foaming brown liquid. Saderna crinkled her nose at the bitter scent.

"What is this? A potion I need to drink before entering?"

Henry's mouth twitched like he was fighting a smile.

"It's just ale," he said as the serving woman placed a large loaf of bread in front of them.

"We're half-mortal, so we need to eat," Aiden said.

Henry tore the loaf of bread into three pieces and handed one to Saderna, who stared at it.

"I don't eat mortal food," she said.

"Your trip through the portal will be more pleasant if you've got some food in you," Henry said.

"Trust me, I've learned it the hard way," Aiden said with a shudder.

Saderna tore a small piece of the bread off and chewed. It tasted bland and dense. She grabbed the tankard and took a drink. The bitter liquid made her want to gag, but she swallowed it anyway. How the humans ate like this was beyond her.

"Before we go into the temple, there are a few things you need to know," Henry said. He slid a small rolled-up paper across the table to Saderna.

Rules for Living in the Mortal Realm:

Do not use your divine name.

Do not use any divine magic without a rune.

Do not use any magic in front of a Vestral.

Do not tell a mortal you're a God/Goddess.

Don't die.

"I'm a goddess. I can't die!" Saderna exclaimed, and Henry shrugged.

"When you're in a Mortal Realm, you are subject to all its laws and restrictions. If you die, your soul could get swept away into the underworld, and your only chance at getting out is if Dearil spares you."

"Sounds like you have experience?"

Henry's eyes darkened, "Yes."

"What happened?"

Henry's mouth formed into a tight line, and he rose from his chair. The light in his eyes faded, and, before Henry could pull a shield up, his aura mingled with hers causing a ripple of guilt and loss to wash over her.

"I'm sorry, I didn't mean to pry." She whispered.

"We should get going," he said.

"But I'm not done yet!" Aiden said with a mouthful of bread. Henry paid him no mind and walked away. Leaving Aiden and Saderna scrambling to catch up.

They followed Henry to the Temple of Portals. The tree hummed with life while the portals within worked their magic. Instead of going up, Henry started down a long winding path toward the roots of the tree. The air became heavier the longer they walked. Her skin tingled as heavy energy swept over her.

"Welcome travelers," A cool voice greeted them from the shadows. "The portals are now awake, though be aware they are quite agitated at having been shut down for so long. Your journey will not be a smooth one."

"Oh no, does this mean?" Aiden glanced at Henry, who was pulling runes out of a pouch attached to his belt. He handed one to Saderna. The stone was a light grey with a combination rune for calm, protection, and a light fall carved into it.

"When the portals get angry, they jump around, and we could be near the ground or hundreds of feet in the air when we come through," Henry said.

The portal was similar to the one that was at the ceremony, but it was made of a dull grey stone and its energy was heavier.

Henry wandered over to a table and secured an axe to his belt. He held up a hand when Saderna started toward the portal.

"Hold on, what name would you like to go by?" Henry asked.

Saderna frowned, and before she could reply, Aiden handed her a small scroll. It was a long list of names. Most of them were too long for her to pronounce, but there was one that jumped out at her.

"Sade," she said and handed the scroll back to Aiden.

"Is that too close to her divine name?" Aiden asked Henry, who shrugged and handed him a sword.

"It was on the scroll, so it should be fine. Now, remember you cannot use your divine name outside of a Divine Realm. You can't even think about it. The same goes for the other gods. If you need to talk about them, use their titles as the humans do."

"What happens if I use a divine name?" Saderna asked.

"The fabric of the world will tear itself apart."

"I see," Saderna swallowed and took a steadying breath. A part of her wanted to run back into her temple, but that wasn't possible. The fates had already decided her path.

Henry stepped through the portal, followed by Aiden. Saderna paused. Her hands brushed the stone, and she took a last look around. She would never step foot here again. She took a breath and stepped through the shimmering field.

The air constricted, and her vision was filled with swirls of grey and dark purple. Her body was becoming heavier with each step. In the distance, a shimmering blue portal appeared, and a pathway lit with dark purple runes appeared at her feet before a dark fog encased the portal.

"Don't stray from the path!" Henry yelled. She peered into the mists, but she couldn't see a thing. A huge dark shadow passed overhead, followed by the sound of enormous wings flapping. Saderna ran for the portal ahead, her body getting heavier with each step.

"Slow down! If you go too fa—" Henry shouted, but Saderna was already headed through the portal before he could finish his sentence.

She pushed through the shimmering ring of magic and walked into nothing but air. She looked down to see the ground rushing towards her. The rune Henry had given her flared brightly, but she was moving too fast for it to work correctly.

She closed her eyes and awaited her fate.

She was sinking in a sea of red, and every time she tried to move to the surface, an invisible fire swept over her skin. Shadowy tendrils reached out to her from below.

"Wake up," a voice crooned.

Was this the afterlife? Had she died from her fall? She took a sharp breath, and to her surprise, she didn't choke on the water.

"Come to me," the voice called again, a portal formed beneath her filled with shadows and broken shards of glass.

"Don't listen to it!" Another voice from above. A gust of air swept her up towards the surface.

"Hello?" She called out. "Where am I?"

The sea boiled violently, and the shadows below her disappeared into a swirling vortex. Faster and faster, she went until she had broken free from the water and a searing light filled her vision. Two blurry figures appeared, casting her in shadows.

"Sade! I need you to focus on your breathing!" One of the blurry figures shouted. It was Henry's voice.

Why is he calling me by that name? My name isn't Sade. It's Sader—

"For the love of all that's holy, do not think about your

divine name!" Henry shouted. Pink sparks filled her vision.

What does he mean not to think about my name? I'm dead, aren't I? No, if she were dead, she would've seen the afterlife by now. The air and her body were too dense.

She drew a breath and nearly screamed at how loud it was. Her heart hammered in her chest, and she feared it was going to jump out.

"Keep focusing!" It was Aiden's voice this time.

Focus? On this ruckus? How did humans stand all the noise? Still, she took a deep breath and then another. Slowly the world around her came into focus. She was lying on the ground, and the sky above was a brilliant shade of blue. A few white fluffy clouds drifted overhead, unaware of the pain she was in. The dirt underneath her was cool and rougher than she imagined it to be.

Dirt. She was lying on top of *dirt*. Excitement hummed in her veins as she dug fingers into the soil.

She tried to roll to her side, but a pair of firm hands kept her from moving. Henry was leaning over her, shaking his head, and a healing rune hovered next to him.

"I'm not done reattaching your mortal body to you," he said and nodded down at her feet. She could see right through them.

"You fell to the ground so hard your mortal form got a bit jostled," Aiden said.

"Oh," was all she could manage.

She turned her attention to the clouds above, and after what felt like eons later, Henry put away the rune.

"You can get up now," he said.

She rose to her feet while Aiden and Henry stood on each side of her. She swayed a bit, and they led her over to a log. Henry handed her a small piece of hard cheese and a small canteen. Thankfully it was filled with water and not ale. She ate in silence, trying not to pay attention to the noises coming from her stomach.

"How do you manage the sounds?" She asked Aiden, while Henry frowned at a map.

"Manage the sounds?" He asked slowly, "I don't understand?"

"Shit," Henry dropped his map and ran over to her. Before she could react, he had a hand on her forehead and a rune in the other. He was so close; she could hear his heartbeat. The rune glowed a soft turquoise, casting a soft light onto his skin.

"What's going on?" She asked.

"Tailor got the tuning wrong," he muttered.

A jolt of electricity swept through her. Her veins were like ice. Henry grabbed her wrists and heat flooded back into her body. Henry's eyes were glowing, and they looked like shining emeralds. Unlike hers, his eyes were a solid color.

"Tuning?" She asked, trying to keep herself from staring at him.

"How sensitive your mortal form is to certain things. Humans are extremely sensitive," Henry said, and he fished out another rune from his pouch.

"This happened to me!" Aiden said cheerfully. "Course my body is natural, but when I was born, my mother had to petition the God of Knowledge to let me see a healer. I was so sensitive I couldn't stand the tiniest of breezes."

"What's so bad about it?"

"Your body came from a tailor, and if it's not tuned correctly, you can die."

"Is everything in this realm designed to kill things?"

"Well…that's the point of a Mortal Realm. Everything here dies eventually," Henry said and backed away. "Take a few more deep breaths."

Her muscles relaxed and her breathing grew easier. She was lucky she hadn't gotten impaled on a tree…

Sade stared at the swaying branches far above her.

A tree. She jumped to her feet and ran over to the nearest one and wrapped her arms around it. The round bark scratched at her skin, but she didn't care. This was something she'd dreamed about for years.

A gentle power hummed around her. It wove itself through every living thing like a giant spider web. She could feel the handiwork of multiple gods within it, unlike the energy in the Divine Realm where everything was separated; here, even the smallest speck of dirt was saturated with it.

She let go of the tree when Henry coughed. Aiden was staring at her with stars in his eyes.

"I always wanted to go into the forest around my temple," she said. Henry's mouth formed a thin line while he picked up his map. With the way his shoulders were quaking she wasn't sure if he was laughing or cursing at her.

"Shall we get going?" Aiden asked.

"Not yet," Henry said. "I'm waiting for the last phase."

"What's the last phase?" Sade asked. She didn't have to wait long to find out when bile rose in her throat. Before she could stop herself, she vomited. When she finished, Aiden handed her a handkerchief.

"Now we can go. We need to get some more supplies,"

Henry said as he eyed her bare feet. "You need a pair of boots; your feet will bleed if you don't protect them."

"I don't need boots; I always went barefoot in my temple."

Aiden and Henry glanced at each other with concerned expressions. Henry shrugged and rolled-up the map.

"Let's get going. We need to get a few more supplies before we head off."

Sade followed behind them, relishing in the dirt beneath her feet and the heat of the sun.

Chapter Six

It wasn't long before Sade was walking like glass was under her feet. To her credit, she didn't complain. She merely wrapped her feet and kept going.

Henry had never seen anyone get so excited about a forest before. Though, he'd never been stuck in one place for twenty years. Watching her look at everything with such joy, he had almost forgotten that she was dangerous. Almost had forgotten that she could tear apart a realm with her power. Almost had forgotten about the dagger strapped on his belt.

He ducked under a low-hanging branch; its movement caused the dagger's sheath to press against his leg. He unclipped it and shoved it into his pack. Aiden raised an eyebrow but turned his attention back to Sade, who was plucking a few wildflowers. Henry pursed his lips. The longer they were here, the harder it would be for her to leave.

The sooner this was over with, the better.

The road became busier the closer they got to town. Meanwhile, Sade was throwing magic around like a fire dancer at a festival.

"Sade, you need to tamp down on your magic. Remember the scroll Henry gave you," Aiden said before Henry could.

Sade tilted her head. "Why?"

"Most countries only allow Vestrals to use magic," Henry said.

"But it's everywhere!" Sade exclaimed, waving toward a plant.

"Don't worry, when we're far away from civilization, you can use all the magic you want!" Aiden said.

Henry bit back a groan when Aiden smiled at her like she'd given him a bag of gold. Gods, this was going to be a long trip if he was enamored with her. However, Sade didn't seem to notice his stares as she took in the town they were approaching.

By Roltian standards, the small town of Larni was just a small tick on a map. None of the buildings had lofty spiral points or even stone walls, but Sade looked at the wooden structures like they were made of gold.

"I've always wanted to see a place like this!" She exclaimed, her face breaking out into a smile.

"This is only a minor backwater town," Henry said, and Sade frowned.

"Don't you think the Divine Realm is nicer?" Aiden asked.

Much to Henry's surprise, she shook her head.

"No, this world is much nicer!" She said and skipped ahead; a few passersby raised their eyebrows at the cheerful goddess.

She merely waved at them and continued down the path.

Aiden watched her with a wistful expression on his face. Henry hurried past him and caught up to Sade.

"We need to drop by the marketplace and get a few supplies."

The God of Knowledge had given him some gold before they left. It was enough to cover their expenses and keep them from having to hunt.

He'd also given Sade her own personal allowance.

They entered the town market, and Sade's eyes widened with wonder. Dozens of merchants had set up stalls with colorful banners depicting their goods.

"Is it all right if I explore?"

Henry hesitated, but the dagger on his belt was silent.

"Yes, I'll get the supplies, and we can meet back here once we're ready," he said. Before Aiden could chime in, Sade twirled and headed into the market.

He grabbed Aiden's arm when he followed.

"No, you don't get to lollygag. I need your help."

"But what if she gets lost?"

Henry raised an eyebrow. "How in the hell would she get lost? This town is tiny."

Aiden opened his mouth, then shut it. It didn't take long for them to gather their supplies. The market was rather bare. He'd hoped to find a tent or two and give Sade some privacy at camp, but they were out of luck. A merchant informed them that a band of adventurers swept through the town a few days ago and taken all the tents.

This trip was getting off to a wonderful start.

"Right, now that we're done, can I join Sade?" Aiden asked as Henry finished shoving some dried meat into his bag.

"Why? Let her explore the town on her own."

Aiden folded his arms across his chest and his gaze swept over the market crowd. His eyes lit up for half a breath but then faded when a human woman swept past them.

Henry couldn't stop himself from frowning. Aiden continued to search the crowd. It was full of humans who were all sporting the same starry-eyed expression as Aiden. Faint wisps of blue and gold wove their way around the town. It transformed the shabby town into something ethereal. A tendril of smoke wrapped around him and almost lulled him into a state of peaceful bliss.

It was Sade's energy, and it explained why Aiden was acting so odd. Her presence was affecting the world around her. Henry reached into his rune pouch and used a dispel rune to clear the air around him, and the faint trails of shimmering light disappeared.

He snapped his fingers to get Aiden's attention, but he merely scowled at him before he went back to observing the mortals. Henry sighed, shoving his rune back into his pouch. He'd have to use more harsh methods to get Aiden to snap out of it.

"You've only known her for a day, and now you're mooning over her? Aiden, you need to shield yourself. You're being influenced by her."

"I'm not going to shield myself. What I feel for her is true!" Aiden shot back; a blush crept across his cheeks. This was bad. Shielding wouldn't help him now.

"You know nothing about her!" Henry snapped.

Aiden crossed his arms. "As I said, her soul is the most beautiful thing in the world."

"Aiden, we need to get her out of this realm as quickly as possible. I can't have you making up insane fantasies about someone you just met!"

"Oh, piss off, Henry. You haven't given me one good reason why we should hurry. The poor thing has been locked up for twenty years!"

This wasn't good. Aiden wasn't snapping out of it.

"She's a lot older than you think."

"Did you hit your head passing through the portal?"

"Sade isn't just the Goddess of Peace. She's also the Goddess of Destruction," Henry said. Aiden stared at him like he'd grown another head.

"You can't expect me to just believe that." Aiden crossed his arms.

"The Sacred Council gave me this information. It's why we're escorting her instead of just giving her a map and showing her where the portal is."

"So, she's a dual-purpose goddess; I don't see the problem."

Henry pinched the bridge of his nose before he continued.

"The reason she was locked up is that she destroyed a Mortal Realm. The Sacred Council has been making her reincarnate, and they wipe her memories."

"You're lying. If this was true, then we would've known."

"They also erased the memories of everyone who isn't in the Sacred Council."

"But she doesn't act like she's about to destroy everything!"

Aiden frowned.

"Use your magic."

A small tendril of green smoke wrapped around him, and Henry opened his mind to it. Aiden's face paled as he connected to Henry's memories of his meeting with the Sacred Council.

"They aren't going to tell her about her past?"

"No, and they want to keep it that way."

"But that's cruel! We have to tell her!" Aiden started toward Sade. Henry grabbed him by the shoulder, guiding him into an alleyway.

"We don't know what she's capable of, and we're only mere half-gods. Do you want to be responsible for the deaths of millions if she loses control?"

Aiden scowled at him while he straightened his tunic.

"No."

"I don't agree with their methods, but we are not going to debate their morality. We need to get her to the Realm of Ruin without incident."

"What if she remembers something?"

Henry took out the dagger from his pack. Aiden's eyes widened, and he shrunk against the wall.

"You cannot be serious!"

"This dagger is enchanted, and it only works on divines. If Sade loses control, this is the only way to stop her."

"You're out of your mind. I can't believe you agreed to this!"

"I had no choice but to agree. My parents' souls are at stake."

Aiden pinched the bridge of his nose and sighed loud enough that a few humans passing by gave them curious stares. They quickly disappeared into the crowd when Henry glared at them.

"You couldn't have negotiated for my parents' souls?" He asked.

"I'm sorry, I wasn't thinking."

Aiden let out a bitter laugh and brushed off a speck of dust from his shoulder.

"You know my father sided with the God of Ruin. They'd never let him out of whatever pit they threw him in when he died," Aiden shook his head. "I won't tell her."

"Thank you."

Aiden nodded toward the marketplace where Sade was now carrying an armful of colorful fabrics and haggling with a blacksmith.

"We should probably stop her."

They quickly made their way over to the stand, where a blacksmith was showing her an array of weapons. Much to Henry's disappointment, there was not an axe in sight.

"This is the finest blade in all of Roltia!" The blacksmith held up a sword with a dull onyx blade. The handle was ornate, carved to look like a dragon's head. A pretty piece, but it would break in heavy combat. It was meant to sit on a mantle.

"I'll take it!" Sade exclaimed with unbridled joy. Aiden eyed Henry like he expected him to stop her. Henry gave him a small shrug; it was her money to do as she wished with.

His hand settled over the dagger, checking to see if there was any sign of her destructive side rising up. Thankfully, the dagger was cold, and no dark energy hovered around Sade.

"Are you sure about this?" Aiden asked Sade.

She gave him a puzzled look.

"What do you mean?"

"That sword is more of a decoration."

Sade smiled. "I know."

The blacksmith cleared his throat, inclining his head towards the line that was forming. Henry guided Sade and Aiden away from the booth.

"The God of War told me it wouldn't hurt to bring the God of Ruin a gift," Sade said while she tied the sword to her belt.

"You think a sword is a good idea? What if it makes him angry?" Henry asked. He could not keep his annoyance from seeping into his tone.

"I was hoping that it would also serve as a warning. I do not want him to meddle in my affairs and it would look bad on him if he refused a gift."

The hairs on the back of Henry's neck stood up while the dagger started humming. He slowly moved his hand toward the bag but stopped himself. Sade had every right to be upset about this. He couldn't spend the entire journey jumping at every negative emotion she felt. The damn dagger was going to drive him mad.

"Then, I hope it works," Henry said, nodding toward the town gate. "I think it's time for us to get a move on."

As they started toward the gate, a throng of people were surrounding a man standing on a bucket. He was holding a large scroll with a painting of a monster on it.

The creature monster was an enormous snake with horns on its head, breathing fire on an unsuspecting sheep. It was something they'd fought before.

"The time has come! We have lived in the shadow of this

beast for two weeks now! How many more of our children need to die before we take action?" The man shouted, and the crowd roared in response.

"We're going to help them, right?" Sade asked. She frowned when Henry nudged her towards the gate.

"We don't have time."

"Yeah, the last time we fought a monster like that, it took us nearly a week to find it and an entire day to kill it," Aiden said. Henry shot him a look of gratitude, but Sade didn't seem convinced.

"We have until the end of the summer to make it to the portal." She crossed her arms and looked back at the crowd. "I cannot leave here knowing these people are not living in peace."

Henry ran a hand through his hair. "We are going to encounter a lot of monsters. We can't stop and fight every single one of them."

"I will not leave this village until these people are safe."

Blue and gold sparks danced around Sade; Henry reached for a shielding rune. He quickly created a bubble around her, and his gaze swept the crowd. When no Vestrals came rushing towards them, he dared a glance at Sade.

Her eyes were bright with anger.

"These people are not living in peace," Sade snarled. "You are interfering with my divine purpose."

"Calm down. I'm not trying to impede on your divine purpose."

Sade's eyes narrowed; a wave of her sparks swept over Henry. His skin burned where the sparks touched him, but they left no marks. He yanked out a calming rune and let the magic seep through him. Aiden rushed over to Sade with a calming rune of his own.

"Henry, did you forget?" Aiden asked.

"Forget what?" Sade asked. The glow in her eyes was fading.

"If a divine goes against their purpose, they will experience pain. Pain that is amplified in a Mortal Realm," Aiden snapped.

Henry sighed. "I forget about that one."

"Of course, you would. You've built up a tolerance."

The glow returned to Sade's eyes. Henry raised up a hand and shook his head.

"You have to realize you cannot bring peace to every single mortal in this realm. We don't have time."

Sade studied him for a long moment. Her magic tried to break through the walls he created in his mind. He stood his ground and stared right back at her. Aiden cleared his throat and gestured towards the mortals leaving the town.

"I hate to interrupt, but if we're going to do this. We need to leave."

Henry started walking again, but Sade grabbed his arm.

"Please. I've done nothing but answer petitions in a temple. I would like to help people in a way that actually means something. I can't bear the thought of more people dying when they didn't need to."

Sade's eyes started brimming with tears. Aiden shot Henry a dirty look and nodded towards the crowd of people.

"I don't see why we can't do it this once," Aiden said.

Henry pursed his lips; a few stragglers from the crowd scurried past. The only weapons they had were pitchforks and sticks. They wouldn't last a minute against that creature. Letting those people die would go against everything he had fought for. With a heavy sigh, he turned back to Sade.

"Fine, we'll go deal with the monster."

In a flash, Sade rushed towards him and pulled him into a hug. Henry stiffened at her touch; he couldn't remember the last time someone had hugged him. Sade quickly released him and stepped back. She looked up at him; her eyes were shining with hope.

"Thank you," she said.

"If we're going to go monster hunting, we'll need to go over the basics of combat. This monster is not something to be trifled with," Henry said.

"Oh, there's no need to worry about that. The God of War made sure I was given knowledge on how to fight," Sade said and reached into a pouch. She pulled out a glimmering rune made from quartz only the Goddess of Runes had access to. "And the Goddess of Runes made sure I knew how to use these."

"I should've known. But there is a difference between having the knowledge of something and actually having to use it. Those two have never faced a monster that could rip your head from your body."

"That's why you're here, to make sure that doesn't happen," Sade said and smiled at Aiden. "Let's get a move on before they get too far."

Henry fell into step behind them. He could only hope having Sade in a combat situation wouldn't trigger whatever force the other gods were afraid of.

Chapter Seven

The forest had gone silent.

A monster was waiting in the shadows taunting the creatures around them. The air was thick with dread and only a few birds flew ahead.

"How long has this monster been here? It feels like this forest has been dealing with this creature for a long time," Sade said.

"Not long, but we've fought monsters here before," Henry said. "It wasn't always like this; there was a time when anyone could walk through any part of these lands without fear. Over the past hundred years, monsters and corrupted spirits have terrorized the land. It's been getting worse every day."

Frustration simmered in his aura.

"But the humans have you two."

"I'm afraid we aren't enough."

"Yeah, we aren't powerful enough to stop all of them," Aiden chimed in.

Sade clenched her fists at her sides; power swelled within, begging to be released and hunt down every monster in this realm. She'd spent her entire existence locked away in a temple, answering frivolous petitions, while Henry and Aiden were here trying to help mortals achieve a peaceful life.

"And what have the other gods done to help?"

Henry let out a long sigh, "The Goddess of the Sea has cleared her domain and a few islands. Everyone else is busy with other duties."

Other duties? What could be more important than ensuring their creations are safe? Was the passage of time wearing down their empathy? Had they become so old they no longer cared about anything outside of their personal gain?

Questions. All she had were questions, and it was unlikely she was going to get answers.

"Enough talk about them," Aiden said and motioned toward a tall oak. "Can you feel that?"

It wasn't the tree Aiden was referring to. It was the drooping shadows hanging onto it. Henry dashed toward the tree; a rune whipped around him, going so fast she could not read it.

"Follow me," Henry said when he'd finished scanning.

"I hate this part," Aiden fell into step beside Sade.

"What part?"

"You'll see."

They followed lines of fractured earth until the forest gave way to a field. A small house, made of stone and wood, sat in the center. It would've made for an idyllic scene if it wasn't for the tendrils of black smoke.

A shimmering energy settled on her skin, ready to protect her from any threat. Henry's gaze slid over to her, and his eyes narrowed.

"Remember, you have to use runes here."

"Sorry," she mumbled, fishing out a protection rune.

Goddess of Peace, please help us. A voice drifted into her thoughts. Sade ran toward the house, ignoring the shouts from Henry and Aiden. She didn't care about the danger, didn't care if a monster jumped out. Someone needed help.

The smell of burning flesh and blood singed her nostrils. The black smoke grew thicker with each step. The voice in her head was getting fainter.

Hold on. I'm coming to help you. She had no idea if the mortal could hear her.

A burst of light cleared the air and revealed the charred corpses of some type of animal she wasn't familiar with. She moved past them toward the house.

"Sade!" Henry yelled from somewhere behind her. She slammed into the door. Wood flew into the air around her, piercing her flesh.

She scanned the room; it was covered in soot and ash. A small human was huddled in the corner. She raced over and gently tapped on their shoulder. The body crumpled into a pile of ash and bone.

"H-help," a weak voice called from another room.

"I'm here!" She replied. The stench of burning flesh was so strong it nearly made her gag.

She entered the other room and found a woman with

charred skin. Her body was so burnt she wasn't sure if she could be healed. Sade knelt next to her and placed a hand on top of her head. It was the only place untouched by flames.

A healing rune floated out of her pouch. Using all of her strength, she filled the rune to its breaking point. The pink swirls descended upon the body, but they could not heal the burnt flesh.

"Leave me be," the human whimpered. Her lungs rattled with every breath she took. Before Sade could try anything else, the human's body went limp.

"Wait, I can save you! Just hold on!" Sade pleaded, but the human's eyes glazed over and she took her last breath. Sade gently closed the human's eyes and rested her head against theirs.

Too late. She hadn't run fast enough.

Energy hummed around her, saturated with fear and death. Before she could stop herself, blue and gold lightning burst from her body. The charred walls of the house shuddered and then exploded outward.

There was so much pain. She'd never experienced this much pain before. Their deaths had been violent and messy. Their screams would echo forever in this world and her mind.

Sade closed her eyes, trying to quell the rage building within her. Swirls of blue and gold stretched out before her like an ocean. On the edge of the horizon, the colors changed to a deep ruby. A figure floated above the mirage and beckoned her to come closer.

Unleash your power and take revenge.

The crimson waters beckoned to her, begging to be released. She reached a hand out.

Wait, the creature isn't here. Why would I continue to unleash my powers? She asked the specter.

Unleash your power.

No, not yet. Not until the monster is found.

Sade pulled the shimmering smoke into herself, watching the red waters disappear. The creature across from her growled but said nothing more before it dissolved.

She opened her eyes. Henry was sprinting towards her. His red hair looked like fire dancing in the wind. A dagger with a copper hilt was in one hand and his axe in the another. He stopped when the crackling energy dissipated.

"I'm sorry, I couldn't help it," she said. The house was now reduced to a mere pile of splinters and dust. The corpses, however, were untouched.

Henry stood still, but orange smoke swirled around her. She let it poke and prod, testing the shields she'd put up to keep herself from causing more trouble.

Aiden soon appeared beside him, his face red with exertion, and he was breathing hard.

"Are you all right?" He scurried over to her side.

Sade nodded. She didn't break eye contact with Henry. His eyes were bright and wary. What was he looking for? Had the monster done something to her mind? Was this realm going to drive her to madness?

She started to break the shields that held her magic at bay. Henry must have sensed it since he stepped back straight and sheathed his weapons. The wariness in his gaze shifted to anger.

"What in the hell were you thinking? You had no idea what was in the house!"

"I heard them. They were begging for help and one of them

petitioned me," she said quietly, and Henry's face fell when he took in the body Sade still knelt beside.

"Gods, they were all still alive?" Aiden said.

"No, only one."

Sade stared at her hands, which were now covered in soot and ash. She failed. She wasn't strong enough to save one mortal.

"You couldn't have saved them," Henry said. His voice was thick with grief. She looked up at him then. He didn't meet her gaze; instead, he picked up an ash-covered rock and blew on it. Sade gasped when she saw the carving of a shattered sword. It was her divine rune.

"How in the world?"

"It seems a Vestral who served you was here," he said, handing her the rune.

The Goddess of Runes hadn't given her a divine rune when she'd made the others. She cradled the stone, and it started to glow.

She closed her eyes and let the rune show her what had happened. A Vestral in a shining cloak made of gold and blue fabric appeared, fighting against the creatures that ravaged the farm. A long claw impaled him in the stomach and the vision faded.

"I will use this to ensure peace returns to your realm," she whispered and gently placed the rune into her pouch.

"Should we put their souls to rest?" Aiden asked.

Henry nodded and used a burnt stick to draw a circle in the ashes. Once that was done, he stepped inside the circle, knelt, and knocked three times.

"God of Death, I call upon you to ferry the souls of the

dead," he said. Aiden groaned while Henry hastened out of the circle.

"You know he hates being summoned like that."

A stiff wind blew up from the ground. She blinked and the God of Death stood before them. He was dressed in a cloak of black and white, his face concealed by a checkered veil. The souls of the dead humans rose from their bodies and began encircling him.

"Henry, how many times do I have to tell you? Just because some mortals in one realm decided that was the best way to get my attention doesn't mean you need to do it every damn time, and I—" The god stopped his tirade when he saw Sade. "Ah, my apologies, goddess."

"What are you going to do?" Sade asked him.

"Take these poor souls to a peaceful end," the god rasped. His voice sent shivers through her body.

His words did little to soothe the raging storm within her. These humans had died for no reason other than a sadistic creature's pleasure. They deserved to live out their lives in peace. Now they would spend the rest of eternity haunted by their memories.

"I will change their memories and make it so each one believes they lived a long, happy life," the God of Death said and nodded to Henry. "If you'll excuse me, I have a realm to run. These poor souls do not need to be in agony any longer."

Henry nodded back, and the God of Death was gone in a blast of icy wind, taking the souls with him. Sade swallowed and stared at the bodies. Henry held up a fire rune, and soon they were nothing more than ashes on the wind.

"We need to find a place to camp before nightfall," Henry said.

The further they got away from the desolate farm, the more her blood boiled. They needed to find the creature before it struck again.

When they found a small clearing Henry thought was suitable, they began setting up their camp. Sade tossed her bedroll onto the ground, not bothering to straighten it.

Aiden quickly set up a campfire, and soon he had a pot of stew boiling over the fire. Sade stared down at the brown and green mush.

"Tomorrow, we'll resume our trek. I think the monster is heading north toward the major farms in the area," Henry said between bites of his stew.

"Tomorrow? What if the creature happens upon a poor traveler and kills them?" Sade asked.

Aiden reached over and patted her on the back. She cringed at the contact. Something about him made her skin crawl.

"It will be fine; you need to recover. Your body cannot sustain a large amount of divine energy for long."

Sade glanced at her hands; nothing was off.

"What do you mean? I feel fine."

Aiden's mouth formed a tight line as Henry handed him his bowl.

"She's a full goddess, Aiden. I doubt she'll have the same energy problems we have," Henry yawned and stretched his arms behind his head.

"Problems?"

"We're half-mortal. If we used the magic levels you did

today, we'd be recovering for the next week."

"I see. Then, perhaps, it'd be best if I continue after the monster while you two rest?"

Henry shook his head. "Remember, you're still in a human body, and you aren't immune to fatigue."

Sade flexed her fingers; her body was fueled by the rage simmering in her bones. She wouldn't sleep until the thing was found and eliminated.

Oh, planning outright murder, are we? That's not very becoming of a peace goddess.

She stiffened at the words. What was this thing?

I'm you.

Sade poked at her stew, unsure if she should tell them she was hearing voices.

"It's all right. I was the same way when I first started working with Henry," Aiden said quietly, oblivious to the invisible specter haunting her thoughts.

"No, you fainted," Henry said with a sparkle in his eyes, "twice."

"How long have you been here?"

Henry passed out a few wooden tankards and poured himself a drink.

"About a hundred years. Henry was born here, he just turned four hundred," Aiden said.

"Oh, I thought you two were brothers."

Henry choked on his drink while Aiden stared at her incredulously.

"What? Why?"

"It's the hair," she said.

"Now that I think about it. You do look like a faded version of myself," Henry said, peering at them over his tankard.

Aiden narrowed his eyes at Sade.

"I'm never going to hear the end of this."

"Sorry," she grinned at him, and Aiden's cheeks turned pink. Henry snorted and muttered something under his breath.

"What was life in the temple like?" Aiden asked, ignoring Henry.

Sade set down her bowl of stew. A pain settled over her chest like it was being squeezed from the inside.

"Quiet. Bedi—The Goddess of Fates was the only one who was authorized to visit me. She only showed up once a year."

"Wait, she only visited once a year?" Aiden exclaimed. Henry crossed his arms and was watching her intently. His green eyes had darkened into a deep jade.

"Yes."

"Who did you talk to?"

Aiden's eyes were now shimmering like he was on the verge of tears. The pressure on her heart increased.

"My plants," Sade squeaked out, the pain in her chest increasing with each breath.

"Aiden, that's enough," Henry said.

"He's fine," Sade gasped and held up a hand when Henry rose from his seat, clutching a healing rune. "I'm fine. It's just… hard to talk about."

"Well, your mortal body isn't fine. Aiden, stop asking her questions."

"I didn't realize you were in charge of me," Aiden shot back. Something passed between the two men causing Henry to grab him by the shoulder. He hauled him to his feet and shoved him toward a thicker part of the forest.

"What the hell are you doing!" Aiden exclaimed.

"We'll be right back," Henry called over his shoulder.

He must've been using a sound rune to muffle their voices. She could only hear the shuffle of feet and a muffled cracking noise when something slammed into a tree.

She wondered if she should interfere, but before she could move, Henry emerged from the forest. He was covered in dead leaves and dirt. He casually ran a hand through his hair, but some stubborn twigs remained.

"Lover's quarrel?"

He ignored the jibe. "Aiden will be taking a walk to calm down."

"He was only asking questions."

"Questions that could cause problems."

"You think I'm going to erupt again like I did at the farm?"

"You could. A human body is a funny thing. They're ruled by emotions, and since you've only been here a day, I doubt you've mastered the art of handling emotions in a few hours."

"Is this why you won't go after the monster tonight?"

"Partially. You need time to cool your head. This monster we're hunting loves to feed off emotions," Henry rolled back his right sleeve. A long white scar snaked up his muscled forearm. "I learned the hard way."

"You can trust me."

Henry snorted. "After you deliberately went against my advice and ran headfirst towards a monster you've never fought before. Why would I trust you?"

Sade ground her teeth and clenched her fists at her sides. He was right, she had ignored his warnings. However, her pride would not let him win.

"Why should I trust *you*? You don't seem to be thrilled at the prospect of escorting me through your realm."

"You shouldn't," Henry deadpanned, "I'm actually working for the God of Ruin and plan on using you for my own personal gain."

Sade blinked once. Twice.

"It's a joke," Henry grumbled.

"Well, it wasn't funny," Sade huffed and rose to her feet.

"Where are you going?" Henry asked, and she inclined her head to her bedroll. He raised his eyebrows, and then a slow grin crossed his face.

"I mean, if you're willing, I won't say no," he said with a wink.

"What! No, I'm going to sleep!" Sade exclaimed. Blood rushed to her face, and she stormed over to her bedroll, tugging the blanket over her head.

What was wrong with him? One moment, he was acting like she was about to explode, and the next, he was teasing her. She already had enough on her plate and dealing with his mood swings was not something she needed.

She lifted the blanket just enough so she could see Henry. He was now staring at the fire. Aiden still wasn't back from his walk. A plan began to form. Once they were asleep, she would find the monster.

Eventually Aiden stumbled back into camp. He and Henry

exchanged a few short words before they headed to their bedrolls. Soon they were both fast asleep. Sade waited until she was sure they were lost in their dreams and wouldn't sense her.

She crept through the woods, following the faint energy trail left by the monster. It wasn't hard to find. She only had to look for pure terror to follow it. The broken branches also helped.

On and on, she pushed; the air became thick with fear and rage. The forest became thicker too. It was almost impossible for her to move through the thick underbrush. Her body ached, and a sharp pain coursed through her legs. Still, she pressed on. She would not let a mere forest keep her from exacting revenge.

Somewhere far beyond her, a wolf howled in the night, sending shivers down her spine.

"I am the Goddess of Peace, and I'm not scared of anything," she muttered and let more magic sweep through her body. It did little to quell the rising fear in her gut.

The monster must be close. It had to be, there was no other explanation. Unless Henry's words about the human form being more susceptible to emotions were true.

She pushed into a clearing. A giant snake was curled up in the center. Smoke rose out of its nostrils, curling around the horns on its head. It cracked open an eye as she got closer.

The creature hissed and bared its fangs at her.

She smiled and prepared to strike.

Chapter Eight

The dream was always the same. His parents were trapped in a cave, calling out to him, begging for him to save them. Henry crawled along the ground, blood oozing from a gash in his side.

A cloaked figure stood overhead, wielding a flaming sword. He braced himself for the blow that always came.

"Henry, wake up!" Aiden shouted.

Henry opened his eyes to find Aiden kneeling over him, his wide eyes filled with panic and fear.

"She's gone."

Henry jumped to his feet, nearly knocking over Aiden, and sprinted across the camp. Weak sunlight filtered in through the trees and highlighted Sade's empty bedroll. He yanked out a seeking rune and tried to tune it to her energy, but her signature was too faint for him to follow.

He ran over to the wards he'd placed around the camp. They were completely empty. Sade must've used the wards to hide her trail. It wasn't something a goddess locked in a temple should know how to do, but magic once learned was hard to forget. Even between lifetimes, a part of her must have remembered it.

Aiden started trembling. His face was stark white.

"Does this mean we're doomed?"

"No, it means she's really damn strong," Henry said. "A hell of a lot stronger than I thought she'd be."

"What?"

Henry yawned and ran a hand down his face, trying to wipe the sleep from his body. He walked over to the fire and poked at the embers.

"What in the hell are you doing, Henry?"

"Getting breakfast," he said and held up a piece of raw boar meat. "Would you like some?"

"Need I remind you that the fucking Goddess of Peace and *Destruction* is going on a rampage? And you're just sitting here? What the hell is wrong with you?" Aiden shouted. He used a water rune to douse the flames.

"Relax, if she was going to destroy our realm, she would've done so at the farm," he patted the dagger at his side. "This thing has been completely silent."

"That's all it took to build your confidence in her! A fucking magical dagger!" Aiden yelled. An angry vortex of forest green and silver sparks formed around him.

"If we're going to take her anywhere, we need to know exactly what we're dealing with. She's stronger than both of us combined, Aiden."

"Your entire spiel last night about being careful with her mortal body was just a bunch of bullshit?"

"No, it was up to her if she wanted to listen to me or not. We're not her jail keepers, Aiden. I will not watch her every damn move. Unlike you."

"You are playing with fire, Henry," Aiden snapped. "Why don't we just tell her about her past and get this over with."

"Do you want the realm to dissolve into nothing? She's going to be here for more than a month. Who knows what the God of Ruin has planned."

"Well, maybe he'll stop now that he knows she's coming to him!"

"Yeah, I don't think so," Henry snorted.

Aiden glared at him and then started toward the woods.

"I'm going to find her and make sure she doesn't kill us all!"

Henry sighed and kicked a piece of wet wood. He knew it was foolish to put Sade into this situation, but he needed to know. The goddess he saw at the farm was not one of chaotic destruction. No, her energy had been focused solely on getting revenge for the humans who'd died at the farm.

Then again, she *had* lost control and destroyed the farmhouse.

With a groan, he headed into the forest, opposite where Aiden had gone. He opened his senses to the forest, focusing on the tiny threads of rage. With each step, his divine rune flared to life, causing orange sparks to trail up his skin.

His energy hummed a song of justice for the deceased and a cry for the head of the monster who'd destroyed their lives.

His divine purpose was something he'd tried to ignore for

centuries. Why was it coming to life now? He'd killed thousands of monsters and mortals, and it'd remained silent. He'd gone to the temples, answered the petitions, and nothing would happen to him.

He wished he paid more attention to some of his mother's lectures. She'd barely had time to transfer her divine energy before…

He collided with a low-hanging branch, and the dark memories faded from his thoughts.

Good, last thing I need is a distraction. He surveyed the surrounding forest. Some of the underbrush looked like someone had hacked it with a dull object. He looked down at the dirt, bare footprints.

"Found you," he said and sprinted through the underbrush.

A gust of wind tossed him into a tree trunk. Gasping for air, he used the tree to stand.

Before him was the strangest sight that he'd ever seen. The snake was pinned to the ground by an invisible force. Sade stood close by, sweat dripping from her forehead as she swung her dull sword at the snake.

No matter how hard she swung, the metal didn't pierce the creature's scales.

"Sade!" He called out; Sade ignored him. He drew closer. Tiny glowing lines crawled along the creature's hide.

"This stupid thing won't die," she said through clenched teeth. Her entire body was trembling.

It wouldn't be long before she collapsed from sheer exhaustion.

"You remember the sword is useless, right?" He reached for

his axe. The runes etched on the metal hummed to life.

"Which is why I'm using it to channel," she said, and Henry's eyes widened when he saw a destruction rune carved into the blade. The light that shone from it was a red so dark it was almost black.

The dagger strapped to his side remained silent. The color was from the rune's essence and not Sade herself.

"Are you going to keep standing there, or are you going to help me?" Sade snapped despite her shaking limbs. Her body was getting close to its breaking point.

Henry nodded and pointed at the center of the snake.

"That's where the heart is."

"Then kill it already!" she shouted, and Henry flung his axe at the spot. The snake shuddered, and its head flopped to the side. Sade released it from her hold and stumbled back.

Sade flopped onto the ground, chest heaving as she used runes to replenish her strength. Henry handed her a piece of hard cheese when her breathing slowed.

She mumbled her thanks before she tore into the food.

While she ate, he went to work on cutting the head off the creature and stuffed into a burlap sack.

"How did you find me?" Sade asked while he hoisted the bag over his shoulder.

"You left a rather easy trail to find," he said, nodding toward the battered underbrush. Sade quickly joined him when he started heading back to camp.

"I'm not sorry."

"I know."

Her brow crinkled. "You're not angry with me?"

"No, I'm impressed. You held off the creature a lot longer than I thought you would. You passed the test with flying colors."

Sade let go of the tree branch she was keeping at bay, Henry ducked to keep it from smacking into his head.

"You were testing me!?" Her voice rose several octaves.

"In my defense, I needed to see how strong you are. I know some people freeze up when they're being tested—"

A wind rune floated out from Sade's pouch and sent him flying into a bush. Thorns tore into his clothes and pierced his skin.

"I was struggling for hours against that damn thing!" She yanked up a sleeve, showing a large bite mark. Blood dripped down her arm and Sade started to tremble. She stumbled over to a log and sat down. Her skin was bone white.

Henry's chest tightened as he watched her try to use her healing rune, but she couldn't get it to activate. He scrambled to his feet, ignoring the pain in his body.

He knelt next to her and gently pressed his healing rune onto her wound. Streaks of pink light wove around them. Sade glanced at him, her dark eyes a mixture of anguish and fury.

"I'm sorry," Henry whispered. "I should've told you and not tried to trick you."

Sade sighed. "I'm sorry as well. I got too caught up in trying to avenge those people and didn't listen."

Henry couldn't stop himself from staring at her. He expected her to have that insufferable pride that nearly every divine had. They would never apologize, yet here she was, apologizing for falling for the trap he'd laid out for her.

He turned his attention to her wound when her face

contorted with agony. Tears brimmed in her eyes as the healing rune fixed an unseen injury. A strange force tugged at his heart, and he suddenly wanted nothing more than to take away her pain. The harder he struggled to release himself from it, the more pressure in his chest increased.

"You know you could definitely beat the God of War in a duel," he said trying to ignore the growing discomfort in his body. He'd never experienced anything like this before. Was he taking on her pain?

Sade raised an eyebrow, the pain in her eyes was fading as a faint flicker of amusement flashed through them. Relief flooded through him at the sight.

"Really? Even though I was almost bested by that monster?"

"You weren't bested, you didn't know how to kill it."

Sade stared at her wound; the rune's light faded leaving a faint scar. Henry tucked the stone back into his pouch. He met her gaze, and her eyes shimmered like tears were threatening to fall. Henry braced himself for a wave of pain, but instead Sade wrapped her arms around him.

"Thank you," she whispered against his shoulder.

"For what?"

"For not treating me like I'm a fragile flower."

Henry couldn't help the chuckle that escaped his lips.

"I'd be a fool if I did."

Her divine presence seeped into his. Sending a wave of gratitude and peace through him. It was something he hadn't felt in years. He took a deep breath, and the scent of lilacs filled his nostrils. His muscles relaxed and he started to feel like he was drifting away on a cloud. Sade pulled back, a lock of hair fell across her face, and he found himself tucking it behind her ear. A blush crept across her cheeks and her gaze dropped to the forest floor.

He froze. What was he doing? Heat flared within him as he realized just how close they were sitting. He stood up, taking care to not knock her over then pretended to check his rune pouch. He'd let himself open too much to her divine presence. The last thing he needed was to turn into Aiden.

"We need to get back to camp," he said. "Aiden might be back by now. He was out of his mind when he found out you were missing."

Sade nodded, but she couldn't hide the disdain that crossed her face.

Ah, so she had noticed Aiden's attitude around her. Sade's eyes narrowed when he let out a quiet laugh.

"What?" She asked.

Henry shook his head. "Aiden doesn't have much experience with women. I've never seen him flirt with anyone and I thought he might be someone who doesn't want romantic companionship. But I guess he prefers goddesses with captivating auras."

"You think I'm captivating?" Her eyes sparkled.

A burst of desperate energy swept past them, saving him from replying. It was coming from the direction of the camp.

"We should make sure he's all right," Henry said. Sade kept pace with him as he hurried through the forest. She glanced at him; curiosity danced in her eyes.

"What?"

"Why don't you act like he does?"

"My mother taught me how to shield myself from divine

influences. Aiden doesn't have any experience dealing with a full divine in this realm. Your presence is rather magnetizing to mortals. Aiden's father went back into the Divine Realm before he was born. He doesn't know how to shield himself properly. I tried to teach him once, but he declined."

"Oh, that's disappointing," she said.

"There is some good news. Once Aiden gets used to your presence, he will likely back off and stop this nonsense."

The tension in Sade's body eased a fraction.

"And how long would that take?"

"I don't know."

The tree ahead of them dissolved into ashes. Henry dropped his sack and grabbed his axe. Sade clutched her dull sword.

"That thing isn't going to help you," he said.

She quickly sheathed it and tugged out an ice rune.

The air cleared to reveal Aiden holding a fire rune not too far from the pile of ashes.

"Where in the hell have you been?" He shouted to Henry. "I thought you were a monster!"

"I'm fine!" She protested when Aiden ran over to her, a healing rune in his hand.

"But you've got a scar!"

"I like to think of it as a souvenir," she said with a sad smile.

"You could've gotten killed!"

"Actually, she was doing just fine," Henry said. He braced himself as Aiden's shoulders tensed. Green and silver sparks danced around him.

"Oh, you don't get to say *anything*, Henry," he snarled and eyed the dagger on Henry's belt.

Don't. You. Dare. Henry sent through his thoughts. Aiden's mouth formed a thin line as he connected to Henry's mortal side. They didn't speak like this often. There was a risk Sade could pick up on their thoughts, but he had no choice.

We do this my way; we're going the safer route and I swear if you put her in any type of danger again. I will tell her.

Gods, she's not a piece of fucking glass, Aiden!

Then maybe you shouldn't have told me about her past!

You would've realized I was hiding something, and I didn't want to risk you questioning me in front of her!

Aiden rolled his eyes and closed off their connection.

"Let's hurry and get to town. We can cry about this over some ale," Henry said.

He fell into step behind them. Aiden tried to place a hand on the small of Sade's back, but she quickly sidestepped him, and Henry found himself moving between them. Sade shot him a look of gratitude. Aiden muttered something under his breath.

Henry started to whistle a tune, trying to clear the awkwardness in the air. But it hung over them like a raincloud.

He couldn't wait to get to a tavern.

❧

To say the townsfolk were grateful would be an understatement.

He ran a hand through his hair while he sifted through the pile of goods they'd been swamped with. Most of the stuff, aside from some tents and a pair of boots that Sade found, wasn't anything useful.

The inn keeper had given them the finest rooms free of charge. Aiden had insisted they stay there for a night and Henry didn't dare protest. Aiden was still furious with him, and he didn't need to poke the fire further.

"What you did was reckless and borderline treasonous," Airi said as she materialized onto a chair. Spirits and the God of Death were the only ones who could move freely between realms. A fact Henry wished weren't true.

Henry kept his gaze on the pile in front of him, smiling to himself when he spotted an axe.

"Let me guess, Aiden filed a complaint," he said while he dug a rune carving tool out of his bag.

"No, I have been watching you."

Henry dropped his tool and looked up at Airi. Instead of the messenger spirit's face, he saw the God of Knowledge's furious one. He'd forgotten about that trick. Like a Vestral, a spirit could be used as a vessel for a divine to speak through. Though the Vestrals kept their own faces.

"You put an entire realm in danger, and you did it with no reservations!"

"Oh, believe me, I had my reservations, but it needed to be done. The God of Ruin won't stop sending creatures. If we come up against anything strong, she needs to be able to defend herself. I can't watch my back and hers at the same time."

"You're playing with a very ancient force. You need to exercise more caution."

"She's not as fragile as you think!"

The god's face drew closer, and a tendril of violet smoke swept around him.

"No, she's not fragile. She's *dangerous.*"

Henry patted the dagger, "I have this remember? You don't

need to watch me so closely; I've got this under control."

"Do not let her reach such a state again or—"

"Or what?" Henry rose to his feet and clenched his fists at his sides. He gestured around the empty room. "You said it yourself, I'm the only one who can lead her to the portal. If you don't like my methods, maybe you should come down here and do it yourself."

"This is your first and only warning Henry. If she reaches those levels again, I will not allow your parents to achieve godhood and will make them wander the void between the realms."

With that the god returned Airi to her original state. The spirit flipped him off before she vanished.

Henry kicked a silver bowl, and it slammed into a wall right as a door opened. Sade poked her head in with an ice rune hovering next to her.

"What is going on? I felt a spirit's presence…"

"I'm fine," he snapped, and Sade started toward him. A wave of peace wrapped around him and, before he could react, his anger melted away like it was nothing. Her wide eyes narrowed; she must've sensed some residual divine energy.

Aiden sauntered into the room, his eyes widening with each step.

"The God of Knowledge was here?" He asked and cast a smirk in Henry's direction. "Seems like he didn't like you putting her in danger either."

Henry pressed his lips together and turned his attention to his new axe. The image of his parents floating around the void between worlds kept flashing in his mind. He started to carve a fire rune into his axe. Sade tried to soothe him again, but this time he was ready for it.

This wouldn't do. He needed her to be focused on wanting to leave this realm as fast as possible. Not trying to calm his frazzled mind.

"I don't care what he thinks," Sade muttered under her breath.

"You should," Henry said and shoved his rune carving tool in his pouch.

"Why? He's kept me locked up in a temple for ages!"

"Twenty years is nothing in the eyes of an immortal," Henry said.

What are you doing? Aiden asked in his thoughts.

What I should have done at the start. We're not here to show her the wonders of this realm Aiden, she has to leave.

Henry—

"What did he tell you?" Sade asked her eyes bright with an emotion Henry didn't want to identify. "Is this because of my behavior at the farm…"

"Yes, because of your behavior at the farm, I had to take drastic actions," he hissed and crossed his arms. He ignored the magic in his blood, boiling to a point it was almost unbearable. His divine purpose strained within him. He ignored it and shoved it down into a dark place in his mind.

Sade stepped forward again, her divine rune floating just above her rune pouch.

"Stop, I don't need your magic. I can calm myself," he said and headed for the door.

"Where are you going?"

"Somewhere that I can carve in peace."

Neither of them followed. Once he was far enough away from Sade's range of influence, Henry's magic exploded with rage.

"Why are you doing this now?" He muttered to his hands, ignoring the befuddled looks from the townsfolk he passed. He quickly made his way into the forest, lest a Vestral added more ruin to his day.

Using a stick, he drew a combination rune in the dirt designed to absorb magic and keep it from setting off Vilmantas's alarms. When he was sure no one could see him, he poured all of his power into his rune. The trees and shrubbery around him became bathed in an orange glow.

A figure made of orange lightning stood in the center of the rune. The heat in Henry's blood increased at the sight.

"What do you want?" He asked the figure.

"You are not fulfilling your divine purpose," the figure said. It was the physical manifestation of his divine self, something he didn't see very often. His divine half usually made itself known through feelings or thoughts.

"I am. I'm escorting her to the Realm of Ruin and getting my parents back," Henry snarled at the figure. He reached for his rune pouch, but the stones slinked away from his fingers.

"That is not an act of justice *or* mercy."

"What in the hell do you want me to do?"

"Help her."

"I am."

"You're not and you know it. If you take her to that realm, you are spelling her certain doom."

"If I don't do this, then my parents will be stuck in the afterlife—" Henry threw up his hands. "Why am I even arguing with you? You're me and we are under orders from the Sacred Council."

"Orders can be disobeyed."

"Enough!" Henry stormed over to the figure. He grabbed it by the throat and forced it back into his body.

His blood boiled to the point he thought steam would start rising from his skin. He collapsed onto his knees and dug his hands into the dirt.

No. He wouldn't listen to that part of himself. Sade had to go. It was the only way peace would be achieved and the only way he'd ever see his parents again. He wasn't going to fail them a second time.

He would not break.

Chapter Nine

Henry hadn't said a word to her or Aiden for days. No matter how hard she tried, she couldn't get him to talk about anything. Not even the weather.

What had the God of Knowledge done to him? She asked Aiden, but he merely shrugged and said Henry was just having a fit about being under someone else's orders.

Whatever it was, Henry was locked in a battle that no one could help him with.

They came to a fork in the road and Henry tugged out his map with a seeking rune hovered over it.

"What the hell!"

Both she and Aiden froze. His voice was hoarse like he'd been screaming, but he'd been silent this whole time.

"What's wrong?" Aiden asked slowly, like he was afraid Henry would fall silent again.

"The portal moved," Henry handed the map to Aiden who paled when Henry tapped a location.

"Oh, Gods. Why?"

Sade took the map from Aiden and waited for something to appear foretelling their certain doom, but nothing happened.

"I don't understand?"

Henry took the map back from her. "The portal is now in the Eastern Marshes."

"So, we get our feet wet. It's not that big of a deal," Sade shrugged and both men stared at her like she'd lost her mind. "What?"

"This means our route has changed and we have to go through the Violet Mountains."

Images of cliffs and lofty peaks cloaked in shades of purple danced in her thoughts.

"It's also home to the skessa," Aiden said and continued when Sade raised her eyebrows. "They're a cross between a troll and giant. They keep to themselves, I've heard rumors they've been acting up."

"They aren't one of the God of Ruins' creations?"

"No, they were created alongside the other creatures in this realm. They're powerful magic users and are extremely territorial. Many humans have waged campaigns of varying success to eliminate them, but most of them come home broken, bleeding, or dead."

Aiden glanced at Henry who'd gone so pale she thought he might faint. He turned away from them and fiddled with something in his bag.

"It's also the location where his parents died," Aiden

whispered. "He hasn't stepped near the mountains since then. He even turned down a bounty from a king to hunt down the skessa."

Sade's heart swelled with sadness; Henry tried to act like he wasn't bothered, but his hands trembled ever so slightly, and his aura emanated with guilt and loss.

"Is there another way?" She tore her gaze away from him and focused on Aiden who shook his head.

"Not unless we want to take a four-month journey skirting around the mountains."

Time, something they did not have. Sade reached for Henry, but she pulled back. She'd already caused him enough trouble. Aiden had noticed the gesture, but held his tongue. A flash of darkness passed over his face.

"I can go alone," she offered, and Henry spun around so fast she felt dizzy watching him. His sadness had been replaced with a grim determination.

"We will get some horses in the next town," he said.

Silence blanketed them again; this was worse than the type she'd experienced at the temple.

"Have you ever ridden a horse before?" Aiden asked, filling the air with the type of conversation she hated. But it was more bearable than the silence.

"Does fashioning a horse out of sticks count?"

"Maybe?" Aiden scratched his chin and glanced at a log.

Sade dared a glance at Henry's back, but he made no sign of being invested in their conversation.

Leave him be, he's not worth your time. The crimson figure flashed before her eyes.

I don't remember asking for your opinion. Her magic strained within her. It wanted nothing more than to bring peace to Henry's tormented soul.

Or maybe it wants to take him out of his misery.

"Would you shut up!" She shouted and clamped a hand over her mouth when she realized she'd said it out loud.

"No one said anything," Aiden's face glossed over with concern. "Are you okay?"

"Yes. I will need some time to answer some petitions when we camp next."

The lie fell easily from her lips. The dark figure in the back of her mind grinned.

"Oh, it's been a few days since you've last listened to them, right? Can't imagine what that would be like. No one petitions me."

"What? Why not?"

"Unlike you or Henry, I don't have a plethora of worshippers at my beck and call. I'm a minor god in the scheme of things, my power levels are that of a spirit." Aiden's expression became wistful, "If I just had one follower…"

"You did, but you smothered them with so much attention they got a big head and then nearly caused an entire civilization to collapse," Henry said with a forced lightness to his tone. He smiled, but it looked off.

"When did this happen?"

"He'd been here almost a year and some nobleman in Acrilla petitioned him. Aiden told him he was a chosen one and destined to lead his country to greatness."

"I thought he'd start a magic school or something," Aiden

grumbled and shoved his hands into his pockets.

"Instead, he tried to assassinate the king and burned down his family's castle. The man ended up with his head on a pike. His death did secure that dynasty's power for another generation. So, in a way, I guess he was destined for something," Henry slowed down and moved beside Sade.

"I got so excited to have someone petition me, I didn't watch for the warning signs," Aiden bowed his head and Sade awkwardly patted him on the back, trying not to have too much physical contact.

"He appeared to him as a talking cloud," Henry grinned, this time it was genuine. "Watching him try to explain his actions to the God of Knowledge was the funniest thing I'd ever seen. So, I took him under my wing after that."

"And now, I'm working with the only god who hates answering petitions and reduced his entire following to one backwater realm," Aiden mumbled. If Henry heard him, he didn't show it.

Sade tilted her head to the side and studied Henry. He kept his gaze on the trail in front of him, his seeking rune held tight in one hand.

"Why don't you answer petitions?"

"Because I prefer to take care of it in person," he gestured to a tree, "I can't sit around and blow sparkles into a pond when things are eating people."

"Do you use Vestrals?"

"Only when things are dire or I can't reach a location in time."

The sounds of steel clashing wafted through the air. Henry

sighed and glanced at his seeking rune.

"Tighten your shields a bit," he said to her.

"Why?"

"Because some humans are fighting a war and I don't want you to become overwhelmed."

"War is something I can handle; I saw it play out hundreds of times in my temple."

But she tightened her shields around her, and Henry's shoulders relaxed. She smiled at him, but he didn't return the gesture. They rounded a bend, and the forest gave way to a large grassy field that stretched beyond the horizon. In the distance, lines of men in shining armor were engaged in combat. Along the edges of the fighting, the souls of dead men watched their comrades with dull eyes.

One by one they turned to watch them skirt the edge of the battlefield. Henry and Aiden were using various runes to mask their presence.

Goddess, why do you turn your eyes from us. Help us find the peace we require. The ghosts called out to her. Sade fought to keep her magic from rising in answer.

"The God of Death will be here shortly, don't pay attention to them," Henry said.

A low hiss filled her ears and both men froze in their tracks. A line of ghosts now stood in their paths. Rage etched into their faces, and all of them were staring at Sade.

"Don't. Move." Henry said, a fire rune floated out of his rune pouch.

"What are the ghosts doing?"

"They aren't ghosts anymore. They've turned into wraiths."

"Spirit, this is not how you will find peace," Aiden said and reached his hand out.

"No, she must pay the price for the blood she stole," a wraith hissed. It was missing an arm and a leg. Its voice sent a thousand tiny icicles down her skin.

"I have taken nothing from you," Sade said, struggling to keep her magic from lashing out.

"You never came to stop this!" Another wraith screamed. This one was a young boy, barely old enough to hold a weapon. A sword was permanently lodged in his stomach. "You could've kept me safe."

"I didn't know this was happening!"

More wraiths surrounded them, pressing them toward the ongoing battle.

"Aiden, do you still have that combination rune from the time we explored the catacombs?" Henry grabbed his axes, his eyes never leaving the wraiths as the runes in the metal lit up.

"I think so!" Aiden frantically shifted through his rune pouch.

The group of wraiths started edging closer and a foul wind filled the air. Sade gagged and covered her mouth, but it did little to hide the stench.

"Whatever happens, don't let them touch you. Goddess or not, these things can drag you into the afterlife," Henry said.

"Can't the God of Death get us out if that happens?"

"It's not that simple."

Sade wanted to press him further, but Henry had his attention on a wraith who was sneaking forward. She would have to ask about it later when they weren't literally staring death in the face. She unsheathed her sword. There was still some energy left in the blade. The rune bathed her in a bloody red glow. Henry cast a glance at her and she could've sworn she saw a glimmer of fear in his eyes.

"Well? Do you have the damn thing or not?" Henry asked Aiden.

"I'm looking for it!"

"Call it out!"

"I can't! It's not responding!"

The wraiths moved closer; Sade didn't need her magic to sense the decay around them. She reached into her pouch, her fingers brushing her divine rune.

"Don't," Henry said.

"But—"

"Sade, you will only make things worse here."

"How do you know that?"

"Because I can feel the God of War's handiwork in this damn mess."

Sade held up her divine rune, and a trickle of smoke flew out. Before she could call it back, a vision of the God of War flashed in her mind. He was holding an enormous sword, drenched in blood and his blood-red eyes beckoned a challenge. He wasn't truly here. His presence was woven tight into the mortals ahead of them.

"Found it!" Aiden shouted. Swirls of black and gold formed a vortex over his head. The wraiths shrank back. "That's right, you annoying bastards, we're not going to the damn afterlife today!"

"Start running toward the horizon and stop when you can't

hear the sounds of battle," Henry leaned down and whispered in her ear.

Sade looked at the wall of wraiths and back at Henry.

"Just trust me on this," he pleaded.

Sade sheathed her sword and sprinted towards the shimmering wraiths. A wave of black and gold swept out in front of her, tossing wraiths to the side and giving her a path out. Cold, hard air pressed against her, trying to keep her in place, but the magic from Aiden's rune held steady.

She crested a hill and spied a town nestled in the forest. Her legs gave out, sending her tumbling down the slope. Her freefall was stopped when she collided with a boulder.

A terrible ringing noise thrummed in her ears as she slumped onto the ground. An invisible weight pressed on her chest, pushing her into the dirt. A whirlwind fueled by blood-red sparks formed around her. The God of War had followed her.

Every fiber of her being hummed with the desire to stop him, but she'd promised Henry she wouldn't.

"Leave me alone!" She shouted to the winds, "I will not interfere in this battle!"

She reached for her rune pouch, willing her divine rune to float out, but it didn't budge. Her fingers brushed the opening, and a surge of power flooded her veins, begging to be let out into the frenzied air around her.

No, she needed to use a rune. She couldn't cause any more trouble.

She pulled out a rune and her heart dropped to her stomach; it was a light rune. That wasn't going to help her get out of this.

Laughter echoed through the wind and white-hot anger surged through her, breaking through the hold she had on her magic. Blue and gold sparks danced on her fingertips, ready to be unleashed.

"You think this is funny?" She yelled and the god's laughter only got louder.

It was then she felt a wisp of power, wrapping around her like a cloak, and pushing back against the maelstrom. A figure appeared in the dust; ribbons of orange lightning arced out of them.

"Sade, can you hear me?" Henry's voice rose above the howling winds.

She could only nod when another wave of pressure pressed against her. In a flash of light, the air cleared, and Henry was beside her. She slowly sat up, using the boulder beside her as leverage. Her body wasn't in too bad of shape, though her lungs burned with each breath she took. But when she tried to stand, one of her legs gave out. Her knee was swollen.

"Easy now," Henry said, a healing rune floated beside them. He gently placed a hand on her leg, and a stream of pink light encased them both.

"Why did he do that? I moved away from the battle," Sade asked, and Henry ran a hand through his hair. Orange sparks floated around him. It was then she noticed his divine rune was floating behind him, keeping something at bay.

"He was being an arse; he likes to mess with people."

"Was it my captivating presence? Did it turn him into Aiden?" She asked, the fury in his eyes lessened slightly and she could have sworn she saw a glimpse of a smile cross his face.

"You just gave me an idea on how I'm going to make sure he pays for this."

"How?"

Henry gave her wink. "You'll have to wait and see."

"But—"

"Henry!" Aiden shouted from atop the hill. He was soon by Henry's side; concern was etched in his features. He reached for his rune pouch, but Henry waved him off.

"No need, she's already healed," he said and rose to his feet. He held out a hand and helped her stand.

"He's gone," Aiden said.

"Good, we need to keep moving," Henry let his divine rune drift back into his pouch. Aiden gave them both an odd look and his gaze traveled down to their hands. Henry quickly let go and mumbled something about healing runes.

"Are we going to get the horses or are we just going to stand here?" Aiden asked.

"Let's go, I want to get the horses before nightfall."

They started to take bets of what type of horses they'd be able to acquire. She cast a glance over her shoulder toward the battlefield, but she was too far away to see anything. Yet, her heart still weighed heavy. She hoped the town would offer her a moment of reprieve.

Whatever thoughts she had about having a moment of peace were dashed the moment they stepped foot in the town. She tried to read the battered sign that had the town's name engraved on it, but it was so worn down the runes were barely legible. Most of the town looked like it had seen better days. The thatched roofs on many houses needed repair and parts of the stone walls were crumbling.

The people around her fared no better. With their sunken eyes and grey skin, they looked more wraith than human.

"Come on, you've got to have more than two horses! Those are too damn slow!" Aiden gestured to two bay horses. He was negotiating with a stable keeper. She was a tall woman, but not as tall as Henry or Aiden, with long golden hair and tanned skin. She was the only human in this place who didn't look like they were about to keel over.

"I'm afraid you are a day too late," she said, and Aiden's shoulders slumped.

Henry brushed him aside and flashed a smile at the woman. Much to Sade's surprise, she smiled back.

"Forgive my friend here, he doesn't know a good horse from a bad one. He's more of a griffin man. I'm afraid we need another horse; we are on an extremely important quest." Henry said, his voice was deeper than it normally was, and his eyes were like liquid emeralds.

"An important quest?" The stable keepers gaze swept up and down Henry's body like she was assessing a trinket. She looked at him through her lashes and a seductive smile spread across her face.

"Extremely dangerous too," Henry added with a gleam in his eyes.

Sade clasped her hands behind her back as her magic boiled within her. She spied a yellow glow from Henry's rune pouch. The fabric made it impossible to tell what rune was activated.

Henry leaned closer to the woman and whispered something in her ear. She giggled and stepped away; her cheeks flushed.

"I'll be right back," she said. She headed into the stables.

Sade moved next to Henry, and the strange yellow glow from his pouch was gone.

"What were you doing to her?" Sade whispered and poked his rune pouch.

"Securing another horse," he said, and Aiden snorted.

"More like securing a new bed to sleep in."

Henry shot Aiden a dark look. "Well, you were about to lose the two horses we could secure."

The stable doors opened again, and the stable keeper walked out with a grim expression.

"Unfortunately, that's all the horses I can spare. The others are either lame or foaling."

Henry gave her a dazzling smile before he tossed her a bag filled with gold. The woman looked down at the gold and then back up at Henry. Before she could say anything, Henry was directing Sade toward the larger horse.

He grabbed a large wooden block and set it beside the horse before he mounted it. He patted the space behind him and grinned.

"Up you go. Unless you want to ride with him?" Henry inclined his head towards Aiden who was struggling to get his horse to stay still long enough for him to mount it.

A shudder swept through Sade, and she hurried over to the block. She pulled herself onto the horse behind Henry and wrapped her arms around his waist. She could feel the hardened muscles of his stomach when she tightened her grip. Her magic flared out and she yanked it back into her, but not before Henry let out a chuckle.

Aiden had to call over the stable keeper to hold on to his horse's bridle. Sade was grateful for the distraction since it kept her from focusing on how close she was to Henry.

"Oi, we don't got all day!" Henry shouted and pointed at the sky. Aiden glared at him, but he was finally able to get onto his horse.

"Thank you," Sade said to the stable keeper. She didn't spare Sade a glance.

"Remember you can come see me anytime," the stable keeper gave Henry a wink then gave Aiden's horse a slap on the rump. With a shrill cry the horse launched forward, and Aiden let out a stream of curses.

Henry nudged the horse forward and they took off at a pace Sade didn't know was possible from a mortal animal. It wasn't long before they were out of the town and onto a dusty road.

Nausea swept over her, and she pressed her face against Henry's shoulder. He smelled of amber and sandalwood. The scent helped keep her from vomiting.

"Are you all right?" Henry asked.

"The world is moving too fast."

"Give it some time. You'll get used to it."

"Why haven't we gotten horses until now?" She asked, trying to keep bile from rising further in her throat.

"I don't normally use horses; I've had too many of them get eaten by the God of Ruin's creatures and they are expensive to buy."

The horses gait faltered, and Sade had to pull herself tight against his back.

"Aiden slow down, let's not injure the horses on their first day!" Henry called out to Aiden, who was using a calming rune on his steed.

Sade rested her head on Henry's shoulder, and her eyes drifted closed.

You failed them. You could've brought peace to them, but you didn't. The crimson figure snarled.

"Don't listen to it," Henry's voice was grave.

"What are you talking about?"

"The reason you hit your limit, is because you went against your divine purpose by running away from the battle. Your mind will make you suffer for it."

"Is this something you've experienced before?"

Henry let out a long breath.

"Unfortunately."

"What do I do?"

"I don't know, I've only experienced it once before. Try to ignore it and move on."

"Is that your answer for most things?"

"Yes, and it usually works."

"Maybe we aren't meant to just ignore it. It *is* the entire reason for our existence."

"Have you ever wondered if you were more than just a physical manifestation of something for mortals to cling to?"

Memories of long days and nights spent locked up in her temple flashed in her mind. Memories of the empty corridors and hours she'd spent staring out into the world around her, wondering if this was what her life was.

"Yes, I would spend hours on the balconies of my temple, wondering what my true purpose was. I doubt whatever created me wanted me to spend eternity staring at a magical pool, no matter how much I enjoyed using it."

"Must've been some pool."

"It was. When I first arrived, I thought the temple was the most beautiful place in the realm. However, as time went on and the loneliness crept in, that pool was one of the only things that kept me from going insane."

"Did they ever tell you why they locked you up?"

"They said my magic had to remain pure for it to work correctly."

Henry's body tensed and Sade could feel a torrent of emotions ranging from rage to guilt before he clamped down on them.

"Remain pure? What in the hell does that mean?"

"I don't know and I'm not sure they knew either. But something changed when the God of Ruin sent back the God of Music. Maybe fate needed me to stay away from everything while my powers solidified?"

There was a period when a new divine was born where their powers were uncontrollable. The time varied between immortals, but Sade's had taken a few years to calm down.

"Maybe," Henry said. His voice sounded hollow.

Sade yawned and rested her head on his shoulder again. The countryside flew by and the further away they got from the battlefield, the more her mind settled.

Chapter Ten

Having Sade ride with him was a mistake.

It took every ounce of his willpower for him to not pay attention to every small movement she made. Her arms around his waist were not helping matters. He'd put too much magic into the charm rune he'd used on the stable keep. Now he was paying the consequences for it. Even the most innocent of touches was driving him mad.

Sade's aura brushed against his and he was overcome with exhaustion. The feeling was enough to drive away the effects of the charm rune. Sade's arms started slipping from his waist and he barely had time to stop her from falling off the horse.

"Aiden, looks like we're camping here for the night!" He called to his friend. They were still out in the plains, which meant it would be harder for a creature to sneak up on them.

Aiden quickly dismounted then helped Henry get Sade off

the horse. She was out cold.

They set up camp with ease. It was something they'd done a thousand times before. Once Sade was in her tent, he tore into a stale loaf of bread and collapsed next to the fire Aiden started.

"Once again, you've put her in danger."

Henry rolled his eyes at Aiden and poured some ale into his tankard.

"And how exactly did I do that?" He looked around the camp, waiting for Airi to show up. When she didn't, he gave Aiden a rueful smile. "Well, it seems the God of Knowledge disagrees."

"My point still stands."

"Your point? You don't have a point, you're just jealous!"

"Jealous? Of what?"

"Sade can hardly stand you and you're simpering over her like a dog."

Aiden's hands clenched at his sides. "I'm not."

"Yes, you are. You need to back off Aiden. She's not going to stay with you and have your children. She has a job to do in the God of Ruin's realm."

"Oh, and you think you're so high and mighty?" Aiden leaned forward, "I sensed your aura when she was riding with you today, Henry. I'm surprised she didn't push you off the horse."

"Well, she didn't. She fell asleep while I was giving her a history lesson."

Aiden started laughing as Henry realized what he'd said. He couldn't stop his own laughter from bursting forth.

Once they had calmed down, Aiden glanced at Sade's tent

and then back at Henry. He was finally free of Sade's influence.

"I didn't realize I was being so intense."

"You owe Sade an apology."

Aiden winced, "I was that bad?"

"Yes."

Aiden was quiet for a moment. "I think the reason it was so intense for me is because I really do want a bond mate."

"What, I'm not good enough for you?"

Aiden shot him a glare. "You're not my type. But maybe Sade is."

"You can't be with her."

"Who says I can't?"

"Last time I checked, a bond could only be formed between the willing."

"Then maybe I can convince her!"

"That's not how that works, and you know it. For all we know, she could be bonded to some minor god that rules over the moon."

"Do you think she'll ever regain her memories?"

"I don't know," he tapped the dagger at his side. "I thought this might trigger something, but she's looked at it several times now."

Something dark was stewing inside of her, straining at the chains the other gods had wrapped around it, but Sade held firm against it. Maybe she believed it was her divine purpose punishing her for going against her reason for existing.

Henry cursed under his breath. Of course, she would feel that way. She wasn't just the Goddess of Peace, but also Destruction. And she had plenty of opportunities to destroy things. Maybe the reason why she was so drained from the battlefield was because of her dual purposes. One side straining to bring things to a harmonious conclusion and the other wanting carnage. It was a battle few could manage without going insane and Sade was merely exhausted.

The part of him that had been afraid of her was now awed by her strength.

"Silver for your thoughts?" Aiden asked.

"This entire situation is a mess."

"You can say that again."

Henry yawned and stretched his limbs.

"Once we get her through the portal, she can do her duty and everything should go back to normal."

"Do you really think she'll be able to get him to stop sending the monsters?"

Henry paused. When he'd first met her, he thought the God of Ruin would walk all over her. Now, he wasn't so sure.

"Who knows, but at least he'll have his hands full."

"I hope she can visit," Aiden said wistfully.

"Seriously Aiden?"

"Sorry, I'll work on it."

"I need to get some sleep," Henry rose and headed to his tent.

Henry jolted from his bedroll. An oily smoke slithered on the ground below him. He grabbed his axes and burst out his tent, ready to fight.

Instead, he came face-to-face with Sade and Aiden, both of

whom had fire runes floating beside them. Aiden had moved the horses close to the fire and scratched calming runes into their saddles.

The grass around them shifted in the breeze. Shadows danced on the edge of the firelight, but nothing emerged from the darkness.

"Can you feel that?" Sade shivered despite the heat from her fire rune.

Henry let his magic loose and found nothing. He walked over to where he'd set up a ward, but there was no sign of anything tampering with it.

"Why aren't they attacking? They usually attack by now." Aiden's voice trembled.

Henry quelled the rising panic within him and summoned his fire rune. Taking a breath, he formed a fireball and let it float high above them. The light illuminated the area around him. Still nothing jumped out at them.

"It was just a dream," Henry said.

"That we all shared?"

"I know some spirits can influence dreams."

He let the fireball fade out of existence and slid his axes back onto his belt.

"Both of you go back to sleep, dawn will be here shortly. I'll keep watch until then."

Sade shook her head. "No, I've gotten enough sleep."

The dark circles under her eyes said the opposite, but Henry wasn't about to start an argument.

"Once dawn arrives, we'll leave."

He and Aiden quickly stripped the tents and prepped

the horses while Sade kept watch. Once they were done, they gathered around the campfire keeping their backs to it as they watched the shadows.

The sun crept slowly across the horizon and, when the stars winked out of sight, he spotted a pair of red eyes watching him on top of the hill. Henry sent out a blast of fire in response, but the fire found nothing to burn.

"The hell was that?" Aiden asked. Henry hurried over to horses and checked the magic levels in the saddles' calming runes.

"I don't know, and I don't want to find out," he mounted the horse and Sade scrambled to get on.

"Something dark is here," Sade said as her body trembled.

Henry frowned and he checked his runes, but they were cold to the touch.

"Aiden, do you sense anything?"

"Nope."

"Sade, can you tell what direction it's coming from?"

"Everywhere."

The hair on the back of Henry's neck stood up. He swallowed and did his best to shove the fear into the back of his mind. He squeezed his legs against his horse's sides and the animal took off at a gallop. Aiden wasn't far behind.

They rode for days, stopping only to catch a wink of sleep and then starting up again. Not a word was said save for Sade letting them know when the feeling of darkness faded. Henry tried in vain to sense what she was sensing, but there was nothing for him to find.

If it weren't for the fact he saw the red eyes, he would've thought Sade was feeling her destructive side.

Which made it more troubling. Why couldn't he or Aiden detect the creature? Had the God of Ruin finally created something powerful enough to defeat a half-god?

He was jolted from his thoughts as the horse slowed. Sweat poured off the creature like it'd been standing under a waterfall. He dug his heels in, trying to get the animal to move faster. The horse gave him a loud snort in response.

"Sade, can you still sense the creature?"

He sucked in a breath as Sade's magic burst out of her in a wave of heat.

"No."

Henry almost fell out of the saddle. He patted the horse's neck, grimacing when it came back drenched in sweat.

"We need to get them cooled down," Aiden called from behind them.

Henry nodded at the line of trees ahead, "There should be a river around here somewhere."

He could hear running water the closer they got to the forest. The horse's ears perked up and moved at a slightly faster walk than it had been. Henry let the animal use its senses to find the water.

Soon they were under the canopy of trees, and their shade provided little relief from the blazing sun, but the promise of water drove them on. Henry wiped a dribble of sweat from his brow.

"This has to be the most hidden creek in existence," Aiden said. A seeking rune hovered beside him.

"Something isn't right," Sade mumbled under her breath. "Henry, stop the horse."

Before the horse was at a complete stop, Sade slid off the saddle. Her divine rune hovered between her hands. A bubble of blue and gold floated around her.

Henry hopped off the horse and gripped the bridle. The calming rune etched into the saddle blazed bright with power as Sade filled it. Aiden quickly joined Henry and together they looked around the forest.

"What is it?"

Sade raised a finger to her lips and motioned for him and Aiden to stay quiet. He watched her weave her magic into the forest's, blue and gold sparks intermingling with brown.

Then she went still, her eyes firmly shut. Henry's gaze flicked back and forth from the forest to the motionless goddess.

This is ridiculous, why can't we sense anything? Aiden growled in his head.

If I had the answer to that question, I'd be richer than most kings.

Gentlemen, I believe I asked you to stay quiet. Sade's voice drifted into his head. She was glaring at both of them. Her presence had woven itself into their mortal halves, protecting their weaker parts from…something.

In silence they stood, and sweat continued to drip off Henry like tiny raindrops.

With sudden burst of movement, Sade created a large circle with them inside. Then, again, she was still, her eyes closed, leaving Henry and Aiden to watch the blue and gold vortex sweep around them.

The sun hit its highest point of the day. Somewhere, a bird sang. Henry was about to lose his mind. His magic itched to be released, but he had no target. No idea what he was up against. All he could do was stare into the forest shimmering with heat and continue to sweat like a pig.

Finally, after what seemed like an eternity, Sade opened her eyes and her rune floated back into her pouch. The air was cooler, and Henry reached for his waterskin.

"What in the hell happened?" Aiden asked her.

"The thing that was chasing us is outside the forest," she said. "It tried to make its way in, but the tree and plant spirits kept it from entering. They were also trying to get us to leave, but I was able to convince them we meant no harm."

Henry's jaw dropped. In all his years, he'd never talked to one plant spirit. He didn't even know they *had* spirits.

"They talk to you?"

"Yes, I can talk to plants," she shrugged. "I had nothing else to do in my temple, so I learned their language and customs."

"Plants have customs?" Aiden squeaked out and Sade nodded gravely. But there was a spark of mischief in her eyes, and she gave him a wink when Aiden wandered over to a tree. He gently touched the bark and started murmuring things to it.

"You realize he'll figure it out eventually, right?" Henry whispered and Sade smiled. The sight caused Henry's heart to speed up like he was under the effects of the charm rune.

"Yes, but the language part *is* true."

"I'm not that stupid."

She grabbed his hand and pulled him over to a tree. She pressed their hands onto the bark and let her aura intermingle with his. A thousand voices started speaking at once and he couldn't hold back a gasp. He tried to separate the sounds, but there were too many. Sade removed her hand from his cutting off the connection.

"Can you teach us?"

"Sure, but first let's get to the stream," she said then called out to Aiden. "The forest spirits have shown me where the water is."

Aiden followed her with a reverence that rivaled the most pious of Vestrals, leaving Henry with the two horses.

"Aiden!" He called after him, but Aiden paid him no mind.

Muttering under his breath, he led the two horses after them, only pausing when they tried to eat the grass. He couldn't be mad at the poor beasts, their coats still glistened with sweat.

It wasn't long before they were at the banks of a gently flowing river. He led the horses over to the water and Aiden helped him take off their saddles.

Sade set up camp while they finished up with the horses.

"She's incredible," Aiden said under his breath.

Henry shrugged. "She's a full goddess. Of course she's going to be more powerful."

"I've never realized how much our power levels differed." Aiden looked down at his hands and clenched them. "It's not fair."

"I asked her to teach us how to talk to plants."

"That's not the damn point, Henry! We have the blood of the divine swimming in our veins, but, because we were unfortunate enough to have a mortal parent, we're not strong enough to do *anything*!"

"Hang on, we've held off the creatures pretty damn well!"

Henry said. Sade was watching them intently. Her head was tilted to the side and her eyes shone with concern.

"Hah, you've held them off. I've been nothing but a weak link," Aiden shoved his hands into his pockets.

Henry rubbed a hand down his face. This was a conversation he'd had in various forms with Aiden over the years. Maybe it was due to his centuries of living, but he didn't care about power. If he had the choice, he would give his divine half to a willing mortal and live out the rest of his days on an island. Alone.

But neither fate nor the God of Knowledge would allow that. Which meant he was stuck like this, forever.

"Aiden, you aren't a weak link. It's not your fault we can't sense the creature. Maybe The God of Ruin's testing Sade, trying to figure out how strong she is before she comes into his realm."

His words fell flat as Aiden shifted in place.

"Never mind, I'm going to take a walk." He glanced at Sade and headed toward a dense part of the forest.

"Where are you going? The water is that way!" Henry shouted, but his words bounced off Aiden's back and he disappeared into the forest.

Gods, I shouldn't have convinced him to stop mooning over Sade.

"Should we go after him?" Sade moved beside him.

"Eh, he gets a little weird whenever he sees something more powerful than him. He'll start off super excited and then have an existential crisis soon after," Henry shrugged, and Sade frowned.

"But you two *are* powerful."

"Not compared to a full blooded divine," Henry flexed his hands at his sides. "I'm a bit more powerful than Aiden because

I'm a dual divine and I have people worshipping me."

"Then we should get more people worshipping both of you!" Sade exclaimed and grabbed his arm pulling him toward the water. He dug his heels in once they reached the river's edge.

"Oh hell no. I'm not going to answer petitions right now. I'm in the middle of a quest."

Sade dropped his arm, and a brief scowl crossed her face.

"Why not?"

"I will not answer anything until you're in the Realm of Ruin."

His head throbbed at his words. His divine purpose surged within him and sucked away more of his magic.

"You need to take your duties seriously! What if someone's life is at stake?" Sade asked.

Henry arched an eyebrow and gestured to the forest.

"That monster that is hunting us is being kept away from the humans. Therefore, I'm committing an act of mercy."

Sade's nose crinkled. "That's a *very* loose thread you're grasping onto."

He shrugged. "Keeps my divine side happy enough."

As if it were waiting for him to summon it, it surged inside him. He tamped down on it before Sade could sense it. She didn't need to know his divine purpose was lighting up like a fire rune whenever she was near.

"Well then if you won't answer your petitions…."

She shot him a wicked grin then a gust of air sent him tumbling into the water.

"You could use a bath. You smell worse than the horses," she said when Henry broke the surface.

She walked away with a swing in her hips, but Henry summoned a rune and used it to pull her into the river.

The goddess glared at him when she emerged from the water.

"What? Can't take a taste of your ow—"

A wave of water smacked him in the face, and he responded with one of his own.

They traded blows of water until they were both red faced from exertion. Sade held up a hand and she trudged over to a sunlit rock and collapsed onto it. Henry sat down next to her, trying not to take note of how her clothes clung to her curves.

"Aiden is missing out," Sade said while Henry used an air rune to dry them both.

He tugged off his boots and poured the water out. Using the air rune, he pulled out the last droplets of water before he pulled them back on. Sade was watching him with a curious expression.

"Do you want me to dry your boots?" He asked. She shook her head and used her air rune to dry them.

"What did you do to the stable keeper to make her give us the horses?"

"Just used a little bit of charm magic. Nothing too special."

"Charm magic?" Sade's eyes lit up. "Can you use it to make someone do whatever you want?"

"Not whatever I want. The rune only enhances my presence and makes it somewhat irresistible. The person I'm trying to charm still has their own freewill and they can refuse it if they want to."

He'd failed more times than he could count with the charm

rune. If he really wanted to take over someone's mind, he'd have to curse them. Something his mother had frequently warned him not to do, since the curse could corrupt him and turn him into the inverted version of himself. He didn't want to find out what the opposite of justice and mercy was.

Sade nodded; her gaze swept down to his rune pouch.

"Have you ever tried to use it on a god?"

"No, I haven't. I think if I tried, they'd kill me."

"But do you think it would work?"

Henry frowned and her shoulders drooped. Was she worried about the God of Ruin?

"I mean it could work," he said before he could stop himself. Sade's eyes lit up again with hope.

"Really?"

"I don't know how well it would work on the God of Ruin, but you could try."

"How did you know I wanted to use it on him?"

"Lucky guess," Henry said and then pulled out the charm rune. Sade reached for it, and he pulled back his arm.

"I want you to test it on me," she said.

"I don't think that's a good idea."

"Why? Are you scared my *captivating* presence would be too much for you to handle?" Sade teased.

Her challenge hung in the air between them. He knew the right thing to do would be to back away and not do anything, but he couldn't resist the mischievous sparkle in her eyes.

"Prepare yourself goddess," he said and let the rune float between them. He tried not to shudder as it filled his body and amplified his divine side.

Sade was watching him with rapt attention. Her gaze swept over him slowly, stoking a fire in his veins. But strangely, her eyes didn't hold a hint of desire in them.

"I don't like it."

Her words were like a splash of ice water. Despite the charm magic thrumming through him, he wanted nothing more than to throw himself in the river.

Gods, since when did his confidence get so rattled? Did he really want Sade to feel something for him, or was it just the charm runes influence?

"Well then, I suppose it won't work on another god," he said. His voice was much hoarser than he liked, and he shoved the rune back into his pouch.

"I don't like that it amplified only one part of you," she said quietly and rested a hand on his arm.

He looked at her again, and the smoldering desire he saw in her eyes startled him. Had the charm rune worked after all? But there was no sign of the charm runes handiwork. There was no yellow glow to her eyes or sparks on her skin, which meant this was much more dangerous than he'd thought.

"Sade," he said and tried to ignore the way her lips parted at the sound of her name. The air between them became electric and that strange magnetic feeling urged him closer to her. He reached for her hand, but he couldn't stop himself from lightly tracing the freckles that dotted her skin.

He had no right to touch her. He was here to be her escort, and, not to mention, he knew who she truly was. But the charm rune's influence was strong and now that Sade's divine self-had latched onto him, he was at her mercy. She was the only one who could snap him out of this trance.

"The charm rune still has a strong hold on me. I'll need you to break it," he said, despite everything inside of him begging him to keep going.

"Right, of course," she said. A faint trail of blue smoke weaved it's way around them, but it had no impact.

"You'll need to distract me. Make me think of something else."

Sade was silent. He dared a glance up at her while she was studying the forest with a strange expression. Henry's heartbeat sped up as a ray of light caressed her face. He swallowed and tore his gaze away before he started tracing those trails of light with his fingers. He somehow managed to scoot a few inches away from her, but it had little effect on the heat in his blood.

This was why his mother had warned him to keep his shields up around other divines. Their influence was difficult to shrug off.

"Have you ever tried to use the charm rune on a monster? Make them want to protect you and others?" She asked.

Laughter bubbled out of him, clearing his mind and allowing Sade to sweep away any traces of the charm rune. He'd tried a calming rune on some monsters before, but perhaps they needed a stronger from of persuasion.

"That's not a bad idea."

The sound of twigs snapping caused them both to look at the riverbank. Aiden burst out of the underbrush. His shirt was torn, and he frantically looked around until his gaze landed on Henry.

"They've made it into the forest!" He shouted.

Henry shared a glance with Sade, but before they could

make it off the rock, a low hiss reverberated through the air. A creature lowered itself from a branch. It had the legs of a spider, the head of beetle, and crimson eyes.

Sade sent a shower of ice shards at it, but the creature was able to knock them back. Henry barely had time to pull Sade into the river to keep the shards from hitting them.

He reached for his axes, but he found himself reaching for the rune pouch and pulling out the charm rune. The monster was in the water now, frozen in place by Sade who was edging toward it with a fire rune. She paused when Henry moved towards her. Sparks danced around the rune as he let it hover in front of him.

Henry stopped a few feet away from the creature. It clacked its mandibles, but it was stuck and couldn't move.

"Let's see if this works," he said with a wink at Sade who beamed. Yellow smoke arced around the fiend. He could feel it's desire to kill him waver, but, before the magic could take hold, a fireball reduced it to cinders.

"What in the hell are you doing Henry? You're supposed to kill the monsters, not seduce them!" Aiden snapped as Henry glared at the ashes floating downstream.

"I wasn't trying to sleep with it! I was trying to see if I could get it fight for us."

"Why in the hell did you think that was a good idea?"

Sade cleared her throat. "Actually it was my idea."

Aiden's jaw dropped as he looked at Sade. "What?"

"It's not a stupid idea if you can create a rune that gets the monsters to not attack. Then we can teach Vestral's how to use them in wards. It would save a lot of time and you wouldn't have to run around and try to save everyone," Sade said with a hint of pride in her tone. Henry couldn't help but smile at her, and Aiden's expression darkened further.

"Maybe Henry's brain got scrambled from using the charm rune, but he didn't tell you that magic is unstable when it's used on animals. It's a failsafe to keep people from using them to do whatever they want," Aiden said. Sade glanced at Henry for confirmation. Disappointment dampened the light in her eyes.

"But these aren't ordinary animals. They were obviously created with magic," Henry retorted. Aiden shook his head.

"Remind me to never leave you two alone ever again. You'll come up with more stupid ideas."

Sade winced and Henry marched forward but paused when he spotted a shadow move in the branches above them. The hairs on the back of his neck stood up. The sound of mandibles clacking filled the air.

"Aiden get the horses! Sade, come on we need to move."

Thankfully Aiden didn't argue, and they headed back to shore, but Sade didn't follow.

"Come on we need to move!"

"I'm stuck!"

Blue and gold smoke swirled around her in a frenzied chaos. Henry dove under the water and found the earth had twisted itself up around her feet. He reached for his divine rune.

Blow after blow he sent to the ground, but something in the dirt absorbed every hit with ease. He kept trying until his lungs burned.

He swam back to the surface and found Sade was also trying to use her divine rune.

"Hey, I don't mean to rush you, but there is an army of

monsters heading straight towards us!" Aiden called from the shore.

"She's stuck!"

"What do you mean stuck?" Aiden's voice rose several octaves.

Henry swallowed his fear and used his rune to check the dagger he'd left tied to the saddle. The weapon was silent.

An eerie calm settled over Sade's face.

"Why are you so calm?" Aiden exploded while Henry reeled his magic back.

"If I thrash around, more mud crawls up my legs," she said her voice void of any emotion. "Get the horses and get to the other side of the river."

Henry didn't spare a glance at Aiden as he waded out of the water and mounted his horse. Using an earth rune, he created a bridge for him and Aiden to cross. Once they were on the other side, he dismounted and handed Aiden the reins. Then he stopped.

Two of the spider-like creatures were standing on the opposite shoreline. They were bigger than the one they'd felled. An inky smoke started to pool around them.

The dagger vibrated.

He didn't have time to grab it before a bubble of fire formed around Sade. Right before the creatures sent a black fog over the water, obscuring his view, the dagger stopped humming.

Chapter Eleven

Fire swirled around her in a vortex as the spider creatures paced along the bank. They'd cloaked her in a curtain of fog that pressed down with the weight of ten horses.

"Sade!" Henry called to her.

"Do not come any closer!" She gripped her divine rune as the creatures paused in their movements. Her feet were still held in place by the dirt. The amount of power needed to break free would push her over the limit, and the last thing she wanted was the God of Knowledge to make another visit.

Let your power loose. Let's destroy them. The crimson figure floated in the fire.

Ignoring the voice, she tried to wiggle her toes and nearly wept when she felt a small root. With her gaze still locked onto the creatures, she called to the spirits of the trees.

"We're sorry divine one, something broke our barriers."

"I'm not worried about that right now; I have two half-divines whose lives are in danger if I can't get out of here."

"But goddess, surely you can free yourself?"

"The amount of power would be astronomical, and I don't want to break the world in two."

"Then please give us a moment to discuss our options."

Oh, so you're scared of your own power? How pathetic! The crimson figure crowed.

Sade called upon every ounce of self-control she had to keep herself calm. The figure merely twirled in the fire like it was attending a summer festival.

"We have a solution, but you're not going to like it."

Images of a raging river flashed in her mind.

"That's fine, I can handle it," Sade patted her rune pouch.

"We will need you to cease all magical activities until we have gotten you away. Your presence interferes with ours; we cannot use it when yours is active."

Sade's heart dropped to her stomach, but she quenched the feeling, and she straightened her shoulders. She was a goddess, not a mortal. She'd survive.

Henry, Aiden. I need you to move down stream and stay away from the edges.

But what about you? Henry was the first to reply, Aiden's connection was too dim for her to reach.

She quickly sent him the images the trees had given her. Henry didn't send anything back, but she soon heard hooves pounding on dirt.

Once she couldn't hear them anymore, she took a breath and sucked all of her magic into her body. She looked around for the crimson figure but found it had disappeared.

Was it possible the thing was connected to her magic? She'd dwell on it after she wasn't dealing with the creatures.

"I'm ready," she told the trees.

The creatures on the banks began clacking their mandibles together. A ball of black and white smoke appeared between them. Skulls formed in the crackling fog. The air cooled and the temperature of the water dropped.

Death magic? But how? Only the God of Death and his Vestrals could use it.

Cold sweat dripped down her neck. If that mist touched her, it was likely she'd be dragged into the afterlife.

"Are you going to do this or not?" Sade yelled at the trees closest to her. The creatures on the shoreline turned their glowing red eyes towards her. They both lifted a leg and the swirls of black and white moved over the water.

The water evaporated as the cloud of death moved. It was slow enough that Sade became more irritated than afraid. She strained against the earth, trying in vain to free herself.

The swirling mist drew closer and closer, the air became so cold she could see her breath, and her body began shivering. She recalled a scroll she'd read back in her temple; about how some mortal forms weren't built for extreme temperatures. She'd already experienced the effects of the summer sun on her body, and she wasn't sure she wanted to feel the effects of winter.

A loud cracking noise filled the air, causing the creatures on the shore to jump. A huge root burst out of the earth and wrapped around the creatures, holding them in place.

Sade covered her ears when a mighty roar rang out from the

forest and a large wave hurtling downstream came into view. She sucked in a breath before the water smashed into her, breaking apart the earth that held her, and scattering the death cloud.

She did her best to keep herself from getting thrashed around too harshly. Her lungs burned, begging for her to take a breath.

A large stick collided with her back, making her scream. Water rushed into her lungs before she could stop herself. Her body convulsed and another object smashed into the side of her head.

Then a vortex of water appeared above her, pulling her out of the river and dumping her on the shoreline at the edge of the forest.

Sade rolled around, the gravel digging into her skin. Pain was everywhere and her lungs burned. Once she could breathe properly, she laid there until her body stopped shaking. She spotted a small plant and reached for it.

"Thank you," she choked out.

The trees above her bowed slightly, but quickly snapped back into place. She started to ask them why when Henry's horse burst through the foliage. A whirlwind of orange sparks hovered around him, making his hair like a raging fire and his eyes glow like stars. The light faded when his eyes met hers.

"Took you long enough," she said. Her voice was hoarse and weak. She swayed and had to steady herself with a low hanging branch.

Henry dismounted his horse at a speed she didn't know was possible and hurried over to her.

"You're bleeding," he said and whipped out a healing rune.

Sade gingerly touched the side of her head. When she pulled back her hands, they were covered with blood.

"This may sting a bit," Henry said and gently placed his hands on her head. The healing rune floated above him, casting a soft pink glow onto them.

Her eyes drifted close, letting the magic do its work and letting her own assist. She opened them when Henry removed his hands.

"I think the other divines are correct. I am easily corrupted."

Henry's eyebrows raised a fraction, and his eyes became guarded.

"What do you mean?"

"Well ever since I've stepped foot in this realm. An apparition has been taunting me. Something is happening to me."

"Sade, this realm can wreak havoc on a divine mind, and you haven't been here very long."

"Have you ever experienced anything similar?"

Henry's mouth tightened, like he was fighting off something deep inside him.

"No. Remember I'm only half-divine. My experience will differ since I have mortal blood," Henry ran a hand through his hair. Exhaustion flickered in his eyes.

"Hold on, where is Aiden?"

"He was right behind me," Henry frowned and called out his seeking rune. He stared at it for a few heartbeats and tapped it with his finger.

"That's odd."

"What is it?"

"It says he's above us."

"That doesn't—"

A drop of blood landed on her arm.

Slowly they both looked up to see Aiden, wrapped in spider silk and dangling from the tree. The source of the blood hadn't come from him, but the horse dangling beside him.

A headless horse.

Faster than she could blink Henry had cut down Aiden and the horse. Once Aiden was on the ground, she rushed over and helped Henry removed the spider silk.

"He's still breathing," she said. Henry used a healing rune to scan his body. No visible signs of injury marked his skin.

"Barely," he pocketed the rune and ran a hand through his hair. His eyes darted around the forest, but no creature came bursting out.

"Are you able to heal him?"

"No, he's been poisoned and that's a healing specialty I haven't yet learned."

"Can I heal him?"

"Some poisons react badly to having magic used on them. We'll need a healer to get the antidote."

"Have you ever seen anything like this?"

"Once, but it was by a human. He cut off the heads of his enemies and tied their bodies to trees. It was a warning to never cross him."

Sade shuddered; what type of human would do such a thing to his own kind? He'd have to be as cold as the God of Death.

The memory of that strange smoke floating towards her sprang forth in her mind. She must've accidently sent the image to Henry, because he shook his head and rocked back on his heels.

"It's not what you think."

"Unless the two creatures were Vestrals to the God of Death, I don't see how?"

"If they got their hands on a divine rune, they can use it. I've seen it before." He didn't elaborate any further as he rose and hoisted Aiden onto his back. "We need to get him to a healer, hopefully the poison won't cause too much damage."

"Hang on, let me see if the plants can help."

Henry raised an eyebrow, but he said nothing while she connected with their essence.

"Do you have any idea what could have poisoned him?" She asked the plants.

"No, the poison in his veins did not come from any of our brethren."

Sade dropped the connection and shook her head at Henry.

"It's not a plant-based poison."

"Wonderful."

He walked over to their remaining horse and draped Aiden's limp body across it. Sade used a fire rune to reduce the dead one to ashes. They didn't need an undead horse following them.

"Thank you for your help," she whispered. Letting the wind blow the ashes over the water. She ran over to Henry and found him holding his map, a grim expression on his face.

"What is it now?"

"The good news is, we're close to a city, and we should be there by nightfall. The bad news…it's nestled in the foothills of the Violet Mountains."

Henry's hands shook as he stuffed the map into a saddlebag. His magic, as usual, was tight against him.

Sade balled her hands into fists. When she'd first been created, she thought her main enemy was the God of War, but perhaps the God of Ruin was the one she'd should've kept a closer eye on.

"Silver for your thoughts?" Henry asked, his tone was light but strained, like he was trying to keep his mind off something.

"When I was in my temple, I would get petitioned by people who'd been affected by the God of Ruin's creatures. But my focus was more on the God of War. I should've kept a closer eye on both of them."

"Do you know why I can't stand the other gods?"

"No?" Sade replied slowly.

"Because they think they can keep an eye on everything. There are thousands of Mortal Realms. How is it divinely possible for you to spread your energy out that thin and still be able to affect things?"

"But it doesn't get thin. I just can't see everything at once."

Henry shrugged. "Same difference. I used to watch my mother spend hours hovering over her sacred pool, trying to grant everyone's petitions. It never worked and she was always so damn tired. Eventually, she started focusing on the major things; occasionally she'd pay particular attention to a mortal, but that was rare."

"You lived with her in the Divine Realm?"

"No, she lived here. With me and my father."

Sade's mouth dropped open, "I didn't know such a thing was possible."

Aiden let out a whimper, but he didn't wake. Small streaks of lime green appeared on his skin.

"We need to hurry," Henry said.

Henry gripped the reins in one hand and fished out a speed rune. He let the smoky sparks settle over them. The wind rushed around them as they ran, not as fast as a galloping horse, but with enough speed it made Sade dizzy.

"Keep your focus on the horizon," Henry shouted over the wind.

Sade gritted her teeth and did as he said. Her divine rune lit up and encased her in a protective bubble. She dared a glance back. The spider-like creatures were crawling down the trees. Dozens more had joined them.

She could only hope her legs wouldn't give out before they reached the town.

⁂

After hours of running and stopping only once to let the horse drink, the Violet Mountains loomed in the distance. Much to her disappointment, the pointy peaks were not covered in purple rocks.

The monsters lurked somewhere far behind them. The closer they got the mountains, the more they drifted back.

Closer to them was a city with high walls, and, unlike the last place they'd been, there was not a loose stone in sight.

"Welcome to Pavento, one of the oldest cities in Roltia," Henry said with a dramatic sweep of his hand. There were tall buildings with decorative spirals peeking over the top of the wall. They moved closer to the gate; it was sealed shut.

"Who goes there!" A rough voice shouted from atop the wall.

"Three travelers who mean no harm!" Henry shouted, "One of us is injured!"

"Step closer to the gate and don't move until the runes stop glowing."

Sade shot Henry a confused look, but he didn't seem perplexed at all.

"Pavento had a shapeshifter problem a couple years ago," he said. A combination rune appeared on either side of the gate, bathing them in a forest green light.

Sade peered at the letters swirling within. It was a modified seeking rune, made to sense if you were human or not.

"But I'm not human," she whispered to Henry.

"Your mortal form *is* human, don't worry. Just focus on your mortal shell and we'll be fine."

She tensed as the green smoke from the runes crawled up her body and tucked her magic deep inside of her.

The runes flickered and changed to an icy blue.

"So, you're Vestrals?" The rough voice called out.

Henry blinked then cursed under his breath.

"I forgot to shield Aiden," he whispered.

"What do we do now?"

"I'm not sure, I've never had this problem before."

"Hello? Are you still there? I will ask one more time. Are you Vestrals?" The rough voice had become more hostile with each word.

"Yes!" Sade blurted out, "We are!"

"And what God or Goddess do you serve?"

"We serve the God of Magic!"

"Please wait one moment while I confirm."

Henry's eyebrows looked like they were going to disappear into his hairline.

"What? The color of the rune changed to the God of Magic's color!" Sade exclaimed and waved her divine rune in his face. "Remember I have blue in mine!"

"I..." Henry sighed and ran a hand through his hair, "I just don't like the God of Magic."

"You don't like any of the gods or goddess."

Henry paused. "Well not *all* of them."

He flashed her a smile and Sade's heart sped up at the sight.

"Excuse me, can you please hurry and get inside?" The rough voice boomed, and the gate opened. They passed through quickly. Once they were through, it closed with a loud thud. They were greeted by large grey and blue buildings that had columns keeping them above the street.

"Why are they built like that?" Sade asked.

"Floods. When the snow melts in the mountains, it swamps the entire area."

"Correct," a gravelly voice said, and a woman in a long grey dress appeared. Her hair, the same shade as the dress, was piled up into a bun on the top of her head. There was not a wrinkle in sight on her skin. "I am Clelia, I'm acting as the city's spokesperson until further notice."

"I'm Henry and this is Sade," Henry said with a slight bow.

"And your companion on the horse?" She asked inclining her head toward Aiden, whose skin was now bright green.

"That's Aiden, he's been poisoned. We need to speak to your healing Vestral."

"We aren't strong enough to remove the poison," Sade

continued.

"Ah, there is no need to rush. Your friend there is under a sleeping spell."

Henry looked like he was about ready to punch a hole in the wall. His eyes lit up with rage and he turned away before the human could see his eyes turn a bright orange. He walked over the horse and pretended he was checking on Aiden.

"That's good news, then? We can find the remedy and be on our way," Sade said.

Clelia's eyes hardened and she waved a hand toward an empty street.

"I'm afraid it's not that simple. We were attacked by a group of scaragnos a week ago and now most of the city is asleep. Including our Liege Lord and Vestrals."

"Scaragnos?"

"That's our name for the spider-beetles."

"And you don't have any idea what the antidote could be?" Henry asked when he faced them. His eyes were back to normal.

"Our Vestrals were among the first poisoned," Clelia looked up at the sky, stars were starting to appear. She placed two fingers in her mouth and gave three sharp whistles.

A young, scraggly looking boy ran out from behind a pillar.

"Take their horse." She looked back at Henry and Sade. "Can you carry your companion?"

Henry nodded and quickly got Aiden off the horse. The boy led the animal away without a word.

"Come with me, we need to get to safety," Clelia shooed them towards a large cobblestone road.

They followed her through the empty streets, most of them

were cloaked in darkness. It didn't take long before they were in front of a large, ornate building. Unlike the columns on most of the other structures, these had runes and flowers carved into them. Glass-stained windows, lit by candles within, bathed the street in a rainbow of colors.

Henry let out a low whistle when they stepped inside. The stone walls were covered in gilded carvings of flowers and scenes from nature. Huge crystal chandeliers cast sparkling light onto the polished stone floors. People were huddled in corners, and they stared at them with curious eyes as they passed.

"This is the Grand Palace, one of the only places of refuge we have left. Most of the wards on the walls have failed since we haven't had a Vestral to charge them," Clelia opened a door ten times the size of Sade. She ushered them into a vast ballroom, crowded with sleeping people, all of whom had green skin.

Henry found an empty corner and gently placed Aiden onto the floor.

"He'll be safe here," Clelia said and motioned for them to leave. She led them down a hall filled with life sized carvings of humans and animals alike.

"What is the state of your temple?" Henry asked.

"It's protected. I will take you tomorrow once the sun is up. The scaragnos have only been attacking us at night so far."

Sade swallowed the lump in her throat as she shared a glance with Henry. If they were here, would the scaragnos attack the humans in the daytime?

"We'll work on getting those wards back and running so that people can return to their homes," Henry said. Clelia opened the door to a large dining hall. Long tables piled high with meat and cheese were scattered around the room.

"They attacked us in the middle of a feast our Lord was holding for his daughter's birthday. Eat up, you'll have a long day tomorrow, and if you get lucky, we won't get attacked," Clelia said.

Sade rushed over to the nearest table and grabbed an ornate silver plate. The metal had been polished to a mirror-like shine.

Once her plate was full of spiced meats and cheeses, she sat down at an empty table; a few humans were sitting at one side. They didn't look up when Henry joined her.

"Do you think we'll find a cure in time?"

"I don't know," Henry said and poked at his food. Sade reached across the table and rested her hands over his.

"We'll make sure he's cured," she whispered.

"This always happens. I can't protect anyone," Henry muttered. "I'm the worst god in existence."

"I think we can both agree that title belongs to the God of Music."

Henry's mouth quivered like he was fighting a smile.

"Yes, he's rather full of himself isn't he?"

"Could you imagine him trying to fight off the monsters with his lyre?"

That made Henry break out into a grin.

"Oh Gods, he'd try to serenade them with a love song or something."

Sade fought back a smile as the humans in the room glared daggers at them. Henry pulled his hands back from hers and raised a tankard in their direction. The human's stony expression didn't change.

"Perhaps joking about the God of Music wasn't the right call," Sade said quietly. Henry ran a hand through his hair then shook his head.

"Some curses can be lifted with a simple joke."

They both glanced at the door, but no one came running into the room shouting that everyone had been cured. Henry shrugged and nodded towards Sade's plate.

"Eat up, who knows when we'll get food like this again."

Sade started to tear into her bread, but Henry didn't move a muscle.

"What is it?"

"Thank you," he said.

"For what?"

"For not letting me wallow."

"Remember, you told me it's not divinely possible to solve everyone's problems at once," she said, and Henry gave her an incredulous look. "What? You don't think I listen to you?"

"No, I just…" He trailed off.

"Are used to dealing with the pretentious arseholes of the Divine Realm," Sade straightened her shoulders and looked down at him from her nose. "Am I pretentious enough now?"

"No, you look like you're constipated," he said dryly, and Sade flung a small piece of bread at him. "Hey!"

"I was trying to look like a snob."

Henry shook his head, amusement danced in his eyes. "I don't think that's possible."

"Oi! Our city has fallen to a dark curse and you two are acting like a couple of idiots!" A man shouted from across the room.

"We know, we are here to find the cure," Sade said. The man glared at her but said nothing more as he went back to drinking.

"Right, let's eat and then get some rest. We've got a lot of work to do in the morning." Henry nudged her plate towards her.

They ate in silence and Sade tried to ignore the rising panic within her. No, she needed to stay focused on finding the cure and making sure whatever plans the God of Ruin had for this city failed.

Chapter Twelve

Even though he was in the finest bed he'd ever laid in; Henry hadn't slept a wink. He checked the windows. Dawn had arrived and with it a bird song. Nothing had attacked the city that night. The scaragnos were likely lying in wait somewhere in the foothills.

He rose and dressed quickly, trying to block out the cheery sounds of the birds outside his window. The floral decor of his room wasn't helping matters either. His room must have belonged to one of the young noblewomen he'd spotted in the room he'd left Aiden in.

His head swam and he rested a hand on an ornately carved bed post.

Once again, his friend was in peril. Though this time, he wasn't sure what to do. Almost an entire city was under the strange spell. In all of his years, he'd never seen anything like it.

Henry clasped his hands behind his back and started to pace. How was he supposed to treat a sleeping poison he knew nothing about? Only the God of Healing would know how to cure such a thing, but his Vestral was out cold and there was no way for him to communicate with Henry.

Unless he used a spirit.

Henry quickly called out a summoning rune, and it immediately flared to life.

"Airi, come quickly I need your help!" He said to the stone. Bracing himself for the spirit's fury, she'd likely still be pissed at him for having the God of Knowledge take her form. Spirits could hold grudges for ages.

Nothing happened.

He tried again and again, but Airi didn't appear. Cold sweat dripped down his forehead. Could the creatures be blocking spirits? He pulled out his divine rune and let the sparks drift around him. Closing his eyes, he focused with everything he had on contacting the other gods.

When he felt a presence, he opened his eyes. Sade was running towards him; blue and gold smoke wove around her in angry waves. She collided into him before he could say anything, and they fell onto the bed. Her magic tore into the pillows sending a cascade of feathers into the air.

"What are you doing?" He asked. Sade looked around the room with a frantic expression.

"I thought you were being attacked; your aura had a high level of despair." Sade said with a slight scowl, her expression was lessened by the fact she was covered in feathers.

"I was trying to reach Airi, but I got no response."

"I tried contacting her too," she said. "Something is blocking us."

Sade drummed her fingers against his chest, lost in thought. It took every ounce of his concentration not to focus on how her body pressed against his. He plucked a feather from her hair and accidently brushed it against her neck. Much to his surprise, Sade let out a giggle. He tried it again, but she grabbed his wrist, pinning it above his head.

"Henry, we need to concentrate on the matter at hand."

"I am, you're absolutely covered in feathers."

"That's not what I mean."

"It's rather distracting. I can't think about anything else now."

Sade plucked the feather from his hand and let it hover between them.

"You are impossible," she said.

A wicked gleam flashed in her eyes, but, before she could do anything, the door opened and Clelia stepped in the room.

"It's time for breakfast," Clelia said slowly. "Unless you two need some more time to finish up?"

"No!" Sade exclaimed and scrambled off him. Before Henry could say anything, she was out the door. Clelia raised an eyebrow when Henry slowly rose from the bed and adjusted his rune pouch.

"I know, I know. We'll pay for it," he grumbled and reached for a calming rune. He followed Clelia down to the dining hall. Sade soon joined them. All the feathers were gone.

They quickly ate breakfast and checked on Aiden. He was still in his comatose state. The sight of which made Henry's guilt almost unbearable. His skin was still the odd shade of green that reminded Henry of vomit. He'd never seen a sleeping curse do this before. Then again it was the God of Ruin's doing, and since he corrupted everything that he touched…

Though it didn't explain how the hell the scaragnos and the shadow vampires were so damn powerful. Maybe another divine was working with him, but he couldn't recall anyone who would be adept at creating monsters.

If Aiden decided not to travel with him after this, he wouldn't hold it against him.

After they checked on Aiden, Clelia took them to the temple. A drab building compared to the Grand Palace, but it held a treasure more valuable than a pile of gold.

"This is incredible," Sade said as they entered the library. It was a tall room with bookshelves lining the walls. A spiral staircase in the center led up to more rooms. It would take them eons to search through everything.

"Over here is where the Vestrals piled all the research about poisons," Clelia said, and Henry made a mental note to make sure he blessed those Vestrals when they awoke.

Henry and Sade both lunged for the table piled high with scrolls and books. He barely started reading when Clelia cleared her throat.

"I was hoping one of you could get the wards up and running?" She asked. Sade set down her scroll, but Henry shook his head and set his down.

"We'll take turns," he said. Sade nodded and turned her attention back to the scroll.

He quickly followed Clelia out into the city proper. A few city dwellers passed by, their gazes hollow and filled with despair.

His divine purpose strained within him. He tamped it down. Getting upset would waste valuable time.

"So, what brings three Vestrals from Sodervia all the way out here?" Clelia asked and Henry didn't need a truth rune to know she was suspicious.

"We were headed to the Violet Mountains."

"And why, pray tell, would you three be stupid enough to do that?"

"We heard about the bounty and wanted to have a go. We're trying to leave our temple, but we can't unless we have a way to support ourselves."

"Retire? I didn't know Vestrals could retire, but I suppose you do things differently in Sodervia?" She asked and Henry cursed inwardly. Most Vestrals stayed within the temple and only an act of egregious offense could have them stripped of their position.

"Yes, it's a new thing our High Vestral wants to try out. She wants to make sure only those who are truly worthy of the gods serve them."

Clelia's gaze narrowed ever so slightly. She probably didn't believe him, but she merely shrugged, and they walked the rest of the way in silence.

"Once the inside wards are done, I'll have you two working on the outside ones. Figure it'd be safer to start within the city," Clelia said, and Henry nodded.

"Thank you, I'll have these working by sunset."

He found the faded marks of a ward and filled it, making sure he matched the icy blue of the God of Magic. If he ever saw that god again, he was never going to hear the end of it.

"Fantastic, I'll come back and check on you in a few hours," Clelia said once he'd finished with one. She glanced over her shoulder before she rounded the corner. Wonderful, a smart human. The last thing they needed was someone questioning their every move.

As he headed toward the next empty ward, a strange tugging on the back of his neck made him pause. He let his seeking rune drift out of his pouch. There was nothing aside from a few rats scurrying in an alleyway.

Gods, keep yourself together. The God of Ruin's creatures were always beatable.

However, time was not something they could win against. Sade had less than a month to get to the portal and he doubted the God of Ruin would extend her time any further.

Gods, why couldn't he just stop his sick parade of monsters and let them get her to the damn portal in peace? Unless…he knew about her past and wanted her to do something drastic so he could use it as an excuse for war.

He traced his hands over a ward, watching it fill with blue light. Maybe he should tell her about her past and see if she could destroy the scaragnos with her anger?

A vision of the city bathed in mortal blood flooded his mind. No, it was too risky, and even then, he wasn't sure how effective divine magic was if the scaragnos were blocking it. Though it did explain why even Sade struggled against them.

He resisted the urge to bang his head against the wall like an adolescent human.

Why couldn't the God of Ruin keep to his own domain? Had he corrupted everything in his realm and now had to reach out to others? And why this one? There were thousands of realms, and he chose the one Henry lived in? Did he have a thing against half-gods?

Whatever it was, he needed to leave his realm alone.

The ward flashed and a crack appeared in the stone. He'd put too much magic into it. He rubbed the back of his neck as he slunk away, hoping no one would notice.

The sun rose higher in the sky as he filled ward after ward. The motion became repetitive, and it allowed his thoughts to wander.

Henry, I think I found something. Sade's voice drifted into his mind.

He sent her an image of his location and it wasn't long before the goddess ran out from an alleyway, clutching a worn scroll in her hands.

"You could've just sent me the information in my head," Henry said while Sade let the scroll unravel.

"I thought it'd be better to show you!" She exclaimed with pride.

Henry looked closer at the scroll; it was a list of various ways to combat sleeping poisons. Some ranging from the mundane tactics like herbal potions to more outrageous ones that involved chicken heads and rope.

It wasn't much, but it was more than they started with.

"Help me get these wards filled and we'll start trying things tonight."

Sade headed toward an empty ward and filled it. The hum of energy was the only sound between them as they moved from ward to ward, ensuring the stone could repel the toughest of creatures.

Even then, was it enough?

"How long can we stay here?" Sade asked.

"Two weeks, otherwise we risk the portal moving."

"But what if we haven't found the cure?"

"I'll come back and find the cure."

"I'm not going to leave here until that happens."

"Sade, you can't risk war between the realms over one tiny mortal one."

"But you live here, and you have fought long enough. You deserve some peace, Henry."

Henry froze. He looked over at the goddess who was watching him with concern.

"Sade—"

She held up a hand and an invisible force kept him from speaking.

"I'm the Goddess of Peace, and if the God of Ruin thinks he can continue to interfere with my divine purpose, then that is a battle I will have with him. If he gets upset because we're a day late, then I'm going to make his life a living hell."

She released him from her hold and went back to filling the wards.

Don't let her go. His inner voice warned.

But he had no choice. Sade was his last hope, his *only* hope at stopping the monsters. He had half a mind to give her the dagger and force the God of Ruin to reincarnate, but the God of Knowledge would have his head if he did that. His parents would likely be locked into the darkest corners of the afterlife and all of his efforts to free them would be in vain.

"Do you always make her do the work while you stand there staring at her like a lovesick suitor?" Clelia said as she walked out of an alley.

He jumped and groaned when his shoulder collided with the wall. He quickly straightened and folded his arms across his chest.

"What are you talking about?" He whispered angrily. Thankfully, Sade was too far away and too engrossed in her task to hear.

"Your face doesn't lie boy; I've seen this a thousand times before."

He bristled at the term boy; he hadn't been one for centuries. But he wasn't about to break the rules for some trite argument.

"Well, your eyes are lying to you," Henry grumbled and headed toward the nearest empty ward. Much to his annoyance, Clelia followed him, giving Sade a wave when they passed her.

"Oh, so that scene I came across this morning was nothing? Is she with someone else? The poisoned one?"

"No!"

Clelia shrugged. "Then what's the problem? You're both young."

"Do you always play matchmaker with people you just met?"

"Yes, I'm the city's matchmaker."

Out of all the humans in the city, the one currently in charge just had to be the matchmaker. The fates had to be messing with him.

Henry scowled and focused on the ward. Sade walked over once she was finished with her ward and showed Clelia the scroll she found.

The elderly human hummed with approval and her eyes watered. Before Henry could start on another ward, she'd pulled them into a hug. Thankfully, she released them quickly.

"May the Gods bless you and your future family," she crowed. "I'll be back with food for both of you."

Sade's brow furrowed as she watched the human scurry away.

"Future family? What does she mean by that?"

"Who knows? Mortals have strange minds," Henry said with a shrug.

"Very strange minds. I'm not planning on being bonded anytime soon," Sade said then frowned at Henry.

"What?"

"Your face is redder than your hair. Do you need a break?"

Gods damn that woman. He didn't need Sade to think he was like Aiden had been. All starry eyed and practically drooling over her.

"I'm fine. It's the heat."

Her eyes narrowed then softened.

"You should take a break and I'll work on the wards."

Henry walked over to a ward.

"We need to get this done."

Sade stared at him for a few moments, but she didn't press him further.

He watched her out of the corner of his eye. The human was wrong. he had no feelings for her outside of admiration and gratitude, and the occasional bout of fear for his life.

Once this was over, he was going to get the Sacred Council to give him a king's bounty and, he was going to stay the hell away from any brown-eyed goddesses.

By the time the sun set, they finished refilling all the wards on the inside of the walls. Now they were in the alchemy room of the temple. It wasn't the largest room, it had no windows, and smelled of decay. Like the library, it was stock full of things they'd need.

Henry had never been in this part of a temple before. He'd always gone to the shrines or the library if needed.

Sade was standing over a large cauldron filled with herbs and tonics the scroll had suggested. They'd been at this for hours; some recipes were duds that exploded once they were complete.

Henry wrinkled his nose at the putrid smell that rose from the bubbling liquid.

"I think this will work; this smell could wake the dead."

Sade grimaced as she used a ladle to fill a vial. Henry held it up in the candlelight. The liquid was a brown and green mixture.

"Either that or it will make them want to stay dead."

Henry picked up another vial he'd made earlier. "Let's go test this out, shall we?"

He used a rune to check the city for any sign of the scaragnos and motioned for Sade to follow when there were none to be found. The monsters were still lurking outside the walls.

Soon they were back in the giant room with the sleeping people. Henry made his way over to the first person who'd gotten attacked. He was a young shepherd who'd been attacked while he was shearing his sheep.

Clelia and a few other people gathered around them as they

readied the limp body. Sade cradled the shepherds head in her lap while Henry poured the first vial into his mouth. He used a healing rune to help get the liquid down his throat.

When nothing happened, they tried the second. The small crowd of people watching them dispersed. Disappointment hung over them like a rain cloud.

"All right, time to try something else," Sade said.

"I think so—"

The boy's body convulsed, and he let out a bloodcurdling shriek. A strange milky film formed on his skin and, before Henry could activate the healing rune, the boy turned to stone.

He'd seen a lot of shit in his lifetime, but this was something he'd never seen before.

"What in the hell is going on!" Clelia cried when three more people turned to stone. Henry stared at his hands; he took a few breaths to keep himself calm then looked up at Clelia with a steady gaze.

"How long ago was he attacked?"

Clelia's hands trembled at her sides.

"A week and a half ago. He was the first one before the monsters attacked the city."

He glanced over at Aiden's still form, then around the room. He rose to his feet and helped Sade stand. Her skin was cool to the touch and her magic was locked up tight. She gave his hand a light squeeze before she let go.

"We'll figure this out."

"Well, you better hurry. I don't want this place to turn into a mausoleum," Clelia said and ushered the remaining humans out of the room.

The souls of the four dead people rose out of their bodies and stared at them expectantly.

"Divine ones, are you going to let us go?" They asked.

Henry knelt and knocked three times. He didn't bother doing a summoning circle. He was too tired to move the bodies around.

"How long does it take for him to arrive?" Sade asked after a few heartbeats.

"Not this long," he said and knocked again.

There was no answer. Not even the God of Death could break through whatever hold the scaragnos had on this city.

He stood and looked over at the souls.

"It seems the scaragnos have taken hold of the magic in this realm and are using it to block the path to the afterlife."

The souls let out a collective sigh before they floated back into their stone bodies. Henry let out a breath of his own. These spirits would not turn into wraiths.

"Let us know when you have reopened the path," one of the souls said as the stone absorbed her form.

Sade moved beside him and gently nudged him toward the door.

"Come on, we need to find this cure."

He followed her into the dark streets. A shadow had him blasting fire at it before Sade could react. He muttered a curse when the fire merely brushed against a stone wall.

Fear gripped his heart and, no matter how hard he tried to push it away, it clung to him like a putrid odor.

The God of Ruin was getting bolder, and they only had so much time to stop his latest escapade.

Sade opened her presence to his. A wave of soothing energy flowed through him, but the gesture did little to soothe his frazzled nerves.

He had no idea how to fix this.

Chapter Thirteen

Days turned into nights and more people transformed into statues. Sade spent hours reading through ancient texts, trying to find the cure. They'd done blood oaths, sacrifices, more potions, and a strange ritual that involved dancing around a bonfire. But nothing worked.

"Why can't we find anything?" Sade groaned and rested her head on the table. Even the crimson figure was silent, and she wasn't sure that it was a good thing.

Henry tossed a book he was reading onto the pile. They'd run out of material the Vestrals had pulled from the shelves and ended up trying to find more information themselves.

"Maybe the cure is in another realm," Henry said.

"Perhaps the God of Ruin experiments on the divines he rules over?"

"After the war ended, not many immortals go to his realm

on their own accord. He'd be an idiot if he experimented on them without having an antidote handy."

Sade sat up. "That's it! I'll go to the Realm of Ruin now. If the cure is there, then I can convince him to give it up as part of the peace treaty!"

Henry shook his head and leaned back in his chair. His eyes were focused on a bookshelf across the room.

"That's a two week trip."

By the time she got to the realm, everyone affected by the poison would be turned to stone. There was also no guarantee the God of Ruin actually had a cure and Sade would have done nothing but waste time.

"Then I suppose I'll just keep reading," she said and reached for a parchment that looked fairly new and quickly threw it onto the reject pile. It was nothing more than a list of poisonous plants.

As they read through more tomes and scrolls, Henry occasionally yawned and rubbed his eyes. She'd tried to get him to rest hours ago, but he ignored her and started reading a rather thick book instead. Guilt still hung around him like a fog, and she wanted nothing more than to take it away. However, that wouldn't happen until they found the cure and, even then, she wasn't sure Henry would ever forgive himself for what happened to Aiden.

"Should we also start looking to see if there is any way the magic in this world can be used to block the Divine Realm's?" Sade asked when she finished reading a scroll on healing techniques. It was useful, but not the sort of information they needed.

Power stirred to life within her, but then it went still.

She looked up at Henry, who was staring at her with alarm.

"Did your magic just…"

"Snuff itself out?"

They jumped to their feet and ran out of the library. They didn't stop until they were on top of the wall and Sade's heart dropped when she took in the scene before her.

The entire city was surrounded by scaragnos and oblong shadows that absorbed the sunlight. There were hundreds of them.

"Holy shit, the shadow vampires," Henry said with a shaky voice.

"The what?"

"Those creatures were the ones who drained Aiden of his magic."

"Wait when did this happen?"

She listened quietly as he recounted the events that led him and Aiden to be in the Divine Realm before the portal blew. When he was finished, Sade pointed to a symbol the creatures were drawing in the dirt. She tried to sense what it was but found nothing.

A flash of irritation shot through her, poking the smoldering embers inside of her and a spark began to grow.

"Can you sense what they're drawing?" She asked Henry. He tried to send a shower of orange sparks over the wall, but they quickly vanished.

"We need to get inside the temple and hope they don't breach the wards."

He started to walk away, pausing when Sade didn't go

with him.

"Henry, you need to get the people into safety."

"I'm not leaving you."

Sade grabbed a fire rune from her pouch and snapped her fingers. A bright blue flame hovered over her hands as a torrent of rage and fear swirled within her. A strange pressure made her head throb, keeping her from using her powers. She pressed back and shoved it aside.

"Henry, I need you to make sure there is nothing aside from me and these damn creatures out here," she said through gritted teeth. Henry's hand rested on the dagger strapped to his waist. He marched over to a small bell that dangled on the inside edge of the wall.

He rang it as loudly as he could, and it wasn't long before Clelia was stumbling up the steps to reach them. Her eyes widened with shock as she took in the sight of the creatures.

"Holy Gods," she said and laid a hand over her heart. "What do we do now?"

Henry rested a hand on her shoulder and nodded toward the palace.

"I need you to get everyone inside the more heavily warded areas," he said gravely.

"Of course."

Clelia ran back down the steps as she started shouting for everyone to get to safety.

"Henry," Sade glared at him.

He stared back, and neither of them blinked.

"I'm not going to lose you to these things."

"You aren't going to lose me," Sade smiled as a surge of

power flowed out of her. She reached for an air rune and slowly backed towards the edge of the wall.

"What if—"

"This will not be another farm incident," she said softly.

"That's not what I'm afraid of."

"Henry, we are the only chance that city has. We cannot let fear rule us now," She searched Henry's face, but he still looked unsure. "Fine, if you want to stay up here, make sure they don't breach the wall."

"What are you going to do?"

She smiled at him and held up her runestone.

"I'm going to take the fight to them."

Henry's eyes widened before he lunged toward her, but he was too slow. She jumped off the edge.

"Sade!" he screamed as she landed feet first on the ground, her fall softened by the air.

The creatures surrounding the wall hissed at her, but they didn't move past the strange runes they'd drawn in the dirt.

The crimson figure floated in front of Sade as she walked closer to the creatures.

Go away.

Come now, you need me now more than ever. Do you want to be turned to stone?

I have nothing to say to you.

She knelt onto the ground and let her magic saturate the dirt around her. Her divine rune hovered at her side. She sent a blast wave of dirt toward the creatures, knocking a few scaragnos back. The shadow creatures were unaffected.

Stop playing games with these things. You're running out of time.

She ignored the figure and pressed forward until she was at the edge of one of the giant runes the creatures had drawn.

It was a combination rune that had a rune for siphoning, magic blocking, and one she couldn't identify.

Wonderful, the God of Ruin was turning into a linguist. Unknown runes were the last thing they needed.

"God of Ruin!" She shouted to the creatures, "Why are you impeding me on my journey? Are you trying to break the treaty?"

The creatures merely hissed at her in response.

Sade ground her teeth as a surge of maroon sparks flew out of her and collided with a shadow creature. The thing wavered for a moment, then exploded in a plume of shadow and smoke.

See? I'm not as bad as you think. The crimson figure floated beside her. The creatures in front of her snarled and growled, but they didn't move.

I don't trust you. Sade gripped her divine rune and pushed out a wave of blue and gold lightning, but it did nothing to monsters.

Why don't you trust me? I'm you.

Because I don't know what you're drawing power from!

Was it her rage? Was there something in the creatures that was corrupting her?

Pressure mounted on her chest and something deep inside of her thrashed about, but it was locked tight.

"On your right!" Henry called from atop the wall. He sent out a stream of orange lightning towards her and knocked a couple scaragnos back.

She turned to see a group of shadows speeding towards her.

Please let me out! The crimson figure pleaded.

Sade ignored it. She used an earth rune to create a wall of rock and dirt that she flung toward the shadow creatures. The shadows easily slipped through the dirt like it was air.

They drew closer and the scaragnos started clicking their mandibles together. The noise made Sade's head throb.

She filled her divine rune almost to the point of breaking and used it to create a circle of cracking fire. The shadow creatures kept moving towards her.

"Sade! Run!" Henry screamed as a wave of bright orange lightning passed over her.

She started to move, but she was too slow, and the shadow creatures had her surrounded in an instant.

"Hello goddess, we desire your energy," the creature hissed. A claw made of hard shadows reached out towards her.

"I must speak to the God of Ruin immediately; this violates the treaty."

The creatures around her laughed. The sound was grating to her ears and made her insides tremble.

"We must feed," the creature replied. A brush of magic told her these things were focused on one thing only, draining her of power.

The creature's pressed in and, in the distance, Henry had jumped down from the wall and was running toward her.

If he got any closer, he risked being drained as well. Then everyone was doomed to die.

The claws of the shadow creatures wrapped around her arms and held her in place as they drew closer. Her vision faded as the creatures feasted. Henry was shouting something, but his voice was muffled by the loud ringing in her ears.

Rage boiled within her, doing everything it could to resist her life force getting sucked out of her. The world slowed and something deep within her cracked open.

"Yes, she is strong," a creature hissed and sent a wave of shadows toward Henry. The force of which threw him back towards the wall.

Sade shuddered and her legs buckled. The creatures held firm and kept her from collapsing. More shadow creatures pressed around her, keeping Henry at bay as they feasted.

Let me out! The crimson creature screamed.

Sade shook her head and shut her eyes. Something deep inside of her buckled.

"Hmm we are close to finishing with this one," a shadow said.

"Yes, we should feast on the orange one."

Sade's eyes flew open. Henry was not far from her standing with a dome of fiery orange swirling around him. He was still screaming something, but she couldn't make out the words. A few creatures broke off from the circle surrounding her and headed towards him. Henry began throwing disks of orange lightning at them. The gesture was in vain as the creatures merely absorbed his blows.

The well of Sade's magic ran dry and the creatures dropped her without any care.

"Henry run!" She screamed as her knees hit the dirt. He became obscured by the shadows.

Something deep inside of her shattered and a renewed flood of energy surged through her. The shadow creatures paused their assault on Henry and rushed towards her.

A wave of crimson smoke shot out of her hands and obliterated the nearest shadow. The creatures let out a shriek and surged towards her. Power flowed out of her, more than she'd ever used before.

The braver shadows lunged at her, but the moment they came in contact with her magic, they were obliterated on the spot.

The world warped around her. She saw millions of delicate threads weaving their way through everything in sight. It was the fabric of the world and the only thing keeping it together. It wouldn't take much to tear it all apart.

Her body trembled with exertion. She'd reached her limit.

"Sade! That's enough! They're gone!" Henry called out to her; his voice muffled like she was underwater.

She looked around her and found not a monster in sight. Her divine rune flickered as she let the power inside of it fade.

No, I was just getting started. The crimson figure cried.

She ignored it. She'd gone too far, and they didn't need her collapsing from exhaustion when there was a city to save.

Once the crimson smoke was gone, Henry ran over to her. He scanned her body like he was looking for injuries, his worried expression faded when he saw none.

"Can you move?" He asked.

Sade nodded and held up a trembling hand.

"I think so. I didn't realize my magic ran so deep."

"You destroyed quite a few of the shadow vampires," he said with a touch of awe. Though his eyes became guarded.

"But not the scaragnos?"

"I'm afraid not. Your magic just bounced off of them."

Sade took a few steps toward the city and her legs gave out. Henry caught her and hauled her to her feet. He wrapped an arm around her waist when she swayed again.

"You need to get some rest."

"I'll rest once we find a cure," she said, and Henry's jaw clenched. "Henry, we have no choice. We need to figure out how to save those people, and Aiden, before it's too late."

Henry muttered a curse under his breath, but before Sade could say anything, he swept her up into his arms.

"It will take us half the day if you try to walk back."

Sade let her head rest against his shoulder, trying not to focus on the tattered magic inside of her.

"Sade," Henry's said.

"Yes?"

"You skirted very close to the point of no return," his eyes glimmered like he was on the verge of tears. "You could've died."

"But I pulled myself back."

"You did, but please promise me you won't go that close again." His voice was hoarse with an emotion she couldn't identify.

"I will try," she whispered.

Henry's aura mingled with hers. Concern radiated from him. Concern for her, but not like she was going to blow up any farmhouses. This was different. More like he actually cared about her wellbeing. She wasn't sure what to make of it. It wasn't something she'd experienced before. So, she closed her eyes and let her body relax against his.

When they made it back to the temple, Henry left her in the library to go check on Aiden and inform Clelia about the monsters.

She yawned as she pulled a book from the shelf. She brushed the dust off the leather binding to reveal gilded runes.

Lady Scargrave's Ultimate Collection of Roltian Folktales. Her excitement faded as she took in the title, and she had no more books to read on poisons or medicine. For such an old city, they were sorely lacking in medical materials.

Once she was settled back at the table, she thumbed through the pages illustrated with various creatures and combination runes said to protect against the creatures. Most of the runes were useless and would probably blow up in someone's face if someone used them.

She reached the end of the book and there was nothing but blank pages.

"Find anything?" Henry asked as he set a plate piled high with meat and cheese next to her. He sat down across from her and started eating from his own plate.

"No."

"Take a break for a moment, you look like you could use some energy," Henry said and pushed a goblet of wine toward her.

"How's Aiden?" She asked as she set the book down and grabbed the goblet.

"Fine, but twenty more people turned to stone," Henry ran a hand through his hair. Dark circles had formed under his eyes.

"We're running out of time," Sade's hands shook, and wine splashed out of the goblet onto the book.

"Damn it!"

She blotted the wine with the hem of her tunic, but the dark stains only got worse.

A ball of shimmering water hovered over the book. Henry had the corresponding runestone floating beside him. Even with magic pulling on it, the wine didn't leave the paper.

"That's…odd," he said.

She traced her fingers along the edges of the wine stain. Creating a trail of golden sparks, the air became electric, but the sensation vanished before she could react.

"Did you feel that?" Henry asked. When Sade nodded, he leaned back in his chair. "Out of all the things we could find in here. Of course, we find the weirdest book."

"Maybe it can help us?"

The powers within the book were old, ancient even.

Henry held up a protection, shielding, and a fire rune.

"Ladies first?"

"What? Don't you want to play dashing hero?"

Henry smirked. "I'd love to, but you're stronger than me."

She reached into her rune pouch and pulled out her divine rune, setting the stone onto a clean part of the page.

Blue and gold sparks sank into the pages. The wine stains vanished as words appeared on the paper. At first, they were a jumbled mess, but slowly they formed into coherent sentences.

Long before we conquered the towering heights.
Came a Goddess filled with fright.
Broken and battered she'd climbed the peaks.
Hoping to find a place of relief.
She climbed and climbed, searching for peace.

Until she found a cave filled with grief.
But the Goddess was not alone and soon she was lying
on the cold stone.
Her enemies tried to vanquish her, but soon she had
them all dead about her.
The world broke as the Goddess screamed and her
soul was ferried to lands unseen.
But not all was lost, for a miracle appeared.
It was a flower so powerful it can cure anything you
hold dear.
Even those whom the God of Death comes to call.
But beware for many have tried to pluck the flower
and all have perished.

The words disappeared and an image of a crimson rose with golden streaks on the petals appeared on the page. Underneath, a list of common healing herbs and boiling instructions also emerged.

"Have you ever seen that before?" Sade asked Henry who was staring at the drawing with wide eyes. "Henry?"

"It can't be," he whispered. His breath was shaky, and his body trembled as he leaned over the table. He flipped the blank page over and he stumbled backwards as a map appeared. A large red x marked a cave on a mountain not far from the city.

"What's wrong? This is great news. If this is true, we can save everyone!"

He looked at her, then his eyes shimmered with grief and fear.

"That's where my parents died," Henry's gaze dropped to the book as Sade closed it.

"Do you want to talk about it?"

Henry said nothing, instead he started to frantically look through a pile of scrolls.

"We have no other options; we have to get that damn flower," Sade said.

"There has to be another way! We can't go to that cave! It's filled with nothing but death!"

Henry stumbled backward like a drunken mortal and crashed into a table. A mountain of scrolls fell on top of him as he collapsed on the floor.

Sade rushed over to him. She grabbed his hands as she knelt beside him. He made no move to push her away, instead he stared at the wall behind her. Lost to memories he kept locked tight in his head.

"I can't do this," Henry whispered.

"You can do this," she lightly squeezed his hands.

"I can't."

"I'm sorry about your parents, but if we don't do this then an entire city and your friend are going to turn to stone."

Henry bowed his head. Her divine purpose strained to bring peace to his tattered soul, but Henry wouldn't let her in. No, it wouldn't be fair to make him go to the place that caused him so much pain.

"Henry, you stay here and gather those common herbs. I'll go to the cave and get the flower," she said as she pulled her magic back inside of her.

His green eyes widened with surprise.

"No, you can't!"

"I can and I will," she rose to her feet and grabbed the book.

"Wait—"

"We're running out of time. I understand the death of your parents affects you greatly, but would they want you to sit idly by and let people perish?"

Henry's mouth formed a thin line and there was a spark of anger in his eyes. She wanted to sigh with relief. She could deal with anger. Grief was an emotion she barely understood, even after listening to thousands of grieving souls searching for peace in her temple.

She didn't have parents and didn't have any strong bonds with anything aside from her plants. When she was created, she had woken up alone.

She would always be alone.

"No, they would want me to fight for them," Henry said after a long moment. His gaze centered on the book, and she tightened her grip on it.

"I can check the temple gardens for the common herbs it mentioned."

Henry nodded and ran a hand through his hair.

"I'll go see if Clelia can secure us some horses," he said.

Sade glanced down at the book that she still cradled and followed him out of the room.

No matter what, she was going to get the cure.

Chapter Fourteen

They left the next morning; Clelia had granted them use of her Liege Lord's stables and she'd given them two horses that she claimed could have a fireball blow past them and they would stay still. The last thing they needed was their horses to bolt at the slightest of breezes.

The Violet Mountains loomed overhead, and Henry tried to keep his thoughts from drifting to his past.

Sade rode ahead on the small trail they were following. Her long braid swayed with the horse's movements. The tranquil scene was a far cry from the one that had taken place the day before. Once again, she'd proven the Sacred Council wrong and pulled back from the destructive power lurking within her.

A power that rivaled the most ancient of divines, and she snuffed out like a candle.

He was beginning to wonder if the other gods had a more

nefarious purpose for forcing her to reincarnate. The more he thought about it, the more annoyed he got. Other immortals had committed countless crimes against the realms, some continuing to do so. Why was Sade being singled out?

Were they truly afraid she'd cause the destruction of everything? Or were they concerned she'd unseat them from their places of power?

"There's a fork in the road, which way do I go?" Sade twisted in her saddle to face him.

"Take the one on the right," he said. He didn't need to consult his map. He had been down this path many times before when he was younger and mortal.

And stupid.

He pushed back the dark memories that threatened to overtake him. When the path widened, he moved his horse beside Sade's. Her divine rune and a seeking rune hovered in front of her.

"They're still following us," she said.

Henry checked his divine rune; a mass of dark and twisted power was not far behind them. The creatures were locked onto them.

"Do you think this will work?"

"I don't think they care about humans anymore, now they've got a half-god and a goddess to hunt," Henry said and let his rune float behind him.

"I hope so," Sade said and waved at a large mossy rock. "Why do they call it the Violet Mountains? There are no purple rocks anywhere."

Henry chuckled; it was a complaint he'd heard quite a few

times when he lived here.

"Patience."

"Why won't you tell me?" She asked with a pout. She tried to poke through his mortal side to get the answer, but he locked it down.

"It would ruin the surprise," he said. He couldn't suppress a smile when she let out a stream of curses under her breath.

Silence fell between them as Sade took in the sights of the mountains looming overhead. Her aura was filled with wonder and awe at the sight.

Meanwhile, he kept his gaze on the road ahead. These mountains meant nothing but death and pain to him.

"Henry?" Sade asked. Her aura wafted around him trying to soothe his battered nerves. He pushed it away. If he softened now, he wouldn't be able to hold back the memories and he needed to be alert.

"I wonder if we'll run into a skessa," he said, keeping his tone light. Sade's mouth twisted into a frown.

"Do you think we will?"

"No idea."

A part of him hoped they would show up and hold off the shadow creatures while they got the flower. But that would require an enormous amount of luck. Something that Henry never had.

They rode until the sun dipped below the tree line.

"We should camp here," Henry said and nodded toward a small clearing. Sade quickly dismounted and started to set up camp.

Henry followed suit and cursed when his legs gave out

underneath him. Sade rushed over and helped him stand.

"Are you injured?"

"I'm just tired."

"Henry—"

"I didn't get much sleep last night."

Her expression filled with concern. Henry stumbled forward, she steadied him with a hand on his shoulder.

"I'm sorry, I know this must be difficult for you."

Henry swallowed the lump in his throat and gently removed her hand.

"We should set up camp," he said.

There wasn't much to set up aside from their bedrolls, campfire, and wards. They'd left the tents in Pavento. It would be easier for them to make a quick getaway without them. It'd been centuries since he'd been near these mountains, who knew what the God of Ruin had lurking in the shadows. Not to mention the skessa…

"They're close to us, but it doesn't feel like they are going to attack us."

Sade's voice broke through his thoughts. The goddess was studying her runes with an intense expression.

"Maybe they want us to let our guard down," he said and glanced into the forest.

"I'll take first watch."

"No, the wards should do the trick. We'll need a full night's sleep. Who knows what we'll face in the morning."

He collapsed onto his bedroll.

He was running out of time. The cave was getting farther and farther with each step. A cloaked figure chased after him with a flaming sword.

"You will not save them!" The figure yelled.

"I will try!"

"Then you are a fool! Your father is already dead, and your mother will join him!"

Henry ignored them and shoved aside a tree branch. His feet slipped on the loose stones as he made it to the cave's entrance. Light from a rune spilled out of the cave and he could hear his mother's cries for help.

"I told you, you cannot go in there," the cloaked figure appeared in front of him.

Henry tackled them; the impact loosened the figure's grip on the sword. He jumped to his feet and grabbed the weapon, flinging it into the forest.

"You will regret this," the cloaked figure snarled. Henry stomped on the figure's knee and ran into the cave.

He stopped short when he saw his father's crumpled form. His mother knelt beside him, a healing rune in her hands. It took Henry a moment to realize his father's left half was burnt so badly his skin had melted. He rushed over and his mother's head snapped up when she heard his footsteps. The anger in her eyes faded to sorrow as she stared at him.

"He's gone," she whispered.

Henry reached out for her, and she shook her head. Pale smoke flowed around her. It was a mixture of orange, black, and white.

"What are you doing?"

"I'm sorry, Henry. I cannot let your father go into the afterlife like this! It's all my fault!" She cried and shoved him away when the ground beneath them buckled. A portal opened.

He screamed as his father's body fell into the opening. His mother gave him a sad smile, before she too disappeared into the earth.

With a cry, Henry jumped toward the portal, but he fell face first onto the cold ground. The doorway his mother had opened was gone.

The cloaked figure appeared beside him then, flaming sword raised.

"I told you to stay away!" The figure hissed and swung.

Pain blinded him and he couldn't stop himself from screaming.

"Henry!"

A voice called from somewhere far away. The earth shook and the cloaked figure disappeared.

"Henry!"

The voice called again.

Henry tried to stand, but the cave was shaking so much it made it impossible. He clawed the ground with his hands, but the gateway to the afterlife didn't open again.

"Henry!"

The voice called out a third time, though it was much closer, and it was almost like it was on top of him. An electric shock coursed through his body, and once the searing pain settled, he realized he wasn't in a cave. He was in a forest lying on a bedroll.

"Henry, can you hear me?"

Sade was beside him, lightly shaking his shoulders. Her

divine rune hovered next to her, covering them in blue and gold sparks.

He blinked and his vision wavered as he struggled to focus. A group of snarling shadow creatures were pacing along the edge of the camp. He checked the wards; they were holding steady.

"What happened?" He asked while Sade wiped the sweat from his brow with a cloth.

"I don't know, I was asleep and then all of a sudden I was trapped in your nightmare."

Henry closed his eyes. His mortal side must've sensed Sade's divine presence and opened up his mind when the nightmare got too intense. She was the Goddess of Peace after all.

"I'm sorry you had to see that."

"I came into your nightmare rather late; your parents had just been sucked into the afterlife. What happened after that?"

Henry sighed. If he didn't tell her now, he doubted she would ever stop asking. An image of her using a Vestral to follow him around for the rest of his life flashed in his mind.

"My mother was looking into a strange magical occurrence. The cave we are going to has an unusual amount of divine magic rifts inside of it. There were rumors the skessa were using them to make themselves stronger and attack the humans. My mother was asked by one of her Vestrals to purge it, but the other divines found out and she was brought before the Sacred Council. She was ordered by the God of Knowledge to stay away from the cave, but more of her Vestrals demanded she clear the rift after a hunting party was killed by the skessa. So, she disobeyed his orders and went to purge the cave."

Henry took a slow breath and batted down the guilt that flared up inside him. Sade squeezed his hand and a wave of peace swept through him, soothing his senses and allowing him to continue.

"She tasked me with standing guard at the bottom of the mountain, and my father was to keep watch at the cave opening. I had warding runes set up to warn me if another divine was close by. Everything was going smoothly at first, but my mother underestimated the power that resides in the cave, and it was taking her far longer than she had said it would. I had been up most of the night getting the wards prepped and I fell asleep."

He couldn't hold back the torrent of images and emotions that sprang forth from deep within him.

"I was woken up by screaming. It was the worst thing I'd ever heard. I ran up to the cave and was assaulted by the cloaked figure with the flaming sword. I was able to throw their sword into the forest and get into the cave. But by the time I reached my parents, my father was already dead and my mother…. Well, I think a part of her died with him. Before I could stop her, she'd opened a portal into the afterlife and went after my father's soul."

"Then the cloaked figure tried to kill you again?" Sade asked.

"No, that was just something from the nightmare. I jumped in after my mother did," Henry sat up and ran a hand through his hair. "Have you ever been in the afterlife?"

Sade shook her head and he wondered if a past life of hers had been to the afterlife.

"Well, it's not a place for a half-god. Part of my body started to rot. Before I succumbed to the afterlife and had my mortal side ripped out of me, the God of Death appeared. Before I knew it, I was in the Divine Realm and the God of Knowledge had given me my mother's divinity."

"And your parents?"

"As punishment for my mother's disobedience, she was thrown into a cage where she would relive her final moments for eternity. My father was placed just outside of her prison where he gets to watch my mother relive her darkest moments. Forever."

Henry's aura flared around him in waves of anger and guilt. If he'd just stayed awake, his parents wouldn't have suffered this fate and he wouldn't have been forced to take on his mother's mantle. His father wouldn't have to watch his mother cry for him when he was only a feet away from her.

"I will not pretend that I know what it feels like to lose someone. I don't. I've only been around twenty years, and I haven't yet formed a family of my own. However, I do know you cannot blame yourself for the choices of others."

"But if I had been awake…"

"You would be dead."

Henry jerked his hands away from hers and glared at the sky. The stars above shone without any care for what happened below. He wished he was up there, away from all this.

He let out a sigh. A part of him knew Sade was right. If he'd been awake, it was more than likely he would've been killed along with his father. Then, they both would've been stuck watching his mother suffer for eternity. Or maybe the God of Knowledge still would've forced his mother's mantle on him.

"It doesn't matter now. What's done is done and nothing will change our fates."

"They had no right to do that. The council is just supposed

to offer support, not rule over us with an iron fist," Sade said.

"I know, but they don't care. There aren't many divines who would dare defy them, and no one wants another war."

Sade's mouth formed a thin line. Her presence grew cold for a second before it returned to its soothing state.

"It still isn't right. Your mother was doing her duty and they interfered in a matter that didn't require their assistance."

Henry studied her; Sade held his gaze.

Had she stood up to the Sacred Council in the past? Was she being punished for some act of defiance? It would explain why they had a dagger created and why she'd been locked in her temple.

"Have you ever thought about rebelling against them?" Henry asked and Sade's eyes widened.

"What? Why would I do that?"

"I mean you were locked up in a temple for twenty years…"

"No! If I did that, it would plunge us all into war, and I don't think I could continue to exist if that happened."

Her magic floated into the wards and filled them with sparkling light. The creatures watching them through the shimmering shield shrank back into the forest.

"Sometimes, I wonder what my life would've been like if I'd been allowed to make my own choices when I was created. Would I have chosen to stay in my temple, or would I have decided to explore? There are so many places in worlds like this that I've only heard whispers of," Sade's tone became wistful as she stared at the sky.

"Even after experiencing the horrors of a Mortal Realm, you still want to explore one?"

Sade rolled onto her side and held up a pebble. Her eyes were full of wonder.

"This place is full of life."

"The Divine Realm also has life."

"Yes, but it's different here. It's…" Sade's nose scrunched up as she trailed off.

"More vibrant?"

Sade's eyes lit up and she nodded. A lock of hair fell onto her face, and he resisted the urge to tuck it behind her ear.

"That's the word I was looking for, I didn't know how to describe it."

Henry chuckled. "You're probably the first goddess to say that. Even my mother preferred the Divine Realm."

"If she hated it so much, then why did she stay here?"

"She fell in love with my father and her fate was sealed when I was born. No half-divines are allowed to be raised in the Divine Realm, unless they give up their mortal side. My mother didn't want me to lose my connection to this world and wanted me to choose if I wanted to stay mortal or not."

"I didn't know you could choose to gain divinity."

"Not many people know. The Sacred Council doesn't want a bunch of mortals trying to become gods."

It was one of the few rules he agreed with.

"And your father? What did he think about all this?"

"My father could never understand why my mother chose him, but he loved her and did whatever he could to help her with fulfilling her divine purpose."

Something inside of Henry lightened as a memory surfaced.

"My mother was often overwhelmed by the amount of

petitions she received. My father would stay by her side until she'd completed them, making sure her mortal form had plenty of food and water. My mother hated when he did this, but he said it was the least he could do for her since she'd given up almost everything for him."

Guilt ate at him; he'd tarnished his mother's legacy by letting all the realms she'd presided over forget about her. He'd spent his entire life watching over one, and he could barely do that.

"If you hadn't been forced to take on your mother's mantle, what would you have done?"

Henry blinked and refocused on their conversation. Sade was watching him with a curious expression.

He shook his head. "It's not anything special. It's nothing that would interest anyone who hasn't lived a long life amongst mortals."

Sade continued to stare at him, her eyes glittered with determination. She moved closer and rested a hand on his arm.

"Whatever it is, it *has* to be better than the mountains of paperwork they make you do in the Divine Realm."

Her magic poked at his aura and he let out a long sigh before he replied.

"I wanted to become a candlemaker."

He tensed waiting for her to laugh and call him foolish, but the curiosity in her eyes only got brighter.

"Why candles?"

"When I was a boy, we spent a winter up in Acrilla. That country is so far north their nights are longer than any place else in the continent. We bought a lot of candles from a Vestral who was also a candlemaker. She created all sorts of marvelous things, her creations rivaled that of the great artists of old. I'd never seen anything like it and haven't since."

He used to spend hours making candles. He'd used all sort of tools ranging from runes to needles, and he'd never been able to replicate her creations.

"And you stopped because of your parents' deaths?'

"No," he paused and took a slow breath. "I…"

"It's fine, you don't have to tell me."

"I asked the Sacred Council to make me the God of Candles. They laughed in my face and practically threw me out of the temple. When I returned home, all of my candles were destroyed, and I was afraid they'd turn me into a frog if I tried to make more."

The words came out of him in a rush. Sade face was a mixture of pity and fury.

"How old were you when they did that?"

"Nine."

"They are *very* lucky we can't contact them right now," Sade snarled.

"It's one of the many reasons I strive to be a thorn in their side."

Sade's expression slowly smoothed over. "I'm sorry. I hope your mother gave them a piece of her mind."

"I never told her. In fact, only me, the Sacred Council, and now you, know about that whole debacle."

"No one else knows. Not even Aiden?"

"Not even Aiden."

"Why?"

"Because my reputation as a fearsome monster hunter

would be ruined if people knew I wanted to make candles. Aiden would never let me hear the end of it."

A low hiss from a shadow creature had them checking the wards. They were still holding strong.

Sade shook her head and muttered something under her breath. Henry laid back onto his bedroll and watched a meteor glide across the sky.

"Thank you," he said while Sade shuffled onto her bedroll.

"For what?"

"Letting me talk about my parents," he paused and swallowed a lump in his throat. "It's been a long time since I've talked about them."

He'd spoken about it with Aiden, but he hadn't expressed much sympathy for his mother. Most didn't. Disobeying a divine decree was an act of treason.

"When you're ready, I'd love to hear more about them. I've never had a family and the subject is absolutely fascinating to me."

Guilt once again crept through him. She likely had a family in one of her past lives. Hell, maybe she had a lover who was still alive, but he'd never know.

"Do you want one?"

"It feels like my life has just begun, but it has crossed my mind. What about you?"

Henry raised an eyebrow and gestured to the forest.

"I doubt anyone would want to join me in this life. It's not a comfortable one and rather dangerous."

"Well, Aiden seems like he enjoys it."

Henry shuddered. "Aiden is like a brother to me and not

once have I ever—"

He trailed off when Sade burst into laughter. It was one of the most beautiful sounds he'd ever heard. Her laughter soon faded, and he wanted to hear it again, but Sade stretched and gave an exaggerated yawn.

"Goodnight, Henry," Sade said with a playful smirk.

She rolled so her back was facing him and soon she was fast asleep.

Henry eyed the monsters watching them from the shadows. They still hadn't moved.

His eyes drooped and soon darkness overtook him. For the first time in centuries, he didn't dream of his parents in the afterlife. Didn't hear their screams or awake in the middle of the night bathed in sweat.

No, this time he dreamt of a goddess with brown eyes flecked with gold and blue.

Chapter Fifteen

The next day went without any problems. The monsters merely watched them from the shadows. Despite their conversation the night before, Henry was mostly silent for the duration of the day.

She could only imagine what was going through his head. The dark cloud that wove itself through his aura had lessened a bit, but one conversation was hardly enough to heal a lifetime of pain. Yet, she still wished she could just take it all away from him. Henry had a good soul, and it wasn't fair that he suffered so.

"We'll make camp at the next meadow," Henry said. His demeanor had lightened a bit and a flicker of excitement danced in his eyes.

"What's in this meadow? You look like you've been given a bag of gold."

"You'll see," he said with a wink.

Sade fought to keep herself from staring at him, so she focused on the path in front of her. What was wrong with her?

It's only because he still isn't at peace, once he is I will move on to something else.

It most certainly wasn't because of the way his eyes lit up when he smiled, or how deeply he cared about the Mortal Realm he called home.

Henry was only meant to be in her life temporarily. She had a destiny to fulfill, and Henry wasn't part of it.

Oh, come now, don't be so dramatic. We don't have to go. The crimson figure's voice called out from somewhere deep in her mind. She pushed it back further. She didn't need to listen to that thing. Once she was settled in her new home, she would take some time and figure out what it was.

She focused on her runes, checking on the creatures that trailed behind them. Their bodies quivered with fear, and a few fell back.

Good. They needed to be afraid of something and she would rather it be her than anything else.

A lone howl broke her concentration and she shot Henry a worried look.

"It's only a wolf," he said. "It's getting dark and they're probably preparing to go on a hunt."

"Do you talk to wolves?"

She searched her memory for such an ability, but she couldn't remember anything from the scrolls she'd read. Then again, none of them had ever mentioned that plants had their own language. She was starting to get the impression that the Goddess of Fates had been *very* selective on her reading material.

"No, but I've lived long enough to know their habits. It's a good sign, the skessa aren't nearby. The wolves fear them and won't go within a hundred miles of them."

"It seems fate is on our side?"

"For now. Don't get comfortable. If you hear the sounds of stones breaking that means a skessa has spotted you."

"And what do I do then?"

"You have two choices, you can either run or fight. Since you are the only hope the people of Pavento have at getting cured, I would choose the first option."

"Have you ever tried talking to them?"

"My mother tried. Many times. It's not easy to talk to something that is hurtling a boulder the size of a horse at you. She always came home covered in bruises and they never backed down or stopped attacking any humans that wandered into the mountains. My father put his foot down after she came home with a sword lodged in her stomach and had to spend two months recovering in the Divine Realm."

Sade flicked her braid off her shoulder.

"Perhaps I can help mend the bridge between the humans and the skessa."

Henry let out a long breath and shook his head.

"There's too much blood on both sides."

"So? I've helped mend the bridge between two warring countries before."

"And how long did that last?"

"What do you mean?"

Henry stopped his horse and motioned for her to do the same.

"The Mortal Realm is not only a realm of decay. It is also a realm of balance. If the scales are tipped toward order, then chaos will prevail. If the scales are tipped toward chaos, then order will prevail. The realm is constantly trying to find the middle ground and there are always figures on both sides trying to swing it the way they want it."

"I always thought it was the God of War trying to get me to fight him."

Henry chuckled. "Well, there is that, but he's not as strong as you think he is. He's a big talker and a bit vain."

"So, you're saying that anything I do to help the mortals is useless because they will always find a way to mess it up?"

"Precisely."

"But isn't that the point? This is why we exist, to help the mortals forge a better path. Maybe someday they will work together and stop fighting?"

"If the mortals no longer need us, does that mean we stop existing?"

Sade looked around the forest. A dragonfly fluttered around a bush.

"I think we'd continue on in some capacity. Look at Aiden, no one worships him and he's fine. Besides, I doubt all the Mortal Realms would suddenly achieve enlightenment at the same time."

"And I doubt our beloved God of Knowledge would allow such a thing to come to pass," he said, and he nudged his horse forward.

"Tell me, how did he become so…influential?"

Henry's expression darkened. "I don't know. I'm not sure I

want to find out."

"Why?"

"Sade, I know you're the living embodiment of peace and want the best for everyone, but there are things that are not worth digging up. My parents paid the price for my mother's disobedience, and I don't want to know what he would do if he found someone digging into his past. I doubt we'd find anything. He's the God of Knowledge after all, and a god as old as him isn't stupid. He's probably removed all traces of bad deeds from everyone's memories."

Sade shuddered. At least with the God of Ruin, one knew what they were coming up against. But gods like the God of Knowledge? That was a different story. Who knew what darkness lurked inside of him.

"I believe whatever he's done will come back to haunt him eventually. The Mortal Realms cannot be the only places with the need to ensure balance is obtained."

The corners of Henry's mouth quirked upwards. "I hope so. That bastard deserves to be taken down a peg or two. The Sacred Council has been ruled by the same divines for centuries. It needs some new blood."

Sade raised an eyebrow. "Perhaps you should consider joining them."

Henry's jaw dropped, and he quickly closed it as he nearly fell off his horse. Sade suppressed a giggle and he cursed under his breath. Once he was steady, he narrowed his eyes at her.

"Why in the hell would I do that?"

"Because you have seen how the decisions made by the Divine Realm affects everything else. You understand the mortals better than anyone. I don't know the others very well, but maybe they need to change things up? Let some newer divines take charge and see what happens?"

Henry didn't reply. He just stared at her.

"Is something wrong?" She asked when he shifted in his saddle and ran a hand through his hair.

"Not to be rude, but you are the most unusual goddess I've ever met," he said after a long moment of silence. "Sometimes I think I'm talking to a mortal and not a goddess."

"Well, I was locked in a tower for most of my existence and I talk to plants. So, I don't think I'll be fitting in at any of the big parties."

Henry snorted. "That makes two of us."

"Honestly, I found the whole ceremony to be a bit dull. No one really cared about me, they only cared about the party."

"Ah, they were probably there to drink wine and gossip. They like to pretend they're better the mortals, but, in all honesty, they are exactly like them."

"So mortal parties are the same?"

"I'm afraid so."

She let out an exaggerated sigh. "I guess I'll skip the celebrations that I'm sure the humans will hold once we bring them the cure."

Henry's gaze flickered toward the summit. The sun was setting, and it bathed the rocks in a warm glow.

"We need to hurry to the meadow. If it gets too dark you won't be able to see the surprise."

"Can't we wait until the morning?"

"It'll be gone by then."

Henry dug his heels into his horse's sides and took off at a gallop. Sade made her horse follow at a slower pace.

The forest surrounding them thinned as they rode up the mountain, and the path became steeper forcing Henry to slow his horse. Just before the trees tapered off, Henry veered off the path into the forest. Sade followed, checking the monsters that trailed behind them. Nothing had changed in that regard.

The trees changed the further they ventured into the forest. They were taller and thick ivy vines wrapped themselves around their trunks.

Henry soon dismounted and Sade followed suit. He quickly set up a few wards and they both watched the creatures chasing them chafe against the invisible barrier.

The ivy had taken over most of the trees. She reached for one of the hanging vines before Henry cleared his throat.

"The meadow is this way," he said and held out a scrap of cloth.

"Why are you holding that?"

"I need to blindfold you."

"Why?"

"Because that's part of the surprise."

She frowned but gave him a short nod. They didn't have time to argue, and if this was how Henry wanted to show the surprise, then she'd let him.

With a speed she didn't know he had, he was behind her, and the cloth was over her eyes. Small pinpricks of light pierced through the darkness, but the cloth was just thick enough she couldn't make out anything.

Henry grabbed her hand and led her through the forest.

He'd shielded his mind so that she couldn't sneak into it.

"Do you always blindfold people you take to this place?"

"Yes, it's part of the allure."

She crinkled her nose; the blind fold scrunched up. She caught a glimpse of Henry's amused face before he tugged it back down.

"I don't think blindfolds are something most people would consider alluring."

Henry chuckled. "That depends on the person."

"What?"

"That's another topic for a different day because we have arrived!" He said and she could practically hear him giving a dramatic bow. Magic swept around her, and the air was saturated with a heavy floral scent.

She felt Henry untying the cloth and soon it fell away from her face.

A meadow filled with violets stood before her, and tiny pinpricks of light emanated from their petals, bathing the meadow in a soft lilac glow.

"The Starlight Violets are the reason why they are called the Violet Mountains," Henry said, his voice was barely above a whisper, as if he didn't want to disturb the tranquil scene before them. "They only bloom in late spring and most of them are gone before summer starts. For some reason, this meadow lasts until the height of summer."

"It's beautiful," Sade whispered as she brushed her fingers on the petals of a nearby flower. The energy within them was ancient and powerful. It was vaguely familiar.

"My mother claimed an ancient goddess favored these

flowers and this used to be her home."

"What do you think?"

"We aren't far from the cave, so whatever is in there is likely keeping these flowers alive," his shoulders drooped, and Sade reached for him. Her aura shifted around him, ready to soothe whatever ailed him, but he gave her a small shake of his head.

"Forgive me, this place shouldn't be tainted by my memories. I wanted to show you something that hasn't been tainted by war or the God of Ruin. I wanted to show you the beautiful side of the realm."

Her heart swelled at his words. Despite the horrid memories that haunted him, he was trying to give her a moment of respite.

Sade rushed over to him and threw her arms around him. He froze and she feared he was going to push her away. But instead, he pulled her close, until her head was resting against his chest and she could hear his heart's rapid beating. She counted his heartbeats as they calmed into a steady rhythm.

She wasn't sure how long they stood there, but she didn't care. For once, she was at peace. For a moment she was able to pretend there was nothing outside of this meadow.

"Thank you," she whispered as they pulled apart. A part of her cried out at the loss of his warmth. "No one has ever done anything like that for me."

Henry's eyes shimmered with an emotion she didn't recognize. Before she could ask him about it, he glanced at the flowers. The light within them was beginning to fade.

Sade followed his gaze and let some magic drift over the flowers. She let it combine with theirs and soon the lilac glow returned.

Henry's eyes sparked with interest. He sent a wave of orange sparks over the flowers, but the plants didn't respond. A flicker of disappointment crossed over his face and Sade reached for his hand.

"You need to learn how to speak to them first," she said and knelt, giving his arm a slight tug. Soon he was sitting beside her with the both of them taking care to not crush any of the delicate blooms.

Henry rubbed the back of his neck.

"What's wrong?"

"What if they don't like me?"

Sade blinked and waited for Henry to make a joke, but his expression was serious as he lightly tapped a flower petal with his free hand.

"They aren't capable of being judgmental, they're plants."

"But—"

Sade rested a finger on his lips and let her aura intertwine with his. She reached out to the violets and let their presence drift into the connection she'd made with Henry.

Henry's entire body convulsed, and she cut off their connection to the plants.

"Sorry, I didn't think it would be that strong," she said, and Henry patted down his hair. He glanced down at their intertwined fingers and shrugged.

"I've had worse," he said, then frowned. "I didn't hear anything."

"Let's try this again," she said and reopened their connection. The flowers sung a song of thanks as they fed off her power. They slowly noticed Henry's presence and his eyes lit up with wonder.

For a moment, she had a glimpse into the man he was before the tragedies that befell him.

"I don't quite understand what they are saying, but I think I get the gist of it."

"That's because they don't know you yet. Once you've earned their trust, they'll be more open with their speech."

Henry rubbed his chin, and a thoughtful look crossed his face.

"How did you discover it?"

She picked at some dead grass. "It was a complete accident. I was trying to create a spirit friend and accidentally tapped into their magic stream. It took me almost a decade before I gained their trust. I would spend hours trying to talk to them, but nothing answered me. I almost gave up until one day I connected to them, and they responded."

She patted the ground beside her and pushed away the dark memories of her time in the temple.

"I think the plants kept me from going mad, and for that, I am eternally grateful."

A soft twinkling filled the air and tiny sparks of silver light floated above the flowers. They swirled in the air and formed strange patterns.

"What are they doing?"

Henry let go of her hand and pointed to the sky, which was now filled with stars. He traced a pattern in the air and the lights in the meadow copied it. Sade glanced at the pattern and then up at the sky. It was an exact copy of a constellation.

"Why are they doing that?"

"The mortals have a legend of an ancient God of the Stars

who gave up his divinity to be with a mortal. They say the flowers are what remains of him," Henry said.

"Why would he do that?"

"Do what?"

"Give up his divinity for a mortal."

"He was in love."

"I wouldn't do that," Sade said, and Henry's gaze snapped up. His nostrils flared and his magic stirred around him. "I would ensure my partner was immortal too."

The tension in Henry's body eased a fraction.

"So, is that what you are going to do after you've ensured the God of Ruin stops sending the monsters? Find yourself a bond mate?"

"I don't think my life is suited for it. I'll likely be sealed away in a temple again and left alone."

Henry nodded, seemingly lost in thought.

"Can plants talk across the realms?" He asked.

"I think so, they have mentioned my plants in my temple before."

Henry's eyes lit up as he stood and walked over to the edge of the meadow.

"Can you connect to that flower?" He asked and pointed at a violet next her.

Sade raised an eyebrow but did as he asked. Henry rested a hand on a nearby tree.

Sade? Can you hear me?

Henry's voice was faint, but she could hear him.

I can. She sent back. Henry made a face. He probably wasn't able to hear her yet.

"I can hear you just fine," she said aloud, and his eyes lit up.

"Fantastic, I'll just have to practice talking to the plants," he said as he sat next to her. "If we can use the plants to talk, I can keep you informed on all the craziness that happens in this place."

Tears welled up in her eyes. "You'd do that for me? Why?"

"Because you shouldn't be isolated and alone," Henry rubbed the back of his neck and started to rise.

For the second time that night she flung her arms around him. Her movement caught Henry off guard, and they tumbled to the ground. Henry was now lying on his back, blinking up at her as she tried to untangle herself.

"You know if you wanted me underneath you, you could just ask," Henry said with a glint of mischief in his eyes. His gaze burned a trail of invisible sparks down her body.

"In your dreams, Henry," she said, trying to quell the fire that was forming under her skin. Henry reached up and brushed a strand of hair from her face. His fingers lightly caressed her cheek, sending a wave of heat through her veins.

Henry stilled his movements and took a long, slow breath. Her gaze fell to his lips, and she wondered what they would feel like against hers.

"I'm sorry, I shouldn't have done that," Henry whispered, breaking her out of the spell he'd put her under. His voice was low and rough, sending shivers down her spine.

"It's fine," she said and quickly moved off him. Henry closed his eyes, and he didn't move for several heart beats. When his eyes opened again, they were back to their normal guarded state. A part of her was disappointed, but she could understand why.

Sure, he could talk to her through the plants, but they would spend the rest of their existence in two different realms. They were meant to pass through each other's lives for a brief moment and nothing more.

Sade tore her gaze away from him and tried to peer into the forest that lined the edges of the meadow. The shadows didn't darken nor did the scaragnos appear in the branches.

"I should go check on the horses," Henry said and nodded at the violets, "enjoy this while it lasts."

Sade sat back down and pulled her knees to her chest. Her fingers traced where Henry's had brushed across her cheek. She closed her eyes and willed it to her memory.

⚜

The next morning, they stood at the mouth of the cave. The horses were safely tucked away and so the creatures wouldn't go after them. The last thing they needed was for them to become a creature's dinner.

Henry was fiddling with his axes. Scaragnos hissed at them from the shadows of the forest below. She pulled her divine rune out of her pouch.

"Are you ready?" She asked Henry when his aura wavered.

"Ready," he said. He took a step forward and slipped on a rock.

"You can wait outside. I'll just dash in there and grab the flowers."

Henry's mouth formed a thin line while he steadied himself.

"I'm going inside, I will not wait here like a coward."

Sade let her aura brush against his. It was a whirlwind of

grief, rage, and fear. She reached for her calming rune and let it seep into their connection. Henry shot her a grateful look as his emotions stabilized.

"Let's go," she fished out a fire rune and let a small fireball float above her palm.

She headed into the cave. The air grew cooler with each step she took, and the stone walls tightened around her. She peered into the inky darkness ahead while blue and gold smoke coiled around her, ready to strike at the first sign of danger. Henry was close behind her; his breathing was haggard, and she could hear his boots scraping against the stone.

"Just a bit farther," he said, and the narrow passageway opened to a large underground cavern. A small stream cut its way through the stone floor around them, and a hole high above them allowed a beam of sunlight to illuminate the cavern.

In the center of the cavern was a small patch of blood-red roses streaked with gold.

"They actually exist," Sade whispered, and she let her fireball fizzle out. The second the fire died; glowing silver lines appeared on the stones around them. They were filled with magic, but it wasn't like any she'd seen before. Unlike the magic that bound the world together, this was on the brink of tearing everything apart.

Was this the anomaly Henry's mother was looking into?

Henry moved next to her. His body was tense, and his knuckles turned white as he gripped his axes. Sade's chest tightened as they moved toward the flowers. Her ears rang as her mind was flooded with faint screams.

"Do you hear that?" She asked Henry.

"Hear what?"

Her divine rune sent out a wave of sparks around her, searching for the source, but it found nothing. The screams became more intense. Then, without warning, they stopped shouting and started begging for mercy.

She stumbled into the water and numerous faces appeared beneath her. They were ghosts trapped under the surface. They reached for her, but their hands passed through her body unable to grab onto her. Had the rifts trapped them here?

"I'm so sorry," she whispered to them, but her words didn't erase the agony from their faces.

"Is something bothering you?" Henry asked.

"I'm fine, this place has a lot of pain. Many lives have been lost here."

Henry's face fell and he started to wade over to her, but she held up a hand. The faces were gone and her mind was clear.

"Let's get these flowers and get out of here," she said and hurried onto dry land. She spotted a small scroll lying on the edge of the grass. A tendril of her magic swept over it. There wasn't any spells or enchantments tied to it, so she picked up and read.

Nice try, but in the end, I will win this game.

The handwriting looked vaguely familiar.

"What in the hell does that mean?" Henry asked when she handed him the scroll. She reached into her rune pouch, seeking out the small piece of paper she'd stashed there. She held it next to the words on the scroll.

The handwriting matched.

"What is that?" Henry asked as Sade twisted the paper in

her hands. She handed it over to him. Henry's eyes darkened while he studied the words.

"It's a note that I found in my chambers after the portal blew up."

"Did you tell anyone about it?"

"No, I wasn't sure if it was the God of Ruin or someone working for him. I honestly forgot about it until now."

Henry's jaw clenched.

"There is no way the God of Ruin could've entered into your chambers without sounding an alarm. So, it had to be someone he was working with."

"But who?"

Henry crossed his arms and shook his head. "The most obvious answer would be the God of Music since he was kicked out, but he's not the sneaky kind."

Sade's stomach churned. "Could it be the God of War? He was brought over as a tribute."

Henry laughed and then choked when Sade glared at him.

"I'm being serious."

"Sorry, just the image of him trying to skulk about the shadows and being all secretive doesn't quite fit the god I know. He'd try, but he wouldn't be able to keep himself from boasting about his plans."

Sade frowned. Henry was right. It was someone who enjoyed these types of games, which left a lot of options. Any of them could be working with the God of Ruin. This was something she would have to untangle later.

A low clicking noise echoed from somewhere deep in the cave, causing goosebumps to form on her skin. A fire rune danced around Henry, and he sent a stream of fire down a passageway.

"We can speculate later, let's get these damn flowers and get the hell out of here."

Sade nodded and reached for the burlap sack. She quickly gathered all the roses she could. The screaming in her mind got worse with each flower she picked.

"We've got company," Henry said, and he tossed a couple flowers into the sack. He jerked his head toward a stalactite. A scaragnos was hanging from it with its crimson eyes glittering with hunger.

Sade grabbed the last of the flowers as Henry sent a wave of fire towards it. The creature let out a shriek as it lost its grip on the stone. The sounds of bones crunching echoed through the cavern.

"Was that the only one?" Sade asked and hoisted the sack over her shoulder.

The sound of clacking mandibles filled the air, followed by a high-pitched scream. Henry yanked out a rune and pulled Sade close to him. He used the rune to form a bubble around them, blocking out the noise.

The beam of sunlight above them flickered, hundreds of scaragnos crawled into the cavern.

It was too late to run; they would have to fight their way out. She used her free hand to call out a fire rune.

"You can run, I'll fight them off," Henry said.

"We're both getting out of here," Sade said. A shadow creature crept out of the darkness.

She took a step towards it, letting the fire swirl around her. The shadow creature let out a hiss and a vortex of dark shadows hurtled towards her. She sucked in a breath, and sent a wave of fire at the monster.

The creature let out a scream and slinked out of the range of her rune.

"Is that all you've got?" She shouted at the creature and dared a quick glance at the scaragnos watching her from the walls. She readied another wave of fire, but, before she could release it, an invisible fist slammed into her chest, sending her flying across the cavern and into a wall.

Gasping for air, she peeled herself off the stones. A blistering pain swept through her, causing her legs to wobble.

"Sade!" She heard Henry cry. A swarm of scaragnos and shadow creatures blocked her view.

Her vision swam with darkness, but she fought it off and she searched for Henry. The sounds of metal slicing against bone filled the air. Finally, she spotted him.

He was standing in the small patch of sunlight, surrounded by scaragnos and the shadow creatures. Runes danced around him as he used them and his axes to keep the creatures at bay.

Sade reached for a rock that jutted out from the wall and tried to stand, but her legs gave out, and she was back on the ground. She grabbed her rune pouch and dumped out all her runes, letting each one flare to life. Her body continued to tremble, and the edges of her vision were laced with crimson.

Not again. We swore this wouldn't ever happen again! The crimson figure shrieked inside of her. The lines in the stone walls glowed a deep ruby, casting a bloody glow throughout the cavern.

She ignored the voice and focused on her runes. Henry was doing his best to keep the creatures away from him, but his powers were waning.

"Henry, put up a shield!" She screamed as she sent a crackling wave of energy towards him. Henry crossed his axes and shifted into a defensive stance. A protection and shielding rune floated in front of him right as her magic slammed into the writhing mass of creatures.

The blow decimated a few of the shadow creatures and turned a scaragnos into a pile of ash.

It wasn't enough.

She sent another wave, hoping the creatures would turn away from Henry and target her instead. But they closed in on Henry until she could barely see the top of his head.

Her heart beat wildly in her chest as she sent another blast. Then suddenly, the creatures closest to Sade moved aside. Henry was on his knees; his hands were locked behind him with one of his axes was embedded in his side.

Henry coughed; blood dribbled down his chin as the shadow creature held him upright.

"Let him go," she snarled.

Sade's vision warped and everything was bathed in crimson as wave after wave of magic burst out of her. The runestones shattered, unable to handle the power she was unleashing.

Henry's aura grew weaker as he struggled to use an ice rune, but the shadow creature reached out and crushed the stone before it reached full power. It reached for the axe embedded in Henry's side and pushed it in further. Henry let out a bloodcurdling scream and the creature let him collapse into a heap on the ground.

Her fingers brushed against the ruby lines in the stone and

a surge of power flooded her veins. The scaragnos let out a shriek and swarmed towards her.

"Henry!" Sade screamed.

A sharp pain erupted in her chest as a vision of a blade being plunged into her heart formed in her mind. She gasped and almost blacked out.

Another vision, this one clear as day found her standing in the cave with no monsters and no flowers. Instead, there was a man lying in a pool of blood as a cloaked figure with a flaming sword stood over him. She vaguely recalled Henry's story of how his parents had perished, but the man in this vision didn't match what she'd seen in Henry's nightmare. This was a different time.

A bloodcurdling scream echoed through the cavern and a stream of sparks flew out of her hands. Cracks formed in the stone as her magic coiled within her. The world around her was beginning to crumble.

"We'll meet again, and this time I'll succeed," the cloaked figure said. The vision warped and faded when the stones broke apart.

With a gasp, Sade untangled herself from the rifts in the cave. This place seemed familiar somehow, like she'd been here before, but that was impossible. It had to be someone else's memory.

She took a long steady breath, trying to make sense of her fractured mind. It was quiet, too quiet. Her vision came into focus, and she searched for Henry in the mass of creatures.

They were all frozen. Nothing was moving, not even the sparkling sunlight.

We don't have much time; you need to wake up before he dies.

The crimson figure appeared in front of her.

"What is going on?"

Be still and listen to your magic.

So she did, letting it merge once again with the rifts in the rock. An overwhelming surge of rage swept through her, and she started to pull back, but the magic sucked her back in.

Another vision swarmed in her mind. She was back at the cave, but everything around her was swallowed by swirling vortexes of darkness. She looked down at her hands and found inky smoke was streaming out of her body.

Millions of voices cried out for her to stop, but she didn't. She couldn't. The rage within her was too great. The earth under her feet buckled and soon she was standing in a black void.

The darkness gave way to the cave she was currently standing in. She held up her hands and sighed with relief when she saw no darkness spewing out of her.

Bile rose in her throat, and she tried to disconnect from her magic, but she caught sight of Henry's body lying on the ground. Even with time frozen, he was getting weaker with each second that passed.

We promised it wouldn't happen again, we can't let it happen again. The crimson figure floated above Henry; it had changed. Now it was her face staring back at her. One of her eyes was a swirling mixture of blue and gold, while the other was crimson. It was her divine purpose, corrupted and twisted by the crimson smoke that swirled around her.

That wasn't me. I'm not that person. This must be a trick! I'm not a monster who would destroy millions of souls. I've been locked in a temple for most of my existence!

No this wasn't her; this was an old memory of some long dead soul that been interwoven into the cave.

We don't have time for this, he's going to die. The figure knelt next to Henry. It swept its hand over him, and she could see his soul was starting to separate from his body.

Her magic flared to life inside of her, pulling the last of it from the stones and her divine purpose into her body. Time resumed, she and watched Henry's chest rise and fall as his breathing slowed. The monsters around him moved towards her.

"Please hold on, I promise I won't let you die," She called out to him.

On the edge of the sunlit stones, she caught a glimpse of a cloaked figure with a flaming sword. The weapon was pointed at Henry.

An ancient terror gripped her entire being as she threw a ball of air at the figure.

"Stay away from him!" She screamed and used the water in the brook to send a stream of water at it. The figure shrugged off her attacks then plunged their sword into Henry's back.

Sade let out a scream and her world exploded in a sea of crimson and gold.

Chapter Sixteen

Henry was keenly aware of two things.

Pain and blood.

His body convulsed when something pierced his back. Blood pounded in his ears, muffling the sounds around him.

Die. A cruel voice hissed in the back of his mind. Tendrils of electricity crawled up and down his spine. He pushed back against it. His magic shuddered within him. Then, without warning, the strange sensation in his back was gone.

He glanced behind him to see there was nothing there.

The dagger rattled in its sheath. Henry pulled it out and looked at it. The blue crystal embedded in the pommel was now a brilliant gold.

A hair-raising scream ripped through the air. Henry looked up to see streams of crimson smoke flowing around Sade. Her eyes had rolled back into her head, and she let out another scream.

He scanned her body, but there were no outward signs of injuries or curses. Whatever was happening was in her mind. It was then he noticed the magic in the walls of the cavern drifting towards Sade.

Shit. What the hell was in the rift that was making her act like that? He needed to get her out of here.

Gritting his teeth, he shoved the dagger back into its sheath and pulled what remained of his magic into his body. Using his healing rune, he concentrated on the wound in his side. He carefully gripped the head of the axe and slowly moved it out. After what felt like eons, the weapon was finally out, and the rune had healed just enough to stem the blood flow.

He reached back to check the wound on his back and found solid flesh instead of a gaping hole. The rune must've healed it as well.

He slowly rose to his feet, taking in the scene around him. Scaragnos and shadow creatures alike were trying to leave the cave, but Sade had woven an invisible wall around the exits. Despite this, the creatures flung themselves toward the barriers. He would've laughed if the situation wasn't so dire. The damn things deserved to have a bit of fear in them.

More magic poured out of Sade, causing the stones to crack.

A scaragnos charged towards him. Henry picked up his axes and prepared to defend himself. The creature got about a foot away before a glimmering barrier made of gold and blue appeared in front of him. The creature slammed into it and let out a shriek before it disintegrated.

Henry blinked and looked down at his hands. That wasn't

his magic. He gently poked the barrier, causing the air to ripple around him. He pulled back his hand when an unbearable amount of fear swept through him.

It wasn't his fear. It was Sade's.

A terrible ripping noise filled the cave. Ribbons of black fog snaked across the ground. The world around him warped and the tearing sounds got louder with each breath he took. The remaining creatures fled, but the dark fog followed them and swallowed them whole. As it rose higher, it consumed the stone ceiling. Rocks fell around him and the mountain shuddered.

This place was turning into a death trap. He needed to get Sade out. He whirled around; adrenaline surged within him. He froze in place when he saw the strange black fog was coming from Sade.

The enchantments in the dagger tugged at his heart, like it was begging for him to bury it in her chest.

A burst of sunlight blinded him. The mountain above him was gone. A terrible wind swept through the remains of the cave. Sade's magic was the only thing keeping him upright. The stones underneath him buckled, but the barrier created a solid place for him to stand.

Henry's heart dropped to his stomach. Despite the throes of destruction she was in, she was still trying to protect him.

"Sade! You need to stop! The monsters are gone!" he shouted. The dagger at his side was becoming unbearably hot.

He sent a wave of calm towards her, but he couldn't penetrate the darkness. He was far too weak. His legs wobbled; his body wouldn't be able to stand for much longer.

"Sade, please stop. You don't need to do this. I'm okay."

He took another step. Even with the barrier, the winds were making it almost impossible to move, but he wouldn't let it win.

Step after step he took, his body growing more unstable with each movement. His magic flickered inside of him like a dying candle. He let a tiny amount out and let it weave itself into the dark mists.

An immense amount of grief and anger flooded through his body as his power wove itself deeper into the abyss. He searched for Sade's center, the core of her divine self, but he only found chaos and fear.

Still, he pressed on. He needed to get past this barrier and get close to her. Her mortal form could only take so much of this before it too would succumb to whatever fate the darkness held.

His body slammed into a wall made from a wriggling mass of shadows. Streaks of crimson started to weave through it.

A flare of orange light surrounded him. He gripped his divine rune and reached for a level of power he'd never used before.

The echoes of souls long dead crying out for justice filled his thoughts. The dagger at his side hummed while he listened to their cries for Sade's blood. His hand hovered over the hilt of the dagger, and the dark smoke around him recoiled like it was preparing to strike.

The barrier around him flared as blue and gold light formed a shimmering wall, keeping the dark tendrils from wrapping around him. The dagger's hum reached an unbearably high pitch. He resisted the urge to fling the thing into the dark fog. He wasn't going to take the chance that it could hurt Sade.

He turned his attention back to the battle waging around

him. The dark smoke tried to eat away at the stone underneath his feet, but the barrier pushed it away and reformed the stone.

It was order and chaos, locked in an eternal battle where no victors emerged. A battle that was buried deep inside of Sade.

He took a long breath and eyed his divine rune. The upright triangle represented mercy and the downward triangle represented justice. Was it truly justice if he plunged a dagger into her heart? Was she that much of a monster that she deserved to be killed repeatedly?

No, he'd seen monsters rip a child's head off with no remorse.

Sade wasn't a monster. She was a goddess with an unbridled amount of power and a past full of pain. If she was a monster, then she wouldn't have cared about the people she'd found at the farm. She wouldn't have fought to protect the mortals she'd come across. And she wouldn't be protecting him now.

He pressed his hands against the golden-blue barrier and rested his forehead against it. Goosebumps formed on his skin as a cool breeze blew over him. He had a choice; he could choose justice for the souls or mercy for her.

How many times had her blood been spilled? How many times had she come to this crucial moment and been struck down? Had anyone ever given her a chance?

Repeating the mistakes of the past would only bring about more pain. That was something he could not stand by and watch. If she truly required justice, then she would receive it, but not in the way the Sacred Council wanted. Not here. Not while she was suffering.

"I choose mercy," he whispered.

Orange lightning surged out of his body, pushing past

the barriers Sade had created. Her mortal form was becoming translucent, but he could still see the terror in her face.

He raced forward. More orange sparks swirled around him, and his divine rune glowed brighter than a star. Tendrils of dark smoke tried to stop him, but he pressed on.

He reached for her hands; they were colder than ice. Her body trembled and another wave of tattered darkness rippled through her clothes.

Her eyes met his, one was crimson and the other gold with blue flecks. He held her gaze and tightened his grip on her hands.

"Henry?" She whispered, her voice was raw with grief and anger. Tears ran down her face and he gently brushed them away.

"I'm alive," he said, trying to keep his voice steady. He ignored the stab of pain in his gut and the headache that was starting to form. His body had reached its limit, but Sade's magic still danced around them in a whirlwind of destruction.

"But they aren't, I..." she trailed off, her eyes glossed over, and she became enthralled by some ancient memory.

"You need to cut off your connection to your magic. Your body can't handle this for much longer," he pleaded.

"They will pay," she hissed.

"Don't go. Don't follow this darkness," Henry's voice cracked. His heart was shattering into millions of pieces. This wasn't something he could help her with. She had to choose.

"I have no choice," she whispered and closed her eyes.

"You have a choice; you always have a choice. Don't let whatever is eating you up inside win. You're stronger than this." His eyes never left her face as he watched her struggle to overcome herself.

Slowly the tattered threads of the world wove itself back together. The air cleared and Henry couldn't stop his jaw from dropping.

The ancient rifts that scarred the stones were gone.

She healed it.

Peace and Destruction. Order and Chaos. That's what she was. It was only now he understood her power. It was one thing to be told of it, but to see it in action…it was terrifying and beautiful all at the same time.

She was one of the most powerful divines in existence, if not the most. And she'd been treated like she was a stain upon all of creation. Why? Other gods had slain mortals and each other. The God of War got to strut about like a peacock, yet he'd received none of the treatment Sade had.

Something wasn't right. There was something he wasn't seeing, or he wasn't being allowed to.

It was enough to make his blood boil.

When Sade opened her eyes, they were brown. No gold or blue flecks to be found. Her mortal form had returned to its normal state, but her hands trembled slightly.

"Are you all right?" Henry asked.

She nodded, her gaze flickered to the sky above them and her brow crinkled.

"Did I blow up an entire mountain?"

"No, you only destroyed the top."

"And the creatures?"

"Dead."

Sade swallowed and looked around the remnants of the cave. The sounds of stones crumbling filled the air as a few remaining stalagmites collapsed. Sade picked up the burlap sack she'd put the flowers into. Henry quietly thanked the fates for that one small mercy. He wasn't sure what they'd do if the flowers had been destroyed.

"Do you want to talk about it?" Henry asked.

She nudged the remains of runestone with her foot. "No, I don't. I need time to process…whatever that was."

His divine purpose strained within him, urging him to tell her the truth, but he pushed it back. This wasn't the time nor the place. Once Aiden and the others were cured, he'd tell her then. Not in this godsforsaken place.

He followed her down the mountain, but his body had enough. A searing pain spread through his back, causing him to jerk backwards.

"Henry!"

Sade was at his side in an instant. She cradled his head in her lap as the rest of his body convulsed.

Shockwaves pulsed through him as his divine side flared to life, keeping his mortal self from succumbing to his injuries. He could feel the icy hand of death coaxing him into the afterlife.

Not today you grimy bastard. Henry pushed against the darkness that danced along the edges of his vision. He could've sworn he heard someone laugh and the ice within him thawed.

"Henry," Sade called out to him, she sounded like she was underwater. "Stay with me."

Sade pulled a healing rune out of his pouch and pressed it against his chest. Pink sparks danced around them, and a scream burst from his lips.

"Don't use any more magic," he managed to say.

The edges of his vision darkened further, and an invisible force pressed against his chest. Then without warning, the pain and the darkness vanished.

He took a few ragged breaths, keeping his gaze on Sade, who was also breathing slowly. He tried to move his arms, but they remained in their twisted state.

"I can't move my arms," he said.

Terror gripped him. If his mortal form was this badly injured, it would take him months, if not years, to recover. If they were attacked now, he wouldn't be able to defend himself.

"You'll be all right," Sade said with a small smile. It didn't wipe away the worry in her eyes as she brushed some hair off his forehead. "I think we've both hit our limit."

"I was just getting started."

Sade pursed her lips, but her eyes flickered with amusement. "Of course, you were."

The sounds of crumbling stones filled the air, followed by a loud crunch. An enormous shadow loomed over them, and Henry's heart nearly stopped.

A giant humanoid came into focus. It peered down at them with only its eyes visible under their cloak. They lowered their hood to reveal a face with dark grey skin and blue eyes.

It was a skessa.

Henry's vision warped as the creature knelt. Sade used her magic to throw a boulder the size of a small horse at the creature, but the skessa caught it with one hand and crushed it.

"That's a skessa, we need to leave now."

She ignored him and stared down the mortal in front of her. Her hands were clenched at her sides.

"Hello divine ones," the skessa said. Its voice reminded Henry of stones falling down a mountain. The mortal held up a hand and Henry's heart faltered. A fire rune had been carved onto the skessa's palm. The rune flared to life and a twisted smile crossed its face.

He tried to move, but darkness overtook him as his body finally succumbed to its injuries.

Chapter Seventeen

Fire streamed out of the skessa's hand and Sade threw herself over Henry's body. She braced herself for the smell of burning flesh and searing pain, but nothing happened.

A loud shriek pierced the air and Sade reached for Henry's axes. They were still covered in his blood. The sight sparked a faint surge of magic inside of her, but she quickly stamped it out. Her body and mind couldn't handle using it right now.

"Don't worry, I've taken care of the last of the spider-beetles," the skessa said and then gave her a soft smile, like it was trying to show it was friendly.

Sade studied the mortal that towered above her. With how Aiden and Henry had acted when they told her about the skessa, she'd expected a terrifying creature. Instead, she faced a giant mortal with grey skin, dark hair that shifted from pure black to a dark blue, and eyes that reminded her of sapphires. Granted, the skessa was enormous and made the largest trees around them look small. Despite the fact it looked like it could crush her in a heartbeat, Sade wasn't afraid of it.

It was a beautiful mortal. Not a monster at all.

You aren't scared of it because you're also a monster. A quiet voice mocked. She shoved it into the darkest corners of her mind and locked it away. She would deal with it later.

She quickly scrambled off Henry, but he didn't move. His eyes were closed and the only sign he was alive was the shallow rise and fall of his chest.

"Goddess, is the half-divine alive? Do I need to send for the healers?" The skessa asked while she checked to see if Henry was still bleeding.

Her body stilled as the skessa's words sank in.

"Why do you think I'm a goddess?" She tried to keep panic from overwhelming her senses. She'd broken enough rules today.

The skessa tilted her head, confusion swept across her face.

"It was foretold in a prophecy that a Goddess cloaked in peace would heal the darkness that plagued the mountain," the skessa said, then nodded toward the forest below them. "And the trees told me you were here."

"Oh," Sade choked out. She would have to have a conversation with the plants about keeping divine identities a secret.

Henry let out a shuddering breath and her gaze swept over his body, looking for any signs of bleeding.

This was her fault. If she hadn't succumbed to whatever was lurking within the cave, Henry wouldn't be teetering on the edge of life and death.

"He needs a skilled healer; I need to get back to the city, lift the curse, and awaken their healing Vestral," she said. She tried to keep the worry out of her voice, but her shaking hands betrayed her.

The skessa nodded. "As you wish, Goddess. I will see about your horses."

"You can call me Sade," she said.

"And I am Tanwen, Fire Priestess of the Cursed Ones," Tanwen paused, then smiled. "Though I suppose we'll have to change our name."

The skessa was soon out of sight and Sade fiddled with the remnants of her runes. She would have to get them replaced before they continued their journey. Or would she? She wouldn't need them in the Realm of Ruin.

She bit her lip. Henry's body looked more fragile with each breath he took.

The sounds of crumbling stone forced her out of her thoughts. Tanwen soon appeared, her face was grim.

"I'm afraid the monsters ate your horses," she bowed her head. "I'm sorry. If my fellow priestesses were with me, we could've stopped them."

A cold sweat dripped down Sade's back as she grabbed the burlap sack.

"How long would it take for us to get back?"

Henry let out a small groan and Tanwen winced. "With his injuries, maybe a week?"

"I don't have a week. An entire city is going to die and so is his friend." Sade covered her face with her hands as hot tears flowed down her face.

Was this punishment for something she'd done? Or was going to do? Nothing made sense.

"Is there a way you can contact the other divine ones?" Tanwen asked.

"I can't. I've used too much magic for my mortal form."

Tanwen let out a low rumble that sounded like a bunch of rocks falling.

"I shall carry you both. It will only take me one night to reach the city."

"Are you sure? Henry told me about the problems between you and the humans."

Tanwen chuckled and eyed Henry with a knowing look.

"I had hoped one who was raised by a divine one and carried their blood would've seen past such nonsense. He's nothing like his mother was," the skessa shook her head like she was shaking off a memory. "But that is in the past."

The skessa held out a hand and Sade's eyes widened at the size. Her hand could fit at least five full-grown men on it. She gently placed Sade on her shoulder. It was hard and did indeed feel like stone.

Tanwen cradled Henry in one of her hands, shielding him from the wind.

Sade fought to keep the contents of her breakfast in her stomach. If she ever came back to this realm, she'd make sure her next mortal form didn't have this weakness. She focused on Henry, watching him for any signs of distress.

"His heart is stabilizing," Tanwen said.

"Good."

She closed her eyes when another wave of nausea swept

through her and didn't open them until Tanwen gently lowered her onto the ground.

"Are you well?" The mortal asked when she ran over to the nearest bush and dry heaved.

"I'm fine," she said once she was sure she wasn't going to vomit. She rushed over to Henry when Tanwen set him down. She peeked at the wound in his stomach and sighed with relief when she saw no blood seeping out.

"So how long have you two been bonded?" Tanwen asked and she sat down on a log, which turned into splinters almost instantly.

"Bonded? We're not bonded. That's a process that requires an oath and mingling of energies, and both parties have to consent…" she trailed off. She and Henry had woven their magic together frequently, but they had taken no oaths and they certainly hadn't agreed to any such nonsense.

The idea of being bonded to Henry wasn't a bad idea, but it would never work with them living in two different realms.

Tanwen held up a hand in a calming gesture. "Perhaps the word means something different to us mortals than to the divine ones. Forgive me, I didn't mean to offend you."

"You meant no harm. There is nothing to apologize for," Sade said. She quickly gathered the materials for a campfire. The mountain air was chilling her bones. Once the fire was blazing, Tanwen moved Henry close.

Sade watched Tanwen utter a petition to the God of Healing. A wave of shame crashed over her when no sign from the god appeared. Were her petitioners also at the temples, hoping for sign? She hadn't thought about her petitioners in days.

"What's wrong? Have I offended you by petitioning another god in your presence?" Tanwen asked when Sade flopped into her bedroll.

"No, I haven't been keeping up with one of my sacred duties."

"I understand. My people had to uphold a duty for a long time and I fear we were not always vigilant."

"You said you were a Fire Priestess of the Cursed Ones. Why were you cursed?"

Tanwen rubbed her chin. The sound of stone scraping against stone set Sade's teeth on edge.

"Because we foolishly sided with the humans. Have you ever heard of the Kesillan Empire?" she asked, and when Sade shook her head, she continued. "They wanted to become gods, and my ancestors decided it was a fantastic idea. So, they sent an envoy with the most powerful priestesses and warriors. They assembled at this very mountain, drawn by the power of the rifts inside of it. At first, they were scared the divine ones would descend upon them and wipe them all out. But the destruction never came, and the preparations continued."

"It took the humans and my people almost a month to prepare for the ceremony that took place. It was then the divine ones enacted their wrath. The human empire was destroyed, and spirits were assigned to the new kingdoms that arose from the ashes. They were to keep the peace and ensure the humans would never dare such a thing again."

"However, my people suffered a different fate. Those who had stayed on our home continent were spared of any punishments. The ones who traveled to help the humans were shackled to the mountain and ordered to keep all mortals away from it. We would only be free when it was healed."

Sade let out a slow breath. There. It was more proof the magic in the mountain wasn't hers. She was the Goddess of Peace, not the pure destruction she'd felt in the stones.

The relief was short lived as her anger toward the other gods grew. Who were they to decide who became immortal? The divine well that fueled their powers was never-ending and wouldn't run out if a few mortals joined in.

And whose idea was it to have the skessa guard a rift caused by unknown source? The longer she was in this realm, the more she could see the flaws of the divine ego and the pain it caused the mortals. There had to be a better way for them to interact with their creations.

"I'm sorry about your people."

Tanwen shrugged. "There must be consequences for our actions. Now that you've healed the rifts, we can return *home*."

Home. A word she would never understand. Sure, she had a temple, but she never chose to live there, and she certainly hadn't chosen to go live in the Realm of Ruin.

She shook off her thoughts when Tanwen let out a soft sigh.

"Tell me about your home," she said.

Tanwen nodded and began describing her homeland. A place with floating cities and rivers so clear they were like glass. Sade's eyes drifted close, and it wasn't long before she was fast asleep.

She awoke in a river of blood.

A strange whining noise pierced the air and a crowd of shadowy specters pressed around her.

"What happened? Where am I?" Sade struggled to stand, but the blood had turned into ice.

"Wake up goddess," one of the figures held up a flaming sword and plunged it into her heart.

A scream escaped her lips and the scene faded. Tanwen's face loomed over her, her fire rune crackled to life in her hand.

"You're awake," the mortal said with a tinge of anger in her voice. She sat back on her heels.

"I am?" she asked as she took in her surroundings. A weak ray of sunlight filtered through the trees. Birds flew above them and filled the forest with their songs.

No, this wasn't a dream. She was truly awake.

She smiled at Tanwen. The mortal didn't return the gesture, instead her eyes radiated fury.

"Who are you?" she rasped.

Sade rubbed the sleep from her eyes.

"I'm the Goddess of Peace," she said and inched her way over to Henry's sleeping form.

"No, what I saw in the nightmare was something far darker than that," A small fireball formed on Tanwen's palm.

Sade reached for her rune pouch, pausing when she remembered only her divine rune remained. She tried to summon her magic, but it stayed dormant.

"It might've been the figure with the fire sword," the words rushed out of her. She couldn't think of anything else to say.

Tanwen closed her palm, and the fire was quickly snuffed

out. The rage didn't leave her face, but it didn't seem to be directed at her.

"You've seen this…thing?"

"Yes."

"That figure has haunted the nightmares of my people for centuries and has led many of them to their deaths."

"What is it?"

"We don't know. I thought it was tied to the mountain and would disappear once the rift was healed. However, since you're having dreams about it, then perhaps it's still around."

Sade clasped her hands together when they started to shake. Whatever the thing was, it needed to be contained. It had caused far too much damage to not only Henry's family, but also the poor skessa.

Was it ever going to end? Was peace something that was only meant to be dreamt about?

"Hopefully it's drawn to my divine presence like the scaragnos and shadow creatures were. If any of your people has a nightmare, or if they are being led to their death, I want them to petition me. I will do whatever I can to help," she said.

Tanwen dropped to her knees and bowed her head.

"Thank you."

Sade smiled, but the mortal didn't move. A trickle of water splashing onto stone was the only indication she was alive. It took her a few heartbeats to realize that Tanwen was crying.

She walked over to her and gently patted the side of her massive knee.

If only I had my magic, I could at least comfort her. She'd hoped the display of devotion would stir the magic within her.

Not enough to cause problems within her mortal shell of course, but just enough to soothe Tanwen. But no sparks danced around her.

"I'm sorry, it's been a long time since a divine one has given us a blessing," Tanwen said.

"I swear your people will always have my blessing," she said and gave the best smile she could manage. This time Tanwen returned the gesture.

"Thank you, now let us hurry down the mountain to get your friend and the humans healed."

They reached the edge of the forest a few hours before sunset. Tanwen helped Sade create a makeshift sled, made from thick branches, for her to pull Henry on.

From a distance, the city looked peaceful, and a few smoke trails told her people were still alive.

"May the God of Healing aid you in your quest," Tanwen said as she gently placed Henry on the branches.

"And may your people have a safe journey home."

Tanwen gave her a sweeping bow and then headed into the forest. She waited until she could no longer hear falling stones then trudged out of the forest.

By the time she was at the city gates, she was covered in sweat. Someone on the wall gave a shout and the gates opened. Clelia rushed out with two stable hands.

"Gods above, you're alive! We feared you perished when the mountain blew," Clelia said.

"The magical rift in the mountain exploded," Sade said, hoping Clelia wouldn't press her too much on the matter. She was too tired to lie.

"Did he get cursed?" Clelia asked as she gently poked Henry's arm. The stable hands took over the sled and started toward the temple.

"No, but we need to get him healed."

"Did you get those flowers? We've lost another ten."

Sade handed her the burlap sack.

"Let's get the potion made."

The smell in the kitchen was one of death and made both women gag.

"Are you sure this is going to heal them?" Clelia asked. She'd covered her mouth with a ragged cloth.

"The book said the flower was the only way."

"Well thank the gods they are all asleep. If they were awake, no one would take it."

Sade peered into the bubbling cauldron. The putrid liquid was a mixture of crimson and brown. Clelia clapped her hands and around a dozen people entered, bowls in hand. Once they were full, they made their way to the grand ball room.

The scene hadn't changed much aside from the mortals who'd turned to stone in her absence. She hurried over to the mortal Clelia indicated was the next one slated to turn to stone.

It was a young boy. He looked so fragile that Sade was afraid she was going to break him as she tilted his head back and carefully poured a bit of the potion into his mouth. Clelia helped her angle the boy so he wouldn't choke on the potion.

Sade watched with bated breath as the child's skin went from a bright green to a deep russet brown. The veins in his arms were still that horrible lime green color. She gave him another dose of the potion and his veins returned to normal.

"Gods above, I think it worked," Clelia whispered and they gently laid him back onto the ground.

"I think so, though the book didn't mention how long it would take."

She rose and Clelia hurried from the room, shouting for more helpers. The mood in the mortals around her had shifted considerably. Hope hung in the air like a thick fog. She smiled and hurried over to the next afflicted human.

Sade trudged into the temple; night had fallen over the city and, with it, exhaustion fell over her like a heavy blanket. Clelia had forced her out of the palace to check on Henry and get some rest.

Henry was on a bedroll in front of the statue for the God of Healing. The stable hands had removed his torn tunic and wrapped his torso in bandages. No pink light emanated from the runes carved into the stone above him. He wasn't healing.

"God of Healing, hear my plea," she whispered as she brushed a hand over Henry's forehead. His skin was hotter than a fire rune. He shuddered and mumbled something she didn't understand. "Please heal him."

The statue above her stared down with its unblinking eyes. No sparks flew out of the stone. The temple was as silent as a tomb.

Was the strange magic from the creatures still lurking around somewhere? Or was this a punishment for some unknown misstep?

Sade reached deep within and tried to gather her magic, but it remained just out of reach. She still needed to heal, and she needed to sleep.

She watched the waning bonfire in the center of the temple and pulled her knees to her chest. Sleep wasn't something she really wanted. She didn't want to dream about the things she saw in the cave.

For once she missed the dreamless nights she had in her old temple, and, for a moment, she understood why the other divines stayed out of the Mortal Realms. Dreams were a terrible thing.

Henry let out a long sigh and she was next to him in an instant. Her eyes roamed his body.

"I'm sorry, I don't know how to help you," she whispered. The only thing she could do was hold his hand and hope the Vestrals would wake up soon.

A whisper of electricity brushed against her skin and her gaze snapped up to the statue, but no light burst out from it. A small orange spark floated past her and brushed against Henry.

She squeezed his hand and the sparks traveled up her arm, sending tingles down her spine.

"Gods, why do I feel like I drank too much wine?"

Sade let out a small gasp as Henry squinted at the ceiling.

"Henry?"

Henry jerked upright. He winced and held his side as he looked around; his eyes were full of panic. His frantic gaze fell upon her, and relief swept over his features.

Sade suppressed the urge to hug him. Instead, she gave his hand a gentle squeeze.

"You're alive," he said, then fell back onto his bedroll with a groan. Sade gingerly checked the bandage. No blood seeped out.

"Don't move, you're still wounded," she said.

"What happened to the skessa?"

She shook her head and gently pressed on his shoulder when he tried to rise again.

"I'll tell you once you've seen the healer. He should be awake soon."

Henry rose again. This time he was fast enough that Sade couldn't stop him. Sade bit back a curse when he waved away her attempts to get him to lie back down.

"What about the people? What about Aiden?"

She pushed back a burst of panic that threatened to overtake her. She'd forgotten to check on him in her rush to make sure Henry was still breathing.

"Clelia and the others are finishing giving everyone the cure."

Henry's eyes brightened into a color of green she didn't know existed.

"You did it," he whispered.

"No, *we* did it."

Her words fell flat on Henry as he looked at her with a mixture of awe and gratitude. His aura wove into hers, lulling her frazzled nerves and drawing her closer to him.

She rested her head on his shoulder when he pulled her close. Her eyes drifted close, and the familiar scent of sandalwood and amber drifted over her.

"Thank you for getting me off the mountain," Henry said when they pulled apart. His eyes were still that brilliant green that made her wonder how he hadn't formed a bond with anyone.

"You would've done the same. Now you should get some rest," she said and rose to her feet. Before she could take a step, her legs gave out from underneath her. She twisted so she didn't fall onto Henry. Instead, she fell face-first onto the stone altar. Stars danced in her vision as a wave of pain overtook her.

"Sade, are you all right?" Henry reached for her, but he let out a groan and fell back onto the bedroll.

Her mouth filled with a metallic taste, and she spat out blood. She gingerly pressed a hand to her lips and found a shallow cut.

"I'm fine, I just need to heal," she said and used the altar to carefully lower herself down onto the stone floor.

Henry shifted so he only took up half the bedroll and patted the space beside him.

"What are you doing?"

"You can't sleep on that floor. The cold will steal the warmth from your bones," he said and nodded toward the dwindling fire. "Unless you think you have enough energy to rekindle that?"

She didn't. So, she laid next to him. The heat from his body lulled her senses and she had to fight the urge to sleep. She started to count the scars on his chest and arms. Most were small and could only be seen if she squinted.

"Sade, I promise I'm not going to burst into flames," Henry said as he looked at her through half lidded eyes.

"Oh, no, it's not that. I was just wondering where you got the scars from."

"Well, you'll have to be specific. I've got a lot."

She traced a silver scar that snaked its way up from his elbow all the way up to his shoulder. Henry's body shivered lightly at her touch.

"That was a gift from the first monster I ever fought," Henry said his voice was strained.

Her fingers brushed another scar on his collarbone.

"Tavern fight."

She couldn't stop herself from tracing the scars that dotted the muscles on his chest.

"That was from a cat," he said, and she looked up at him. A mixture of amusement and desire flared in his eyes.

"A cat?"

"When I was sixteen, I was sweet on a girl who had this cat that got stuck high up on a rock. She begged me to rescue it and I foolishly agreed. Damn thing clawed me up so bad, my mother had to take me to a healer."

Sade couldn't help the laugh that escaped her. The powerful half-god she'd come to know had been easily defeated by such a small animal.

"I'm sorry," she said as her laughter faded, and she wiped a few tears from her eyes.

When he didn't respond, her gaze snapped to his face. He was staring at her with an expression that made a wave of electricity sweep across her skin.

She couldn't hold back a yawn, and the intensity in his gaze softened.

"Would you look at us? Two divines who are supposed to be the epitome of power and we look like we can barely fight our way out of a tavern," Henry said with a grin, and he draped part of his blanket over her. He didn't seem concerned about their proximity at all. Something inside of him had changed. The storm clouds that haunted his aura had been lifted.

"It's a good thing the other divines can't see us right now. Can you imagine the gossip?"

"We'd be the scandal of the century," Henry's voice rose in pitch. "My dearest goddess, did you hear about the two divines who became so weak they could barely walk?"

"I heard they took a nap in front of the God of Healing's statue in the hopes he would heal them," Sade said with an equally high pitch.

Silence passed between them for a moment before they both burst into laughter.

Sade wiped the tears from her eyes and Henry's laughter faded. He had fallen asleep. A faint flicker of his magic stirred around her, lulling her senses like he was trying to get her to join him. But the thought of having to endure another nightmare was enough to keep her eyes open.

Instead, she watched the light from the dying fire dance across Henry's sleeping form. His strong features were marred by the expression of pain etched in his face. It was a sight that sent a wave of guilt through her. This was her fault. If she'd been strong enough to not lose it at the cave, he'd be fine.

"I promise you, this won't happen again," she whispered and lightly brushed his arm. Henry mumbled something in his sleep.

You can't protect him. The dark voice said from a place she couldn't reach.

Who are you?

Her only answer was a burst of laughter that sent chills down her spine.

Chapter Eighteen

Henry glared at his summoning rune. He'd been trying all morning to get in touch with the other gods, but they were still silent.

"Do you feel anything?" Sade asked. No runes danced around her; the goddess hadn't been able to replace hers, so she was keeping watch for any Vestrals. The summoning rune wasn't something the humans used. It was one of several runes the Goddess of Runes kept hidden from mortals. If they were caught with it, there would be severe consequences, but they had to take the risk. They needed to know if the God of Death would be there to fetch the souls of the dead.

If he wasn't, they risked having a wraith outbreak, and none of them were in any shape to deal with that.

"Nothing." He glanced at Aiden, who shook his head. He let out a sigh and shoved the rune into his pouch.

"Can we get that skessa friend of yours to try?"

Sade had told them all about the skessa who'd helped get her down the mountain. Henry couldn't believe none of the other divines had told him about the curse and let him believe they were nothing more than monsters.

"She is probably halfway to the sea by now," Sade said and peeked out the window. "We've got company."

Aiden shoved his rune into his pouch while Sade pretended to be deeply engrossed in a scroll. Henry merely leaned back in his chair and tried to ignore the throbbing in his side.

A few moments later, Clelia stepped through the threshold.

"I've been looking everywhere for you three. Are you ready to attend the ceremony?" She gave Sade and Aiden a pointed look.

"Yes, we are," Henry said as he struggled to stand.

Clelia pressed her lips together. "You should stay here."

"I want to pay my respects to the dead," Henry said and used the back of the chair to steady himself. Sade and Aiden were by his side in an instant.

"We'll keep an eye on him," Sade said brightly. Clelia muttered something under her breath as they walked out into the street. The crowd was dressed in varying tones of black and white.

Henry slowly walked behind the enormous crowd as they made a solemn procession to the temple. He had to lean against a pillar once they walked under the building.

"Go get some rest, Aiden and I can attend," Sade whispered as the Vestral to the God of Death flung open the temple doors. A horn sounded from somewhere in the crowd and they parted to allow the humans carrying the stone bodies through.

"I want to make sure their souls are ferried through," he said. He glimpsed a soul hovering just above one of the stone bodies. It needed to get to the afterlife before they became a wraith or ended up stuck in an eternal loop.

"I haven't been able to get in contact with the other gods. I fear the dead may not be able to leave."

"Great, so our chances of them becoming wraiths grow with each passing second," Aiden grumbled and moved beside them. There was no trace of the poison left on his skin.

"How do we know if they will become wraiths or not?" Sade asked as they followed the crowd into the temple.

Henry shrugged and immediately regretted it as another flash of pain swept through him.

"We don't, that's something the God of Death keeps very tight lipped about," he said through gritted teeth and ignored the disapproving stare from a healing Vestral. They followed the crowd down into the crypts. Combination runes meant to keep out water glittered in the torch light.

"I hate going into these things," Aiden muttered under his breath. "I keep thinking a draugr is going to jump out at me and tear out my insides."

Sade's eyes widened. "A what?"

Henry glared at Aiden and softened his expression when he looked back at Sade.

"It's an undead creature and they are only created if they aren't buried properly. Most crypts are fine."

Aiden muttered something under his breath while Sade eyed an elaborate tomb. A wisp of blue smoke danced and wrapped around her. There was no trace of the goddess he'd seen in the cave. Her energy now was a strange mixture of her peaceful side and the reckless sparks of destruction. Had the two sides merged in the cave?

He caught her eye and saw a flash of determination in them before it shifted back into fear. Her magic stilled and he could barely sense it.

She can control it. Henry diverted his gaze to the humans in front of him. He couldn't keep the sheer awe from rising within him. The goddess beside him had held the fabric of the world with her hands and she let it go.

The other divines claimed she was so dangerous that she had to be locked away or forced to be reborn if she stepped out of line. They were wrong.

The goddess he'd come to know wasn't someone that treated her duties lightly. Even with her missing memories, he doubted her core self would change that much.

And why was it that only the Sacred Council knew about her past? If Sade had destroyed a realm with no remorse, wouldn't they make sure most divines knew about her punishment? They'd done it with his mother and father.

Sade brushed her fingers across a protection rune carved into the wall before they headed deeper into the crypt. The movement sent a slight wave of sparks over him and another memory from the cave rose from the murky depths of his mind.

Even in the throes of destruction, she still tried to keep him safe. A goddess bent on pure mayhem wouldn't have done that, and he would've perished alongside the monsters.

Knots formed in the pit of his stomach.

What if she had been trying to protect a realm from something, and, in the process, accidentally destroyed it?

He felt the faintest flare of his divine purpose. He reached for it, but the magic slipped away from him like it was afraid it had even activated.

"Henry? Do you need to go back?" Sade lightly tapped his shoulder. He glanced at her as the crowd disappeared around a bend.

"I'm fine. Sorry, I was thinking," he said. A slight frown crossed her face, but she didn't press him further.

They entered an enormous cavern that looked more like a large underground arena.

Aiden let out a low whistle. "I was wondering where they were going to put everyone."

They hastily found an empty bench and waited for the ceremony to begin. The people carrying the stone bodies halted in the center of the arena and a Vestral to the God of Death walked around them with their divine rune.

"Oh, God of Death, we beg of you to ferry the souls to the afterlife," the Vestral said.

Henry tensed as the soul floated above its body. Thankfully, none of the mortals could see it. If they did, they'd likely panic at its wraith-like appearance.

An icy wind blew up from the ground and it sucked the soul into an invisible whirlwind and vanished.

He breathed a sigh of relief; the God of Death had heard them. His relief quickly turned to concern. If the other gods could hear them, then why hadn't they answered the summons earlier?

"This is ridiculous. I was just fine at the funeral," Henry muttered. He was sitting on a stone bench tucked under a large window. A crowd of humans were scattered throughout the grand ballroom.

"I don't care. You're lucky I'm even allowing you to be here. Now drink the damn thing." A Vestral loomed over him and shoved a silver goblet into his hands. The Vestral was a good head taller than Henry and the scars on his face told him he wasn't a stranger to a fight.

Henry quickly swallowed the bitter liquid and handed the goblet back to him.

"Remember to just sit and watch," the Vestral said before he spun on his heel and disappeared into the crowd.

"You look like we're still attending the funeral," Aiden said. He slid next to Henry and handed him a tankard of ale.

"I just drank a potion that tasted like death." Henry took a long drink; the ale wasn't quite strong enough to wash away the lingering taste of the potion.

"Well, at least Sade looks like she's enjoying herself," Aiden said with a nod.

A small group of human males surrounded the goddess, one of whom was gesturing wildly as they told a story. Henry caught her eye as she took a sip from her goblet. The goddess flashed him a smile before she turned her attention back to the human.

The human cast Henry a sidelong glance as he leaned closer to Sade and whispered something in her ear. She flushed a bright red. A flash of jealousy surged through him as the human raised her hand to his lips and kissed it.

He pushed back against that feeling. Sade was a goddess, and it was only natural that the mortals be drawn to her. And her presence was practically irresistible tonight.

She radiated pure joy, something not even the most cold-hearted mortal could resist being near.

He took another drink of the ale as guilt swelled within him. Enough was enough. Once they were out of Pavento, he was going to tell her.

Oh finally. It only took you having a near death experience to stop being so damn stubborn. Maybe we should have those more often. His divine purpose crowed within him.

"Shut up," he muttered under his breath.

"I didn't say anything?" Aiden briefly rested a hand on his forehead. "Are you okay?"

"I'm fine." He tilted his tankard to find it empty.

"I'll get you another," Aiden said and hurried away.

Henry closed his eyes and rested his head against the window. He wanted nothing more than to curl up in a bed and sleep. He hadn't felt like this since he'd been forced to become a god.

Someone blew a trumpet. The sound jolted him out of his thoughts, and he opened his eyes to see a man and a woman enter the ballroom.

The man was dressed in a light purple tunic, embroidered with thousands of Starlight Violets embellished with tiny diamonds. The woman at his side was wearing a flowing dress made from lilac colored silk. It, too, was embroidered with the Starlight Violets, though hers shimmered with light.

"Presenting their Graces, the Duke and Duchess of Pavento," a herald shouted, and the humans curtseyed.

"Do not let our presence damper your festivities," the duke shouted and held up a goblet then threw it onto the ground. "Tonight, we dance and honor the gracious God of Magic for curing us!"

Henry bristled at their words, but it wasn't something that surprised him. Vestrals were seen as nothing more than vessels for the gods and didn't deserve any praise. And they didn't need to draw any more attention to themselves.

The crowd cheered as the two nobles drifted over to some fancy chairs a servant had prepared for them.

"Tis a right shame. They thank the gods, but not the humans who did all the work," Clelia said as she emerged from the crowd.

Henry had to bite back a smile at her words. Instead, he gave a nonchalant shrug of his shoulder. A sharp pain jabbed at his side and he couldn't stop the gasp that escaped him. Clelia's face became clouded with worry.

"It's fine," he said through gritted teeth.

"Why are you here? You should be in bed," Clelia scolded when he let out another groan. She moved aside as Sade rushed over to him, concern etched in her features.

"Should I call for the healing Vestral?" she asked as her eyes scanned his body.

"No, I just moved too quickly," he said. Sade studied him for a long moment.

"You'll tell me if you feel any worse?" she asked and she gently pressed a hand on his forehead.

"I promise."

She gave him a soft smile. Her hand drifted down to his cheek where it lingered for half a heartbeat before she went back into the crowd. Henry's skin burned where she had touched it. His blood heated, and he stared at the chandeliers above him. He started counting the crystals to keep himself contained.

Gods, I really need to visit a brothel.

"Your face is redder than your hair," Clelia howled once Sade was out of earshot. "You really spent days alone with her and you're still at square one?"

"Clelia, stop trying to pair us together. It's not going to happen and there is nothing going on between us."

Clelia's gaze swept over the crowd of mortals that swirled around the room. Someone started plucking at a lyre. The God of Music would've wept tears of agony at the sound.

"Ah, it seems our dear bard was one of those who turned to stone." Clelia winced, and then her sharp eyes were back on him. "You need to tell her how you feel."

"There is nothing I need to tell her."

Disappointment crossed Clelia's features.

"Take it from me, boy. If you don't act soon, you will lose her."

Henry's jaw clenched. Thankfully, Aiden arrived holding two overflowing tankards, and Clelia gave him a nod before she left.

"What took you so long?" Henry grumbled and snatched a tankard from him.

"What, no thanks? Do you know how hard I had to fight to get the ale?" Aiden sat next to him in a huff.

Henry didn't answer as he took a drink. The human playing the lyre finally figured out how to play a simple folk song, and the mortals started dancing. A few mortals had grabbed Sade and pulled her into a dancing circle. He couldn't help but smile at the genuine delight that crossed her face.

Perhaps this party wasn't so bad.

As the night went on, the music got worse, and Henry was running out of ale. He glanced out the window. Night had fallen hours ago.

He winced when the mortal hit yet another unpleasant note, but the humans were too drunk to notice. As the music traveled through the air, the dancing mortals slowed down. Another note and they slowed further.

Henry glanced down at his tankard. The ripples in the liquid barely moved. He looked back at the dancers, and they were all frozen in place.

This was bad. Divine magic was flooding the ballroom in a way he hadn't seen since his parents were carted off to the afterlife.

"Sade! Aiden!" He called out. Aiden was first to emerge from the crowd, concern was etched into his face. Sade was right behind him.

"What is going on?" Sade asked.

"We're in trouble," Henry said as he struggled to stand.

"Big trouble," Aiden added.

"Shouldn't we be preparing to fight?"

Airi shimmered into existence, along with another

messenger spirit. Henry's heart dropped as their forms shifted. The God of Knowledge appeared first, his face marred by a cold fury, and then the Goddess of Fate also appeared. Her face, however, was filled with relief.

"I told you they were fine," she said as the God of Knowledge's glaring gaze swept over them. Henry then noticed the god's normally long hair was cropped short. It looked like something had bitten it off.

"You've been missing for almost two months!" the god exclaimed.

Henry shared a glance with Sade as Aiden's jaw dropped. "Missing?"

"We thought you were dead, but the God of Death couldn't find your souls. Do you realize how close we came to war over this?" the god spat.

"I don't understand. How did we go missing?"

"You were stuck in a time bubble. For whatever reason, this area has been moving slower than the rest of the realm," the Goddess of Fates said, and she bowed her head. "Forgive me, I didn't see it."

The God of Knowledge gave her a slight look of disdain before he leveled his gaze at Henry.

"And would you care to explain why the rift in the mountain is gone?"

Sade moved, so she was standing in front of him. She held her head high, but her hands trembled as she clasped them behind her back.

"I fixed it and I freed the skessa who were bound to the mountain."

For the first time in his existence, Henry watched the God of Knowledge fumble for words.

"That's wonderful news," the Goddess of Fate said with a genuine smile.

"No, it's not. You didn't have the authorization to do any sort of mass healing ritual," the God of Knowledge said.

"I'm a goddess, and last I checked, the Sacred Council was only meant to offer guidance. Not rule us with an iron fist."

The god looked over her shoulder at Henry.

"You are a bad influence."

Henry couldn't stop the grin that swept across his face. A blast of air hit him in the gut and sent him flying into the wall.

He rolled on the ground, gasping for air as Sade and Aiden rushed over to him. Blood seeped into his tunic and dripped onto the floor.

Aiden pulled out a healing rune while Sade stared at the wound in his side. When her eyes met his, there was a faint glimmer of crimson and gold in them. He shook his head ever so slightly.

"You are in no position to mock me, Henry," the god said.

"Leave him alone," Sade whipped around sending sparks of gold toward him.

The god held up a hand and the wave of light dissipated.

"Enough!" The Goddess of Fates stormed between them. She glared at the God of Knowledge. "We came here to check on them and now we must inform the God of Ruin that the treaty still stands."

The god's jaw twitched; his eyes were so dark that his pupils weren't visible.

"You are lucky we need you for the treaty, goddess," he said, and his gaze flickered to the dagger on Henry's belt.

Bastard. Did he want to force Sade to be reborn just because she stood up to him? Had the entire thing about keeping everyone safe been a lie?

"And if I wasn't?" Sade asked coolly. Her challenge hung in the air and Henry wondered if he was going to tell her the truth.

The God of Knowledge cracked his neck as he hovered closer to Sade.

"You've crossed a line, goddess. You used magic that could've destroyed this realm, and you've violated multiple rules on healing magical rifts."

"No, Tanwen told me a peace goddess was supposed to come down and free them."

The God of Knowledge cast a sidelong glance at the Goddess of Fates.

"Is this true?"

"I don't remember giving a prophecy to the skessa, but I do keep a record of every prophecy I've given. I'll have my subordinates check my records," the goddess said.

"Fine, but prophecy or no, you did break the rules and revealed yourself to a mortal. For that, you must be punished. I will have the God of Ruin take away your plants."

"Don't do this," the Goddess of Fates blurted out as she grabbed the god's arm. "We need to leave now."

In a flash, the goddess's form rippled and the messenger spirit she was using to channel through vanished from sight.

Sade tensed like she was about to attack, and Henry rested a hand on her shoulder.

"Don't do it, he's not worth it," he whispered. Tears formed in her eyes, but she kept her hands clenched at her side.

"That's a tad extreme, don't you think?" Henry asked the god who narrowed his eyes.

"I wasn't asking for your opinion on this matter."

"You can't do this. You can't take away the one thing that brings me happiness," Sade said. Despite her tears and rage, her power remained locked in her.

"Happiness is something for the mortals. You must rise above these emotions and embrace your duty. Don't make me come down here again, or the consequences will be much more severe."

In a flash of light, he was gone. Sade trudged over to a bench and collapsed onto it. The world around them unfroze, and the party resumed with the mortals blissfully unaware of what had taken place.

"I'll go get some ale," Aiden said after he helped Henry over to the bench. He quickly disappeared into the crowd, leaving Henry with Sade who was watching the dancers. The joy that emanated from her was gone. Her eyes searched the crowd, but they were unfocused.

Henry wanted nothing more than to storm back into the Divine Realm and throw the God of Knowledge into a pit. Was he trying to make Sade fall apart? She didn't need this.

Sade sniffled and wiped away a couple tears. Henry pushed back his anger and focused on the goddess beside him. He let the emotions in the crowd sweep into his body. Then, once he was completely saturated with them, he reached for her hand and let his aura weave into hers.

Sade's eyes widened. He braced himself for her to cut off their connection, but she didn't. Instead, she scooted closer to him and rested her head on his shoulder.

"Thank you," she whispered.

He gently squeezed her hand, and they watched the dancers twirl around the ballroom.

"Are you sure you can't stay longer? We have an opening for a Vestral to the God of Magic," Clelia said. Henry tightened the straps on his saddlebags. Sade and Aiden were preparing their own horses.

"No, we still have that bounty we need to collect on," Henry said, and Clelia frowned.

"You're still going to go after the skessa? In your state?" She shook her head. "You young folk get crazier with each passing year."

Henry reached into his gold pouch and handed her some coins. She tried to give it back to him.

"Thank you for helping us save the city. We wouldn't have been able to do this without you," he said.

"I know," Clelia said with a smile and pocketed the gold. Sade walked over. It was like a rain cloud had settled over her, but she gave Clelia a warm smile.

"Thank you, Clelia. We'll miss you terribly," she said.

"Oh, come on now. You must promise me that you'll come and visit sometime?"

Henry cleared his throat when the light in Sade's eyes died.

"Of course, we'll come and visit," he said and glanced at

Sade. "I think it's time we head out."

Sade nodded and practically ran over to her horse. Clelia started to leave but halted in her steps.

"Don't forget to tell her," she said.

"I won't," he flashed her a grin before he dug his heels into his horse's side and the animal took off at a gallop.

The landscape rushed by as they headed toward the mountain pass. He needed to tell Sade about her past before she entered the Realm of Ruin. He just needed to gain the courage to do it.

Chapter Nineteen

They made it through the mountain pass with no incidents. No monsters haunted them in the shadows and they had no surprise visits from the God of Knowledge.

As they descended the mountain, the landscape changed drastically. The towering trees were replaced by ones that were bent and twisted in all sorts of directions. The natural magic of the realm was barely a whisper here.

"What's wrong with the land?"

"Ah, the Eastern Marshes are where the great Kesillan Empire did most of their experiments. They ruined the land with their arrogance," Henry said with a quiet anger.

"Most of the people live on the far east side of the marsh. The land there is more stable," Aiden added as they passed the remains of a town. Ghosts flittered about like they were still living; unaware they were stuck in an eternal loop.

Her heart broke at the sight, but there was nothing she could do. Death wasn't her domain, and she didn't want to know what the God of Death would do if she tried to free the ghosts.

"Right, so we've got what? One day left?" Henry asked once they were past the ruins.

"I think so, unless the rune you're using is wrong," Aiden said with a strange look in his eyes. "Oh, are you thinking what I'm thinking?"

Sade tried to listen in on their thoughts via their mortal side, but both men had cut her out.

"Marsh rabbit," they said, and Sade could practically hear their mouths water.

"What's so special about this rabbit?" she asked.

"Imagine a meat so tender it makes you want to cry," Aiden said with a wistfulness in his voice. He glanced at Henry. "You sir are in no shape to go hunting."

Henry bristled and sat up straighter in his saddle.

"I'm doing just fine, thank you. It's just a bruise at this point."

Sade shared a concerned glance with Aiden.

"Henry, maybe you should let Aiden go and you can help me prepare camp," she said.

They started having one of those silent conversations again, leaving her to admire the scenery.

"Fine, Aiden can hunt, but I get to be the one to cook it," Henry said after a while. Something in his voice was off, but he flashed her a grin when she looked over at him.

It wasn't long 'til they found a dry patch of land and Aiden hurried off into the marshland, claiming he'd be back before sunset. Sade worked with Henry to set up camp. Now that they had no monsters chasing them, they could set up the tents.

Henry was unusually quiet; he didn't make any jokes about camping in the mud or even talk about the weather. He went about his duties with a solemness she'd never seen before.

"Do you need sometime alone?"

Henry looked up from the rope he was tying around a tent stake. He blinked as his eyes refocused. It was like he'd forgotten she was there.

"Sorry, I was just thinking about tomorrow."

She couldn't suppress the shudder that swept through her. By this time tomorrow, she would be in a completely different realm.

"I've been trying not to think about it," she whispered.

Henry's expression softened. "I'm sorry, I should've kept my mouth shut."

"No, it's fine." She looked around the small camp they'd created. "Believe it or not, I'm going to miss this place."

Henry grinned at her, causing her heart to race at the sight.

"The crazy magic and near-death experiences didn't turn you off?"

"No, I think it added to it, and the company hasn't been so bad either," she said, then smiled back.

"Hold on, I'll be right back." Henry's eyes sparkled as he dropped his rope and hurried over to his horse. He pulled something out of his saddlebag, then glanced back at her.

"Close your eyes and hold out your hands," he said.

She squeezed them shut, and it wasn't long before Henry pressed something into her hands.

"You can open them now."

He'd given her a small wooden bowl that glittered with glowing silver life runes. They were carved all along the outside and had a cloth covered the top of the bowl. She pulled it off to reveal a small Starlight Violet.

"How? I thought they were done for the year."

"I grabbed one while you were sleeping in the meadow. I wasn't sure if it survived the attack in the cave, but somehow it did. Now you'll have a plant with you in the Realm of Ruin."

She bit her lip and watched the light from the runes ripple across the petals. Her eyes watered when she looked at Henry. He was watching her with an unreadable expression.

"Thank you," she said and pulled him into a hug, taking care to not drop the bowl.

"You're welcome," he whispered. She closed her eyes and rested her head on his shoulder. That peace she'd experienced back at the meadow once again swept through her.

Would she ever feel this again? The Realm of Ruin was likely to be a harsh place and full of many terrifying creatures. Her arms tightened around him as tears welled up in her eyes.

"Sade, what's wrong?" Henry leaned back; his eyes were bright with concern.

"I don't want to go," she said, as more tears continued to fall. Henry didn't say anything. He brushed the tears from her face and a soothing wave drifted out from him.

"I don't want you to go either." He said it so quietly she thought she'd imagined it, but, with the way his body stiffened, she knew she wasn't just hearing things, and she likely wasn't supposed to hear what he said.

Neither of them said a word as they stared at each other.

Henry's eyes had darkened into a shimmering forest green.

Sparks hovered between them, a mixture of orange, blue, and gold. She shivered as it raced along her skin. Henry tightened his grip on her waist and pulled her closer till their bodies were pressing so tightly she wasn't sure where she ended and he began.

Her heart raced as she tried to piece together her thoughts. Her gaze traveled down his face, memorizing every inch of it till she came to his lips.

"Sade," Henry breathed out. Their faces had gotten so close. The warmth of his breath on her skin sent shivers down her spine.

She could hear the question in her name. If she stepped away now, they could both move on and let the fire that danced between them die.

That would be the safe choice, and the one she knew would cause them the least amount of pain. But the way he was looking at her, like she was the most important person in all of creation, had her giving him the slightest of nods.

Henry froze like he was battling something deep within himself, but whatever it was lost as he leaned down and kissed her. The touch of his lips on hers sent shockwaves through her body.

Their auras wove together, and she felt like she was floating. The dark thoughts that had been following her since the cave were pushed away and replaced with bliss.

She never wanted to leave here. The treaty be damned.

Fire raced through her veins as her lungs burned. She'd forgotten to keep breathing. Reluctantly, she pulled away and Henry rested his forehead against hers. His eyes still had that burning fire within them.

Before she could kiss him again, the tree beside them exploded.

Henry shoved her behind him and took the brunt of the blast. A shielding rune hovered above his pouch and the splinters fell harmlessly around them. Henry muttered something under his breath and summoned his runes. She peeked past his shoulder and saw Aiden staring at them like he'd just witnessed a murder.

Her magic told her there were no monsters nearby.

"It's just Aiden," she said to Henry. His body stiffened.

"What in the hell is going on?" Aiden's face was now filled with fury.

"I can explain," Henry said as he faced Aiden, letting his runes drift back into his pouch.

"Hypocrite," Aiden snapped.

"Aiden what—" her words died on her tongue when Aiden's fist smashed into Henry's jaw, sending him flying into the debris of the tree. She tried to summon her magic, but it refused to cooperate.

"You fucking lied to me!" Aiden shouted as Henry hopped to his feet.

"Aiden—" Henry started, but Aiden kept going.

"You told me to go hunt so you could tell her about her destructive side! And I come back to find out you've gone behind my back and started courting her! How could you? You knew I fancied her!"

Henry's reply was lost to her as Aiden's words danced in her thoughts. Her magic boiled inside of her as the visions she'd seen in the cave flooded her memories.

"What do you mean my destructive side?"

The fury in Aiden's face morphed into horror as his skin turned bone white. Henry's eyes were full of nothing but guilt, and he dropped his gaze when her eyes met his.

Knots formed in her stomach as they had one of those telepathic conversations. She didn't have the energy to understand what they were saying. She wasn't sure if she wanted to know.

"There's something I need to tell you," Henry said.

She closed her eyes and took a breath, steadying herself for whatever was coming next.

"What?"

"Before I took you through the portal, the Sacred Council summoned me. They told me this isn't your first incarnation, but it was the first one where you didn't remember anything. So, they locked you up in that temple to keep you from remembering things."

Something cold and dark stirred deep within her, breaking through chains that had been wrapped around her soul. She pulled her magic toward her, but it shrank back into the strange darkness that threatened to overtake her.

The visions she saw in the cave flashed through her mind and she struggled to focus on Henry's words. Once her mind had stabilized enough, she returned her attention to him.

"What do they not want me to remember?"

"That you're not just the Goddess of Peace. You're also the Goddess of Destruction and you—"

She couldn't stop the hysterical laughter that burst out of

her, and Henry fell silent. The sound washed away the darkness that gripped her heart. Henry's expression remained solemn.

"Peace and destruction cannot exist in one person. The two sides would drive them mad and then break them apart," she said once the laughter had died down.

"Sade, I know this is hard to believe—"

"It's literally impossible!"

Henry unsheathed the dagger he kept at his side and let it float in front of him. The blue crystal embedded in the copper pommel glowed as it moved closer.

She stumbled back as an invisible hand wrapped around her heart. Fear coursed through her as she stared at the dagger. A hazy vision arose in her mind and transformed the world into a place she didn't recognize. She tried to move, but glimmering chains held her body in place.

"This is all your fault," a voice hissed. Three hazy figures loomed over her. The dagger hovered above her chest and, no matter how hard she tried, she couldn't escape.

"Do you have any idea what you've done?" Another voice, this one sounded familiar.

"Let me go!" She strained against the chains that held her.

The dagger plunged into her heart and the haze around the three figures lifted to reveal the God of Knowledge, the God of Magic, and the Goddess of Fates. They were all looking at her like she was the scum of creation.

Pain spread through her body as her heart failed and in the blink of an eye, she was back in the marsh. Her body had collapsed in a heap. One hand gripped her tunic right above her heart and the other was still clinging to the bowl.

"I'm sorry," Henry knelt beside her. The dagger nowhere in sight. Aiden was a few feet away, watching them with his arms crossed.

She lurched forward as another spasm of pain swept through her. Henry wrapped an arm around her waist and pulled her close to him. His presence flooded through hers and let her fractured mind settle for a moment.

"What did I do?" She asked when she pulled away.

"You destroyed a realm."

She blinked. Once, twice. It was the only thing she could do as a cold numbness swept through her, snuffing out any trace of power inside of her.

The pain in her heart increased, but she couldn't make a sound. Millions of voices screamed in her head, some begging for mercy, and others cursing her name.

Monster. A voice called out from the abyss within her.

Countless mortals had suffered and died because of her. An entire realm was gone, and she could barely remember it. The voice was right. She wasn't a goddess. She was a monster.

"Sade, can you hear me?" Henry asked as he gently wiped the tears from her face. His magic once again wove itself through her, pushing aside the storm that threatened to overtake her. Tears threatened to fall as she gripped his tunic like a lifeline. Slowly, the screams of the mortals who'd perished faded, and in its place was a hollow pit.

It was her magic at the cave, she was sure of it. She'd done something there eons ago and her actions were still harming people today. It was her fault his parents had ended up in the afterlife. She was the cause of all his suffering, and she couldn't even tell him why it happened.

"Don't." She jumped to her feet.

"Sade, you need to stop and take a breath. I know this is a lot to take in."

"Stop looking at me like I'm worth saving. I'm the reason the rift in the mountain was created. I am nothing more than a monster."

She stared down at the Starlight Violet, watching the light weave through the petals.

"Sade, you're not a monster. You're a goddess."

Her grip tightened on the wood bowl. She kept her gaze firmly on the flower in front of her. This wouldn't do. Despite Henry's beliefs, her memories told a different story. She wasn't the bringer of peace; she was the bringer of death.

She looked at him. His eyes were shining with strength and hope. She wanted to believe him, wanted to believe she was a goddess worth being followed. But she wasn't. Her peaceful side hadn't been able to stop her from obliterating an entire realm.

Henry deserved someone who wasn't going to make his life worse. She needed him to see it.

She steeled herself, hardening her heart for what she was going to do next.

"Aiden is right, you are a hypocrite."

Henry blinked. "What?"

"You waltz around this realm, pretending like you are attending to your duties, but you're just really pretending you're still human. If you really were the God of Justice and Mercy, you would've told me about this the moment my feet hit the soil. You let me believe a lie and you walk around with a weapon that's caused me nothing but pain and suffering."

The light in Henry's eyes died. She hated herself for it, but she had no choice. He needed to understand she was nothing more than a monster and to stay away.

"You're no better than the divines you claim to hate. You're just like them."

Henry bowed his head. His hands trembled at his sides.

"Hold on—" Aiden started, but his words died on his lips when she glared at him.

"That goes for you as well," she snapped. "And for the record, I would never choose you to be my bond mate."

Aiden's eyes flashed; his mouth formed a thin line as she brushed past Henry.

"I did it to save my parents and give them a chance at life again. It was the only reason I took them up on the offer," Henry whispered. His voice was hoarse, and it almost made her stop.

But she didn't stop walking. She couldn't stop.

The cold numbness inside of her wavered as she headed out of the camp. She needed to get out of here before her façade broke. She didn't stop until her legs burned and her breath became ragged. After what felt like hours later, she collapsed onto a half sunken log. Her fingers dug into the bark as she stared at the clouds.

You should be angry with him. You should show them the full might of your powers instead of cowering in the marshes. A voice called from the abyss.

How could she be angry at him? He was trying to save his loved ones from a fate they didn't deserve.

No, she was mad at the other gods. The ones who would

use such a connection and force someone to carry out the work they didn't want to do. Henry was a mere pawn in their game.

She peered at the water, waiting to see if her eyes would change color, but they remained a deep brown. No magic glowed within them.

Who was she? Was she truly a dual goddess? It wasn't unheard of, but usually the aspects complimented each other. Destruction and peace were not things that lived in harmony. They would always fight for dominance within her.

How could her peaceful side let her destroy a realm? Wouldn't that have broken her as well? Shouldn't she be a soulless husk drifting away in the afterlife? How was it fair to the countless mortals she'd killed that she got to live another life?

All she ever got were more questions. She needed answers now more than ever.

"Will someone please come down here and tell me what's going on? I know someone is watching!" she shouted at the sky, hoping someone would appear in front of her.

Anger coursed through her. They couldn't do it; they couldn't come here and tell her about her past. Did they prefer to just stab her whenever they got the chance? Was it easier to have her restart over and over again rather than trying to actually fix her?

Something broke inside of her and crimson sparks raced across her fingertips. It was a mere echo of the power she experienced at the cave.

A burst of blue and gold rushed out of her, stifling the crimson as it tried to weave its way into the fabric of the world. Why couldn't it have done that at the cave? Why was that side of her so damn weak?

She squeezed her eyes shut as she reached for her divine rune. Her hand gripped the cool stone as she fought the darkness within her.

No, she would not let it win. Not here.

Monster. That cruel voice in the back of her mind cackled with glee. A wave of power tried to push itself out of her.

She pushed back as hard as she could, shoving the glittering sparks back into the darkness.

A flash of silver caught her eye, and she braced herself for the presence of another divine. Instead, she was met with the steely eyes of a grey hawk as it flew in lazy circles above her.

"Cowards. You aren't worthy of being called gods!"

Her words were lost to the wind as it picked up. She stared at the divine rune in her hands. The broken sword, once a shining symbol of peace, was now tainted by the truth of who she really was. It was also a symbol of destruction.

She squeezed the divine rune with all of her strength, letting the magic in the rune flow into her hands and back into the stone. Blue light flecked with gold danced around her. It didn't take long for fractures to form in the stone, and, with a loud crack, the rune shattered.

Blood dripped down her arm as she stared at the shards, now coated in crimson. She dropped the remnants of the rune into the water.

She didn't deserve any of it. She should've been thrown into the deepest pit at the edge of time and left to rot.

A monster is all you are and is all you ever will be. That strange voice from the abyss called out to her. She didn't fight it.

She couldn't.

She curled up into a ball as the visions of the cave flooded her thoughts while letting her own fade into the background.

Chapter Twenty

Henry adjusted his cloak as a cool gust of wind swept its way through the marshes. A dense fog was rolling in, the sight of which dampened his mood further. Sade hadn't said one word since she trudged back into camp the night before. She merely stared straight ahead, her eyes unfocused.

Guilt ripped through him. He'd spent the entire time worrying that she was going to destroy the world. Instead, she was destroying herself. Her presence had faded to the point he couldn't sense it, and her rune pouch was gone.

He caught Aiden's eye; he gave Henry a look that made him want to crawl under a rock.

Hypocrite. Aiden sent into his mind. It was the only thing he'd said to Henry over the past day.

It was just a kiss.

Hypocritical bastard.

Great, now he had two words he was going to be tortured with for the rest of eternity. This is, if Aiden chose to travel with him after this. Henry let out a sigh and cut off their connection. He'd lost his friend and Sade because of a kiss. A kiss that a part of him didn't regret.

This entire thing was a mess, and he didn't know how to fix it. He was sure Aiden would come around eventually, but Sade…

He grabbed his map and almost tore it in half as he opened it. His seeking rune floated out of his pouch. They'd reach the portal by sundown.

He started to put his map away, but his rune fell to the ground instead of going back into his pouch. Muttering under his breath he hopped off his horse. He reached for the rune at the same time a surge of magic flooded his veins and sent him flying face first into the mud.

His divine purpose strained within him. It wanted nothing more than to keep Sade in this realm, but that was impossible.

He locked it out of his mind and wiped the mud from his face. He grabbed the rune and shoved it into his pouch as muffled laughter drifted over him.

He looked to Sade first, but the goddess was doing her best impression of a statue and staring at the horizon. Aiden was the one who had a hand clamped over his mouth. He shot him a glare and waited for him to stop laughing.

"I think it's time for us to give the horses a break and I need to clean up."

He tied his horse to a scraggly tree and stalked off into marshes. The sounds of Aiden's laughter rose with each step he took.

Once he found a reasonably clear puddle of water, he paused when he caught sight of his reflection. He was completely covered in mud. No wonder Aiden hadn't been able to control himself, he looked like a swamp creature.

Grabbing a water rune, he quickly cleaned himself off. His hand brushed against the dagger at his side. He froze.

He'd packed the damn thing away once Sade knew about it. How did it get back onto his belt? No wonder Sade wasn't looking at him.

"I had Airi move it, to remind you of the duty you failed," the God of Knowledge's voice broke through his thoughts.

Henry's head snapped up; the god was hovering a few feet away. His face was covered in scratches, an odd sight. Normally divines in their true form never showed signs of injury. What in the hell was going on in the Divine Realm? Had someone finally stood up to the Sacred Council?

"You look like shit; did you lose a bet?"

The god bristled and with the snap of a finger the scratches were gone.

"My appearance is none of your concern," the god clasped his hands behind his back. "You failed to keep this realm safe."

Henry snorted and gestured to the marshes around him. "How? Sade is going to be in the God of Ruin's halls tonight and your precious little treaty will be intact."

"While the dagger was being put back onto your belt, it showed Airi your little adventure in the cave. How you ignored its warnings and decided to take matters into your own hands."

Henry's mouth went dry. Had the dagger been enchanted to keep track of everything he did? It didn't matter. He wasn't going to back down. Even if Sade hated him, he would not let this bastard ruin her life anymore. He drew his shoulders back and gathered what little magic he could to calm his nerves.

"She didn't destroy the realm when we were in the cave, and she didn't destroy it when she found out this isn't her first existence. Why are you so afraid of her?"

The world stilled as rage crossed the god's face, and Henry could've sworn he saw a tiny amount of fear.

"What do you mean she found out?" The god hissed.

"I told her."

Silence hung between them, like creation itself was waiting to see what the God of Knowledge was going to do next. Instead of rage, the god looked at him with an icy calm. Henry stared right back at him; orange sparks slithered on his skin.

"You are lucky my bond mate won't allow me to throw your parents back into the afterlife. You've put every single realm in danger with your actions."

"Sade isn't dangerous."

"How many times do I have to say it? She destroyed a realm!"

"You've never told me why. Yes, she is powerful and destructive, but she's not just the Goddess of Destruction. She's also the Goddess of Peace, and believe me I've also seen that side of hers at work!"

The God of Knowledge stared at him for a long moment and Henry wondered if the god was going to disappear. Instead, defeat crossed his face.

"I don't know why she destroyed the realm."

Chills ran down his spine and he couldn't keep his jaw from dropping open.

The god who was supposed to know everything didn't know why Sade had destroyed a realm, and he punished her anyways? He'd used the dagger on her countless times and let her live most of this existence alone.

Gods above, I'm living in a mad world. Nothing makes sense anymore. The sheer arrogance of the god in front of him was mind boggling. It was enough to make him wonder if he should switch sides.

"How in the hell is that possible?" he asked once the shock wore down.

"I might have known at one point, but it seems I've forgotten."

Henry clenched his fists at his sides. Electricity boiled just under his skin begging him to unleash it on the god.

"Sade has suffered because of you, and you don't even remember why!"

"If it was important, then I would've remembered. I am knowledge itself, and if it isn't something that I need to know, I forget it."

Henry couldn't stop the crackling wave that arced out of him. The god let out a sigh as he let it wash over him and pushed it into the ground.

"How dare you! You've been keeping her locked up and lying to her for what? Because you're scared? You don't even know what to be scared of. For all we know, Sade could've been fighting to keep us safe from something and destroying the realm was the only thing she could do!"

He wished the goddess had given him more details about her visions, but she'd kept them to herself. Now he could only speculate, and he doubted she'd be giving more details about her experience.

The god arced an eyebrow. "It doesn't matter if I remember the real reason or not, she violated our most sacred rule. Surely as the God of Justice and Mercy, you can understand. I am enacting proper justice for the souls she killed."

"It's not justice if you don't remember why she destroyed the realm. How can we be certain she was the one who did it? If you can't remember, that means your memories have been tampered with."

He let out a bitter laugh. "I never thought you would be coming to her defense. The god who shirks his duties is now trying to protect the goddess who destroyed a realm."

"She doesn't need my protection. She's perfectly capable of taking care of herself. Thanks to you, Sade thinks she's a monster," Henry spat.

"Your faith in her would be amusing if this situation wasn't so dire." The god glanced back at something Henry couldn't see. "I'm afraid my time here has come to an end. Once you've delivered Sade to the portal, Airi will come to collect the dagger and she will inform you on the status of your parents' souls."

The god vanished, leaving Airi in his wake. Henry headed back to the others but paused mid-stride when he noticed the spirit hadn't left.

"What is it?" he asked.

"The Goddess of Fates has asked me to give you a message," she said then continued when Henry gave her a nod. "Do not give back the dagger. Make sure you destroy it once Sade is out of the realm."

Henry eyed the dagger; he could've sworn the damn thing shrunk into its sheath.

"Why now?"

"Because it can only be destroyed in a Mortal Realm and we are running out of time," Airi's form wavered. "I'm sorry, I don't have any more information."

In a gust of wind, her form dissipated, leaving him alone. He trudged back to the horses. He shoved the dagger into a saddlebag and the tension in Sade's shoulders lessened ever so slightly. But the goddess still had that half dead look to her.

Damn that god, and damn himself for not noticing the dagger. Knots formed in his stomach. How was she going to fare in the Realm of Ruin? Would it corrupt her and eat away till there was nothing left?

"You missed a few spots," Aiden said as Henry mounted his horse. He ignored him and a heavy silence fell over the group.

He glanced at the shadows, hoping a monster would jump out and give them something to do except ride in that awful quiet.

But nothing jumped out, and Henry was left to deal with his tumultuous thoughts.

Don't let her go. The wind whispered. Henry tightened the grip on the reins 'til his knuckles were white. His divine purpose had been hounding him for hours, and it had only gotten worse the closer they got to the portal.

His magic waned, and it was taking an enormous amount of effort to use his seeking rune. He didn't dare ask Aiden; he didn't want to give him more fuel to use against him.

Yet the closer they got, the more he wanted to turn and run. Sade needed more time away from the politics and the conniving immortals that surely dwelled in the Realm of Ruin. It wasn't fair that she had to walk into such a place with a gaping wound in her soul.

He grabbed his seeking rune and frowned at the stone when it didn't light up. Closing his eyes he reached for the small flame within him, but it slipped from his grasp.

He gritted his teeth; his divine purpose was acting like a child. Sade had to go, there was no other option. Why couldn't his divine self understand this?

Hypocrite.

Without his magic, he couldn't keep Aiden's thoughts from intruding into his.

The longer the word bounced around in his skull, the more he started to wonder. He'd thought Aiden's feelings were merely the result of Sade's influence on the mortal world, but he was wrong. Aiden still had a torch for her and couldn't blame his friend for being upset at finding him and Sade. He'd broken his trust.

Hypocrite.

But what he could blame was himself. He wasn't going to deny he was attracted to her. His dreams had certainty taken an interesting turn the past few weeks, but that's all it was. Physical attraction.

It wasn't like he was going to try and bond himself to her.

The muddy road eventually dried, and he could hear the faint hum of a portal. They were getting close.

He motioned for the others to dismount. Horses and other animals didn't like being near the portals.

Henry watched Sade out of the corner of his eye. Her cool exterior had given way to apprehension. Her hands trembled as she pulled something out of her saddlebag. Henry stifled a gasp when he saw the bowl that carried the violet in her hands.

She hadn't gotten rid of it like he thought she had. Did this mean she didn't hate him? The goddess gripped the bowl as she turned her attention to Henry.

Her eyes still had the lifeless haze, but there was a slight glimmer of determination in them.

"I'm ready," she said.

Henry tried to speak. The words would not come out as a heavy weight had settled over his mouth. His divine purpose sprang to life and Henry once again struggled to regain control of his body.

Please just stop, let me speak to her. He pleaded with his divine half. The weight on his tongue lessened and he took a breath. Sade was staring at him.

"Are you okay?" she asked and there was a tinge of concern in her tone.

"I'm fine," he said and gave her a small smile.

These were her last moments of freedom. He wasn't going to make it about him. He would deal with his divine purpose later. Even if she hated him for all of eternity, he wanted to make sure she was going to be okay.

Sade didn't look convinced, but she didn't press him further.

His gaze dropped down to the violet she was holding.

"Are we all going to stand here until the sun sets?" Aiden said as he stood beside Sade. Shock crossed his features when he noticed the violet, but it was quickly replaced by indifference.

Henry nodded toward an area with thick underbrush.

"I think the portal is in there," he said. Aiden and Sade looked at him like he'd grown three heads.

"What do you mean you think, what are you hiding Henry?" Aiden snapped.

"Nothing, the map just wasn't clear."

Green smoke arced out of Aiden and penetrated Henry's skin. Aiden let out a gasp.

"Gods above, your magic is gone!"

Sade looked at him with alarm. Her cold exterior had vanished.

"No need to be so dramatic, remember I'm still recovering so my body can't handle my magic and the portal's at the same time."

He shot Aiden a glare, willing him to stop talking, but Aiden wasn't inside his head.

"How long has this been going on for?"

"Just today, I swear."

Aiden snorted. "Forgive me if I don't believe you." He turned to Sade with a glum expression. "How can we believe him? When he's done nothing but lie?"

Sade didn't spare him a glance as she stormed into the thicket. Henry hurried after her, and Aiden was right behind him.

He almost slammed into Sade when she suddenly stopped.

He looked over her shoulder and saw the portal on the other side of a muddy clearing. It was like the ones in the Divine Realm, but its stones were cracked and looked like they were going to fall apart at any moment.

Three immortals in tattered cloaks stood near the shimmering portal. They would've passed for humans if it weren't for the fact that the lower half of them were a writhing mass of snakelike shadows. The sight was not as strange as the magic that wove around them. It resembled oil and had a putrid smell. Henry's mortal side recoiled at the sight. He didn't want to know what that energy felt like.

"That is the most disgusting thing I've ever seen or smelled," Sade said. Her voice was so quiet, Henry thought he might've imagined it.

"Yeah, it feels like something is rotting, but also not?" Aiden's brow furrowed. "This is the strangest magic I've ever seen."

The trio moved closer, the sagging skin on their faces swayed with their movements. It looked like it was ready to fall off at any moment. Henry swallowed the bile that rose in his throat at the sight of their rotting flesh.

"Ah, we've been waiting for you," one of the immortals rasped.

Before he could stop himself, Henry stepped in front of Sade and tried to quell his rising nausea.

Was this the fate that awaited Sade? Would she slowly rot from the inside out and turn into…whatever those things were? Was this why his divine purpose didn't want her to go? Was this rotten magic going to harm her?

"Can you give us a moment? I need to do a cleansing ritual

before Sade leaves the realm."

"Cleansing ritual? The God of Knowledge didn't inform us of such a thing."

"Ah, that's because he doesn't come here in a mortal form. We went into a very hazardous part of the realm where a special magic attached to her skin. If it's not cleansed from her mortal form, it could break apart the portal, and you'll all die horrible deaths."

The immortal frowned then waved a hand as they moved back to the portal.

"You have five minutes."

He spun on his heel to find Sade and Aiden staring at him.

"What cleansing ritual?" Aiden asked, Henry ignored him and focused on Sade.

"Do you want to go?"

"If I don't go then the realms will plunge into war. I've already caused enough damage. I cannot bear to be the cause of more suffering," Sade whispered.

"But it's not fair to you," Henry said, and Sade's eyes watered. He reached out to her, but she backed away as she wiped away a few tears. That hollow look swept back over her features.

He couldn't do this. That realm was going to destroy her.

"I should've told you about your past the moment you stepped foot in this realm. I'm sorry, I was…I am a coward and don't deserve my godhood. But I cannot stand here and watch you sacrifice yourself for a bunch of divines who don't care about you."

"I'm not doing this for them."

"Sade—"

With a flick of her wrist, she pulled out a sound rune from his pouch and silenced him.

"Thank you for getting me to this point. I will do my best to get the God of Ruin to stop sending the monsters." Her voice was colder than ice and each word hit him like an arrow.

A weight settled in his heart as Sade walked toward the portal. Every fiber of his being screamed at him to stop her, but he stood rooted in place.

No. This was her choice. He would not take her free will away. He wasn't going to be like the others and keep her on a leash. Even after all this, Sade still wanted to complete her duty. She still wanted to bring peace to all the realms. Who was he to deny her that?

She was better than him. He'd spent most of his life avoiding his duties to the mortals who worshipped him. He'd been running from his destiny while Sade faced hers head on.

"I'm going to destroy the dagger!" The words left his mouth before he was fully aware of what he was doing. Aiden let out a startled gasp behind him, but he didn't take his eyes off Sade.

She whirled around, but before she could say anything her escort shoved her through the portal. And with a gust of wind, it was gone.

For a moment, the only thing he could hear was his own breathing. A terrible cracking noise filled his ears and something tore itself away from his soul.

The weight in his heart had become unbearable and he wanted to rip it out of his chest. He'd felt something like this before, when his parents had been forced to stay in the afterlife. But this was different. His magic was being sucked out of him.

Without it, he couldn't talk to her through the plants. He'd never get to hear about her life in the Realm of Ruin. He'd never hear her laugh or watch her eyes widen with wonder as she took in the world around her. He'd never get to kiss her again or hold her in his arms.

He was a hypocrite. His feelings for her were more than a passing fancy and now they had no chance to grow.

Another wave of searing pain had him dropping to his knees. Muddy water seeped through his clothes as he struggled to regain his composure.

His divine purpose materialized in front of him wielding a sword made of orange lightning. The figure said nothing. It just stared at him with icy rage.

Henry bowed his head.

"There was nothing I could do, she had to go," he whispered.

A cool soothing wave swept over him, and the vision of his divine side faded. Aiden knelt beside him and patted his shoulder.

"Don't do this right now," he snarled at him. But Aiden had no malice in his features. He looked at Henry with pity.

"I'm sorry."

"Oh, fuck off Aiden. I don't want to talk to you right now." He grabbed Aiden's arm and used him as leverage to stand.

"Listen—"

"No, I don't need to listen. I'm going to destroy this fucking dagger and then find the closest tavern. I'm going to get so drunk that this whole damn thing will feel like a fever dream."

Aiden held up a hand, but Henry flipped him off and stormed away, stopping ever so often to catch his breath as the invisible fire ravaged his body. He kept pushing through the marshes, ignoring the voices inside of his head that screamed he needed to get her out.

But there was nothing he could do. Sade was going to complete her destiny.

A destiny he couldn't be a part of.

Chapter Twenty-One

"I need to go back. Henry cannot destroy that dagger! It could kill him!" she pleaded with her escorts as they led her through the void. Unlike the precarious passageway from the Divine Realm, they were on a cobblestone road flanked by rivers of lava.

The immortal closest to her gave her a look so cold it chilled her bones, despite the heat from the flaming rivers.

"We cannot return. The portal has closed," it said.

A quick glance over her shoulder showed the stones that once held a glimmering pool of energy between them were now lit only by the lava. She tightened her grip on the bowl. If Henry's magic was still gone, he wouldn't hear her warning in time.

Silver light slithered on the violet's petals. A few drops of it landed on her skin, sending a cascade of soothing energy through her, but it didn't help wipe away the guilt and shame she carried.

"Excuse me, goddess, but we are on a tight schedule. Can you please keep moving?" Another immortal asked in a much nicer tone than its companion. This one's skin also wasn't as decrepit.

They hurried past a gurgling fountain of lava and into the crackling portal. As she emerged through the passage, every nerve in her body tingled, and it wasn't long before her insides felt like they were going to melt. A flash of light blinded her, and the pain reached a point it was almost unbearable.

When her vision returned, she found herself in a Temple of Portals. It was almost identical to the one in the Divine Realm, except for the small ribbons of oily smoke that wound its way through the wooden walls.

The portal behind her closed with a loud cracking noise. It was then she noticed her escort was gone. She tightened her grip on her bowl.

A hidden door opened, and a tall immortal stepped into the room. Their skin was covered in bark and tiny branches were growing out of their arms. It had no eyes or mouth to speak of. It was one of the temple's priests.

Hello goddess, we apologize, but it seems your escort vaporized on the way back. The priest said in her mind. The magic they were using was identical to the one the plants in the other realms used.

She cast a glance at the now dormant portal as goosebumps formed on her skin. That would explain the painful sensations she'd experienced moving through the portal.

"Wonderful. Who is going to show me around now?"

We haven't been given that information.

"Right, so I'll just wander around on my own."

The priest swayed from side to side.

Before you leave us, you must surrender your mortal form. It will not survive outside of the Temple of Portals.

Sade frowned and stared at her hands. She studied the minor scars and bruises she'd obtained over the past couple of months.

"I don't know how to. Do you have a tailor?"

Unfortunately, our tailor has gone missing after an ill-advised trip to the Raging Sea. It should be easy. Just connect your energy to ours and it should slide right off.

"Is there any other way?"

The priest once again made that strange swaying motion.

No. Please hurry. We have other duties to attend to.

With a heavy sigh, she connected to their magic and let it weave itself through her divine form. She closed her eyes as her skin warped and a terrible ripping noise filled the air.

Her heartbeat faded into the background and the ripping noise subsided. She took a few breaths, and her body was lighter. When she opened her eyes, she found the world to be even duller than before.

She held up her hands. Her skin had no blemishes. No reminders of the realm she'd come to love. She was back in her divine form, no longer bound by the confines of mortality. Electricity surged through her body. The familiar blue and gold was now marred with crimson. Thankfully, it faded and blended in with her skin.

Fantastic, now your human form will be stored in the unlikely event you will return to a Mortal Realm. The priest said as a door flew open and a heavily armed sentry entered. Its armor was the color of a night sky and had tiny rubies embedded in the metal. A large sword was strapped to its back, which thankfully remained sheathed.

"We have detected an unauthorized weapon."

Sade pulled her bowl close to her chest. "It's a flower!"

"I am referring to the sword strapped to your belt."

"Oh, the sword? The sword is a gift for the God of Ruin."

"A gift? Who told you to bring him a gift?" A cool voice drifted from the door. A tall woman moved into the room, stopping a few feet away from Sade. She wore a flowing sleeveless dress that had thousands of glittering diamonds embedded throughout. Swirls of smoke made it look like tiny clouds were inside the gems.

Sade instinctively reached for her rune pouch. Her hand clenched into a fist when she remembered she didn't have any runes.

The woman snapped her fingers and Sade's sword appeared in her hand. She unsheathed it and ran a hand down the edge of the blade.

"The God of War put you up to this, didn't he?" the woman asked. Her eyes never left the blade, but Sade detected a tinge of wistfulness in them.

"He said it would bring good tidings?"

The woman snorted and handed the sword to the sentry.

"If you had arrived on time, Casimir might have found it slightly amusing."

Sade bit the inside of her cheeks to keep herself from gasping at the sound of his name. She'd grown so used to using their titles in the Mortal Realm. It was another thing she'd have to adjust to.

She trailed off as she eyed the bowl in Sade's hands, and her eyes lit up with curiosity. "Oh, what's this?"

Sade shifted so the woman couldn't see the flower.

"This was a parting gift from...a friend."

She couldn't bring herself to say Henry's name out loud, and a part of her wanted to keep him safe from...whoever she was. For all she knew, this goddess was helping Casimir create the creatures.

"You...brought a flower into the Realm of Ruin?" The woman stared at her for a few moments before she burst into laughter. She patted Sade on the back and nodded at the sentry, who backed off. "Oh, you're going to be so much more fun than that sulking musician."

"Who are you?"

"Einar never mentioned me?" The woman frowned. "Wait, you're the one who was locked up in a temple from the moment she was created, right?"

Some of the tension left her body. If the divines here thought she was just the Goddess of Peace, then she had a fighting chance. She didn't want to know what would happen if they found out about her more sinister side. But it also meant she would have a hard time finding any answers to her past.

"Yes."

"I'm Levina. Goddess of Storms and Einar's sister."

She kept her shock to herself. The God of War had a family? It wasn't uncommon, but she'd never imagined he would have one. Then again there was a great deal she didn't know.

"I'm Sade."

Levina arced an eyebrow. "Sade? I thought your name was Saderna."

"Sade is the name I chose for the Mortal Realm, and I'd rather be called that."

The goddess didn't look very impressed.

"Remind me to never have you name anything for me." She glanced at the priest, who was swaying in place. "Right, enough small talk. Casimir will not be happy with me if I hold things up."

Sade followed her out of the temple. Unlike the one in the Divine Realm, this temple was in the middle of a raging river and a rickety looking bridge connected it to the city proper.

She had to bite the inside of her cheeks to keep from gasping in horror at the scene in front of her. The place was in complete shambles and looked more like a war-torn village than a city ruled by a god. The immortals they passed spoke softly and averted their gazes when she smiled at them.

"By all that is divine, what are you doing?" Levina hissed and grabbed her arm.

"Saying hello?"

"Not that, your magic!"

A mixture of blue, gold, and crimson were weaving a bubble around her, pushing back against the oily magic of the realm.

It was a strange sight for her to watch her magic create a protective bubble all on its own. She'd become so used to using runes, she'd almost forgotten what it was like to use her powers outside of the Mortal Realm. She tried to rein it in, but it wouldn't listen, and it spread out from her body. It swept across the stone buildings, and, for a brief second, everything looked vibrant and healthy. Then as quickly as it had appeared, the area returned to normal.

"What did you just do?" Levina growled. Her eyes were glowing a deep ruby and the light cast a bloody glow on her skin. Now she could see the resemblance to the God of War.

"I don't know!" Sade clenched her bowl as the goddess's magic tried to penetrate Sade's. After what felt like eons, the goddess threw her hands up in frustration and stormed up the palace steps.

The air became thicker, and if she'd been in her mortal form, she doubted she'd be able to move at all.

The palace itself was a sad copy of the one in the Divine Realm. No ornate runes were carved on the walls, and the windows were dusty and muted. The immortals who roamed the halls kept to the shadows, even their steps were muffled.

She could see why Zimri didn't want to stay here, but she was used to silence and found it somewhat comforting.

Levina paused at a pair of excessively large doors. A rune in the shape of an exploding sphere was carved into them.

"Are you ready?" she asked, and before Sade could reply, she flung the doors open.

The room was mostly empty, save for a table in the center. A tall, white-haired male was hunched over it. The sound of metal clattering against wood echoed across the room. The man straightened when Levina shut the door.

"The elusive Goddess of Peace finally graces me with her presence."

"Hello Casimir." Sade quickly hid the bowl behind her back

as the god faced her. His skin had a greenish tint to it, and it was littered with sores. His blue eyes were bloodshot, and a milky film spread over them as he moved closer.

"You are not as terrifying as I'd thought you'd be. I thought Vilmantas locked you up in the tower because he couldn't bear the sight of you," Casimir chuckled. He kept moving closer. Sade wanted to turn and run, but she couldn't let him sense her fear.

"I need to talk to you about your activities in the realm I passed through."

"Ah, there it is." Casimir grinned as he shared a knowing look with Levina. "Even though you were locked in a temple for twenty years, you're just like the other tributes we receive. All business and no fun."

Sade cast a glance around the mostly empty room. From what she'd seen of this realm so far, having any sort of fun looked to be the last thing on anyone's mind.

"This is important. Countless lives are at stake and people I care about have gotten hurt—"

In the blink of an eye, the god was behind her and the bowl was in his hands.

"Give that back! That was a gift!" Sade snarled as the god stared in wonder at the violet.

"A Starlight Violet? I thought Vilmantas wanted all of your plants destroyed…" The god's brow furrowed as he poked at the petals.

"He said the plants in my temple were going to be destroyed. This plant is from the Mortal Realm." Sade reached for the bowl, but the god kept it just out of her grasp.

"Why would you want to keep this? It's going to die at some

point, not even your life runes can make it immortal."

The flower wilted as a stream of oily smoke poured out of the god's hands.

"Stop it!" Magic flooded her veins as she yanked the bowl away. A stream of golden blue streamed from her fingertips, filling the life rune to the point of bursting, but her efforts were in vain. The flower was permanently damaged.

Casimir and Levina burst into laughter. Sade's entire body trembled as she struggled to keep herself from flinging a fireball at them.

"Oh, this is rich. I've never seen anyone, aside from the Goddess of the Harvest, get so attached to a plant," Casimir said as he regained his composure.

Sade pressed her lips together and kept her focus on the flower.

"I guess this is what happens when you lock a goddess in a temple. You get attached to all sorts of weird things," Levina snickered.

Anger flared within her. It begged her to show them the real reason she'd been locked up for so long. It would be so easy to just reach out and tear this crumbling realm apart.

She swallowed as horror and guilt swept away the dark thoughts. No, she was here to ensure peace between the realms continued for eternity. She would not let herself sink to that level of destruction ever again.

"I'm not here to be laughed at like a court jester," she said through gritted teeth. "I'm here to ensure the peace between realms continues and you are breaking that peace by sending the creatures."

Casimir rolled his eyes and clapped his hands. More tables appeared laden with food and drink. Thankfully it looked fresh and not half rotten.

"I will not be conducting any business today." He gestured to a table laden with what looked like boar meat. He grabbed a goblet of wine and handed it to her. "Take a moment and relax. I'm sure you are famished after your journey?"

The hairs on the back of her neck stood up as she caught a faint glimmer of oil inside the red liquid. If she drank it, would she succumb to the realm's influence? Would she become as lifeless as the other divines she'd seen?

It wasn't a risk she wanted to take, so she gently set the goblet down and gave him an apologetic smile.

"I'm afraid I don't like to eat or drink while I'm in my divine form."

A flicker of annoyance clouded Casimir's face before he gave her a tight smile. He clapped his hands; a swarm of immortals entered the room and practically pounced on the food.

"Then I'm afraid your audience with me ends for today," he said as he eyed the light that still snaked across her skin. She couldn't help but shiver at the darkness that clouded his eyes. "You can't keep that up forever, Saderna."

"My name," she snarled, "is Sade."

Casimir howled with laughter, causing the divines in the room to jump. A glare from Levina had them quickly resume shoving food down their throats. It was then Sade noticed most of them had tears in their eyes and their hands trembled like they were fighting to keep themselves from eating. Was the God of Ruin forcing them?

Crimson sparks arced out of her, pushing Casimir's magic out of the room and freeing the others from their invisible trap. The god stopped laughing as a stunned expression crossed his face. The immortals fled, and a few gave her some grateful looks when they passed.

"Oh, now you've done it," Levina said in a sing-song tone as Casimir's shock morphed into fury.

Sade ignored her and focused all her energy on the god in front of her.

"I don't give a damn about what you want to call yourself, but you just stepped over a line. I am the one who is in charge of this realm," Casimir snapped.

"I can't help it. I'm the Goddess of Peace and those people weren't at peace. If you don't like it, then don't do those kinds of things in front of me," Sade said and folded her arms across her chest.

Casimir's mouth formed a thin line and his body tensed. Sade braced herself for a blast of wind, but it never came. Levina walked over to him and wrapped an arm around his waist.

"Darling, don't look so upset. You have been complaining about how boring things are around here," Levina cooed as she stroked the god's cheek. "Remember when the God of Dancing arrived? It took him ages to settle down. This is nothing we haven't seen before."

Sade swallowed a wave of bile. Those two were bonded? No wonder Einar hadn't mentioned her.

Casimir's mouth quirked upwards. "Ah yes, I remember the spontaneous dancing was rather fun."

"Exactly! You'll just have to become more creative at

circumventing her powers until she settles in." Levina smiled and gave him a quick peck on his cheek.

"I suppose it could be fun…" The light that shone in Casimir's eyes dwindled when he met Sade's gaze. "I think I understand why Vilmantas had you locked up. Your presence is rather annoying."

Sade gave him the brightest smile she could muster. She could deal with him thinking her magic was annoying. It was better than him knowing she was also the Goddess of Destruction.

"That's right. I just cause nothing but peace and harmony wherever I go."

Casimir shuddered. "Levina, please escort our new guest to her temple. I've had enough of her 'peace and harmony' for the day."

"But—"

Smoke drifted over Casimir's skin and cast the god in shadows. "I said I am done for the day."

Levina grabbed her arm and pulled her out of the room before she could say anything. Sade yanked her arm away the moment they stepped in the hall; the door slammed shut behind them.

"You did well for your first meeting. Casimir can be… overwhelming," Levina said. Her voice broke through the almost sacred silence of the hall.

"Thank you," Sade said and looked down at her flower. The petals had continued to droop and one looked ready to fall off.

"I don't know why you're so attached to the damn flower, but the sooner you let go of any attachments to that realm, the better. This is your home now and the longer you resist, the more painful it will become," Levina said as she led her through an iron gate and into a courtyard that had a bridge on the end.

The bridge hovered over the river that she'd seen weaving throughout the city and under the temple of portals. At the end of it was a building that looked like it'd been scorched in a fire. Her heart dropped to her feet as she recognized the runes carved into the stone.

It was her temple.

She took off at a run. Levina shouted at her to stop, but she didn't listen, and it wasn't long before she was standing in front of the door. Or what was left of it. She grabbed the handle and the door opened with a groan.

Inside, the temple was worse. Every stone was covered in soot, and ashes floated into the air with each step she took. Everything inside the temple was destroyed. All her scrolls and the few trinkets she had were now piles of embers and ash.

Her body trembled with rage as she opened the door to her sacred pool.

This room had endured most of the destruction. The glass ceiling was gone. The plants she'd taken so long to cultivate and care for were either on fire or shriveled up. The walls were crumbling and looked like the smallest gust of wind would take them out.

The only thing that hadn't been destroyed was the pool and a letter that floated on the water. She frowned and set aside her bowl. A quick tug with her magic had the paper was in her hands almost instantly. Strangely, it wasn't wet at all. The words matched the ones in the previous letters she'd gotten.

Thought I'd redecorate the place. Now it truly is more fitting for the Goddess of Destruction.

The letter fell from her hands as she trembled with rage and guilt. Was the person who did this someone she'd wronged in the past?

Levina let out a low whistle when she stepped into the room.

"Wow, this *definitely* wasn't like this when it first showed up. Except for the plants of course, they arrived like that."

Sade gritted her teeth and fought to keep herself from throwing the goddess out of the room. She needed answers, and that would only cause more problems.

"Do you know who would've done this?"

"This realm is full of many nefarious immortals. Your time would be better spent repairing it and putting in some wards."

Sade scanned the walls. The runes that had kept her from leaving the temple were nowhere in sight.

For the first time in this existence, she wished the damn things were still there.

Levina cleared her throat.

"I'm sorry about your temple, but I have things to do. I can't stand here and watch you wallow in misery all day."

Sade nodded, and the goddess swept out of the room.

She waited until her footsteps faded and cleaned out one of the vases. Once she had removed the dead foliage, she refilled the life rune on the vase and planted the violet.

The flower swayed in the breeze that was now flowing through the temple.

It would be so easy for her to connect to the flower and

try to contact Henry, but the plant was barely clinging to life. It probably wouldn't survive if she tried to speak through it.

With a heavy sigh, she drew her knees up to her chest and stared at the clouds. She wiped away tears that fell. Her temple, what she once saw as nothing more than a prison, had been her only hope for a place of refuge in this godsforsaken realm. Now it was a solemn reminder of her past.

A past that was mired in the mists of time, and she had only begun to pierce the veil. However, if this mysterious note giver knew about her past, that meant others did too, and they wouldn't be as forgiving as Henry.

Her past was equally, if not more dangerous, than her destructive side. Because something was hunting her, and she had no idea when it would strike. She could only hope whatever it was would leave Henry out of it.

Chapter Twenty-Two

Henry squinted into his tankard, checking for any leftover ale. When he saw none, he motioned for the tavern maid to bring him more.

It had been three weeks since Sade had gone into the Realm of Ruin. He hadn't seen Aiden since he'd left the portal.

The dagger was still in one piece and his magic still wasn't responding. So, he had to resort to more mundane methods to destroy it. He'd tried smashing it with rocks, throwing it off cliffs, and hired a blacksmith to melt it down. The blacksmith almost died when his forge exploded, but the dagger escaped with zero damage.

It was yet another notch in his list of failures. He wouldn't have been surprised if the God of Knowledge took away his divinity based on his track record. Who would want to worship a god that wasn't strong enough to destroy a magical dagger?

He eyed the weapon in question, then he placed it on the table. At this point, if someone came and stole it, he wouldn't care. But no human noticed its presence. In fact, no one noticed him. It was like he was invisible. He was just another mortal enjoying their ale.

It would've been perfect, except for the gnawing guilt that continued to eat away at his insides. It differed from the guilt he carried about his parents. This was fueled by his divine purpose.

Look, we can't do this forever; can you please give me back my magic? Sade is gone and there is no point in throwing a fit. He focused on his divine side, but, where he once had no problem accessing that part of himself, he now faced a giant, impenetrable wall.

"Gods, I'm four hundred years old and a part of me still acts like a child," he mumbled as the tavern maid poured some more ale into his tankard.

"How much?" he asked as he eyed the large jug on her shoulders.

"If you want the jug, that'll be ten gold pieces," she said.

He grabbed a handful of gold from his pouch and let the coins clink onto the table. The woman's eyes widened in shock, but it wasn't long before she hastily pocketed the money.

"If there is anything else I can do for you, let me know," she said with a knowing glint in her eyes as they swept down his body. She gave him a wink before she went to check on her other patrons.

Henry studied her for a moment, then went back to drinking his ale. Not long ago, he would've jumped at her offer. She certainly wasn't an ugly mortal, and it would definitely help him release some tension. But he couldn't shake the image of Sade's face from his mind, and the remorse that welled up within him cooled his blood.

Perhaps he just needed some more time, then he'd be able to have some fun.

He was halfway through the jug when he noticed a few unsavory characters watching him from a table across the room. He tipped his tankard at them before he downed the ale in one gulp. His little show with the gold had likely drawn their attention.

Time to go. He thought and buckled the dagger back onto his belt. He tried to stand, but his vision warped, and he had to lean on the table for support.

He'd drunk a bit too much and, since his magic wasn't active, his body would feel the effects of the ale a lot more strongly than it normally would've.

"Hand it over," a low voice growled as the tip of a sword lightly pressed into his chest. Henry stared down at the metal and poked it.

"There are a lot of things in this room that could be handed over. I'm going to need you to be a *bit* more specific," Henry said and mustered the cheekiest grin he could. He locked eyes with the sword's owner, and his grin quickly faded.

The man was tall, taller than any human Henry had ever seen, and he looked like he could tear the doors off the tavern with ease. He eyed the men still sitting at the table. All of them were weaklings compared to the man in front of him.

Of course, it just had to be the most terrifying man in this damn tavern who decided to rob him. If he had his powers, his opponent would be easy to fight, but now that he had only his axes to defend him…

He regretted every damn word that came out of his mouth.

"Give me the gold," the man said, and pressed the sword harder into his chest.

"Can I give you half? I'll also throw in the jug. I can't just give you all my gold, I have to live."

"Then maybe you shouldn't be such a smart arse." The man's eyes narrowed, and Henry nodded.

"All right, fine. I'll give you the gold." In a fluid motion, Henry had his axes in hand, and he knocked the sword away. "But you'll have to fight me for it."

He took a step back. His vision warped, and he reached for a nearby chair, but the man was faster. He grabbed Henry by his collar and flung him at a nearby dice table. The six men who'd been playing stared at him with a mixture of shock and anger as the dice and their tankards fell off the table.

"What in the hell are you doing? We're trying to play a very important game here!" A dice player hissed.

Stars danced in his vision as he struggled to get off the table. His hands slipped on the small puddles of ale.

"Give me the damn gold!" the swordsman bellowed and swung his sword. Henry barely had time to move before the sword ended up embedded in a groove on the table.

"Oi! Did you steal from him?" One of the dice players asked.

"No, he's trying to steal from me!" Henry kicked at the swordsman's hand as he struggled to pull out his sword.

The dice players looked at him, and then back at the swordsman. Henry muttered a curse under his breath as they brandished various weapons.

"How much gold does he got?" One of the younger dice players asked.

"Enough to buy Jeni's services," the swordsman said as he inclined his head toward the tavern maid, who was quickly making herself scarce.

"Gentlemen, we don't need to come to blows," Henry said as he tried in vain to call up his runes. If he could get his charm rune to work, he'd be able to talk himself out of this.

Come on, I need you to stop pouting and give me my magic back! He shouted at his divine side, but the damn thing tightened the restrictions it had on his powers.

The men around him pounced onto the table and fell back with a groan as they all collided against each other. Henry rolled off the table. Someone grabbed his foot and he kicked hard; the sound of bones crunching filled the air followed by a string of curses.

The tavern erupted into pure chaos as other people joined in the fight. Henry ducked as someone lobbed a chair at him. He spotted the burly swordsman throwing a man into a wall.

"All this over some stupid coins," he mumbled to himself and sighed with relief when he spotted the door. He willed his legs to move, but he slipped on a puddle of ale as a bright burst of light erupted from the center of the room.

When it subsided, Henry found himself hovering above the ground. Orange sparks swept across his skin, but it wasn't coming from inside of him. The magic suddenly vanished and sent him crashing onto the floor. The bones in his nose cracked, and there was a brief flash of pain. He gingerly touched his nose.

It was crooked.

"What in the hell is going on here?" A shrill voice asked as Henry struggled to stand. A task that was almost impossible since his hands were slick with blood and ale, but he was able to use a chair to pull himself up.

He quickly took in the scene of the tavern as he pressed a cloth to his nose. An older woman in a bright orange cloak was glaring at everyone. Two silver triangles, one upright and one upside down, were embroidered on the right side of her cloak.

She was a Vestral for him. Wonderful. Out of all the gods this realm worshipped, one who worked for him just had to show up.

"A fight," the swordsman spoke up.

The Vestral sighed, and, from the weary look on her face, Henry could tell this was something she dealt with regularly.

"And what did I say about fights?" the Vestral asked the swordsman.

"That the next time you came in here, you'd banish the aggressor from the town," the swordsman said.

He started to make his way toward the door as the Vestral scanned the room.

"And who started it?"

All eyes in the room fell on Henry.

The Vestral stormed over to him as her eyes glowed orange.

"Hang on, I'm just passing through. There is no need to throw me out," he said.

"The God of Justice and Mercy would not look kindly on me if I didn't enact justice in this case."

Gods above, since when did his Vestrals act so high and

mighty? He certainly didn't care about tavern fights. No, what he cared about was his gold being stolen.

"Hang on, the fight was justified! They were going to rob me!"

The Vestral's eyes narrowed and with a flick of her wrist an air rune floated up out of her pouch.

"Rules are rules," she said, and a gust of air had him out the door and landing face first onto the cobblestone street.

He rolled onto his back, struggling to breathe as the Vestral loomed over him.

"You have until sunrise to sober up. If you are not gone by the time the rooster crows, I will not hesitate to lock you into the stocks for a week," she said before she turned on her heel and went back into the tavern.

When he got his magic back, he was going to have a very serious conversation with this Vestral. Where was her act of mercy? Leaving him to bleed on the street wasn't something he'd want them to do.

And this was yet another thing that was his fault. He hadn't taken his duties seriously enough and now his Vestrals were monitoring taverns like they were the most precious place in the realm. Then again, he had been drinking a lot the past few days. Maybe they picked up on that somehow?

"Correct. Even though you cannot access it, your divine side will still influence your Vestrals."

Henry's heart nearly stopped beating. It was a voice he hadn't heard in centuries. A low hum filled the air as two messenger spirits appeared. Their forms rippled and their appearance changed.

And for the first time in centuries, his parents stood before him.

He forgot how to breathe. He just stared at them. His father hadn't changed, though his red hair looked brighter, and his grey eyes were now filled with life instead of the soulless husks they'd been in the afterlife.

He was extremely surprised to see his mother hadn't changed her appearance too much. Her green eyes were now blue, and her hair was a deeper shade of brown.

But that didn't really matter. What mattered was that they were finally free of the afterlife.

"Hello Henry," his father said as his mother gave him a tentative smile.

Henry couldn't stop the tears from flowing. All the pain and guilt he'd carried burst out of him. His parents hovered closer, like they were afraid of coming near him. He wasn't sure how long he sat there, bawling his eyes out, but eventually the tears dried.

"I'm sorry, I failed you and I've failed your legacy," he said once he was sure he could speak without crying.

His mother knelt in front of him and tried to grab his hand, but her spirit form passed right through him. She gave him an apologetic smile.

"You didn't fail us, Henry. You did exactly what you were fated to do," his mother said.

"What do you mean by fated?"

His mother glanced at his father, who gave her a solemn nod.

"We knew that one day we'd be forced into the afterlife and

that you would become the next God of Justice and Mercy."

All the pain and suffering they'd all gone through was because of some stupid fate? He'd spent the last three hundred and seventy-nine years wallowing in guilt and anger for what?

"You didn't think it would be a good idea to fucking tell me about this?" he asked through gritted teeth.

"Believe me, we wanted to, but the Goddess of Fates made us swear a blood oath to keep silent," his father said. "If we hadn't gone along with it, this realm would've been destroyed…again."

Henry frowned; his gaze darted between them.

"This realm was destroyed?"

"Yes, the Goddess of Peace and Destruction destroyed it. Fortunately, the God of Knowledge and the God of Magic were able to resurrect it."

That would explain the rift and why Sade exploded at the cave. It must've triggered a memory. But if the realm had been rebuilt, why didn't the God of Knowledge tell him? Did he want Henry to think of Sade as nothing but a monster?

"Sade destroyed this realm?" Henry said slowly and his mother chuckled at Sade's chosen name. He shared a confused glance with his father.

"She hasn't gotten better at naming things," his mother said, "but yes she did."

"Why?"

The light in his mother's eyes dimmed.

"Unfortunately, that information has been lost to the fog of time."

The God of Knowledge had said something similar the last time he'd spoken to him. Something wasn't right. Sade was powerful, but she wasn't powerful enough to erase people's memories. No, this was something else. Something sinister was lurking in the dark and playing with people's minds.

"Sade isn't a monster; she wouldn't destroy an entire realm for no reason! There has to be some way to find out what happened."

"The only one who has a chance at figuring it out is Sade. She's the only one who still has the memories inside of her." His mother glanced at something behind her. "I'm afraid we're running out of time. The Goddess of Marriage has graciously allowed us use of her messenger spirits, but we have duties to attend to."

The tumultuous sea that was his thoughts quieted at her words. He didn't even know what godhood's they'd been given.

"I'm the Goddess of Dreams and your father is the God of Sleep. We're rather low on the power scale, but I have a plan to raise us up," his mother said. Henry held back a sigh. Without his divine side active, she could read every thought he had without issue.

"I don't need to be higher on the power scale," his father said. "I've gone from being a powerless human to a god who is able to put people to sleep with a mere thought."

"But imagine if you could put an entire army to sleep!"

His father crossed his arms. He didn't seem too thrilled with the idea.

"Henry, you need to get her out of that damn realm," his mother said as their forms started to fade.

"What? But the treaty—"

"Is a load of horse shit. Eventually, we will go to war. We

cannot have the magic inside of her become corrupted. I cannot believe the God of Knowledge was stupid enough to let her go, but she needs to get out of there before it changes her."

Henry shook his head. "I can't go. She barely spoke to me once she found out about her past. I'm the last person she wants to talk to."

"Henry, for whatever reason, you are the only one who's been able to pull her out of her destructive state. Put aside your personal feelings and do your damn duty."

"I'll try."

"You better do more than just try. I didn't spend almost four centuries in the afterlife so you could just *try*."

His mother definitely hadn't lost her bluntness.

Before he could reply, his parents were gone, leaving Henry to sway in the wind. He tried to take a step forward, but, between the fight and the alcohol, his body didn't know what way was up or down. So, he ended up back on the ground.

His head throbbed as he tried to make sense of all that had just transpired. He couldn't just waltz into the Realm of Ruin and demand that Sade come with him. She'd likely throw him out herself.

He rested his head against the cobblestone. It was cool to the touch and helped soothe his growing headache. Why him? Why did the fates decide that he, a mere half-god, was supposed to keep Sade from destroying things?

The memory of her in the cave flashed through his mind. The absolute pain the goddess had been in was almost incomprehensible to him. Was she in pain now? Was the realm's influence already eating away at her until she was but a shell of who she was? She was trying to fulfill her destiny and ensure the realms had peace.

And what was he doing? Laying on a street and feeling sorry for himself?

No. He needed to get Sade and find who was really causing all this mayhem.

"Look, I'm going to correct my mistake. Can I have my powers back?" he said, not caring if someone heard him.

A faint flicker of magic sprung to life within him, just enough to invigorate his tired muscles and give him strength to stand.

Before he could move, a wave of ice water splashed onto him.

"What the hell?" he sputtered as more water crashed onto him, clearing his head and making it so he could stand without the world shifting.

"Hello Henry," Aiden said as he set down a couple of buckets.

"What do you want?" Henry asked. Aiden looked like hell. His clothes were torn, and his face had numerous scratches on them.

"I wanted to apologize for being an arse," Aiden said and held up a hand when Henry started to speak. "You were right. I was jealous and made some stupid decisions."

Henry squeezed the water out of his tunic before he let out a long sigh.

"I was also being a hypocritical idiot and didn't want to face what I was feeling. I'm sorry for not being honest with you."

Aiden smiled and clapped him on the shoulder.

"You reek of ale. I thought you were going to destroy the dagger," Aiden said as he used a rune to pull the water out of his clothes.

"I tried; my magic still hasn't returned. The damn thing is invincible." Henry paused and eyed Aiden's rune pouch.

"Oh, hell no, I'm not going to even try. I've had enough damage done to my body this year to last me for eternity."

"Speaking of which, what in the hell happened to your face?"

Aiden ran a hand through his hair. "I was ambushed in the forest; a bunch of creatures came at me, and I barely escaped."

Henry's blood ran cold. If the creatures were back, that meant Sade hadn't been able to convince the God of Ruin to stop sending them. Did that also mean she'd already succumbed to the realm's influence?

"I'll help you kill the creatures and then we need to get Sade out of the Realm of Ruin."

"That's great, the creatures are—" Aiden paused as the rest of Henry's words sank in. "Wait, why do you want to get Sade? What about the treaty?"

"Screw the treaty. Do you really want to find out what happens when her destructive side and the God of Ruin's magic mix?"

Aiden muttered something under his breath when the Vestral from earlier left the tavern. Henry's body tensed, but the Vestral didn't spare them a glance as she stumbled down the street.

"No, I don't," Aiden said, and motioned to the gate. "Let's go hunt down those creatures and go get Sade."

"Are you sure they're here?" Henry asked Aiden as they crept through the forest. Aiden nodded. His eyes were fixed on a seeking rune that cast a silvery glow on his face.

Henry tightened his grip on his axes. His magic was slowly seeping back into his body. At this rate it would take months for him to get back to full strength.

He scanned the trees around them. No creatures lurked in the shadows. The hair on the back of his neck stood up. Something was off. His divine side shouldn't be struggling to connect.

"Hang on! Sorry, they're over there." Aiden pointed to a cluster of dead trees. His mortal side balked at the sight; it didn't want to go in there.

Gods, I've fought monsters in much more frightening places than a damn forest. The voices in his head screamed at him to back away. He ignored them and sprinted over to the trees. He spent some time hacking away at some dead underbrush, but he didn't see anything amiss.

He started to backtrack when he saw a faint glimmer of light from inside a nearby bush. He glanced over at Aiden, who was still scowling at his seeking rune. Henry carefully pulled back at the branches. A dispel rune had been carved into the bark.

His eyes slowly traced the glowing lines and his mouth dipped into a frown. It wasn't an ordinary dispel rune. His name had been added into it. It was a combination rune meant to keep his powers at bay.

Henry jerked away from the bush as icy hands grabbed hold of his wrists. A shadow creature slithered out of the bush.

"Aiden! We've got company!" He shouted and braced himself for a torrent of air. But it never came. The shadow creature tightened its grip and Henry's axes fell to the ground. The creature spun him around so that he was facing Aiden, who was staring at him with a feral grin.

He held up the seeking rune in his hand, and the stone shimmered as magic rippled across the surface. It burned away the carving of the seeking rune to reveal an identical rune to the one Henry found carved in the bush.

"What in the hell is going on?" Henry strained against the shadow creatures hold.

It couldn't be. Aiden couldn't be working for the God of Ruin. This had to be a trick.

Aiden stalked forward and unhooked the dagger from Henry's belt. He walked away and then, without warning, he whirled around and struck the side of Henry's head with the dagger's pommel.

When he awoke, he found himself bound to a chair in the middle of a dimly lit room. Judging by the damp earth smell, it was somewhere underground. The heaviness in the air told him he wasn't in a Divine Realm, but he wasn't sure that was a good thing.

Across from him was another chair. This one had a skeleton chained to it.

Aiden was sitting at a table, making yarn with a drop

spindle. A few shadow creatures hovered not too far from him. One creature gently tapped on the table and Aiden glanced over at him.

"You fucking traitor!" Henry yelled. He strained against the chains that bound him to the chair, but they didn't move an inch.

"Ah, the damsel has finally awoken from his beauty sleep." Aiden smirked and waved his spindle at him. He flipped it over and unscrewed the dull wooden end to reveal a needle hidden underneath. The shadow creatures shrunk back at the sight.

"Am I supposed to be scared of that?" Henry raised an eyebrow; the creatures feared a mere spindle? Nothing made sense anymore.

"This spindle is cursed. It was created by a witch as revenge against those who didn't invite her to a party for some spoiled princess. I stole it before she could use it. Why use such powerful magic over such a mundane thing?"

Aiden sighed and replaced the wooden end. "The needle holds a sleeping curse a million times more potent than the magic I used in Pavento, though it doesn't turn your body into stone. When you're under this curse, nothing can hurt you and nothing can wake you up. It's quite a rush, using such an object to create such a simple thing as yarn."

"Are you going to use the damn thing on me or not? I don't care about your stupid hobbies," Henry snarled.

Aiden laughed and tossed the spindle onto the table. He rolled-up his sleeves and a shadow creature handed him a knife.

"I'm not going to use the damn spindle on you. It's a one-time use and I don't want to waste it. Especially on a washed-up failure of a half-god." Aiden walked over to the skeleton and tapped the skull with his knife. "I'm going to make you wish you ended up like my friend here. Unless you want to join us?"

"I would rather die than join the God of Ruin," Henry spat.

Aiden shrugged. "Your loss."

"Why don't you just kill me? Save yourself the trouble."

"Because I need someone to do my experiments on," Aiden said, and gave him a sinister smile. "I've been dreaming about this day for a long time. I spent so many hours listening to you whine and complain about your state in life, having to pretend I was so much weaker than you. To make matters worse, I watched you court the goddess who was supposed to be my bond mate."

Henry laughed. "Sade would never want to be bonded to you; she was repulsed by you the moment she laid eyes on you. Something deep within her must've recognized you and it probably wasn't a good memory."

He wasn't sure if that last part was true, but he had an inkling it was, and it was worth it to watch Aiden's face transform into a scowl.

"You do not know how bonds work. You've spent your entire life avoiding them. There are many ways to bond two people together. Not all of them involve love or lust or whatever the hell it is you 'feel' for her. Sade was meant to be mine long before creation decided you were supposed to be born."

"Then why isn't she your bond mate now?"

Aiden pursed his lips. "Things became… complicated. But the past doesn't matter. Sade will be my bond mate, whether she likes it or not."

Henry pushed against his restraints, hoping his magic would flood his veins and allow him to break free. But he couldn't feel a drop of it.

"You're going to wear yourself out if you keep doing that," Aiden said as he walked over to Henry's side and used the knife to slice his palm open. He reached into his rune pouch, pulled out Henry's divine rune, and pressed it into the cut.

"I can't believe the God of Truth decided that the God of Ruin was the better option," Henry said through clenched teeth.

"Oh, about that. I'm not the God of Truth," he pointed his bloodied knife at the skeleton, "that's the God of Truth. I'm the God of Deception."

Henry stared at the skeleton. A trail of light slithered across the bones. Horror flooded through him. The god was still alive. If his body and soul were stuck here, it explained why he hadn't been reborn or found in the afterlife.

"How have you been able to trick us? You're a half-god. You can't change your appearance." He paused. "Unless you're not a half-god."

Aiden lifted the divine rune. It dripped with Henry's blood.

"No, I am a half-god. I can't change my appearance, but I can mimic another's magic."

Henry rolled his eyes. "So? I can change mine to match the color of any other god. It's nothing new."

Aiden smiled and blue sparks danced across his fingertips. Henry wanted to vomit as he felt the brush of Sade's magic against his skin.

"Between that, creating these monsters to hide my movements, and using you to convince the others that my similarities to the God of Deception were just a coincidence, this was the easiest con I've ever pulled off."

"You created the monsters?" Henry's mind flashed to hundreds of villages that had been wrecked by the creatures he'd fought. All those poor souls.

"You know, it's been so much fun watching you run around and blame the God of Ruin when I've been with you this entire time."

Bile rose in this throat. The countless mortals who'd perished had all been because of the god in front of him.

What would become of Sade when she tried to get the God of Ruin to stop sending the monsters? Would he charge her with blasphemy and throw her into a pit?

"Why are you doing this?"

Aiden wagged his finger at him. "Ah, I don't think so. The only thing you need to know is that your time as the God of Justice and Mercy is coming to an end. You are now nothing more than my prisoner."

He snapped his fingers and a shadow creature appeared next to him with a tiny potion bottle. Aiden swiftly uncorked it and emptied the contents into the cut on Henry's palm.

Henry couldn't stop the scream that escaped his lips as liquid fire spread through his bloodstream.

"That poison is a new concoction of mine. It's supposed to have the user feel like they are on fire. The last couple of humans I tried it on burst into flames." Aiden waved over another shadow creature. "Keep an eye on him, I've got a meeting in the Realm of Ruin to attend."

"When Sade figures this out, she's going to tear you apart and I'll be there to hold you down!" Henry called after him, but Aiden stalked from the room without another word, leaving

Henry to deal with the poison in his veins.

How did he miss this? Aiden had been one of the few people Henry trusted. He thought he'd gained a brother when Aiden joined him, but it was all a lie, and he was an utter fool. He'd been too stupid and blind to see it. He failed to protect the realm and let the true monster walk right in.

His thoughts were silenced as another wave of pain swept through him.

Chapter Twenty-Three

S ade tapped her fingers against her leg. She was sitting on a bench nestled under a dead tree, watching Casimir and Levina hold court.

They were seated on large thrones that looked seconds away from falling apart. Immortals paraded in front of the couple, offering gifts or badly worded poetry. Every divine in the realm had to attend this ridiculous ceremony. Despite the decay, they were more arrogant than the divines in the other realm. At least Vilmantas didn't force everyone to kiss his feet. She grimaced as a creature held up Levina's foot and slobbered all over it.

I get to spend eternity watching this every month. She glanced down at her hands; her powers were still pushing against the realm's. It was getting harder to keep it at bay and she'd only been here a few weeks. She'd put a few wards up in her temple in a feeble attempt to create a safe area. It was working, but she'd no idea how long it would last.

She still hadn't been able to convince Casimir to stop sending the creatures. In fact, she hadn't been able to say a word to him other than hello. The god claimed he was too busy to hold a meeting with her.

A sentry walked over to her; she gritted her teeth at the sound of rusted metal squeaking against the stone.

"Casimir would like to speak to you."

The crowd parted as she walked over to the thrones. Both divines were dressed in opulent finery that glittered with dispel runes, keeping the decay of the realm from ruining the fine fabrics.

"My dear ones, today I would like to announce the arrival of the newest tribute from the Divine Realm. Please give a warm welcome to the Goddess of Peace," Casimir said. A smattering of applause broke out in the crowd as he snapped his fingers.

A decaying immortal brought a rickety chair and set it next to Casimir's throne. The god patted the seat, and a sentry pushed her forward. Once she was seated, Casimir leaned towards her.

"This was the welcome I was going to give you had you arrived on time," he said. "But better late than never."

"Casimir, I need to talk to you."

Casimir raised a finger to his lips as a three eyed immortal stepped forward with a lyre.

"Hush, you'll ruin the show," he said and focused his attention on the divine when it screamed.

Sade blinked, and it took her a moment to realize the thing was trying to sing. She waited until they stopped, then she poked Casimir's arm. The god glanced at her with an annoyed look on his face, but he said nothing and returned his attention to the crowd.

No. She wasn't going to just sit here and wait for him to speak to her. She hopped off her chair, and the immortal that was currently standing in front of the thrones glared at her.

"I waited all day for this! You can—"

Crimson smoke swirled around her, and the immortal stepped back. She whirled around to face Casimir and Levina, both of whom looked mildly amused.

"Casimir, you have violated the treaty by sending those creatures to terrorize the mortals. You need to stop, or I swear there will be consequences."

Casimir's face turned to stone as clouds formed around Levina. She tensed, waiting for them to blast her with fire or call for the sentries.

Unleash me, let's show them our true power. She stilled as she glimpsed the crimson figure. She hadn't seen it since that fateful day in the cave.

Her dark thoughts were cut short by an uproar of laughter. Casimir, Levina, and everyone else present were laughing.

At her.

She started to leave, but Casimir raised his hand and wiped away a few tears with the other.

"Why do you think I can create monsters?" the god asked as he rose from his throne.

"Because it's in your nature to ruin things, and the creatures I battled had your signature all over them."

Casimir sighed and motioned for a sentry to stand next to him. He placed a hand on his shoulder. At first nothing happened, but then the oily smoke ate away at the sentry's armor. It wasn't long before they were left standing in a tattered tunic, but Casimir didn't stop there.

The sentry shook as blisters appeared on his skin.

"I cannot create anything; I can only eat away at what is already created," Casimir said as he released the sentry from his grip. "Why you insist that I am this evil god who is terrorizing realms is beyond me."

If Casimir wasn't the one creating the creatures, then who was? There were thousands of immortals here. She didn't have time to question every single one.

This is why we need to just destroy the whole damn thing. The crimson figure whispered.

Sade focused on Casimir. "If you're not the one creating the monsters, then we need to find the divine who is making them and ensure they are punished."

"No one in my realm is making any damn monsters. And why do you care so much about this particular Mortal Realm? There are millions of them."

"The God of Justice and Mercy lives there," Sade snapped. "I don't think he'll tolerate this much longer."

Casimir laughed again. "You mean that piddly excuse for a divine is guarding that realm? Now I'm glad it's being infested with monsters, that so-called god needs to be put in his place."

Sade clenched her fists. Her powers were a raging storm inside of her, but she needed to keep it leashed.

"If you do not help me find who is creating the monsters, then I will consider the treaty to be broken."

Casimir's eyes twitched and his skin started to bubble.

A horn blew somewhere in the distance. Casimir's magic snapped back into his body, and he glanced at Levina when she rose from her throne.

"Something's happened at the Temple of Portals!" she said as another horn blast sounded. The crowd erupted in panic and Casimir watched them scramble away with a scowl.

"What did you do? Did you send a messenger spirit to Vilmantas and complain about your stupid monsters?" he asked Sade.

"You know I don't have any messenger spirits." Sade crossed her arms.

"Listen, we can argue about this later, but we need to make sure the portals haven't been damaged." Levina moved in between them.

Before Casimir could stop her, Sade took off toward the temple. Levina and Casimir were right behind her.

When she arrived at the tree, there was no sign of damage or an army of gods swarming through the portals. A lone priest stood at the entrance.

Casimir pushed Sade out of the way and stormed over to the priest.

"What is going on? Why are you ruining my day?"

The priest bowed. "We had an unauthorized portal opening. Don't worry, we were able to seal the room."

"Take us to it," Levina said.

Sade started to follow them, but Casimir whispered something to the priest and a burst of air gently pushed her away from the door. It slid shut before she could rush in.

"Oh, for the love of all that is divine, let me in!" she shouted and banged on the door.

When that didn't work, she tried connecting to the tree. It wouldn't let her in, and another wave of invisible energy pushed her away.

After what felt like eons, the door opened, and a priest emerged.

"Please follow me."

She followed the priest through the maze of hallways until they were standing at the door to the room she'd come through when she first arrived. Her heart beat wildly. A part of her hoped Henry had come to visit, but she knew it was highly unlikely.

The priest opened the door and Sade's heart dropped to her feet. Aiden was curled up in a ball on the floor as Casimir and Levina stared at him. He was covered in blood and his clothes were shredded.

She rushed to his side, and he winced when she gently touched his shoulder.

"Aiden! What's happened? Where is Henry?" she asked as he opened his eyes. They were bloodshot and feverish.

"Sade?" he whispered. He tried to sit up, but he coughed up blood instead. Oily smoke crawled up his skin and blisters started to form. She covered Aiden in her protective bubble, and his skin returned to normal.

She grabbed his rune pouch and pulled out a dispel rune. She filled it to the breaking point and pressed it into his hand.

"Aiden, I need you to tell me what happened! Where is Henry?" She trailed off when Aiden passed out. Her eyes flickered to the portal.

"Is he dead?" Levina asked.

"No." Sade looked at Casimir, who was studying her with a grim expression. "He needs a healer and I need to go find Henry."

"The healer I can help with, but you are forbidden from leaving this realm." Casimir snapped his fingers and the portal closed.

"Henry is in trouble!" She shot to her feet.

"I don't care." Casimir shrugged and moved so some priests could carry Aiden out of the room.

"Please, I beg of you to let me go find him." Sade dropped to her knees and grabbed the hem of his tunic. "I won't ask for anything else. I'll even stop asking about the monsters."

Casimir's eyes flickered back and forth from the portal.

"My answer still stands," he said and left the room. Levina followed him and gave Sade an apologetic smile before the door shut.

⊱❧⊰

They placed Aiden in one of the rooms within the palace that had minimal damage. Sade spent the next few days painting dispel runes on the walls and fueling them with her power. As she fueled the runes, the shield protecting her body weakened further.

She sat next to the bed, watching Aiden's chest rise and fall. Guilt gnawed at her; she hadn't been able to stop the monsters from returning to the realm. Now Aiden was fighting for his life in a place that would easily kill him, and she had no idea where Henry was.

She tried using the magic in the temple to find him, but she'd found nothing.

He's fine. Maybe he took a break and went on a solo trip. Or maybe he's reuniting with his parents. Yet, no matter how hard she tried, she couldn't shake the feeling that something was wrong.

Her eyes drifted to the dagger with the copper hilt strapped to his belt. The memory of him declaring he was going to destroy it danced in her mind.

If the dagger was here and he wasn't, did that mean the enchantments in the dagger killed him?

She took a breath, trying to calm the rising panic within her. There had to be a perfectly logical explanation for all of this. She was just overreacting.

"Sade?" Aiden asked, his eyes cracked open. "Can I get some water?"

She grabbed a goblet and helped him sit up enough so he could drink from it.

"Thank you," he rasped and took a long drink. It was the longest drink she'd ever seen anyone take. When he was done, she had to keep herself from ripping the goblet from his hands.

"Is Henry all right?"

Aiden stared at her for a few moments. Sade's mouth went dry as his eyes started to water, and his lips trembled.

"He's gone," he said quietly. "We were hunting in the forest, and we came across a nasty group of creatures we'd never fought before. I told Henry to run, because he was still having problems accessing his magic. The stubborn fool told me he'd fight them off with his axes."

Aiden paused and wiped away a few tears from his face. He took a deep breath before he continued.

"At first things went well, but we got separated. By the

time I made my way over to him, he was in trouble. Once the monsters were defeated, I tried to get him to a healer, but it was too late." Aiden reached into his rune pouch and held up Henry's divine rune. It was completely covered in blood.

"He wanted you to have this, and he wanted you to know he was sorry for not being able to destroy the dagger."

He offered the rune to Sade, and she rolled it over in her palm. The light inside of the rune was dimming with each breath she took.

"He's a half-god, surely he'll be reborn," she whispered.

Aiden shook his head. "If he was going to be reborn, his rune wouldn't be fading like that."

Her entire body went numb and the light in the two triangles flickered. It was like watching a fire die, and there was no way she could rekindle it.

She stood up and clutched the stone to her chest.

"I don't believe this; he can't be dead!" She started backing towards the door and Aiden tried to rise.

"Sade, don't do this to yourself."

She ran out of the room and didn't stop until she was in her temple. Her magic flared out of her as she knelt next to the pot that held the Starlight Violet.

"I need to speak to Henry," she whispered to the plant.

Sparks of silver danced along the petals as the flower processed her request. She carefully wiped the blood off Henry's divine rune and placed in next to the violet. A dim orange glow illuminated the flower as the rune continued to wane.

Her heart sped up as the violet stilled.

We're afraid we cannot locate the man you've inquired about.

The flower whispered into her mind.

Try again and use the divine rune. It might help you.

The magic in the flower whirled around the rune before it resumed its search. Her hands clutched the sides of the pot like it was the only thing keeping her from falling into a dark ravine.

The person you are trying to locate doesn't exist.

"No," she growled at the plant. Wiping away the hot tears that streamed down her face. "You need to keep trying. He must be out there somewhere."

No matter how hard she made the plant search, it couldn't find him.

We cannot continue searching, our magic is being depleted. One of the remaining petals broke off. It was brown by the time it settled on the soil.

A heavy weight pressed against her heart, squeezing her until she felt like she was going to split into two separate halves. She backed away from the pot as the rune finally died out.

Her temple had become quieter than a tomb, and all she could hear was her breathing. A sob escaped her lips as she curled up on the floor.

The ember of hope she'd been holding onto was snuffed out by the flood of grief that overtook her. The one person that believed she wasn't a monster had paid the price with his life.

She destroyed him, just like she destroyed a realm.

Her blood cooled, and it wasn't long before her skin was like ice.

Goddess of Peace, hear my plea… A voice drifted out from her sacred pool.

She didn't care. She wasn't a goddess; she was a monster

that couldn't even protect the man she cared about the most. Let the other divines find someone who was worthy of being the Goddess of Peace.

With shaking limbs, she rose from her spot on the floor and stormed out of the room. She slammed the door behind her.

Her skin tingled; the magic of the realm was seeping into her soul. A faint burst of her own wasn't enough to fight it off, but she didn't care. Let the realm turn her into a husk. It was what she deserved.

Hush now, little goddess, we'll take away the pain. The realm whispered as it wove itself into every fiber of her being.

She welcomed it with open arms.

Chapter Twenty-Four

Henry watched a shadow creature pour a vial of scarlet liquid into the cut they'd created on his arm. He waited for the rush of excruciating pain to overwhelm his senses, but it didn't come.

They must have lessened the effects of the hidden dispel rune since he could sense his divine side. However, his magic remained out of reach.

Day after day, the creatures poked and prodded him with all sorts of concoctions. It was enough to drive him insane; he feared he would if this went on for much longer. There was only so much he could take.

He hadn't seen Aiden since he'd been brought here. He was likely wreaking havoc somewhere. The only thing he couldn't figure out was why he needed his divine rune. Was he going to do something horrible and blame it on him? And what about the dagger? He doubted he was going to use it on Sade since he was trying to make her his bond mate. Maybe he was going to sneak into the Divine Realm and stab the God of Knowledge with it?

Whatever he was going to do, it likely wasn't good.

The shadow creature made a low hissing noise and scribbled something onto a scroll that hovered nearby. It floated over to the table and grabbed another vial.

"What are you doing with that one?" Another shadow creature floated into the room.

"These poisons aren't working the way they're supposed to. The scroll says it's supposed to create euphoria, but he's not acting very excited," the creature holding the vial said.

Wonderful. Aiden wanted him to feel good while being tortured. No wonder Sade had been repulsed by him. Some part of her must have remembered he was a sick bastard.

"Hmm, maybe we've done too much? Perhaps we should give him a break. Let the other poisons leave his body, and then we'll try this again."

"But I'm out of herbs for the new one," the other creature whined. "Would you mind watching him while I go forage?"

"Why? He's not going anywhere and if he did, we'd find him."

Both shadow creatures made an odd humming noise, then left the room, and, for the first time in weeks, Henry was alone. He glanced around, double checking if anything else was lurking in the corners before he looked at the skeleton across from him.

Henry felt sorry for the god. His body had become a literal prison and his identity had been stolen from him.

"Do you have any ideas on how I can get out of here?" He

asked it. The pale smoke that ran up and down the bones flared, but Henry didn't hear any voices inside his head.

"Well, this has been an enlightening conversation." He studied the clasps around his wrist and tried to yank his arm free. Pain shot through him, and a small amount of blood trickled down the side of the chair. The skin on his wrists was completely raw.

A loud creaking noise caught his attention. The chair with the skeleton had somehow turned around.

I've finally lost it. No matter how much he blinked, it didn't return to its earlier position.

The skeleton made a terrible cracking noise, and Henry winced as the skeleton's head swiveled so it was now facing him. The jaw moved like it was trying to talk, but, since he was nothing more than a pile of bones, he only made a clacking noise.

"Stop it!" Henry hissed and eyed the door. "Are you trying to alert the damn creatures?"

The skeleton hung its head and didn't move for a moment.

"What are you doing?" He asked when it started to nod aggressively.

Henry followed its gaze down to where its hands were bound to the back of the chair. Two runestones were tied to the skeleton's hands. Henry could barely make out the carvings on them, but he could tell they were identical to the combination rune that blocked his magic when Aiden captured him. Whatever power was left in the god was fueling the runes.

He could still move his legs and, if he could get close enough, he'd be able to kick the runes out of the skeleton's hands and break the connection.

Before he could say anything, the skeleton shook, and its hands clattered to the floor. The light in the runestone sputtered and died out. A trickle of power surged through his veins.

The skeleton's head snapped up and its jaw closed. It gave Henry a nod before it twisted its head back into its normal position.

Well, that was one way to deal with the rune problem.

"Thank you. I promise when this is over, I'll come back for you," Henry said.

He took a breath, and, when he exhaled, the chains that bound him broke. He slowly rose to his feet, and his muscles screamed in protest as he stumbled over to the table the shadow creatures were using. His body was not in good enough shape to use magic at the levels he needed in a fight, and he had no time to make runes. He was going to need another weapon, but his axes were nowhere in sight.

The only things on the table were a bunch of vials filled with liquids he knew nothing about, and Aiden's cursed spindle. He quickly grabbed it. It was surprisingly heavy and would likely knock someone out if he hit them hard enough. Though he doubted that would work against a shadow creature.

"Here goes nothing," he muttered and headed through the door. He found himself in a tunnel that looked to go on for ages. The only light to be found was at the opening of the shaft and the small amount that spilled out from the room he'd escaped.

Each step he took was like walking through mud. His bones creaked with every movement he made, and it took all his willpower to keep quiet. If he started screaming, he might as well go back and tie himself up.

So, he pushed on until he was at the edge of the tunnel and found himself staring down a mountain goat. Henry held up the spindle, and the animal bleated at him before it bounded away. He watched it disappear over the crest of a hill and shook his head.

"Gods, it's just a goat. I need to stay calm," he muttered to himself. He looked around, trying to find something he could use as a landmark to find this place later. He didn't have time to create a location rune. The only thing he knew was that he was in a forested valley, surrounded by mountains. Which meant he could be anywhere on the damn continent.

If there was a divine in charge of luck, it clearly had a vendetta against him.

He moved away from the tunnel entrance as fast as he could. He didn't want to be here when the shadow creatures came back.

By the time the sun set, he was not as far from the tunnel entrance as he would've liked, but his body couldn't go for much longer. His stomach growled as he created a pile of dead pine needles and dirt. He'd forgotten to grab some food in his rush to escape.

An icy wind blew and caused him to shiver. If it snowed, it could bury him in his sleep. Most of the trees here were evergreens, so he couldn't use them to see how much longer he had. He scratched his chin. He'd grown a full beard during his time with the shadow creatures, so it had to be at least two months. Which meant winter could decide to arrive any day. He needed to get the hell out of here.

He nestled into his pile of leaves and took a deep breath.

Sleep wouldn't come easily to him, but he had to try.

Now the question was, did he dare try to go into the Realm of Ruin, or did he wait until he could summon the other gods?

An image of Sade screaming in pain flashed in his mind. He couldn't risk the other divines not believing him. His parents would, but since they were only minor deities, their words wouldn't hold much weight.

He'd get Sade out first and then go bother the others. If they didn't believe him, then at least she'd be safe, and they could both figure out what to do next.

If she wanted to. He wouldn't blame her if she went into a remote realm and shut everything out. In that case, he'd figure something else out.

He eyed the tree next to him and let some magic drift towards it, but he pulled it back when he heard a twig snap. A low rattling noise caused the hairs on the back of his neck to stand up.

With a groan, he rose from his makeshift bed and grabbed a nearby stick. Between that and the spindle, he might have somewhat of a chance. The rattling noise pierced the night air again, this time it was much closer.

He unscrewed the wooden top on the spindle, exposing the needle. The metal glinted in the moonlight, and a feeling of unease spread through him. How the hell Aiden spun yarn with this thing was beyond him. He could barely walk through a crypt without freaking out.

Then again, the man he knew was a complete lie. He probably got off on the idea of holding such a cursed object so close to himself. Henry shuddered at the idea and directed his attention to the monster that was currently stalking him.

"How about you reveal yourself and we get this over with? I have things to do and you're not on my list," Henry shouted.

The trees rocked, and Henry shifted into a defensive stance. His legs shook with effort. He wouldn't be able to stand for much longer. He was glad no one else was here to see him like this, preparing to fight off a monster with something used to make yarn.

Gods, I should've run for the hills. But he probably wouldn't have made it far and would've been in worse shape to fight.

The earth underneath him bulged, and he barely had time to jump out of the way as a giant serpent burst out of the ground. It wasn't a typical giant snake. It had four legs and streaks of lightning magic crawled across its grey scales, which marked it as a beithir, one of the deadliest natural creatures in this realm. They were a rare sight; he'd only seen one since he became a divine. And that one had been picked apart by a mountain griffin.

A quick glance at the sky told him no griffins were going to swoop down and save him.

He was thoroughly fucked. There was no way he could fight the thing off with a mere spindle and a stick.

The beithir hissed at him, showing off the fangs that were as long as he was tall. Venom dripped from them like a waterfall and created a pool of glistening liquid on the ground. The dead pine needles sizzled as the venom ate through them.

Henry spun on his heels and ran as fast as he could. Fire raced through his muscles as the beithir chased after him. He headed for a part of the forest that was thick with thorny bushes and rocks.

If he couldn't fight it off directly, maybe he could use the landscape against it. He pushed through the thicket into a large meadow. He made it to the center when the beithir burst out of the trees and used its tail to block his escape.

"All right, fine. I guess I'll fight my way out," he grumbled. Gripping the spindle, he spun and faced the creature. To his great surprise, the snake reeled back like he'd hit it.

He eyed the needle and almost dropped it when an inky magic started to swirl around the pointy tip.

At least Aiden hadn't lied about that. All that magic because some stupid mortal didn't get invited to a party.

What am I doing? I need to focus on the creature in front of me, not stare at a cursed needle.

Straightening his shoulders, he tried to focus on the beithir, but he was finding it impossible to keep his thoughts coherent. This was bad. His body had reached its limit, and he was staring down a snake the size of a small house.

Gods, why couldn't it have been the size of a regular snake? If he survived this, he was going to have a long chat with whoever created this creature.

He took another step toward the snake, keeping the spindle in front of him. The snake hissed at him, but the fear of the magic in the spindle kept it from striking.

It slammed one of its massive feet onto the ground and Henry had to grab onto a tree to keep himself from falling. The needle almost pierced his flesh. Seeing an opening, the creature lunged at him, stopping short when Henry pointed the cursed spindle at it.

When the thing didn't hiss at him, he realized it was frozen.

Ice crystals formed on its scales as he frantically scanned the forest for the source of the magic. He kept his back pressed against the tree.

"I was wondering where my spindle went," Aiden said as he stepped out from the shadows.

"You're too late. I've already summoned the other gods and they're going to stop you," Henry said.

Aiden laughed and shook his head. "You know, you've never been a very good liar."

Henry gripped the spindle as Aiden moved towards him. A couple of scaragnos emerged from the shadows. They pounced on the beithir, tearing away its scales to get to the flesh underneath.

"Now, Henry, we can do this the easy way or the hard way," Aiden said. Forest green smoke that looked like it'd been mixed with oil slithered around him. A divine rune floated in front of him. It was snake wrapped around an overturned goblet.

"What did you do with my runestone?" Henry asked, and a sinister smile crossed over Aiden's face.

"I gave it to Sade. She thinks you're dead."

A whirlwind of orange lightning burst out of him, sending Aiden flying backwards. He slipped in the puddle of venom and almost fell into the beithir's mouth.

"You manipulative son of a bitch," Henry snarled. Power flowed out of him; his body screamed at him to stop, but he didn't care.

"Oh, don't be so dramatic."

With a flick of his wrist, Aiden had a fire rune floating in front of him. Henry gritted his teeth and pushed with everything he had against the flames that threatened to roast him like a boar.

Sweat mixed with blood seeped from every pore and into his eyes. He wouldn't last much longer. Without a runestone to channel through, it would start eating away at him like the scaragnos were eating the beithir.

"You know she's moved on rather quickly from you. She's been waltzing around the realm without a care in the world. I guess she doesn't care about you that much," Aiden smirked. He hadn't even broken a sweat.

The magic inside of him stilled. Aiden was trying to rile him up until he literally burned himself out.

At this point, he would be stupid to think he could escape and get to Sade. No, he needed her to know he was still alive and to come find him. He dropped the stick he was holding and pressed his hand against the tree.

"That's all you've got?" Aiden said. He stalked toward him like a wolf about to pounce.

"I'm just warming up."

"We both know you're done." An air rune floated out of his rune pouch. A burst of wind pushed him away from the tree.

Henry tried in vain to connect to the trees, but, since he wasn't touching any plants, he couldn't connect.

"Did you think I wasn't going to notice you trying to connect to the tree?" Aiden said. "There's no point—"

The beithir's tail slammed into him, throwing him to the side. The scaragnos clung to its scales as it spewed venom at them. The creature disappeared into the forest, taking the scaragnos with it.

Aiden rose to his feet, his face marred by hatred.

Henry dove for a nearby tree and pressed his hands against

it. There was no time for him to check if he'd connected properly.

Sade, I'm alive. You need to get out of that realm. Don't listen to Aiden, he's been working with the God of Ruin this entire time and he's the—

Before he could continue, the tree exploded, sending thousands of splinters into his flesh. His ears rang and his body hit the ground with a loud thump. The spindle fell from his hand. He reached for it. Before he could pull it close, Aiden's boot slammed onto his hand, shattering bone. Henry couldn't stop the scream that escaped his lips.

He eyed the needle. It gleamed in the moonlight and, with a sinking stomach, he knew what he had to do as Aiden stood over him.

"I was going to go easy on you, but now you've made a mess. You better hope Sade doesn't hear your message, or I swear I'm going to turn you into the first half-god, half-spider."

Henry gathered every bit of magic he had and blasted Aiden with it. He grabbed the spindle with his good hand and stood before Aiden grabbed him by his tunic collar.

"You're going to pay for that," Aiden snarled. A fire rune floated up beside him. Henry moved the spindle behind his back.

"No, I'm not," Henry said, and he pricked his finger on the needle.

He couldn't help the smile that crossed his face as he dropped the spindle and held up his hand. A tiny drop of blood raced down his palm. Aiden's eyes widened. He shoved Henry back onto the ground as he grabbed the spindle.

The veins on Henry's arms turned black as his mortal side was ripped out of him. His divine side let out a burst of orange light, trying to pull his mortal side back to him, but it was no use. Not even gods were immune from curses.

Shadows danced on the edges of his vision. Aiden screamed something at him. His voice was muffled by the roaring in Henry's ears. The half-god unleashed a wave of fire, but the curse absorbed it, allowing the flames to flow harmlessly over Henry's body.

Sleep now. A voice crooned.

As the darkness overtook his vision, he panicked. What if the tree's magic didn't reach Sade? What if she'd succumbed to the realm's magic?

If it failed, he needed to make sure he had a backup. And the only way he could try to reach her was with a petition. He'd never done one before, and he was pretty sure petitioning another god was against some ancient divine law. But he had no choice.

Goddess of Peace, hear my plea.

It was both a petition and a reminder that she wasn't just the Goddess of Destruction. He could only hope his words were enough; he had no idea how to attach emotions or memories or whatever else the mortals did.

His thoughts scattered and the curse lulled him into the abyss. It wasn't long before he was deep into a dreamless sleep.

Chapter Twenty-Five

Sade sipped from a goblet as she watched a pair of immortals squabble over a board game. She relished the tingling wave that swept through her body, lulling her senses to the point she felt almost nothing. The wine she was drinking was the specialty of the realm, designed to eat away the emotions inside and leave the drinker in a numb state. The only drawback was the effect wasn't permanent.

She was sitting in the largest tavern in the city, a crumbling building that was one breeze away from collapsing.

Aiden sat across from her, mulling over his ale. He'd just returned from a trip to the Mortal Realm. Despite the dispel rune that was hovering beside him, the stone would eventually break. Which meant he had to leave the realm to carve a new stone and recharge it. The half-god had been in a sour mood all day.

"Have you been back in your temple at all?" he asked.

Sade raised her eyebrows. "No, I haven't. Why is there some important petition that I missed?"

She hadn't been in there since she learned about Henry. Her petitions were likely piling up, but she didn't care. It was safer for her and all mortals if she kept away from them. She was a living curse.

"No, I was just trying to make small talk."

Aiden took a long sip from his tankard. The gloomy look on his face was gone.

Despite the effects of her drink, Sade still had a tinge of repulsion whenever he was around. She knew it was petty. He had nowhere to go, and he'd lost his friend. But the way he'd reacted when he found her and Henry was forever etched in her mind.

"How is the realm? Any more monsters?" She asked as she poured herself another glass of wine. The liquid pushed away the memory of her first and last kiss with Henry and muffled the sadness that threatened to overtake her.

"The attacks are becoming less common; I think the God of Ruin is moving on to other things."

Sade swirled the wine in her goblet. Now that Henry was gone, and Aiden didn't seem to be too interested in protecting the Mortal Realm, she thought the divine who was sending the monsters would've seized the opportunity and took over. But nothing happened.

"And the dagger? Have you made any progress?"

Aiden shook his head. "No, I'm going to try a new technique and see if it'll work."

An awkward silence fell between them. Talking to Aiden was a chore and it didn't help that he looked like a duller version of Henry. She took another swig of her wine.

"By all that is divine, you two look like you're attending the most boring party in the world," Levina said as she swept into the tavern and marched over to their table.

"I'm afraid I'm not one for talking these days," Sade said. She took another sip, but Levina snapped her fingers, and the drinks were gone. "My, my, are you still mourning that half-god? He must've done a number on you to get you so attached to him."

Sade was grateful that the wine diminished her anger. Otherwise, she might've thrown her out the window. She'd done her best to avoid her and Casimir. It'd been easy to do since they were too busy fawning over each other and acting like they were star-crossed lovers. But, as with everything in this place, it didn't quite hit the mark and they acted more like fools.

Not even love was safe from the influence of the realm.

"Can't a goddess just come into a tavern and enjoy a nice goblet of wine?" she asked, keeping her voice cool.

Levina crinkled her nose as she cast a disapproving glance around the room, like she was too good for the place.

"Casimir wants to see you," she said to Aiden and then she glanced at Sade. "*Both* of you."

Sade bit back a sigh. "Can't it wait? I have things to do."

Levina snorted. "Your wine can wait."

Not wanting to get into a fight, Sade followed her back to the palace. Aiden was close behind her.

They found Casimir standing on a balcony overlooking the city. The railings were covered in an emerald moss. The color reminded her of Henry's eyes. She shook her head and focused on the god in front of her.

"Ah, there you are," Casimir said as he smiled at Aiden. His smile faded when he looked at Sade. She braced herself for a reprimand.

"Why are you drinking wine at a shitty tavern and won't touch a drop of what I offer at our feasts? I thought you didn't '*drink in your divine form*,'" he said that last part with an unusually high-pitched voice.

Sade gave him a halfhearted smile. "Things change."

"Oh darling, don't be too upset. She's still in mourning for that one half-god. At least her magic isn't making her look like a walking sun," Levina said with a pointed glance at Sade's arms.

Power stirred somewhere deep inside of her, but it was quickly lulled back to sleep by the wine in her veins.

"Ah, that's true." He turned to Aiden. "Have you thought about my offer?"

"Yes, and I accept."

Sade frowned as the two clasped arms and Levina let out a happy sigh.

"Accept what?"

"Aiden has decided to join us and be our liaison to the other realms," Casimir said as he puffed out his chest. He looked like he'd been told the God of Knowledge had ceased to exist.

Sade's eyes darted to Aiden, who gave her an apologetic smile.

"What are you doing? Why are you joining him?"

"Because Henry told me with his dying breath to take care of you, and it's hard for me to do that if I can't live here."

A horrified gasp left her lips. The wine's dulling effects on her emotions were already wearing off.

"No, I won't allow it. You cannot ruin your life," she said. Aiden walked over, capturing her hands with his. She swallowed and resisted the urge to yank them away.

The last thing she needed was someone to take care of her. She wasn't worth the effort.

"Sade, I made my friend a promise and I will not break it," Aiden said. He gently squeezed her hands, then let go.

"Well, now that's settled," Levina cut in before Sade could respond. "We should throw a ball to celebrate!"

"Only if we can get some decent music," Casimir grumbled. "I'm so tired of listening to the drivel that our subjects make."

"I could bring in some bards from my realm, give them some dispel runes, and they should be fine for the night," Aiden said.

Sade couldn't believe what she was hearing. Aiden was willing to risk bringing mortals here for what? A night of perverse pleasure?

"What are you doing?" she hissed at him while Levina and Casimir conversed amongst themselves.

"If I'm going to live here, I need to make a good first impression," Aiden whispered.

"Bringing mortals to this realm is a death sentence and you know it."

Aiden shrugged. The gesture caused a flurry of magic to bubble up inside of her, but the influence of the realm proved too strong, and back into its prison it went.

"This is just for one night. If any mortal shows any signs of being affected by the realm, I will escort them out."

Sade trembled with anger, but she kept her mouth shut.

"Hmm and can you guarantee they'll actually be good?" Casimir asked, "Because we had the bloody God of Music here, and he couldn't stand us or hold a damn tune."

Aiden nodded. "I can. I will cast a spell on them that will make them think they got summoned by the King of Roltia."

Casimir studied Aiden for a long moment before he nodded.

"If you can ensure such a thing, then I will grant your request."

"This is a stupid idea. You could kill people!"

Aiden's jaw clenched, but it was Casimir who spoke next as a couple of sentries appeared next to her.

"I'm afraid your audience with me is over for the day, goddess."

"I will not allow this to happen!"

"You have no such authority," Casimir growled. He moved closer. "You are nothing but a tribute from another realm while Aiden has joined me willingly. You've done nothing but wallow around my city, acting as if your stupid feelings are more important than anything else. This is my realm, and what I say goes."

With a wave of his hand, the sentries dragged her off the balcony and slammed the door shut behind them.

Anger boiled in her blood, burning away the lingering effects of the wine. For the first time in weeks, her head was clear. She pushed the sentries off her and stormed out of the palace.

She couldn't believe it; Aiden was going to risk the lives of mortals all for a bloody party.

"Sade! Wait!" Aiden called out to her, but she didn't stop.

He ran in front of her, turning so he was running down the steps backwards.

"What are you doing? You should be cavorting with your new friends," she snapped.

"I need you to listen to me," Aiden tapped the hilt of the dagger at his side. "This is the only way to destroy the dagger."

"What?"

"Look, if I can earn his trust, then perhaps I can get him to use his magic to destroy it. He ruins everything, so why not get him to turn the dagger into a rusty heap?"

It wasn't a bad idea by itself, but using innocent mortals was appalling to both her destructive and peaceful sides. If they agreed on something, then she knew it was bad.

"I cannot condone this. I don't care what Henry told you."

Aiden's shoulders drooped. "Come on Sade, please give me a chance."

Aiden gave her a pleading look, but she brushed past him.

"I will not take part in this."

She hurried down the rest of the steps and fled into the city.

A flash of red caught her attention and her heart sped up. Without thinking, she pushed through the crowd of immortals, ignoring their curses and glares. Another flash of that fiery red had her sprinting down the street.

She rounded a corner and froze. The immortal she'd been chasing was wearing a tattered red scarf. It gave her a puzzled expression before it disappeared into the crowd.

What am I doing? He's dead. It's been two months. I need to pull myself together.

But she couldn't. Not in this place where her soul was being slowly torn apart. The only place she stood a chance at feeling normal was in her temple, but she didn't want to enter it. Not only would she have to face the physical reminders of the half-god she'd grown to care about in a way she shouldn't have; she would have to face the mortals and their numerous petitions.

She would have to listen to them worship her and pretend she deserved such praise.

A bitter laugh escaped her lips as she leaned against a wall. Immortals pressed in around her. All of them had the same lifeless look on their faces. Her gaze dropped to her hands as the oily magic wove in and out of her skin.

Her temple, the place that had been designed to hold her captive, was the only place she could go to hold off the effects of the realm.

The fates had an awful sense of humor.

She wandered through the city, keeping her head down and letting the influence of the realm push away her thoughts. If this place was going to break her, it was taking its sweet time.

Goddess. A contorted voice drifted in the wind. Or was it her thoughts? She couldn't tell.

When she raised her head, she found herself staring down a cloaked figure, a flaming sword at their side.

Fear seized her heart, and she tried to summon her magic. The figure moved closer. Its sword dragging on the stone, sending a shower of sparks into the air.

"What do you want? Are you the one who's creating the monsters?" Sade asked as she backed up. Her powers were still being suffocated by the realm.

The figure merely swung its sword in a figure-eight pattern, then charged at her.

Sade ran. None of the immortals around her reacted to the figure with the flaming sword, which made it difficult for her to move quickly. A wave of heat flashed overhead. She dared a glance back to see the sword spewing out fire.

Despite this display, the crowd continued to move like normal. A milky film appeared in their eyes as oily smoke wove around her, trying to coax her into the same dreamlike state. She pushed against it. If she succumbed further, she had no chance against the cloaked specter.

A crackling noise filled the air as lightning streaked past her. The smell of burning flesh wafted through the air. A divine had burst into flames.

Sade didn't spare another glance at the cloaked figure as she ran to her temple. Her skin tingled as the air thickened.

A blast of wind had her stumbling and struggling to stay upright. If she'd been in her mortal form, she wouldn't have been able to continue. Another blast hit, but this one was slower. Everything was starting to move at a snail's pace.

Was the realm going into lockdown? She waited for Casimir to appear, but the god didn't show. Maybe he didn't care that an unknown immortal was trying to kill her. He did, after all, seem more interested in what Aiden had to say.

After what felt like ages, she made it to the entrance of her temple. It was then she dared to look back. Her heart dropped to her stomach; the hooded figure was crawling across the bridge, weighed down by an invisible force.

She rested a hand on her temple walls and let its energy surge through her. Pushing back against the realm's influence, crackling crimson light flowed down her arms. It looked a little too much like blood. The cloaked figure moved faster the closer they got to her temple. She sent a burst of air at them, but they used their sword to bat it away.

What in the hell is this thing? A spirit? A god? Her thoughts raced as she entered her temple, barring the door shut.

"You won't be able to hide from me forever, Goddess," its voice drifted through the door.

"Did I wrong you in one of my past lives?" Sade pressed a hand to the door, letting a few golden sparks seep through it. She tried to connect to the cloaked figure's mind, but it was locked tight.

The door buckled as the sword pierced its way through, and the flames lapped at the wood. Sade grabbed onto the sword and gripped the blade. Fire washed over her like water as blood dripped down her arms. She pushed into it until the metal warped and the sword snapped in half.

A hair-raising screech sounded from outside the door, and she peered through the smoldering opening. The cloaked figure was cradling their sword like a mother would a child. Then, with a flash of blinding light, they vanished.

Sade rested her head on the door. Her magic raced through her, healing injuries as it went. She moved away from the door and stared at the entrance to her sacred pool. Countless petitions awaited her in there as did the memories of Henry she tried so hard to forget.

Why was she grieving him like this? Was it because what they had was something that never had a chance to fully blossom?

Her feet moved on their own accord, and she found herself

mere inches from the door.

Go, we have neglected the mortals for so long. They need us. Her divine purpose whispered; it must've been her peaceful side.

No, I cannot. I am not worthy of being worshiped. She backed away, ready to flee. A chorus of voices rushed into her thoughts; millions of souls cried out for her blessing.

"I can't do this. I'm sorry," she said.

Goddess of Peace, hear my plea.

She froze mid-stride. That was Henry's voice.

But that was impossible.

Yet, she entered the room and gasped at the sight in front of her. The room was full of floating silver lights, and the Starlight Violet shone like a miniature star.

She stood at the threshold, transfixed by the scene before her. A few of the lights hovered close to her. She reached out and an image of a moonlit forest flashed in her mind.

Sade.

It was Henry's voice again; it was filled with fear and determination. She reached out to another light. This one showed her an image of a giant snake with legs. She wasn't sure if it was a creature of the realm or a monster that'd been created.

What was this? Why was she seeing this now? The plant could've shown her this when she'd found out Henry had died. She moved closer to the violet; Henry's divine rune was still nestled on the soil beside it. Neither of the triangles were lit up.

The lights dove into her pool. Blurry images of Henry running through a forest as the giant snake creature chased him appeared on the surface of the water.

He was in rough shape, his movements were stiff, and

it looked like he was having trouble breathing. His body was coated in blood, and the beard he'd grown made him look almost unrecognizable. But his green eyes were hard with determination as the snake creature trapped him. The images flew by faster, most of it was just blurry images of the giant snake.

He dove for a tree. She gripped the edges of the pool, wishing she could reach into the water and pull him out.

Sade, I'm alive. You need to get out of that realm. Don't listen to Aiden, he's been working with the God of Ruin this entire time and he's the—

The water rippled as the tree Henry was speaking to exploded and Aiden stalked toward him with the intent to kill written all over his face. The images suddenly cut off, leaving her to stare at her expression.

"Where is the rest of it?" She exclaimed and ran over to the violet.

The flower was now shriveled and brown. Destroyed by the sheer amount of magic that had flooded through it. Sade knelt next to the vase, replaying Henry's words over and over in her mind.

Henry was alive and Aiden had been working with the God of Ruin. She'd thought his sudden loyalty to Casimir was odd, but the whole thing had been a show for her.

Was he the one creating the monsters?

She paced around the room, her mind swirling with questions, and her blood boiling with rage. She needed to find Henry, However, if she left, then the treaty between realms would be void, and they would plunge into war.

Why are you trying to keep these realms safe? Let them both burn. Her divine purpose whispered. It emerged from her pool, a figure of glittering crimson magic. A splash of blue had taken over part of its face.

"I've already destroyed a realm and—"

The figure rippled, and the crimson was eaten away by the blue. A flash of gold swirled around it.

Enough about the damn realm being destroyed. We don't have enough information to keep beating ourselves up like this. Henry needs you. Find him, and then you can figure out how to stop the war afterwards. Despite its harsh words, the figure's magic was gentle.

Sade looked down at her hands. "What if I break again? I already came too close in the cave."

Look around you. We cannot live here. Peace will not be obtained by you allowing yourself to turn into a husk.

"But the souls I destroyed…it's not fair to them."

If we're truly responsible for whatever happened, then we will find a proper way to atone. For now, we need to stop wallowing in self-pity and start doing our damn duties.

The figure vanished when someone started pounding on a door.

"Sade!" Aiden shouted.

Her magic coiled within her. Had he sensed the plant magic? Did he know about the message? He had the dagger. Was he coming in here to force her to be reborn?

No, she couldn't panic yet. She needed him to think she was upset about something else. She eyed the dead violet.

"By all that is divine, this better work," she muttered. She dug up the violet and placed it into the wooden bowl.

Aiden continued pounding at the door as she made her way

to her temple's entrance. She kept thinking of Henry's haggard face and the pain he was in. Tears formed in her eyes and by the time she opened the door, she was crying.

"Sade! Are you—" Aiden paused as he took her in. His gaze flickered down to the bowl, then back up to her face.

"I left it alone for too long. It's dead," she wailed and the tension in Aiden's body melted away. She could've sworn she saw a glimmer of triumph in his eyes.

"I'm sorry," he said. For a moment, she almost believed the sorrow in his voice was genuine.

He wrapped his arms around her and pulled her into a hug. She kept the bowl wedged between them, making sure they didn't get too close. Her blood boiled, and it took everything she had to keep from blasting him off the bridge.

She eyed the dagger on his belt. It would be so easy to reach for it and stab him.

But she wasn't ready. She needed to make sure the portal to the Mortal Realm was open. And the only time it would be was when that blasted ball was taking place.

She needed to do something that created enough chaos so no one could stop her from leaving or care.

"Right, I should get back," Aiden said when she stepped out of his embrace. She gave him a small nod, and he left without another word.

Aiden retreated down the bridge, but she couldn't keep her eyes off the dagger. The blue crystal embedded in the pommel glinted in the waning sunlight.

Even though she longed to use it on Aiden, he wasn't a big enough figure in this realm to cause panic if she plunged it into his heart during the ball. No, she needed to take out someone who would ensure absolute chaos.

She had to kill the God of Ruin.

Chapter Twenty-Six

While the rest of the realm prepared to attend the ball, Sade prepared to escape it. She channeled into her Vestrals to see what the weather was like and what humans wore during that season. Winter had come early to the Mortal Realm, so she scoured the markets in the city and found a well-worn, heavy-duty cloak, winter clothes, and boots. She stashed everything near the Temple of Portals, since she wouldn't have time to run back to hers.

But what about the mortals who were going to enter the realm? How are they going to get out? Her divine purpose had been nagging her about this all morning.

That was something she wasn't sure about. Her divine purpose, or at least half of it, didn't think anything she thought of was a good idea.

The thing she was most concerned about was her magic.

She had to figure out how to keep the effects of the Realm of Ruin at bay. It was proving to be an arduous task. She wondered if she should wear a dispel rune, but she had no runestones. She tried to make some from the rubble in her temple, but they turned to dust the moment she set foot outside. The only other place she could get some were from a Mortal Realm, and she didn't want to ask Aiden to get her any. If he suspected anything was amiss, she feared he would tell Casimir, and they'd use the dagger on her.

So, she sat in a rundown courtyard, practicing pushing her magic away.

The patter of footsteps on stone made her pull her magic back in and let the realms sweep into her veins. She hated the sensation of the oily smoke slithering over her skin, turning her body into a living prison.

"Ah, there you are! I've been looking all over for you," Levina said. She cocked her head to the side. "You look different. Are you finally done mourning that pathetic half-god?"

Sade gave her a tentative smile.

"Yes, I am."

"Good, then we must get you prepared for the ball and the ceremony."

"What ceremony?"

Levina leaned towards her. A conspiratorial spark glimmered in her eyes. "Don't tell anyone, but Casimir has decided to forge a bond between you and Aiden."

Sade reeled back. "What! He can't do that!"

"Why not?"

"B-because I refuse! Bonds can only be created between

consenting parties."

Levina held up a small scroll. "Didn't you sign the agreement to become the tribute? It's in there."

Sade took the scroll and carefully read the tiny print. It was nestled between long paragraphs about decorum and oaths to keep the peace. She had skimmed over this when she'd signed it and had paid little attention to the contents. Now she was regretting it.

"This isn't fair. There is so much text and most of it is just dry bureaucracy!"

"It's not my fault you didn't read it thoroughly, but you signed it, so you are bound to the terms," Levina said. With a snap of her fingers, the scroll vanished.

Sade's hands trembled at her sides. She wasn't sure who was worse, Vilmantas with his condescending arrogance, or Casimir with his love of forcing people to do whatever he wished. They didn't care if their actions hurt others, so long as they remained in power.

She let her rage cool and harden into determination. Levina was watching her with a guarded expression. She got the feeling if she said the wrong thing, she'd be in trouble.

"I'm sorry for reacting so harshly. I was caught off guard," she said and mustered the brightest smile she could. "I've always wanted to be bonded to someone."

"I thought it would be better if you knew beforehand. It would ensure you didn't react in a way that was detrimental to our image and your future," Levina said, and her gaze flickered over her clothes. "We need to get you ready."

Sade followed her back into the palace, and they entered

a room filled with gowns and other accessories. Crude dispel runes embroidered on the fabrics kept the influence of the realm at bay.

Levina clapped her hands, and a humanoid immortal stepped out of the shadows with a resigned look on their face.

"Help our dear friend find something suitable to wear," Levina said before she swept out of the room.

The divine glanced at her, then at the racks of dresses.

"Right, let's get started, shall we?"

A few hours later, Sade was standing outside the ballroom, waiting to be announced. She had settled on a dress made from an opaque indigo fabric with golden leaves embroidered on it. It was strapless with cutouts on her torso that showed off her skin underneath. Unlike the other dresses she'd seen with skirts that could barely fit through the door, hers flowed at her sides and had slits that ran up the sides of her legs. She'd chosen it so she could run.

"Wow you look amazing."

Aiden was now standing beside her. He was dressed in a sharply cut tunic made of dark green and silver. The dagger was at his side, along with the sword he'd used to fight the creatures with. She hated the way his eyes roamed her body. It made her want to throw a fireball at him.

She merely dropped her gaze, and, in an effort to look embarrassed, fiddled with the fabric.

"Are you ready?" She asked as the doors opened. Aiden offered her his arm, and they stepped through. A tall immortal with grey scales announced their names and ushered them into the crowd.

It was the most beautiful room she'd seen in this realm. There were high arched ceilings with paintings of immortals flying around a city that looked to be made of diamonds. The walls were covered in carvings of ivy and various woodland creatures while the windows had crimson velvet drapes that reached from the floor to the ceiling.

Dispel runes floated around chandeliers made from crystal and glass with thousands of light runes etched into the glass ornaments. The light runes flickered like candles, casting an ethereal glow on the room.

She studied the crowd milling about the room. Most of the immortals had taken on a human appearance, but a few kept their true forms.

"The architecture is rather mortal, wouldn't you say?" An immortal said to another as they walked past. Both of them wore voluminous gowns that showed off bits of scale and fur.

"I heard Casimir was inspired by a Mortal Realm going through something called a Renaissance."

The pair disappeared into the crowd as Aiden led Sade to a spot under the window. He ran a hand through his hair, and he gave her a sheepish look.

"There is something I need to tell you." When she nodded, he continued, "Casimir has decided we should become bond mates."

Sade swallowed the bile that rose and plastered a smile on her face.

"I know, Levina told me."

Aiden sighed. "Look, I know I'm not Henry, but I did promise him I would look after you, and this is the best way."

It amazed her how easy it was for him to lie.

"I understand," she said and focused on the group of mortals who were sitting in a corner with glazed looks on their faces. The light from the dispel runes on their instruments shimmered as they played a tune she didn't recognize.

"Do you want to dance?" Aiden asked, inclining his head toward the crowd where some divines had started to dance. Some moved in time with the music, while others struggled to keep from knocking over others in their oversized ball gowns.

"I think I'll watch this time around; would you mind getting me some wine?"

Aiden started to say something, but he must've decided against it as he gave her a sweeping bow and went in search of the wine.

Sade leaned against the wall, watching the immortals become lost in the music. The melody wrapped around her, urging her to let go and join the crowd.

She searched the crowd for Casimir and Levina. Her eyes fell upon the thrones at one end of the ballroom, but the chairs were empty.

A trumpet sounded and the doors flew open.

"Announcing their divine majesties: The God of Ruin and the Goddess of Storms!" A sentry shouted then bowed as the two divines swept past him.

Both were covered head to toe in glimmering gold fabrics and wearing matching halo crowns. Casimir's tunic was in the same cut as Aiden's, but it was dripping with diamonds. Levina had a gown so wide she probably could've made two more dresses from the fabric. Her diamonds had tiny fires on the inside, making her look like a walking candle.

The dancers stopped their movements, and they all dipped into a curtsey or bowed. Sade rolled her eyes at the sight. They were all divines; they shouldn't be bowing like that.

We need to get out of here. Her destructive side whispered.

As much as she wanted to run, she had to be patient and wait.

Aiden emerged from the crowd then, carrying two goblets of wine.

"This might taste weird," he said when she took her goblet.

"Why?"

"The enchantments used to enhance it doesn't work here while the dispel runes are active."

She swirled the wine, watching for any signs of the oil. When she saw none, she took a careful sip as Aiden downed his and made a face.

"By all that is divine, how can you stand this stuff?" he asked while he waved over an immortal standing in the corner and handed them his goblet.

"I don't, but I find it more tolerable than ale."

She tightened her grip on her goblet and she resisted the urge to grab the dagger. Casimir and Levina had finally made their way up to their thrones. Levina was having a hard time sitting as her gown ballooned up around her.

Laughter bubbled up out of her as she took in the sight. Thankfully, the music started up so only Aiden could hear her.

"I think she got a dress that matches her ego," Aiden said

once she calmed down. His eyes took her in again with a look that made her stomach crawl. She focused her attention on the whirling dancers.

By all that was divine, couldn't he bother someone else?

She was glad she was going to be out of this place soon.

The night wore on, and Sade was getting impatient. Every second she wasted here meant Henry was going to suffer longer.

She stayed at her spot along the wall. Aiden eventually got bored and danced with a few others. Surprisingly, he was actually good at it and soon garnered the attention of every non-bonded divine in the room.

"Excuse me, would you like to dance?" A tall, lithe immortal with grey skin bowed as he approached her.

She gave him the iciest glare she could, and he quickly retreated. A sentry marched forward, and she wondered if she'd broken some stupid law.

"Casimir wants to see you," the sentry said.

Her heart sped up as she approached the throne. Levina had squeezed herself into her chair, but the goddess looked miserable. She eyed Sade's dress with envy.

"I knew I should've chosen a dress with a slimmer skirt," she said with a pout. Casimir shrugged and gave Sade a stern look.

"My dear bond mate has informed me you are already aware of the ceremony."

"That is correct," she said, keeping her tone as neutral as possible.

"Well, I don't see any reason why we can't get started. Now

where is Aiden?" Casimir said as he searched the crowd for the half-god.

He was flirting with a goddess who had eight eyes, six on her head and two on her hand. He must have sensed Casimir was looking at him since he hurried over to Sade's side.

Casimir clapped his hands, and a trumpet blew, quieting the crowd around them.

"My dear gentle ones, tonight is not just a night to celebrate our newest alliance. Tonight, we celebrate the bonding of two divines, the God of Truth, and the Goddess of Peace and Destruction."

Sade's heart stopped beating. He knew who she was. All this time she'd spent trying to hide who she was and it was all for nothing.

Casimir leaned back in his chair as she stared at him.

"What are you talking about? I'm the Goddess of Peace," she said, and Casimir threw back his head and laughed.

"Oh, come now, goddess, Aiden told me everything. There is no need to keep up this pointless charade." Casimir clapped his hands and a pair of immortals made from silver smoke appeared next to the thrones. "Because, once you are bonded, I plan on using your power to take what rightfully belongs to me. You can either fight it or join me in fighting."

Sade clenched her fists at her sides. "I will not join you."

"You are making the wrong choice. The Sacred Council clearly doesn't care about you. Why do you side with them?" Levina asked. She looked genuinely curious.

"I'm not siding with them either."

Casimir's brow furrowed. "Then who?"

"Enough of this!" Aiden said, and he stormed over to her and grabbed her by the wrist. "You promised me we would be bonded, now do it already."

Sade resisted the urge to yank her arm away. She needed to be close to the dagger.

"Very well," Casimir sighed and made a sweeping gesture to the smoky immortals. "You may begin."

As the smokey divines moved towards them, Sade reached for the dagger at the same time she used her magic to blast Aiden away.

Everything froze.

Sade tried to move, but the enchantments in the dagger kept her feet planted on the ground.

"Let me go!"

The dagger showed her a vision of her banging away at a forge. A sword with a hilt identical to the dagger was strapped to her side.

She created it. The dagger was hers.

If she had been able to move, she would've thrown up. The Sacred Council had taken something she created and used it against her.

Her eyes darted to Casimir. Despite being frozen, his face was full of rage and fear.

"Right now isn't the best time to be giving me such revelations," she said to the dagger. "I need to get out of here."

The blue crystal changed into a deep ruby. Runes carved into the blade lit up and formed a single word.

Destroy.

Before she could react, the crystal glowed a brilliant gold

and another set of runes lit up on the metal.

Reincarnate.

The world returned to normal, and Casimir's magic tore into the dispel runes above her, showering him with bits of stone.

"Destroy," she whispered to her weapon.

In a flash she was moving again, pressing against Casimir's magic with the dagger's crystal bathing her in a bloody glow. A wall of putrid smoke surged towards her.

She reached within and poured every ounce of destruction magic she had at it. Sparks flew in the air as her magic tore Casimir's apart, eating away at it like it was nothing.

The rage in the god's face turned into fear. His eyes focused on the dagger.

"You don't have to do this!" Casimir pleaded as an invisible force pinned him to his chair. "I'll let you go. You can leave here, and I promise I won't bother you."

Levina struggled to rise from her throne and sent a blast of air that brushed Sade's back. She leapt onto Casimir and screamed as electricity surged through her body.

"You won't defeat me this easily," Casimir snarled and gripped her wrists. His power flooded through her and she struggled to keep Casimir from pushing her off him.

The dagger pulsed in her hand, almost like it was coaxing her to let go of it. An image of it sticking out of the god's chest flashed in her mind.

Sade hesitated. Could she trust this thing? She tried to free her wrists, but Casimir's tightened his grip.

Please don't kill me. She whispered to the dagger and let go.

The dagger plunged itself straight into Casimir's heart.

The god gasped. He barely had time to react before the life faded from his eyes.

She pulled the dagger out of him and stumbled off of the throne. Blood dripped off the blade and onto the floor. The ballroom had fallen silent, then erupted into chaos as everyone scrambled to leave.

"How dare you kill him, you insolent wretch!" Levina let out a bloodcurdling scream as she struggled to stand, but the goddess's dress was keeping her locked in her chair.

Taking a breath, she prepared to flee, but then she spotted a trail of oily smoke oozing out of Casimir's body. Someone started clapping their hands. Aiden was watching her with a gleeful expression.

"Well done, Sade," he stalked towards Casimir's corpse. "You've done all my work for me."

"What are you doing?" Sade asked as she inched toward the door. Someone slammed into her and almost knocked her off her feet. The crowd was still panicking behind her, and she cast a glance at the terrified mortals who were now huddled in the corner. Their dispel runes had faded from their instruments.

"Taking my rightful place," Aiden said and glanced at Levina as she continued to struggle. With a wave of his hand, the goddess's eyes drooped, and she passed out. "I've been trying to take over this place for eons, and you just handed it over to me on a silver platter."

"Why do you want this realm?"

"Oh Sade, you've fallen so far from the goddess I used to know."

"Answer the damn question."

"Power, of course. Do I have to spell every little thing out to you?"

Aiden rested a hand on Casimir's head. The god's body convulsed before it became a puddle of oil that Aiden swept into his body.

"Do you really think being the embodiment of Truth and Ruin is going to work? I can barely control my dual purposes."

"Gods above, you're more annoying than Henry. I'm not the bloody God of Truth. I'm the God of Deception, and now I'm also the God of Ruin." Aiden held up a hand, and Sade waited for a blast of magic to arise out of him. But it never came.

She stormed towards him.

"Where is Henry?"

"I'll never tell," he said with a grin, and Sade threw a ball of lightning at him. Aiden gripped the side of the throne to keep himself upright.

She readied another wave of lightening, but the sound of flesh being torn apart behind her made her cast a glance over her shoulder. The mortals who'd been huddled in the corner were now food for the scaragnos.

Horror flooded through her as she realized all the divines who hadn't made it out, minus Levina, had been transformed into the spider-like creatures.

"Now, Sade," Aiden cracked his neck. "We can do this the easy way, or we can do this the hard way. Join me, become my bond mate, and I will let Henry live. If you refuse, then I'll have to force you to become my bond mate, and Henry will die."

More dispel runes shattered above them and she could feel the realm's influence growing stronger. She eyed the chandelier and let a small amount of her magic filter into it.

"I refuse."

Aiden sighed. "You always do this, you know. You make my life so much more difficult than it needs to be."

"What are you talking about?"

"Ah, you really don't remember, do you?" Aiden shook his head. "You've always tried to play the hero and rise above your baser instincts. But you'll never be able to shake off the truth of who you are, Sade. You'll *always* be the villain."

Sade took a breath and pushed back against the guilt that welled up within her. She wanted to learn more about her past, but Aiden was the last divine in all of creation that she wanted to learn it from.

No, she was going to find out her past on her own terms.

A shimmering wave of blue arced out of her, forming a line that wrapped itself around the chandelier and slammed it into Aiden. He screamed in agony as the glass pierced his skin.

Sade fled the room as fast as she could. She dove through the door as the chandelier shattered on the wall above her. The scaragnos were right behind her, their mandibles nipping at her heels.

"You won't make it out of here alive!" Aiden's voice echoed down the hall.

She ran as fast as she could, using short blasts of air to propel herself forward. It wasn't enough. The scaragnos were still right beside her. She wanted to stop and blast them with a fireball, but she couldn't stop moving.

The magic in the realm pressed against her with a strength she didn't know was possible. She barely made it to the bridge that connected to the temple. Her body struggled to move, trying to fight against the sheer power of the realm. Since Aiden was now a dual divine, did that mean the realm's influence was stronger?

It was a question she didn't want an answer to.

She grabbed the bag she'd hidden in a crate that was near the bridge. A scaragnos grabbed onto it with its spider silk.

Sade sent a weak wave of fire at the creature and almost set her bag on fire, but it was enough to free her bag from its clutches.

The air thickened further, pushing against her as she crossed the bridge. She fought against it with all the strength she could muster. Her feet slipped, causing her to slam onto the wood.

"Sade!" Aiden's voice drifted over her; she dared a glance behind her to see him running at full speed. It wouldn't be long before he reached the bridge.

She scrambled to her feet. Fear surged within her, and her magic billowed around her.

After what felt like ages, she made it to the other side, and relief flooded through her. The relief turned into horror when she saw the door to the temple was sealed shut.

"No, I'm not going to die here," she said to herself and pushed with all her might against the door. Sparks flew out of her hands. They ate through the wood and made a hole just big enough for her to enter.

I'm sorry. She said to the tree as she crawled into the temple. The tree didn't reply. The plants probably hated her at this point.

She pulled herself through and saw a pair of priests

watching her from behind a corner.

"I'm not going to hurt you," she said and held up her hands.

The priests took one look at her dagger and fled.

She sighed and hurried down the hall.

"Sade, you need to stop right now!"

"Go to hell!" she shouted and continued her sprint through the maze of hallways. She skidded to a halt in front of the door and checked the runes that were written next to it.

It was Henry's realm. She kicked the door down and the portal loomed before her. She rushed towards it and was about to step through when something wrapped around her torso and yanked her away.

Aiden stepped through the doorway. Sweat fell from his forehead like raindrops. His magic was flickering like his body was having trouble adjusting to being a dual divine.

She dove again for the portal and slammed into an invisible wall.

"You will not leave this realm," Aiden hissed. A tendril of oily smoke drifted over to the portal. He tried to close it, but the stones resisted.

"Are you having some performance problems? No wonder you have to force me to be your bond mate." Sade smirked as he tried again, but only blisters formed on his skin.

"You pretentious bitch!" Aiden snarled as he unsheathed his sword. He charged towards her, but his legs buckled, and he ended up in a heap on the floor.

It would be so easy for her to end him right then and there. She started towards him; her knuckles white as she gripped the dagger.

Then the portal made a strange whining noise. The oily magic of the realm was weaving through the stones. It wouldn't be long before it was deactivated and she was trapped here. She had to make a choice, either kill Aiden or save Henry.

Cursing under her breath, she shoved the dagger into her bag and sprinted to the portal. Crimson lightning arced out of her hands as it merged into the portal stones.

"Go ahead, go through, but I'll be right on your heels," Aiden said. "And I swear I will turn that damn realm into a smoldering pile of embers. You will have nowhere to hide and nowhere to run."

"You won't be going anywhere." Sade smirked as she let her destruction magic nestle itself further into the portal.

Much like she had at the cave, she could feel the numerous threads that bound the realms together. There were thousands, if not, millions of them.

Anyone of them could connect to the Mortal Realm at any time. She needed to be sure that no divine could access this realm until she found Henry and uncovered her past. She reached for the heart of the tangled threads, the center where they all emerged from, and tore it in half.

The walls of the room buckled and sap started dripping down the walls. The room shook, and there was a horrible screeching noise.

"I'm so sorry," she whispered to the tree, and she hoisted her bag over her shoulder.

"What in the hell did you just do?!" Aiden yelled. His screams were lost to her as she jumped through the portal, pulling the rocks with her. The rocks disintegrated before they reached the void.

She stumbled onto the path that led to the other gateway. Lava bubbled up on the sides of the path as she sprinted towards it. A terrible scratching noise made it almost impossible for her to move, but she kept pressing on and didn't dare a glance back.

"Please don't place me in the middle of the sea," she said to the stones before she passed through the shimmering field.

Thankfully, the portal was close to the ground and not near any hazardous areas. She scanned her body. There were no signs of it turning translucent. Her mortal form had managed to attach itself correctly. Once she sure she was stable, she assessed her surroundings.

She'd been dropped off in the middle of a snow-covered field with no sign of any mortals. Her gaze drifted to the night sky above her. She recognized the four guiding stars, but that was about it.

Goosebumps formed on her skin, and she quickly changed. She would need to either find shelter or start a fire. Then she could plan her next steps.

"Sade."

Her head snapped up when Airi shimmered into existence, along with a couple other messenger spirits. Her heart dropped as the God of Knowledge, the God of War, and the Goddess of Fates appeared.

"Would you mind telling me why you destroyed our entire portal network?" The God of Knowledge asked, his demeanor was eerily calm.

"To keep the God of Deception and Ruin from destroying this world and forcing me to be his bond mate," she said, and she rested a hand on the hilt of her dagger.

"The God of Deception is alive?" the God of War asked.

"Yes, he was pretending to be the God of Truth. He became a dual divine after I killed the God of Ruin."

The God of War let out a low whistle while the other two divines stared at her in shock.

"How did this happen?" The God of Knowledge looked at the Goddess of Fates with an odd expression. He still had that strangely calm demeanor, which was starting to worry her.

"I didn't see it. I'm sorry."

The god rubbed a hand down his face.

"Would you mind telling me why you decided to not tell me about my past?" Sade asked.

The God of War glanced between them, confusion was etched on his face.

"That is not open for discussion," the God of Knowledge said through gritted teeth.

"I think it is. You used my own dagger against me, and you've kept the fact that I'm not just the Goddess of Peace hidden for eons. *Why?*"

He stiffened; a flicker of rage drifted across his face.

"You are in no position to ask me anything. You're the one who has not only destroyed a realm, but now you've destroyed the bridges between realms. You're lucky a divine wasn't traveling between worlds, otherwise you'd have their blood on their hands as well."

The God of War held up a hand. "Hang on, did you say she *destroyed* a realm?"

"I'm also the Goddess of Destruction," Sade said, and the

god's eyes widened.

"So how—"

"Don't say another word." The God of Knowledge glared at him.

Sade straightened her posture. She didn't have time to stand here and be lectured by divines who had no business lecturing her.

"I don't have time to listen to this. I need to find Henry."

"Wait, what happened to Henry?" the God of War asked.

"Aiden captured him; I think he's somewhere in this realm."

A strange look fell over the god's face.

"Are you done? Because I have important business to discuss," the God of Knowledge hissed. When the other god didn't reply, he turned back to Sade.

"Goddess, you have committed grave crimes against the realms. You have broken the treaty, slain a god, and destroyed the portals. Do you have anything to say for yourself?"

"Go fuck yourself," Sade snapped.

The god pursed his lips before he continued, "You are hereby declared a fugitive and all the Spirits of the Realm's will be authorized to use force against you. I will allow the other divines to use their Vestrals to hunt you down and bring you to justice."

With that, the god vanished, and the Goddess of Fates quickly followed him. The God of War stood there for a moment longer with a troubled look on his face.

"Sade, can you hold on a moment?" He asked when she started to turn away.

"What?"

"I will do what I can to convince our eternally pissed off overlords to back down. Barring that, I will use my Vestrals to help you if you need it."

Sade frowned. "Why would you do this?"

"Because Henry is my friend, and, if he's missing, he needs to be found. If he trusted you, even after he knew about you, then I trust you."

The god left before she could respond.

She reached into her bag and pulled out Henry's divine rune. The triangles etched into the stone were still cold. No light glittered inside of them. She held the rune close to her chest and took a long slow breath.

"Hold on Henry," she whispered. "I will find you."

Chapter Twenty-Seven

Somewhere in the void between worlds.

Tisiphone hurried through the deserted halls of the palace. Most of the residents were outside, marveling in the beauty of the destruction of the portals and the web that kept their realm hidden.

She flung open the doors to the balcony, revealing a half-naked divine sitting on the railing. It was, Madoc, the God of Madness. The god had chosen a muscular human male form with jet black hair that brushed his shoulders.

"The lovely Goddess of Vengeance returns; I trust this is your doing?" he asked as he pointed up at the sky.

She scowled and threw her broken sword on the ground. Madoc quirked an eyebrow.

"She destroyed my sword," she snapped.

"Well, did she get my messages at least? Those little notes I asked you to leave while you stoked the fires of chaos?" the god asked.

"Yes, but they didn't do anything. I don't think she remembers you. I told you it was a stupid idea."

Madoc pointed at the sky. "It worked out, didn't it? The portals are destroyed and, with it, the chains that kept our world away from the others. Our wonderful little world can finally breathe that *fresh* void air. Soon the Realm of Madness will rise again."

He hopped off the railing and summoned a robe.

"What do you plan on doing next? Are we going to invade the Divine Realm and enact justice against the God of Knowledge?"

Madoc laughed and tapped her nose.

"Oh, you're so adorable, but no. We're not going to invade them… yet. I have my eyes on a different prize," he said, and he walked over to the carving on the wall. It was a divine rune made to look like a shattered sword, the symbol of the Goddess of Peace and Destruction.

When he looked over at her, there was a glint of madness in his eyes.

"It's time for my daughter to return home."

Pronunciation Guide

Bedisa: Beh-diy-saa

Casimir: Kaa-ziy-mih-r

Einar: Eye-nar

Sade: Sah-day

Vilmantas: Vil-mahn-tas

Glossary

Common magic:
Magic imbued into the Mortal Realm and not as powerful as divine magic. *Also known as natural magic.*

Combination rune:
A rune with two or more words.

Dual divine:
God or goddess with two divine purposes.

Divine magic:
Magic granted/used by the gods. Mortals can use it, but only a fully attuned Vestral or an unrefined can.

Divine name:
Name granted to a god or goddess during their creation. Cannot be used in a Mortal Realm.

Divine purpose:
What the god or goddess rules over. Can manifest as a separate entity or thought, is usually dormant in Divine Realms.

Divine rune:
The symbol of the god or goddess who uses it. Also can be used in a runestone by a Vestral or divine.

Rune:

Used for writing or runestones.

Spirit of the Realm:

A spirit who helps rule the kingdom they were assigned to.

Vestral:

An individual who has undergone and survived the attunement process. Used by gods to channel divine magic safely in Mortal Realms.

Acknowledgements

Some might say that writing is a solitary art, and in some ways it's true. But I've learned the creation of a book is actually a group effort.

I would first like to thank my mom and dad for being rockstars. I know I have spent countless hours talking your ear off about some inane writing problem, but despite my ramblings you have given me your unwavering support. And for that I am eternally grateful.

To my amazing siblings, much like mom and dad, I've spent a lot of time grumbling about the writing process to you. Yet, you still cheer me on and I am extremely thankful for your support.

To my friends, thank you for supporting me through this process!

I would like to give a huge thank you to my fabulous beta readers: Jessa, Sarah, and Bettina. Thank you for taking the time to read and give such amazing feedback! The story would not be where it is today without you!

To my fantastic editors, Jacelyn and Brittany, thank you for your hard work! You made my lackluster prose shine!

To Dani, thank you so much for your help with the book blurb!

To Lauren, founder of Paperbacks & Co, and the ladies of Paperbacks & Co. Thank you for all of your support and advice you've given over the past year. I've made so many new friends and I can't wait to see everyone succeed at their goals!

And I would like to thank you, dear reader, for taking the time to read this book!

About the Author

Rachel L. Brown has been reading and writing for as long as she can remember. Some might say she was born with a book in her hand.

Rachel lives outside of Austin, Texas with her cat and dog. When she's not writing or reading, she spends most of her time down by the lake.

www.ingramcontent.com/pod-product-compliance
Lightning Source LLC
Chambersburg PA
CBHW020910110726
47900CB00001B/90